Unexpected

By

Emma Henry

ISBN: 9798687492096

For Thierry

ACKNOWLEDGEMENTS

After many abandoned attempts, this is my first finished novel and it would not have been possible without the unstinting support of my other half, Thierry, who always believed throughout the long (very long) years it took to write this book.

I am also indebted to my friends and family who read the manuscript, offering invaluable insight and advice, and assisted with an endless series of titles, blurbs, book covers and other unexpectedly (!) troublesome tasks without which this book would never have seen the light of day; Philippa, Becky, Jules, Gregg, Rufus, Annie, Dot, Charlotte, Didi, Pippa, Aileen, Jane, Helen, Jon, Katie, Piers......I thank you all.

Finally, I wish to thank all those who generously publish free help on the 'how to' of a first timer in the self-publishing world, as well as Publish Nation who helped me make this all a reality. I would have been lost without you.

STELLAR
/ ˈstel.ər/
Adjective: something truly awesome or magical

PROLOGUE

'Good morning 4B.' Mrs Peacock, Headmistress of Palmerton Primary, stands before the class, a wide, masculine stance, chin tucked in preparation should a display of disapproval be required.

'Good morning Mrs Peacock.' 4B sing back in wobbly discord.

'Today, I am happy to introduce you to your new classmate and friend, Nina, who joins us all the way from Sweden.'

There is an expectant pause, the rustle of fidgeting as everyone tries to get a better look. Sweden? That's foreign, right?

'Well?' She spreads her arms and raises up her palms, appealing to the masses.

'Good morning, Nee-nah,' they mumble back.

'We are very excited to have Nina joining us at Palmerton and I know you will all welcome her over the coming days and help her to feel at home.'

All eyes are now back on Nina, a whisper of a girl, two long twigs for legs, bobbly knees, shaggy mop of white blond hair in stark contrast to her tanned skin. Privately, Mrs Peacock thinks she looks like a lit match; she just hopes she doesn't get blown out on her watch.

'Nina does not speak much English yet, but she will learn fast with your patience and assistance.' The army of eyes flick back and forth between the lit match and Mrs P. 'Any questions 4B?'

A lone hand goes up. 'Is that where Abba come from Miss?' Amy Mallet, Abba awareness inherited from a mother who attended the legendary 1979 Abba concert at Wembley, is not one to let an interesting moment pass without having a say in it.

'Yes, Amy, that is where Abba come from.'

'Cor.'

'High praise indeed, Amy.'

'Miss?'

'It's Mrs Peacock, Amy.'

'Mrs Peacock Miss. Abba speak English, Miss.'

'They do indeed Amy and so will Nina in no time at all. Now, Nina, this is your teacher, Miss Clark,' says Mrs Peacock, towing a reluctant Nina forward to introduce her to Miss Clark, a proud doughy 22-year-old from Slough. Miss Clark bends down, her face close to Nina's.

'Hel-lo Ni-nah, well-cum to ow-er cl-arse,' she enunciates slowly and loudly.

'She's not stupid Miss Clark, nor is she deaf.' Mrs Peacock pulls Nina back to a safe distance. She has had first-hand experience of Miss Clark's morning breath in the staff room and it can't be healthy for such a shred of a girl.

Nina's face remains impassive as she scans the room, desperately searching for a friendly face. At the very back, she spots two girls wedged into a small desk together, both with unbelievable amounts of wild hair, one dark, one red. They are whispering together, occasionally pulling back a hank of hair to study Nina before conferring some more. She looks at them, hope lighting in her chest.

'Now, Miss Clark, where is Nina going to sit?' Mrs Peacock asks.

'Um, in view of the, you know, I thought she could join -'

'Here, Mrs Peacock.' The dark-haired girl is on her feet, hand in the air. 'Mrs Peacock. Here.' She squashes herself against her friend leaving just enough room for a small one.

Nina doesn't need any further invitation, there is a flash of white as she sprints down the classroom, past the curious faces and a disappointed Amy, tripping over stray feet and an abandoned book, over to the two girls at the back where she squeezes herself onto the end of the seat.

'I'm Stella.' says the dark-haired girl, patting her new friend. 'And this is Kim.'

PART ONE
THE LONGEST DAY

CHAPTER 1

Status quo
Noun: the existing or actual state of affairs

So, here it is.

An hour ago, Jackson, love-of, texted me to say his friend Callum is coming for drinks tonight and to get myself home. Pronto. Now when Jackson asks (tells) me to do something, I usually get on it. ASAP.

Life is much easier that way.

Only today when he messaged, I was stuck in the office finishing up an urgent report for the boss, a report that I had been trying and failing to finish up all day because the boss is, a) never happy and, b) always unhappy. Changes had been made and remade and unmade, a frustrating exercise made all the more so given that he is currently in Finland, staying at the Hotel Finn – they really stretched themselves thinking up that name – and travels without a smart phone or an iPad or a computer. Nothing useful in other words.

The boss, Malcolm Clay, known (un)fondly as Feet-of, has an ultra-basic, Nokia brick; the one we all used back in the Stone Age of modern technology. He believes this *old school* approach gives him kudos as someone hip and thrifty, out-of-step yet somehow ahead of the crowd. It doesn't. It just makes life a living hell for the PA – me – as I spend half my life feeding pages into an ancient fax machine and waiting for them to burp their way into existence (on another ancient fax machine) somewhere else.

So, when Jackson's text sprang into being, I bravely said that I was tied up at work and would be home later. Jackson insisted and I ended up doing what I always do when Jackson insists; I obeyed. Shoving the latest updates into the reluctant fax machine, I legged it out of the office before the boss could phone with yet more changes.

And here I am, at home, as requested, almost on time and studiously ignoring the eleven missed calls from Finland.

What I don't know is where the hell Jackson is, although I am looking forward to a rare moment of smug triumph when he finds I got home before him.

Callum, who moved to New York a few years ago in a hail of self-congratulatory plaudits, is back in Blighty - a whole year earlier than anticipated. Which is a shame. I was delighted when he flew off across the pond even if I did have to endure an extended period of (hotly denied) sulking from Jackson, hugely miffed to have missed out on the chance for a move to the Big Apple. What I don't know is why he is back, although I would be prepared to hazard a guess and say that the US Immigration came to their senses and realised that Callum was a first-class dickhead and should be allowed to sully the land of the free and home to the brave no longer.

I am also interested as to why Jackson has invited him for drinks, unless it's to get the gory details first and do some gloating – which would make perfect sense, come to think of it - and why he is so adamant I should be here.

Waitress?

Note taker?

Spare part?

I check my phone in case an update from Jackson has slid into being without my knowledge – it hasn't – and then I eye the wine fridge. Jackson, hiding misogynistic tendencies behind outdated social values, considers it a crime for women to drink alone, or to even *start* drinking alone; an absurd doctrine that I chose to ignore. Besides, a few gulps of something cold and fruity right now would go a long way to smoothing off my fractured edges before Callum gets here. Jackson only drinks red wine, which leaves me some space for manoeuvre in amongst the whites. He draws the line at rosé – my favourite - and won't have it in the house, so I have been forced to restrict consumption to evenings out with the girlfriends, Kim and Nina, although these days it is usually just Kim and me. Getting Nina out of her office and into a bar lately involves a lengthy negotiation conducted well in advance. Do not even think about a last-minute spur-of-the-moment drink, the one where you get to 5.25pm after a monumentally crap day, text the girls for an emergency pick-me-up and hoof it to the appointed bar lickety-split. Nina never makes those any more. I don't think she even leaves her office before about 10pm these days. Voluntarily.

It is all about the job.

Only it is not a job, *it's a career, Stella.*

Glass of wine in hand, I call Jackson but he doesn't pick up. Maybe he is somewhere on the Underground, rumbling through the honeycomb of tunnels where we all know it is not worth even trying to use your phone. Apart from the fact there is no network, there is not enough space in the crush to safely use a phone. Last time I tried, I dropped it while cemented firmly in an upright position by the hordes and never saw it again.

Doorbell!

Dammit, that must be Callum. He has beaten Jackson to it. If there is one thing I do not want to do, would pay good money not to do, even for a minute, is deal with Callum on my own. Maybe I should just pretend I'm not back yet, couldn't get away, got stuck on the Tube, fainted in the crush on the platform.....

Then again, I can just see Jackson's face when he finds Callum kicking his heels on the front door step and me hiding out in the guest bathroom. Not gonna go well. So, taking a final swig of wine, I hide the glass in a cupboard behind a pack of pasta and make my way slowly downstairs, pulling open the front door and cobbling together a welcoming smile.

3

There he is in all his smug glory.

A sinkhole, God? Any chance?

I say hello and he says hello, and then we both stand there looking uneasily at each other. This is going to be excruciating if Jackson doesn't get a wiggle on. I give a last desperate glance towards the end of the road, praying that he will be striding towards us – he isn't - take a deep breath and invite Callum in. He looks as reluctant as I feel but eventually steps past me and makes his way up the stairs to the living room; we live in one of those weird buildings where the front door is downstairs, with the rest of the flat is upstairs. I believe this is called a duplex although *multiplex* would be a more accurate description of our home, a vast expanse of real estate with stunning views out over Primrose Hill. I love living here, I really do; it's convenient and close to town, not to mention palatial, I just wish Kim and Nina lived closer by.

Kim lives with Bart – yes really, Polish, short for Bartosz – south of the river near Wimbledon (Bart since becoming an ardent tennis fan) and Nina lives in a converted warehouse in the Docklands. Although it would be fair to say that *warehouse* is something of an undersell; the place is a spectacular modern / vintage mishmash with huge floor-to-ceiling windows overlooking the Thames. The view couldn't be more different from ours although it still captures the attention, especially at night with the jagged city skyline reflected out over the water. Not that she is ever there to appreciate the view. Building that career in the city involves long hours, with evenings and weekends dedicated to getting the edge on her colleagues by holing up in the office while they are foolishly enjoying some down time.

Callum stands now in front of the wall-to-wall plate-glass window, legs apart, hands on his hips, admiring the view and nodding his head in approval.

'Not too shabby at all. I could enjoy this view every morning before work.'

Thankfully you don't, I think, digging deep to summon the level of sincerity required to respond cordially. 'It's not bad is it? You get the full four seasons out of this window. Spring is gorgeous, but autumn is my favourite. It's stunning. Now, what can I get you to drink?'

He ignores me, turning back to the view and I have a sudden panic that he might have gone all *healthy living* in New York and is going to ask for a glacial water from Tibet, with a slice of cucumber and a side of parsley.

Which would mean a giant G&T posing as a glass of sparkling water for me.

'Callum? Something to drink?' I try again.

He swivels around, clapping his hands and rubbing them together in anticipation. 'Glass of one of Jackson's reds would sort me out nicely,' he says, managing to make it sound as if I have just asked him for rampant sex on the sofa.

Bolting off to the sanctuary of the kitchen, I pull open the wine fridge. Is he expecting me to open one of Jackson's top-shelf wines? Some of them up there are worth more, much more, than my monthly salary and are strictly out-of-bounds. Hedging, I go upper-middle and pull out a bottle at random; Chateau Lafleur, 2009. No idea, but I like the name. Jackson has tried on occasion to educate me about wine, but when you mainly drink with your girlfriends in wine bars, or at home alone (I know, I know....), it is hard to remember what you are meant to be appreciating; something fruity and unchallenging that can be swigged with gusto tends to be the overriding objective.

Speaking of which - this Lafleur stuff is fantastic.

A quick check on Vivino reveals it's a snip at a mere £450 a bottle. For fuck's sake! I should have gone lower-middle; this stuff is far too good for Callum.

Right, olives, salted cashews, guacamole, Kettle chips and, pride of place, my special wasabi peanuts from Japan – they are quasi-inedible but good entertainment value in the uninitiated. I pour two large glasses of Lafleur and put them on the tray; I don't want him to see the bottle in case he thinks I opened it to impress him. Or worse, please him.

Pushing open the door with my hip, I find him on the phone, still gazing out at the view.

'Chill, I've got it,' he says with a throaty chuckle. 'You owe me one. We'll sort paperwork tomorrow. Ciao.'

'Good news?' I slide the tray carefully on to the table, terrified of spilling the precious nectar, and hand him a glass.

'Very. I have somewhere to live,' he says, taking a sip of wine then showing off by swilling it about and gurgling.

'That was quick. Where will you be living?' I ask, the epitome of po-lite.

'Right here in Primrose Hill,' he says with a sly smirk, taking another sip.

My heart goes into freefall. 'Really?' I try to speak calmly, but it comes out as a fraught bark, like a dog who's just discovered a new cat flap on his back door. 'How lovely. Jackson will be thrilled.' Which is a complete lie. Jackson doesn't do *thrilled*.

'Oh, I doubt we'll see much of each other.' He turns back to the window. 'I'm looking forward to this view though. I lived in the Village in New York. Greenwich Village. *The* place to live of course, awash with delis and books shops but short on the green stuff. Costs a bloody fortune too. Not that I couldn't afford it, but you get seriously more floor space for your money here, and trees. And I'm looking forward to running around the park.' He pats his stomach as I simultaneously pull mine in. I rarely walk around the park let alone run, though I am partial to a spot of sunbathing on the rare occasions that the sun and the weekend agree to a joint appearance.

'I read there's an outdoor gym. Any good?' he asks. 'You need a decent workout to burn off the day. In an ideal world, it would be morning and evening, but there's simply not enough hours in the day in my business. When do you work out?'

'Lunchtime,' I say. Total fabrication.

'Chance would be a fine thing. I expect you have two-hour lunch breaks every day. At my level that's not permitted. Every minute counts.'

I look at him in disbelief. 'Bullshit! You guys are permanently on three-hour lunches in the name of entertaining a client.'

He dismisses me, saying crossly, 'you have no idea what real work is.'

'You what? We do all the work while you guys waltz about doing fuck-all and pocketing all the money.'

'Answering the odd phone call and typing a letter. Hardly *all the work.*'

'You know nothing about my job,' I snap, gulping some more wine to calm my nerves, already frazzled after, oh, all of five minutes with this dickhead.

'You work for that Clay.' He takes a handful of cashews and starts throwing them a little way into the air and catching them in his mouth in a show of bored nonchalance. 'Poisonous personality, but he's clever, I'll give him that. Made something of himself against all the odds.'

Hello? Pot. Kettle. Black.

'Still got a shocking reputation though. Thought you might have moved on,' he pauses, then making sure to catch my eye, continues, 'moved up.' His lips make a tiny popping sound on the *p*. 'He pulled any more spectacular bargains out of the hat while everyone else was looking the other way?'

He drones on, inevitably moving back on to the subject of himself. 'I found myself Senior Floor Manager within months. And let me tell you, Slymann's New York office is the most aggressively competitive environment I've ever worked in. Makes the London office feel like kindergarten in comparison. Your wits about you twenty-four seven. I used to take the contents of my trashcan home with me to burn. I had a real live fireplace, wood logs and all the works, perfect for burning tell-tale scraps. Glass of Napa's finest Pinot Noir, feet up, personal debrief, good end to the day. Been telling Jackson and he's finally.....'

I tune out, concentrating on finding all the olives with the red pepper stuffing and alternating with sips of the lush wine. When Callum got the job over there, Jackson insisted ad nauseum that he was not interested in New York – he doth protest too much methought, until he got very persuasive about Hong Kong. *'Asia is where it's at,'* he said on repeat, elaborating on the future of the markets out East, especially the all-powerful Chinese. He was so compelling I became convinced he was hatching a move to Hong Kong and it seemed only reasonable to start preparations. There are a ton of very informative ex-pat forums on the internet and I became a regular, genning up on where to live and the best schools for learning Mandarin. It was only when Kim found me flat hunting in the Sai Ying Pun area – popular with ex-pats living in the city – that I was forced to acknowledge that I was perhaps getting ahead of myself.

'......uber extended hours, requires full cerebral commitment and you can expect an IPO bake-off every Friday for months on end. It's a tough climate.' He fixes me with a penetrating stare, eyes bulging, and I feign interest while trying to work out why he is suddenly talking about baking.

'Bake-offs,' I murmur. 'Well, I never!'

'You don't even know what a bake-off is, do you?' he says, swilling his wine and oozing so much supercilious self-satisfaction that there is only one thing for it.

I hold out the wasabi peanuts, thrilling as he takes a handful and pops in four or five. At once.

There is a delicious delay as his bleached teeth crunch through the bright green shell before the cut and burn of the pungent wasabi kicks into action. I watch closely as the magic vapours get to work, cleaning out his sinuses and blazing a trail through to his unsuspecting brain. His nostrils flare, red blotches stain the pale cheeks, a repressed cough and, oh, is that a bead of sweat I spy upon the suspiciously smooth brow?

He is tough, I'll give him that. His chewing is determined, unwavering, punctuated only occasionally by a choke of pain. Finally, a lone tear dribbling forlornly down to his chin, he raises his glass to me in an unspoken *touché,* draining it – a waste, he won't taste anything for hours – then handing it to me for a refill.

He doesn't speak, can't speak, vocal cords no doubt burnt to a crisp.

When I come back with two more generous glasses, he has disappeared. His leather folder was on the floor by the window and I see it's gone too. My heart gives a double bump as I wonder if he has really just walked out, picturing Jackson's face when he gets here and finds me with an open bottle of Lafleur and no Callum. I put down the wine and slump onto a chair – a frail antique thing that Jackson has told me many times never to sit on – just as Callum reappears, strolling casually out of our bedroom with a tape measure in his hand. He is unperturbed to find me there, pulling out a pad of paper and noting something down.

'Checking who has the biggest bed?' I quip.

'Very droll,' he mutters, coming over and grabbing a glass of wine. He sucks up almost half before turning his back on me and staring out at the park; an ever-evolving view in the fading light, the darkening colours changing the tableau minute-by-minute.

I send up another silent plea for Jackson to get back here, now. I have done my bit.

Dragging his eyes away from the window and no doubt wondering what to say next, Callum spots a photo that stands on a low table. My favourite. Kim, Nina and I, taken about ten years ago when we were young, lithe and carefree. Untroubled.

Inseparable. If there was a fire, this is what I would grab first, only don't tell Jackson; he is not one for photos and keepsakes, no family pictures, no university shots, no nothing. But I love this picture of me and my girls. We were packing up to leave after a week's holiday in Crete; our skin is tanned, our smiles are bright, our cares are fleeting. The owner of the small apartment we had rented, Mr Zoumpoulakis, was checking we hadn't trashed the place when we asked him to take a picture of us, huddling together on the tiny balcony, the bright turquoise of the Aegean Sea blurring into the cloudless sky behind us. Our arms were tight around each other as we grinned into the camera. Best friends forever.

'When was this taken?' he asks.

'About ten years ago. Crete.'

'That's Kim, right?' he taps a manicured nail on the glass and I nod silently. 'And Nina of course. She hardly looks any different now.' His tone is admiring, which is typical but not unusual.

'Neither does Kim,' I say, wanting to even up the scores.

He looks at me, a tiny smile tugging at the corner of his mouth. 'Working for Clay taking its toll?'

I try not to let the hurt register on my face, feeling the strain as I attempt a weary, untroubled, laugh.

'Just kidding,' he says, although his eyes say otherwise. 'I saw Nina recently in New York and thought she was looking better than ever.'

I look up in surprise. 'She never mentioned it.'

'Keeping under the radar, I expect.'

I am put out. Not just because Nina never said she was going to New York - Kim and I always have a list of requests, mainly involving Bergdorf Goodman's beauty department - but because Callum knows more about my friend than me. And what does he mean, under the radar?

'She's doing well, going places,' he adds, the comparison with me unmistakeable.

'She is,' I murmur, wondering if we are opening a session of the Nina Appreciation Society.

'Up for promotion too. Incredible woman.'

'Indeed.' I keep my voice low, steady, but he has rocked me again. I had no idea Nina was up for promotion. She is not a serial bragger, but she would be excited enough about a promotion to tell us, Kim and me, surely? We have always been each other's first port of call for news, the good, the bad and the downright grisly. It is true that we have seen less of her lately; nonetheless, how come we have been kept out of such a large loop?

'She did look lovely. Certain blush on her pale Scandinavian cheek.' He grins and I feel a bit sick. 'Radiant.' He puts his hand on his heart and briefly closes his eyes. 'Just radiant.' His voice is no more than a whisper as a shiver of unease tiptoes its way down my spine.

Callum and Nina?

Apart from the all-consuming job that leaves no time for dallying with hopeful candidates, Nina has sworn off all men since she dumped the all-too-amiable Angus. Kim and I loved Angus, Bart worshipped him, even Jackson tolerated him and he is hard to please. We were distraught when she called it a day while never getting to the bottom of *why*? We dug and pried but Nina was giving away nothing. Bart thought it was the loafers and cords he wore on weekends, Jackson refused to indulge in such trivial speculation and Kim and I leant heavily towards the idea that Angus was just too *nice*.

'Being nice doesn't pay, Stella,' she likes to lecture me.

There was no side to Angus, no agenda, no malice. Wealthy, educated, family seat in the country, a leading something-or-other in the City, handsome enough; he was a good bet. I had even suffered fleeting moments of virtual infidelity to Jackson on more than one occasion – a distant ache for his simple undemanding niceness. I love Jackson, but

I am the first to admit that he is not always *nice* and *demanding* is his middle name.

I clear my throat, keeping my tone light. 'Good to hear she was looking so radiant.' The word feels strange in my mouth, inappropriate, implying that she might be expecting a happy event and if there is one thing Nina never ever wants, it is children.

'Can't be easy having a friend like Nina,' he says, back on the insults.

'It's very easy. Thank you for your concern.' I look him in the eye and say slowly, 'You wouldn't know, but it is possible to be ambitious, successful and beautiful, yet still be a good friend. She's like a sister to me.'

He snorts disbelievingly. 'Sisters have a complicated chemistry sometimes.'

'It's very uncomplicated, thanks.'

'Love is complicated too,' he drawls soberly. 'Gravitation cannot be held responsible for people......' his voice fades out.

Oh, fuck. Now what is he talking about? 'Gravitation? Sorry, you've lost me.'

He gives deep sigh. 'Einstein.'

'Right.' Nope, still no idea.

'Look it up.'

He finishes his wine and announces he has to go. I make a feeble attempt to persuade him to wait for Jackson, which he thankfully ignores and two minutes later, he has gone. I sit for a moment on the bottom step, my head in my hands, mind buzzing like a demented fly, bashing again and again against the same impenetrable truth. Nina and Callum. My feisty, daring, darling friend. Why him?

There has got to be a mistake. Wandering back up to the kitchen where the wine is, I call Kim.

'Hey sweetie, how's it going?' she asks.

'He's gone.'

'Who? Jackson?'

'No, Callum. Jackson's not even here yet.'

'Typical.'

'Look, Callum was being really creepy about Nina and, well,' I hesitate, 'I know this is going to sound weird, but I think something might be going on between them.'

Kim laughs out loud. 'Don't be soft. Nina wouldn't touch him if he was the last man alive on earth.'

'I know, I know. It's just that he kept going on and on about how gorgeous and amazing she is, said he saw her in New York. Said she is - '

She cuts me off, 'Nina hasn't been to New York for an age.'

'That's what I thought. He insists she was there recently. Keeping under the radar, he said. Something about a promotion.'

'Promotion? Hang on, putting you on speaker phone, Bart's here.'

'Stella my Bella, how is Calamity?'

'Painful as ever, Bart, worse if that's possible. New York has not improved him.'

He tuts sympathetically. 'Why he back?'

'I have no idea, but he's going to live around here somewhere, Primrose Hill. I'll probably bump into him in the deli on Saturdays pontificating about coffee beans. He was so full of himself and he wouldn't stop talking about Nina. Then he started quoting Einstein.'

'Einstein?' Bart sounds interested. 'How so?'

'Something about gravitation and responsibility. Told me to look it up.'

'Gravitation cannot be responsible for people falling in love,' murmurs Bart. 'Albert Einstein.'

How does he know this?

'Come again, Bart?' Kim sounds worried.

'Gravitation cannot be responsible for people falling in love.'

'Did he say that, Stells?'

'Something like that.'

And just like that my evening, already devoid of sun and light, takes on an altogether darker and more troubling aspect. Nina and Callum? It can't be true. Nina has class, something Callum wouldn't recognise if it knocked on the door and formally introduced itself. She also has a life plan, one that can be boiled down to; career, aim high; husband, aim higher. Although no one with their sanity intact could possibly consider committing to Callum, even if he has been promoted beyond all rationale and reason.

I must be missing something. And where is bloody Jackson? An absolute stickler for punctuality, it is unlike him to even be late, let alone a no-show. Unease slithers through me, and not because I think he has been taken ill or had an accident - but because I don't.

What I need is a distraction, I need to occupy my mind. TV and a cup of tea. And food. Maybe a bowl of pesto pasta on the sofa; something I can only do if Jackson's out and, as we have established, that is the case tonight. Filling the kettle, my eye falls on the luscious Lafleur. I pour what is left into my glass and take a few deep sips, enjoying the luxury of drinking such a heavenly wine on my own, without pretence or restraint. The kettle boils and I stuff a teabag into a mug and pour in the water, swilling it about with a teaspoon and opening the fridge for the milk.

No milk. Which is typical. There is little worse in life than black tea.

Then I look at the wine fridge. If I were to open another bottle and drink half, no one, not even Jackson, needs to know.

Hiding the first Lafleur bottle in my handbag to dispose of tomorrow, I open a second and pour myself an enormous glass, taking it through to the living room and turning on Netflix.

CHAPTER 2

Missing

/mɪsɪŋ/

Adjective: (a person) absent from somewhere, especially their home, and of unknown whereabouts

Jackson is missing. See above.

He didn't come back last night and is therefore absent from the place we call home. Whereabouts unknown.

And, to be completely honest, he didn't come home on Monday night either, I just didn't know it at the time, being asleep and therefore unaware. I only found out this morning for sure when I counted his pants and now, I wish I hadn't bothered. Ignorance is everything. Knowledge is loaded with misgivings and dark imaginings; unhelpful in the extreme.

Someone slumps into the seat beside me, elbowing my fragile head.

'Jesus! Watch out!' I wince, putting a hand to my head.

A London bus into central London during the commuter hours is no place to be fighting a debilitating hangover. I get a scowl and a middle finger in return from a spotty youth, greasy hair in a lank fringe between his grimace and the outside world.

'Fuck you,' I think, too cowardly to actually say it out loud. At least I look better than you even if the only thing between me and your heinous hair is half a can of dry shampoo and a (slightly) better cut.

Hunching away from him, I look out of the grimy window into the early morning grey. The movement of the bus is enhancing the general queasiness saturating every cell in my body and I sense a sheen of sweat breaking out in unusual places. Surely hangovers are meant to get progressively better

15

as the body processes the alcohol, not worse. I dab impotently at my slick forehead with the back of my hand and wonder what I am doing here. Why didn't I just call in sick? I *am* sick. Sicker than I can remember being, ever. Self-inflicted for sure but that doesn't detract from the all-pervading nausea.

Feeling someone's eyes on me, I look up and find the spotted horror staring at me.

'Boyfriend beat you up?' he sneers.

'What? No!' I turn my back and fix my gaze on the muted reflection in the filthy window, carefully touching my sore eye. Boyfriend wasn't even there, you moron. Boyfriend is missing.

Whereabouts un-fucking-known.

My head is throbbing with pain, every beat of my heart ricocheting off my skull and knocking out a distress signal in my own private Morse code. I would give my arm right now for a drink of water, a sip, a dip of my tongue in the cool, life-saving liquid. I once looked up why hangovers make us feel so bad, only now I can't remember, which is hardly surprising given I barely know my own name this morning.

An annoying noise seeps into my conscience and I turn to find that the Greater Spotted has plugged in his earbuds and is listening to some hellish dinosaur screeching over a barrage of tortured guitar and disconnected drumbeats. The inadequate little earpieces do little to temper the racket and the effect is like nails down the blackboard of my misery. Recklessly, I tug at a wire and the little bud pops out of his ear with a clammy sucking sound.

'Turn it down,' I hiss at him, swallowing back a wave of bile and retching on a revolting stench of stale alcohol.

Is that me?

'Cunt, you stink,' he spits. 'Now, fuck off and don't touch me again.' And with that he screws the bud back in and turns up the volume.

Cannot believe he used the c-word. On public transport. Before 10am. Surely there is a watershed for that kind of language? Turning my back to him, I huff discreetly into my hand and take a quick sniff.

Crap. I stink.

And I gargled twice with the strongest of the Listerine collection before leaving the house. I start rummaging through my handbag for something, anything, that might take the edge off.

What I find is an empty wine bottle.

Shame that I resorted to such a tactic fizzes over me. Telling myself that it is all Jackson's fault, I send up a quick prayer for some help getting through the day just as a microscopic hand glides into view from behind me, holding – hallelujah! - a packet of Extra Strong Mints. Taking one gratefully, I peer around to see who my rescuer might be and gaze into the bright beady eyes of the most wrinkled human being I have ever seen. Her skin is folded into thousands of tiny pleats, laddering down her neck where they pile up at the bottom giving a ruched effect. Offsetting the whole is a jaunty purple beret with an orange pompom.

'Take the packet, you're going to need them. I can smell you from here,' she says in a soft voice with a faint cockney bent. I lean in a little closer to hear better. 'Stay back, love, let that mint do its work.' She puts up a hand to ward me off.

I recoil. 'Is it that bad?'

'I tol' you, you stink.' A contribution from the Greater Spotted. He can bloody talk, emanating as he is a fetid odour of unwashed teenage existence. That hair alone is probably housing a colony of fat, bloated nits, not to mention what might be living in the other nooks and crannies.

At least I made an effort. Aside from the Listerine, I attempted a shower. In fact, rarely have I needed a shower more, only it didn't go well. Walking up face down on the sofa, glued to Jackson's precious Robert Cavalli black leather cushions with dribble, it took me a minute to orientate myself. Rational thought had to fight the crushing headache and queasy sea of unease washing around in my stomach and threatening to surge back up. As reality seeped in, embellished by vivid images that flashed in and out, I became aware that I was very late, that there was no news from Jackson and that I had the worst hangover ever. I also needed to pee urgently, drink large quantities of water, inhale a mug of tea, dose up with painkillers and take a hot shower.

And we don't just have any shower, we have a fancy, ruinously expensive model that Jackson imported from Sweden – which is excessive when you have an IKEA around the corner – that pummels you from every angle, including a special jet that is designed to massage the face with alternating hot and cold water, thus pepping up the circulation, eliminating toxins and ridding you of all those dastardly dead skin cells that pile up on a daily basis. Bring it on, I thought.

At the double please.

Peeing and rehydrating fatigues completed, I got in the shower, dialled it up to Max and pressed Go.

What hit me was a wall of water so powerful it almost took out my eye. And that was the good bit. Because the water was stuck on hot. Boiling hot. Scaldingly hot and I couldn't get away, pinned as I was against the glass wall by the flood. Shrieking, I skittered about, arms flailing, hands clawing and clasping for the door, unable to escape the inferno. Finally, as panic got the upper hand, I threw myself at one of the walls – which turned out to be the door, ripping it off its hinges and crashing with it to the floor. On all fours, and thus under the scorching cascade, I eventually managed to get the bloody thing turned off, slumping pathetically onto the sea of shattered glass and water. There was blood too and some hair, which I found attached to a piece of the door.

Not a good start to an already bad day.

Extra Strong. Does what it says on the packet. I can feel the minty fumes reaching out to the hidden corners where sneaky pockets of stench might hide out. I crunch the little sliver at the end and pop in another. If I eat the whole packet maybe, just maybe, I can overpower the stink of wine by sheer volume of dissolved mint.

Out of the window, the traffic stops and starts while horns beep at the reckless Lycra clad commuters on their skinny two-wheelers, weaving in and out, racing time and tempting fate at every junction. At Marylebone, a wave of nausea brings me up short and I wonder if I have overdone the mints? But what is a little extra bilious unease compared to the horror of turning up at the office reeking of last night, every breath a sour eulogy to the humble grape. Opening my mouth, I force in another chunky white disc.

Greater Spotted gets off at the next stop, managing to radiate youthful discontent as he shoves past a pregnant woman and elbows an old man in a flat cap out of his path. Next to me, quick as a wink, a purple beret slips in to his place.

She beams at me, happy.

'You're looking a bit worn out love,' she says, keenly. 'What happened to that eye?'

'Bad night. Bad morning,' I say, keeping it simple. I am not in the mood to start conversing with a stranger.

'Nasty fall you had back there.' She gives my hand a pat. 'Saw you go down, didn't stand a chance. Need your wits about you first thing or you get mown down.'

Her sympathy makes a dent in my disinterest. Carnage, having made mincemeat of me in the shower, came back for another go at the bus stop. I was easy prey. Tired and disorientated, I was in no shape for the demands of a morning commute into central London. Running late, I hit the rush hour at its peak and found myself at the bus stop with a restless crowd, all determined to get on the next bus – a bus that would not have room for everyone. As it swooped in to the curb, there was a surge forward and it was every man for himself, women and children be dammed. Before I had even registered what was happening, I was fighting the tide, going backwards instead

19

of forwards, my feet tripping on the people behind me. From there, it didn't take much, a low-flying briefcase caught me out and I was soon sprawled on the damp pavement as the doors hissed shut and the bus pulled out into the busy traffic.

'Bunch of barbarians,' goes on my companion. 'It was like a scene out of Braveheart. I watched that last week on the Beeb. That Russell Crown's a dish, isn't he?'

My sluggish brain struggles to keep up with the change of topic. Braveheart? 'The film?' I question. 'With Mel Gibson?'

'Gibson is it? I thought he was a Russell.'

'Russell Crowe? Gladiator?'

'Is that the one? Big sword, men in skirts, lots of blood.'

My head is too fogged up to work this out so I settle for an elaborate shrug. 'Could be either.'

'You are a little red, if you don't mind me saying.' She leans in for a closer look. 'Was it one of those tanning machines? My sister dozed off once and was burnt to a crisp. She was peeling for weeks. Got her Gavin to pull off the dead skin, while she watched Jeremy Kyle.'

'That's gross,' I say, choking back another wave of bile.

'He'd collect the bits on a saucer.'

'Stop!'

'Then feed them to the cat, Gengis. He sicked up a skin ball behind the sofa in the end, poor thing.'

'Enough already!' I don't mean to shout but the skin ball pushed me over the edge.

'I've got a new cream that you could try, if you like. Anti-aging too. There's a nice lady at the Boots on Oxford Street who is happy to advise, very knowledgeable. She recommended this blue eyeshadow. Look.' She turns to me and closes her eyes, revealing a papery eyelid delicately coated in a vibrant blue powder that is fast sinking into the creases. It makes for a faintly striped effect.

'That's a lovely colour. Suits you.'

'Doesn't it?' she smiles, happily. 'I've got a purple colour too, goes a treat with my beret but I thought I'd mix it up today.' She gives her beret a tweak. 'I'm Iris by the way.'

I look at her open expectant expression and sigh, 'Stella. Nice to meet you Iris.' I stand up. 'This is my stop though, so I'll say goodbye.'

'I'll come with you. See you to the door. Careful, love, you're swaying.'

Of course, I am bloody swaying! Have you ever tried standing in a fast-moving London bus without swaying? I try and detach myself as the bus doors open, try physically pushing her back in, but Iris, attached to me as firmly as a limpet to a rock in stormy seas, is going nowhere. She is what you might call a force of nature, probably a spy during the war, parachuting into occupied France, booby-trapping the enemy and torturing prisoners for information. Germans didn't stand a chance.

She sticks with me all the way to Claybourne House – named after our glorious leader. Fourteen floors of Central London real-estate of which we occupy two, the rest being rented out for vast sums of money to various companies including two solicitors, a tax consultancy, an insurance broker and a travel agent. Inside I get a concerned greeting from the security guard, a strapping young British Jamaican called Devon, as gentle as he is tall, who is not used to me arriving at this late hour. He then calls Iris over to sign her in, the purple beret just about reaching his waist, while I make a beeline for the hub of the building; the Brazilian Coffee Hut, manned by Marco – not as tall but just as kind as Devon.

Coffee. Heaven in a cup. My heart settles at the thought and no one makes a better coffee than Marco. I would bet a month's salary on him in a coffee contest, a Battle of the Baristas. They are the very fuel that our office runs on and he himself makes the world a better place. In the eight years that I have worked here, I have never seen him take a day off, yet he is unfailingly cheerful, polite, courteous. I stop by for a chat and a latté every day, sometimes twice, three times in emergencies.

'Miss Stellaaaa!' Marco greets me effusively. 'You late, you neva late.'

This is true. I am always the first in, ahead of the crowd, getting a lead on the day. I like watching everyone arrive, catching a glimpse before they get their office face on. You would be amazed what you can learn, the unfiltered gestures, the hidden quirks or, in Bob's case, the hipflask discreetly slipped into the bottom drawer.

'Not a good day, Marco.'

'Ah, Stella, I sorry. You latté?' Marco looks at me, cardboard cup at the ready.

'With an extra shot. Please. No, make that two. Two extra shots.'

Marco's eyebrows shoot up as he growls in surprise, 'extra shot!'

'What's an extra shot?' A purple beret materialises at my left shoulder, orange pom-pom bobbing.

'Extra shot of coffee. Gives it more caffeine, more oomph.' I give Iris a brief summary.

'Ooh, I could do with some oomph. One for me too, please,' she says, giving Marco a big smile, wrinkles lining up in attention.

'Stella?' Marco looks at me, questioning. 'This lady with you?'

'Er, well, kind of. This is Iris. Iris, meet Marco.' I look around for Noemia, his niece who he employs to help out. 'No Noemia today, Marco? She sick again?'

He shakes his head. 'No Noemia today. No Noemia tomorrow. She go Frankfurt. Boyfriend.' He comes out to greet Iris, swooping down low and giving her tiny paw a quick kiss. 'Friend of Stella, friend of Marco.'

Iris looks delighted at this show of chivalry, eyes flicking from me to Marco and back again.

'I thought her boyfriend was from Wolverhampton?'

'New boyfriend,' he elaborates, smiling. 'I need new help. Adver-*tize*-ment.' He points to a scrap of paper sellotaped to the front of the till, which reads, *Help.*

Cryptic to say the least.

'Someone is going to need to read between the lines there, Marco,' I say, taking a pen and adding, *wanted,* underneath. 'Now, latté for me, lots of shots and a normal coffee for Iris. She has enough oomph for two already. What would you like, Iris?'

She settles for Marco's recommendation of a Hazelnut cappuccino and he gets busy, glancing at me from time to time, a frown trenching his forehead. Eventually, he airs his concern, 'I worry. You sick. What happen?'

'Many things happen, Marco, and not one of them is good. Do you have something for headache, as well?' I can feel desperation starting to leak out of every pore and the office First Aid Kit, safeguarded by Clarissa, will offer nothing more than an ineffectual aspirin.

'I drug for pain. Very good drug.' He puts our coffees on the counter then disappears from sight, muttering quietly as various cupboards and drawers are opened, eventually popping back up with a dirty box in his hand. 'Duas.'

'Two? What are they?' I peer dubiously at the packet. It is all in Spanish or Portuguese.

'Is good. No pain.' He waves his hands in the air expressively. 'Also food. Very im-pour-tantay.'

'I need to eat? Right.' I quickly scan the choice, but I know already what I want. Breathless with anticipation I order a *Morning Muffin.* Not a day has gone by for the last few years that I haven't clocked the Morning Muffin, a beauty the size of a small cantaloupe melon and strictly off limits. Jackson can be very persuasive about what muffins can do to the top of your waistband and I have been unwilling to take the risk.

'Oh la la, Stella, crazy girl. And cookie for I-reese.'

He bags it all up and refuses to let me pay for the food, so I leave a huge tip instead to make up the difference. Can't have Marco funding my crisis. I have already taken mints and make-up advice from Iris, who I am not sure has much to spare given the worn state of her duffel coat and the scuffed Doc Martens, one of them with a half a sole flapping loose. She looks enchanted though with her coffee and cookie and I get an unexpected jolt of pleasure. Not a sentiment I was expecting today, not unless Jackson re-appears spilling effusive apologies and carrying a large bouquet of flowers – something he has bought but twice in our five years together. Not that I have been counting.

Although of course I have; it is hard not to when you've only got to two.

Thanking Iris for the mints, I bend down to give her a quick peck on the cheek, breathing in a waft of scent so familiar I stop dead trying to locate the name.

'What is that?' I ask her. 'Your perfume?'

'Do you like it? It's called Charlie. Found it in the British Heart Foundation. Almost new too.'

'It was my first ever perfume,' I say with a smile, heading off towards the lifts.

Time to face the office crowd, no doubt huddled around my desk laying bets as to what time I will arrive. We are partial to a wager in this office, anything to inject a splinter of interest into the day and relieve the boredom of our crushingly dull jobs. We don't stop at a paltry sweepstake for the football World Cup as per your average British institution either. No, we do the World Cup, European Cup, FA Cup, Grand National, Gold Cup, four tennis Majors, Olympic Triathlon (summer), Olympic Curling (winter) and a new addition a couple of years ago, the Vendée Globe round-the-world sailing race. This epic of man v nature provides exceptional value with over two months of entertainment, clustered daily around Bob's computer to see how our plucky sailors were doing. We got so involved, Clarissa was posting weather alerts for Cape Horn on the office noticeboard and we all spent hours googling the doldrums. When my pick, Tanguy de Lamotte, crossed the line an impressive twenty days after the winner, I was so relieved I bought the whole office a glass of Prosecco in the Bunch. The only downside is you have to wait four years between editions.

Leaning against the lift wall, I catch sight of myself in the mirror opposite. Holy crap. It is not good.

Divert, divert, divert.

I make the safety of the office bathroom unnoticed and find a woeful blotchy face highlighted in all its sad glory by the artificial light. How can this be? Before I left the house, I layered on some of the markets most expensive products, carefully moisturising and priming and prepping and concealing and covering, yet here we are with no sign of said unguents. Where have they all gone? My eyes, one of which took a hammering somewhere between the shower and the floor, are small and piggy, bloodshot, with no sign whatsofuckingever of the mascara I plastered on a short while ago. And my hair; oh, my hair. I don't love much about myself, but I do love my hair. On a good day, it is dark and glossy (thanks to Jackson's Aveda shampoos) with enough natural curl that it doesn't fall flat. Now though, the dry shampoo has had an electric shock effect and I look like I've had a very bad perm, circa 1984.

Sitting on the loo, I consider just calling it a day. Sneaking back into the lift, shuffling around the edge of the lobby, back on to the bus......home. Only I will spend all day obsessing about Jackson, wondering where he is, what he is doing, why he hasn't called and of course checking my phone every ten seconds. At least here, there will be people, work, the boss, gossip. I need to remain calm and everything will be OK. Swilling down a couple of Marco's pills with some tap water, I look at my watch, trying and failing to remember what time Clay is due back from Helsinki.

Dear God, please let his flight be delayed, or hijacked, love Stella.

Not that anyone would pay a ransom for Feet-of-Clay; they would be unplugging the phone and popping open the champagne.

Right. Office face on.

Fake it Stella, fake it.

CHAPTER 3

Tonic

/ˈtɒnɪk/

Noun: a medicinal substance taken to give a feeling of health and well-being

Installed safely behind my desk, I wonder if I might have got away with it and allow myself a short micro-doze to recuperate. Good for the health and indispensable in times of gross fatigue and alcohol mismanagement.

'Stella?'

That is Clarissa. In charge of office admin, gossip and do-gooding.

'Stella?'

Reluctantly I open my eyes to find half the office forming a wall around my desk, eyes to the fore.

Oh, bollocks. Here we go. 'This is a nice welcoming committee. Most thoughtful. Really you shouldn't have bothered. Take a good look and then get back to your desks people.' Everyone takes a good look, but no one goes back to their desk. 'The boss will be back at any minute and you know how he hates to find us away from the front line,' I add, a deterrent that has no effect whatsoever.

'What the fuck, Stella?' Clarissa erupts loudly. 'I mean, what the fuck?'

'Swear box, Clarissa.' From Bob, who manages marketing and the office swear box. He is rigorous in his monitoring of our language and has created an Excel spreadsheet, which he updates every month to keep up with current trends. Takings are later given to our local, the Bunch of Grapes, in exchange for alcohol.

'Swear box amnesty for ten minutes while we assess the situation,' announces Clarissa, coming around to me and easing her substantial bottom onto my desk. The wood creaks in protest as it adjusts to accommodate her weight; Clarissa lives at the fat end of curvaceous and when she parks her amplitude in the vicinity you are forced to take notice.

'Nice of you to turn up Stella. God, you look rough. Hangover?' From Nathaniel, full-time office creep and part-time marketing assistant. A weasel who somehow negotiated a body transplant at birth.

'Always a pleasure, Nat. Any tips? You have more experience with hangovers than most. You had one every day last week.' I blow him a kiss and he stomps off back to his cubicle.

'Now, Stells. I mean, seriously now, what the fuck is going on?' Clarissa has her uber-concerned face on, which in truth is very similar to her nosy face.

'I'm fine, really.'

'It's 10 o'clock! And Nat's right for once, you look rough as hell.'

'Never better.'

'Bullshit,' she throws back at me.

'You're just taking advantage now, Clarissa,' Bob admonishes.

'Shut up Bob. This is an emergency.'

'I'm peachy,' I insist as firmly as I can without moving my head. 'Fit as.'

'Clearly fucking not!'

She means well, I know she does, but this is too much attention. I simply cannot deal with them all now. 'Clarissa.' I attempt a severe look, which hurts my head, pain zinging into my temples. 'If I don't drink my coffee soon, I will kill someone.'

She narrows her eyes at me. 'Why are you so red? Are you having a hot flush? Is it early on-set menopause? Or a rash? You could be contagious. We should call a doctor. Ringo's done a First Aid course. I'll call him.'

I sigh. I am getting nowhere.

'Sonia, call Ringo,' Clarissa instructs Sonia, admin assistant and resident dormouse, who reaches for the phone.

'Put the phone down, Sonia,' I say sharply, wincing as a shaft of pain does a full circumference of my skull before settling behind my dodgy eye.

'He's a St John's Ambulance reservist,' objects Clarissa. 'Practically a professional.'

'No! Absolutely not! I'm fine and I've just taken some pain killers.'

The last person I want to see up-close-and-personal is Ringo. He is part of the accounts team known as the Beatles: John, Paul, George and Barry, aka Ringo. Minus the charisma. And the cool shirts. He might be a genius with numbers but his personality and wardrobe lack the same flair and, to top it all, he has the worst case of bad breath. Ever. I am sure back in the Stone Age, before the invention of the toothbrush and Colgate, some poor man had a piece of rotting woolly mammoth stuck in his furry back molar that would have caused some discomfort to his fellow cave-dwellers, but Ringo has taken the syndrome to whole new malodorous heights.

Talk about the killer blow; I am not letting him anywhere near me.

Clarissa is looking at me intently. I try again, speaking slowly and quietly. 'Not now Clarissa. It's been a tough morning and I just want to get on with some work before Mr Clay gets here.' I stare at her, my eyes pleading.

She gives a tiny nod and stands up, slipping off the desk with a grace that defies her size. 'Back to your desks everyone,' she says, clapping her hands and ushering people away like a policewoman at the scene of a crash. 'Nothing to see here. Move away. Stella needs some space.'

I take a huge gulp of coffee and switch on my computer, silently mouthing a thank you to her. The last thing I feel like doing is work, but I need to occupy my mind.

Half an hour later and I have done precisely nothing except check my phone for messages every ten seconds. No news, in case you are interested. Concentration is impossible as a never-ending parade of possible scenarios flickers through my head like the news updates at the bottom of the screen on CNN. So, when my desk phone buzzes, I snatch it up, praying its news. Good news.

'Stella,' I bark.

'Relax, it's only me,' Clarissa hisses theatrically. 'Just checked the Heathrow arrivals and *the Eagle has landed*,'

'What are you talking about?'

'Clay is on his way. His flight has arrived.'

'Why didn't you say so?'

'I just did! The countdown has started, you have sixty minutes, that is six zero, to touch down. Let me know if can be of assistance and I'll abseil in.' And she hangs up.

Did she say abseil? That's all I need, Clarissa turning all 007 on me; I haven't got the energy. In fact, am feeling a bit weird. Spacey. It could be Marco's pills, or it could be the fact that I have consumed nothing for almost 24 hours except two bottles of wine, possibly three, some olives and a packet of mints. I take another slug of my latté, which, by the way, is fantastically good with the extra shot, heavy and rich, a tiny caffeine hit in every gulp. Sixty minutes. I have an hour before the boss gets in, an hour to get myself into shape or into a frame of mind to pretend I am in shape. Praying for a miracle of energy, I remember the muffin, lying like a sleeping giant in the bag on my desk. Closing my eyes in anticipation, I take a huge bite, groaning as my mouth floods with sugar and vanilla and cinnamon and caramel and a host of other creamalicious delights.

This thing is heaven.

Muffin - latté - muffin - latté. An imperceptible tightening of my waistband with every swallow.

Fuck you, Jackson, I think to myself bravely.

Fortified, I reply to a couple of unimportant emails and make a half-hearted attempt to tidy my desk. It lives in a state of what I like to call controlled chaos, although there are times when it strays into what the boss refers to as *the unholy mess.* There are various piles of paper to which I attribute important titles like, *Urgent, Must Do* and *Don't forget.* At the bottom of the Urgent pile I find a collection of crusty old sheets of paper relating to pressing issues I thought I had dealt with weeks ago. Months. Feeling reckless after so much caffeine, I discreetly take most of them to the shredder via a circuitous route to avoid walking past Clarissa's beady eyes. The rest I put back on the top of the Urgent pile with the addition of a new *Uber Urgent* post-it and one particularly gnarly number that I pass to Sonia with a casually scribbled note; *please follow up.*

Easy peasy.

My desk looks positively angelic now, exposed patches of the worktop squinting in the dazzling office lights after so long in the dark. Encouraged, I press on, cleaning my phone with a wet wipe - disgusting, black as the plague - before spending a meticulous few minutes dusting off my keyboard. Also disgusting. I am trying to dig out a large morsel of muffin from beneath the space bar when my phone peeps. I pounce on it, convinced it must be Jackson this time.

No such luck. It's Kim.

Kim: *what time did J get in? hope u gave him shit*

Me: *didn't come home*

Kim: *he stayed in town?*

Me: *no idea. Cant get hold of him*

Kim: *bastard*

Me: *yep*

Kim: *try him at the office*

Kim: *got to run sorry meeting xx*

I know she is right but calling his office feels like a last resort. And if he is there, then what? Even if he was holed up all night in some tortuous multi-billion dollar negotiation, surely he could have sent me a message. A short text. He hasn't exactly got to send out a carrier pigeon.

And although I am desperate for news, a part of me doesn't want to know.

Kim is practical though and unsentimental where Jackson is concerned. Affection for him has dwindled over the five years we have been together and now sits sadly somewhere near the bottom of the scale. She gets on with him though, mainly for my sake, which is more than can be said for Nina. She was excited when I first introduced her, calling him my first *proper* (in her eyes) boyfriend; he was employed, home-owning, rich, handsome – virtues that none of the previous ones had managed. It didn't last long though, Nina's approval. Jackson sees himself as the alpha-male, he likes to control and dominate, which is fine when you have a willing pushover like me but less so when you are up against an alpha-female who will be controlled and dominated over her dead body. There have been some colossal clashes. Clashes frequently won by Nina who takes on the role of the iceberg with chilly aplomb, sinking Jackson's confident Titanic time and again.

Nina will be savage when she hears what is going on and, being an advocate of the Tough School of Love, will not hold back from letting me know what she thinks.

I look again at Kim's text. Should I call his office? Dare I call? Do I really want to know?

'You look as if you've been mugged,' says Nathaniel, coming by to have another pop.

Telling him where to stick it, I pick up the phone and dial. Imagine if Jackson was mugged last night and is now lying unconscious? His phone was stolen but the nurses found a business card in his pocket and called his office to let them know....

His direct line rings and rings, but no one picks up, so I dial his PA, Carly, who answers immediately with a chirpy, 'Carly speaking!'

'Oh, Carly, hi, it's Stella, what a relief you're there. I can't get hold of Jackson, think something might be up with his mobile, God forbid, you know what he's like with that bloody phone, sorry, forget the bloody bit, just popped out, it's just that phone is practically welded to his hand and it's always charged, you now that, I know that, we all know that! Ha, ha. Anyway, I only need a minute, something urgent has come up. Could you put me through, I won't be a tick?' I am barrelling on, unable to stem the flow.

Carly is more succinct. 'I'm sorry Stella, he's busy.'

Fuck fuck fuck. That means he is there. If he is busy, he must be at the office. No longer missing then – whereabouts confirmed.

'Oh, er, just for a minute?'

'I can't Stella.'

'Then could you give him a message to call me?'

'I'm sorry, he said no messages.'

'Carly, it's Stella. I'm not just *anyone*.' I take a deep breath. Begging is just around the corner and I don't want to beg. 'I absolutely have to speak to him so, when he's no longer busy, could you ask him to give me a call?'

'Look, I won't be seeing him today, Stella.'

I pounce on this. 'So, he's not there? He's not in the office? Do you even know where he is?' I snap out the questions.

'I can't tell you,' she snips back.

'He's not in hospital, is he?' This is so embarrassing.

'Hospital? Is he sick?'

'Oh, for fuck's sake, I'm asking you if he's sick?'

'Not that I know of.'

33

'Look, Carly, it's me, Stella, I really need to speak with Jackson. Please.' Here comes the begging.

'I'm sorry -'

'Just help me out here. Girl-to-girl.'

'I'm sorry -'

'Stop saying you're sorry and tell me where the fuck he is!' I bellow. Christ, now the whole office will have tuned in to what is going on Chez Stella. I peep around the computer screen and find Clarissa and Sonia both staring at me open mouthed. I give a quick wave and duck back out of sight.

'Carly, so sorry,' I murmur, trying and failing to sound sincere. She knows me, we have shared wine in the pub, crisps, and I can't stand that she is hiding stuff.

'I don't think there's any call to speak to me like that,' she pipes, prime and proper. 'It's your life, Stella, your mess, you sort it out.' And she hangs up.

I sit there gaping at the phone. Jackson has primed his secretary to fob me off and she did it! Where is her sense of girl solidarity? I want to get over there, grab her stupid curls and smash her stupid head into her stupid fucking computer until she has half the alphabet embedded in her forehead. For life.

Then she might open up a bit.

Slumping slowly forward until my head is on my desk, I close my eyes, overwhelmed with fatigue. Trying to hold up my crumbling life is exhausting.

Just going to have a teeny tiny power nap.

I am floating.

I am a cloud.

I am Zen of Zen.

I am....

Silence of phone is distracting me.

Put phone in drawer, shut drawer, lock drawer, hide key.

Ommmmmmmmmmmmmm.....

'Stella?' A deep male voice breaks into my bubble.

'Hello? Jackson?' I try and open my eyes only there are little weights dangling from each and every eyelash.

'It's Miles. Are you OK?' the voice says. A hand on my arm. 'Stella?'

Miles? I reluctantly force my head off the desk, rubbing my eyes and blinking them again and again, trying to reconnect with the outside world. I squint at the man leaning over me. 'Who are you again?'

'Miles,' he says, moving back a little, no doubt slayed by my fetid breath.

Miles? I sit up straight and suck in my tummy. 'Golden boy?'

He smiles, a hazy light emanating from his head, which could be his natural golden aura or could be the office lights.

'You look dazed. Shall I get you some water?' He leans in close again and I find myself tilting towards him as if pulled by some magnetic force. He smells delicious and I try and sneak a few silent sniffs. 'Stella, are you sure you're OK? Your right eye is swollen and you look as if you might have a fever.?' He puts a hand to my forehead and for a beat I let myself sink into that caring touch.

'All is well,' I say, drawing reluctantly back. 'No drama, no fever. Tiny blip in the shower this morning, minor mishap at the bus stop. Nothing serious.' I give him a light shove to keep him away from the toxic smells emanating from me. 'Look, if you want to help, I'd kill for another coffee.'

He lasers me with a searching look. 'Sure, I'll get it.'

'With an extra shot. No, two. Two extra shots.'

'Got it. Don't move.'

Chance would be a fine thing. I have become completely detached from my legs and walking is not currently an option. More importantly, why would I want to move when Miles Appleton is bringing me coffee? Known as Golden Boy, he is the office heartthrob, partly because he is drop dead gorgeous and party because he is *nice* (in the very best sense of the word); young (exact age has yet to be confirmed), friendly (without being ingratiating), chatty (perfect level of interest in office gossip), charismatic (oozing from every pore), up-to-speed on all things sporty (very useful for office bets) and because he is by far the brightest star in the office. None of us could believe our luck when he turned up one Monday morning last year under the watchful eye of Robyn. Never one to mollycoddle the new arrivals, Robyn made an exception for Miles and remained glued to his side for a week, unperturbed by the daily ribbing from Clarissa:

'Miles out of your league, Robyn.'

'He's miles too good for this place.'

'She'd walk a million miles for one of your smiles.'

You get the gist.

When he gets back, I am busy crawling about under my desk, an activity which has revealed a new ailment.....my right knee has broken through the fog and is demanding I stop crawling about on it. The problem is I can't find my phone anywhere and I know it has to be here. Somewhere.

'My phone. I had it. Check the bin would you.'

He has a rummage, but it is not there.

'Let's dial your number. Quickest way.'

He picks up the office phone and looks to me for the number to dial. I look back at him, my mind blank. Not the foggiest; there is a black hole where this information should be. Feeling like a fool, I delicately waggle my head trying shake the numbers free, as Miles stretches over me to get one of my business cards and dials. A faint buzzing noise emanates from my desk. The drawer! I remember putting it there now. Vaguely. Miles tries to pull it open, but it is stuck fast. He tugs again.

'Locking the phone in the office drawer? Is that your idea or Mr Clay's? Where's the key?'

The key! I had the key, I locked the drawer, pulled it out and........

Miles is gazing at me intently, waiting, as the silence stretches out. I had the key and I put it.....my eyes scan my desk, now all-too-free of bits of paper and handy clutter that could hide a key. I peer into the small jar housing the paperclips. Nada.

'You must know, if you locked it,' he says, all too reasonably.

I shake my head. Trying not to laugh he takes two paperclips, unfolds them and squats down to get going picking the lock, wedging himself against my left leg. I allow myself to linger for just a few seconds, making sure to get plenty of lungfuls of his delicious smell before backing carefully off. After a few fragrant filled minutes, he pulls open the drawer.

And there lies my phone.

No messages. No missed calls. In case you are wondering.

Feeling the pressure of Jackson's disappearance anew, I call Kim for a pep talk.

'Hey Stella, any news? I'm really busy, can't stop for long.' She sounds puffed, as if running.

'He's up to something, Kim,' I cry. 'The PA, Carly, she fobbed me off. He's not there and she won't say where he is and she won't give him a message. She told me it was my mess and I had to sort it out.'

A weighty silence greets this outburst. I can't blame her. What is there to say?

'Can we meet for a sandwich at lunch?' I am suddenly desperate to see her. I need reassurance, I need sympathy. Understanding. Luckily, Nina is always unavailable during working hours so I won't have to endure a tough love session. It is one of her new rules; no personal calls, texts, WhatsApps, during working hours.

'No chance. I'm drowning here,' says Kim.

37

Tears well, instant and unexpected. Crap. I refuse to cry, not here, not in the office, I can't sink that low. There is a long pause as I am unable to respond, trying desperately to rein in the mounting tide.

After what feels like an hour, I manage a weak, wobbly, 'no problem'.

'Oh God, you sound so sad. Let's do it. Pret at 12.30?'

'Bunch of Grapes?' I need the pub. My hangover is hankering for a hair-of-the-dog.

'That bad? Bunch it is then, 12.30. Gotta run.'

'Stella!' Feet-of is standing right in front of me, knocking on my computer screen.

How long has he been there? He doesn't look as if he has just flown in from Finland, business class, he looks as if he has been on a geography field trip around the Pennines. Crumpled jacket over mismatched non-descript trousers, grey shirt that might have started life as a white one, and a nasty orange tie. His hair, what is left of it, is tufting out over his ears, which usually means he forgot to take his Brylcreem and I will no doubt be sent off on an emergency mission to Boots.

'My office, now,' he grumbles.

I reluctantly prepare to leave the shelter of my desk, sliding my feet into my beautiful shoes, a rare present from Jackson. They are Louboutin's, the real McCoy; velvety red soles, skyscraper *get-me* heels, power-in-a-shoe. Impossible to walk in of course but they do give me a lift, in every sense of the word, and I attempt a strut, head held high.

Fake it, Stella.

He has installed himself behind the oversized desk as I carefully close the door. Trying to make up for his lack of stature - physical, mental and spiritual – he ordered a giant slab of furniture that would happily accommodate four or five people with room to spare, plus a ridiculous wing-back chair complete with a round greasy patch where his head touches the leather. A patch he has had me try to clean on more than one occasion - something so far beyond my job description it is not even in the same postcode.

His eyes are assessing as he watches me. 'Is there something you want to tell me?'

Silence. My mind is flitting about, wondering what, of the many things that have gone wrong today, he is going to pick me up on.

'You're not looking your best,' he says, disapproval radiating across the expanse of wood between us. 'I don't know if your hair is intentional, it's hard to tell these days, but it's not appropriate for the office. For *my* office. You know I take personal appearance very seriously.' This from the man who regularly carries half his breakfast around on this tie. 'And, if I'm not mistaken, you have a black eye?'

I sigh. No one mentioned it was black now.

'Not the kind of image I wish my personal assistant to present and we have Savills coming this afternoon.' He gives a dramatic huff, flapping his tie around to underline his displeasure. 'It's all most disconcerting. See what you can do. And.' He flaps some more. 'You have a leaf. On your bottom.' He looks away in embarrassment.

'A leaf?'

'A leaf, Stella.'

'Right. Noted,' I mutter. 'Hair, face, leaf. I'm on it.'

Backing towards the door, I find the offending article and carry it like a sacrificial offering back to my desk where Clarissa pounces before I have even had time to sit down.

'What happened?' she whispers at me, glowing from the excitement.

'Why the fuck didn't you tell me I had a leaf stuck to my arse?' I hiss, waving the leaf at her.

'A leaf? I didn't notice. Honestly. There's so much going on with you today, Stells.'

'How could you miss a fucking leaf?'

'That's enough,' roars Bob, brandishing the swear box and marching over. 'Stella, I've been more than lenient but enough is enough. I'm giving you a special discounted rate given the, er, difficult circumstances that you find yourself in this morning, *but.*' He holds up a finger. 'I've lost count of the number of times you have used the f word so put in a fiver and we'll call it quits.'

Day. Light. Robbery.

'Harsh but fair,' says Clarissa. 'We'll be able to go to the Bunch soon. I've put in at least that today.'

'How could you miss a leaf?' I repeat, handing Bob my purse.

'Come on Stells,' she begs. 'You, Miss-perfect-never-late-toe-the-line-at-all-times, turn up mid-morning, looking like a pile of shit, purple face, black eye, wild hair. We love you, you hold this place together, but we missed the leaf. The face is drawing all the attention.'

CHAPTER 4

Maelstrom
/ˈmeɪl.strɒm/
Noun: a frightening situation, full of turmoil and strong emotions

Kim isn't there when I arrive at the Bunch of Grapes so I take advantage to order a glass of Sauvignon Blanc without any disapproving comments. A small one, even if I am tempted to go all-out with a large one. And a bowl of fat chips. Marco did tell me to eat and the muffin is but a thing of the past.

Stress does marvellous things for the metabolism, don't you know?

Now, where to sit? Clutching my glass with two hands, I make for the back corner. Don't want to risk office eavesdroppers getting hold of even more grist for the gossip mill. As it is, I bet that right now, this second, they are converged around Clarissa's desk, oohing and aahing over the walking catastrophe that is Stella Halfpenny this morning.

Which is exactly what Kim does when she arrives.

'Blimey Stella. What the hell has happened?' She pats my mad hair, peering at my face. 'Have you been mugged?' She dumps her bag on the table, eyes fixed on the freak exhibit. 'Why didn't you say and when, for God's sake? You were home last night waiting for twinkle toes.' She leans in again and studies my face before suddenly standing up, shocked, hand to her mouth. 'Christ, he didn't hit you, did he? Stella, tell me he didn't.'

'Yeah, right. I told you, he didn't even fucking come home.'

She nods, remembering. 'Maybe he's been called overseas or is trapped in a strip club with an important client waiting for the firemen to break in and free them,' she says, expanding on her long-held theory that anyone involved in the financial markets spends half their life in seedy clubs watching pole dancers.

I shake my head sadly, taking a slug of wine.

She bends down again, her face close to mine and I get a hint of *Terre* by Hermes, Bart's aftershave, which she likes to wear. 'That black eye's going to be a corker.'

'Tell me something I don't know,' I say, crossly. 'Just get a drink and sit down. Quietly.'

'Right. Don't move. I'll be right back.' She pinches my cheek and strides off to the bar. Kim is not beautiful in the way that Nina is, but she can still turn heads. Nature gave her red curly hair, tamed now to auburn glossy waves courtesy of an extortionately expensive celebrity hairdresser, freckled skin and what could be termed a *strong* nose. Her legs are long and her body lithe, seemingly unaffected by the passing years and today clothed in a crisp white shirt and a pair of dark grey tailored trousers. She looks understated yet chic; two things I most definitely am not today.

She returns clutching a tomato juice and a bowl of hummus with some celery sticks, setting them on the table between us.

I glare at her in disgust. 'Would you like to adjust your halo before sitting down?'

'What?'

'Tomato juice and celery? Really?'

The waiter chooses this moment to rock up with my chips, bolstered on either side by bowls of ketchup and mayonnaise. We both spend a few seconds gazing at the chips, glistening with grease and salt, before I generously push them into the middle of the table next to the cherubic celery.

42

'Holy crap, Stella, now I really am worried. Wednesday lunchtime and you're on the wine and chips. What happened to all that mid-week abstinence you've been boasting about lately?' She takes a sip of tomato juice and grimaces. 'All that crap about grabbing a sandwich together for lunch. You are in need my friend. Now give. What the hell is going on? Tell sweet Kim all about it.'

I feel the tears that I've been holding back all morning threaten. They gather and swell, a couple of big fat juicy ones bursting forth and rolling down my cheeks. Wiping them away, I take a large gulp of wine, then eat a couple of chips, dipping the first in the ketchup and the second in the mayo. Kim watches me carefully, waiting for me to compose myself.

'It's hard to know where to start. Jackson didn't come home last night.'

'Yes, we've covered that. Bastard. Don't forget this is Jackson we're talking about; Jackson does what Jackson wants. You know that, you've always known that. There's bound to be a simple explanation.'

I scowl at her. 'One night maybe but not two.'

That gets her attention. 'What d'you mean, two?' she demands. 'He didn't come back Monday either? Why didn't you say?'

'Well,' I hesitate, not wanting to go further. Well-hidden family secrets will be divulged. 'I wasn't sure at first.'

'You're going to have to explain yourself.'

'Well, sometimes he comes home after I've gone to bed and leaves again before I've woken up.'

She looks at me sadly. 'You've never told me that.'

'Well, I'm telling you now.'

'So, what makes you think he didn't come back on Monday?'

'Thirteen pairs of Calvin Kleins,' I mumble into my wine.

Kim frowns, as well she might. 'Did you say Calvin Kleins? Would you care to elaborate?'

43

I clear my throat and pop in another chip. Here we go. 'Jackson has fourteen pairs of Calvin Klein pants, tight black trunks, size medium, worn in rotation. He wears one a day and they are washed at the weekend. Therefore, by this morning, Wednesday, there should have been eleven left, pairs fourteen and thirteen being in the wash basket and number twelve busy keeping the crown jewels warm.'

Kim's eyes are open wide in disbelief. 'Tell me you are fucking kidding.'

'I wish I was. I wash them every weekend, dry, fold and restock the drawer. But an unlucky thirteen means he didn't come back on Monday night, or last night, and is therefore gambolling about in a three-day old pair of pants.' I peer into my wine glass, which is almost empty, before adding, 'Grubby bastard.'

'Counting the pants. Move over Miss Marple,' Kim says, starting to enjoy herself. 'Ms Halfpenny and the Mystery of the Missing Skivvies. Stella, you are *on* it. Now, tell me what his office said.'

'Oh, I had a *lovely* chat with Carly, his PA. A dodgy and unreliable witness for the defence, if ever there was one. Couldn't even lie convincingly. Jackson should really give her some coaching. She said he was in, until she admitted he was out. All day. Unavailable. No, I can't even give him a fucking message. Then she said, *it's your mess, you sort it out.*' I try to mimic Carly's precise diction, but it just comes out as a shrill squeak. 'She said those very words.'

'Fuck. Those jocks of his are going to be rank if he doesn't come back soon.' Despite myself, I give a honk of laughter. God Bless Kim. We sit in silence for a minute eating chips, the celery an unwanted sideshow. 'Accident? Having a boil removed from his butt? Disorientated in A&E?' Kim suggests.

'Don't be stupid. Jackson wouldn't be caught dead in A&E.'

'You're right. Such a snob. And don't say it is part of his charm, it isn't. Time to quit covering for him.'

I blanch, stung.

'Sorry sweetheart, but it's true. Anyway, take me through last night, A to Z, don't spare the detail.'

With no wine left and an empty chip bowl, I have no further delay tactics available so I might as well get on with it. Besides, I need my girls on board and Kim can bring Nina up-to-speed later, saving me the bother. So, I unload my sorry tale starting with the mad dash to be home in time for Callum and finishing with the drawer key.

'Crikey, Stells,' she breathes, when I am done. 'And your poor face. If he'd bought a normal shower like a normal person this would never have happened.'

'Normal is for the common people,' I say.

Kim's face lights up and she gives a quick burst of Paul Young's *Love of the Common People*.

'Not heard that for ages. They don't play Paul Young anymore, do they? Right, let me get some more drinks and then we'll make a plan.'

She is back in a flash with two glasses of wine, tomato juice abandoned. We clink and she takes a deep draft, smacking her lips and sighing with pleasure. 'Lunch time drinking. Nothing better. Now, are you sure you haven't missed a message or a call. It doesn't sound like Jackson not to turn up when he says he will without good reason.'

'Who do you take me for? I have checked my phone ten thousand times. I have turned it off, on, off again. I have updated everything, deleted apps and reinstalled apps. Na-fucking-da. On the other hand, he must have a hundred text messages and missed calls sitting in his phone from me and he didn't bother to reply to one. Not. One. The fucker.'

'Maybe that's why he's gone all quiet. You know Jackson hates that stuff, hates texts, hates being hassled. You baited him and he's punishing you.'

45

'Baited? What kind of word is that?' I ask, indignant.

'It's like baiting a bear.'

'Don't call Jackson a bear.'

'A pissed off Jackson is like a mother bear with a hangover who has lost her baby cub after someone stole all the honey,' she says, looking mighty pleased with herself. 'And imagine how much more pissed off he is going to be when he finds the broken shower. How did you *do* it? That thing was solid.'

'You know how people get superhuman strength when their dog is stuck under a bus and they lift it up without breaking sweat?' Kim nods, looking attentive. 'Well that was me, I had to get out of that boiling water, I was desperate and just ran, shoved, I have no idea, but down it went and there was I on the floor in a pile of broken shower, nose-to-nose with the bin. Needs a wipe under the pedal by the way, must have a word with the cleaner; she is failing in her duty to pander to Jackson's impossibly high standards.'

We take a minute to reflect on Jackson's household mania.

'My eye hurts.' I place a finger gently on my eyelid and feel the tiny thump of a pulse. 'And I may have lost some hair. Can you see a bald patch?' Kim takes a second to inspect my head, thankfully shaking hers. 'And Marco gave me some painkillers. I think they might be quite strong, probably pure cocaine or heroin or something. Crack. Crystal meth. Parts of me have gone quite numb. Is my eye twitching?'

'He'd never give you anything dodgy. He's a diamond, that Marco. You've probably had too many coffees. I do think we should get you to a doctor for a check-up though. Then home, your home, so we can wait for Jackson. Bart will be there and I'll call Nina. She's going to be all over this when she hears. The gloves are gonna come off. She'll have him kneecapped or nudged down some steep steps.' She puts her hand on her heart, her face solemn. 'A tragic accident M 'Lord,

46

he stumbled, arse went over tit. There was nothing we could do.'

We argue back and forth for a while about the doctor. I am relieved to skip the office, delirious at the thought of abandoning work and retiring to my sofa – and getting home to tidy up before Jackson gets there – but I don't want to waste half a day in A&E. Kim eventually gives in, remembering that she has to deliver a contract to her boss this afternoon in Marylebone, which we can do en route to Primrose Hill. Plans made, she heads over to Claybourne House to get my house keys – hopefully easy to locate on my newly tidied desk - while I wait in the pub, stoically refraining from another trip to the bar.

I might have chosen my boyfriend badly but no one can fault my friends. Kim and Nina. They are the scaffolding to my flaky core, the frame around my life that that has supported me for as long as I can remember. Our friendship has held firm since we met in primary school. As a scrappy six-year-old, hopelessly shy and lacking in self-assurance, I occupied a lonely world peopled with unintimidating imaginary friends. Until Kim arrived; a fearless, confident vortex that pulled me into the real world, our differences somehow fitting together perfectly. Then Nina turned up one day fresh off the boat from Sweden, thin as a pin, shock of white hair and, most importantly, untold Abba connections. With little discussion required, we opened the door to our little club and snaffled her before anyone else could, Kim's break time Finger of Fudge making up for our unappealing hair and my brown clothes. We formed an impenetrable unit thereafter, rebuffing all pretenders who wanted in without mercy.

They both filled the family-shaped hole in my life, bringing a warmth and stability that had been entirely absent until then. My unhappy home life consisted of me, Stella, and Babs. Babs was, is - I believe she is still alive, living in Spain with a dodgy character called Tony - my mother, not that there was anything remotely maternal about her. She was Babs to everyone, me included and, well, she simply was not a very nice person. Selfish. Uninterested. Uncaring. Uneverything, including sober. Babs at some level of inebriation was the norm for little Stella. Only one thing could keep her vaguely sober – money, or lack of. She worked a job at the local bookies from where it was but a short hop to her drinking hole of choice, the Beer Tap. She would set up shop on her stool in the corner, facing the door to keep an eye on traffic coming in and out, holding court and inhaling pints of her favourite beer: Stella Artois.

Now you know my middle name.

To supplement her meagre income, she would hook unlikely suspects in the bookies over the 3.50pm at Chepstow and invite them to retire to the pub for a swift half or ten. A big spender would ensure her some free pints on another night, thus helping to cover her alcoholic requirements. Every night there would come a point when she would, in the space of a minute, transform from merry to maudlin, pinching ten pence pieces from the tip jar on the bar and playing Dolly Parton's Jolene on the jukebox, over and over, ripping into anyone that had the nerve to complain.

The pub was home for much of the time in my early years, Babs being uninclined to give up her evening pints for motherhood. As a baby, I have been told, she liked to keep me in a basket behind her stool like a pet dog, shushing me if I made a noise. As I got to toddler stage, I was allowed to roam the floor, seeking attention and discarded peanuts, anything to avoid Babs who gave me no attention but was fond of trying to hit my head with a well-aimed dry roasted. The locals affectionately called me Half Pint, although Babs preferred to call me the Runt, or the fucking Runt, depending on how much beer she had consumed.

In the end it was Eric, the landlord, who took charge, putting me out back in his living room with a video, half a lemonade and a packet of cheese and onion. I watched Care Bears on repeat before I was deemed old enough to move onto Eric's own favourites: Oklahoma, South Pacific and Singing in the Rain. I loved the musicals, not only were they way more fun, but Eric would come and sit with me sometimes, tucking me under his arm and singing along. I remember how safe I used to feel there, enjoying the rumble in his chest as he sang and I would try to learn the words so I could sing with him. My musical taste was severely skewed as a result; I liked to think I was Nellie Forbush, *washing that man right outa my hair,* which was confusing for any potential girlfriends who preferred Britney or Ace of Base. When Eric's daughter, Sally, moved back to work in the pub, she took me under her wing, introducing me to the 1985 Live Aid concert - oh-so-thrilling - but secretly I missed those evenings when it was just Eric and me, cuddled up, watching together.

I never said a word to anyone about my unorthodox situation, partly because I knew it wasn't *normal* – and when you are a kid, you want to be like everyone else - but mainly because I was scared of Babs. Then I met Nina and Kim and everything changed; I found myself releasing a steady drip of information about my evenings at home alone or out the back of the pub and before long the Fishers (Kim's family) and the Bergdahls (Nina's) had rallied round, extending their family embrace to include little Stella Halfpenny. I would eat supper with Kim's family, wonderful home cooked meals: shepherd's pie, fish cakes, bangers and mash. I can still remember the first time I ate with them, Mr Fisher stabbing an extra sausage with his fork and sliding it on to my plate, while Mrs Fisher piled on another mountain of fluffy mash, made with real potatoes that I had helped peel. I hadn't known that mash was made from proper potatoes until that evening. Mash, for me, came from a packet. After supper I would help with the washing up, revelling in the community of the shared chores. Supper over, I sometimes moved across to Nina's house where I had a bed on her top bunk. I even had my own set of sheets with a pattern of flowers around the edge and a matching pillow case. How I prized those sheets, carefully making the bed every morning, folding down the top sheet so that the flowers ran in an ordered line across the bed.

Kim and Nina. Family.

What Kim failed to mention earlier was the exact location in Marylebone where she has to deliver a pile of contracts to her boss, busy conducting business with a Qatari national who has taken over the entire top floor of a hotel called Hemplewood Place. Had I known, I would have sought alternative transport. This is a hotel that holds memories for me, precious memories, memories that I would usually be happy to mull over, to relive, to savour.

Just not today.

You see, I have been to the Hemplewood once before. With Jackson.

Long ago, when we first met, he used to take me to exciting places that had previously been way out of my league. Hemplewood Place felt like the high point; a fabulously over-the-top afternoon tea in the infamous Inner Courtyard. This wondrous eatery sits in the heart of the hotel, a magnificent glass dome offering uninterrupted views of the London sky. It is, was, a tiny slice of paradise in the heart of Central London. Today, though, I don't feel up to paradise, don't want to see its mocking splendour, taste those once sweet memories.

In the back of a black cab, Kim is inspecting her face in a small mirror, dabbing daintily at her nose with a powder compact. As I watch her keeping the rush of freckles on dim, she turns to me. 'What?'

I shake my head.

'Want me to work some magic on you?'

I shake my head. 'No point. I've tried. I plastered on layers of expensive face products this morning and they'd all fallen off by the time I got to the office. They need to develop a lotion that will stick to greasy hangover skin, seeping with last night's alcohol. Clear gap in the market. I should contact Estée Lauder and offer my services as chief consultant and guinea pig.'

She looks at me critically. 'Maybe it's better that way, then if Jackson turns up later and finds you looking wrecked, he'll realise his actions have consequences. It would do him good to learn some remorse.'

Ha! As if. Remorse doesn't feature in his repertoire; he was born without the remorseful gene. Along with guilt and shame. All missing. Although it is one of the things that attracted me to him, that self-assurance, that confidence. Made me feel safe. Plus, I have more than enough remorse, guilt and shame for the two of us, it would be a waste of energy to double up.

'That's fourteen quid, love.' The driver opens the window between the front and back of the cab, his eyes pausing for a beat on my sorry face.

'Do you want to wait here? I won't be long,' Kim asks.

'How long?'

'Ten minutes, fifteen max.'

'I'll have to charge you,' the taxi driver butts in. 'I've a family to feed.'

Kim gives him a sweet coy look. 'Five minutes then. Not a second more.'

'Still charging. Five minutes is another fare.'

Swearing loudly, Kim orders me out as I wave her off and limp pathetically in to the hotel after her, my dodgy knee now begging for a flat shoe.

The hotel reception is busy, awash with over-dressed middle-aged couples of varying nationalities demanding room upgrades, so I plough on through to the inner courtyard. I was resplendent that day with Jackson, if I do say so myself, in a hip trouser suit from Whistles, which was part-funded by Nina. Personally, I couldn't believe my luck. I kept crossing my fingers, praying and thinking, *I've made it! A proper boyfriend with a proper job, solvent, a home owner.* As the ticked boxes stacked up, I had to push away the persistent worry about my lack of boxes, wondering if in a successful partnership (successful marriage, actually; I was getting way ahead of myself) the boxes were bundled into a joint account, Jackson's stash making up for my lack of. Self-confidence has not always been my strong suit, so I had a tendency, pre-Jackson, to find myself boyfriends who could have been described as *unsuccessful* or *needy.* There is nothing an insecure woman likes more than a needy boyfriend, we come into our own, papering over our own fears by trying to fix someone else's.

Nina called them penniless losers, leeches, freeloaders and, the greatest sin of all, unambitious.

'Eyes to the sky, Stella,' she would say. 'Aim for the stars.'

Now, as I look out over the restaurant, I feel calmed by the muted hum of discreet conversation, the soft-stepping waiters, porcelain tea cups teetering onto wafer-thin saucers and the faint chink of crystal glasses being touched in celebration.

Closing my eyes, I drift off to that day almost five years ago.

It was a Thursday afternoon and I had left work early citing an appointment with the dentist; unoriginal but the boss was severely weakened by recent root canal treatment, so I was on safe ground. I headed over to Oxford Street and ducked into the hallowed halls of the Selfridges beauty department for a makeover. Years before, when I first came to London, I used to work in Selfridges; first in Haberdashery, then Shoes – hallelujah, the perks – before stagnating in Stationery. A few of my old colleagues were still working there, loyal devotees to the Selfridges brand and Maria, still in Shoes, had secured me a spot for an overhaul at the Bobbie Brown counter. A cheery young man did such a good job transforming me that I ended up buying most of the products – a purchase way beyond my means, but I was on a high that shielded me from such mundane realities.

And on to the Hemplewood. Champagne, heavenly food almost too beautiful to eat and, best of all, the luxury of Jackson's attention on me, and only me. He wanted me then, at that moment, on that day, Jackson wanted me.

My reverie is interrupted by a familiar voice. I look around me, certain I can hear Nina. I'd know that voice anywhere. Swivelling about I catch sight of her distinct white mane of hair. She is being directed to a table across the restaurant and strides off confidently. Not in her office then and available for support services to a girlfriend-in-need. Except she is probably schmoozing an obscenely rich American with a huge stash of cash just begging to be invested. Our friends over the pond love Nina, an English accent coupled with her ethereal Scandinavian beauty and a razor-sharp brain. I try to see who she is meeting as she disappears behind a pillar guarded by what looks like a fir tree, but it's impossible to see.

The fact that I can't see who she is meeting gives me an itch.

What if it's Callum? Seeing him twice in less than twenty-four hours would be what is known as *overkill* and not good for the already fragile Halfpenny health.

To avoid being accosted by the head honcho directing operations, I wait until he is busy seating people and then slip into the courtyard. Ahead of me, Nina is being seated by a deferential waiter, while another – they are everywhere – is speaking to her companion, who I can't see yet, hidden as he is by the fir tree.

Half way there, I lose my nerve. Do I really want to deal with Callum now? Last night was bad enough and there are no wasabi nuts here to take the edge off his arrogance. I hesitate, undecided.

'Can I help you, Madam?'

I jump about a foot in the air. 'Jesus, you nearly gave me a heart attack.'

'I prefer the Spanish pronunciation, Madam, *Hay-soos.* Do you have a reservation?' A po-faced waiter with an impressive helmet of gleaming black hair looms over me.

'Er, no. But, my -'

'I am afraid we are fully booked, Madam,' he says, now eyeballing the top of my head.

'Is it my hair?'

'Excuse me?'

'My hair. Is that why you're fully booked?' Logic has left the room and his magnificent thatch is making me paranoid. Not a hair out of place.

'This has nothing to do with your chosen hairstyle, Madam. However, we are fully booked. There is a sizeable delegation from Qatar with us today.'

'Well, I will in fact be joining friends,' I say with conviction, flicking an eye over at Nina who is already deep in conversation. How come she hasn't intuitively felt my pain?

'Very good,' says my well-coiffed friend. 'May I escort you?'

'I'm good, thank you,' I say, heading off over the final expanse of beautiful floor tiles - Italian probably, Middle Eastern possibly, Bart would know. He is encyclopaedic where tiles are concerned. He is encyclopaedic about many things but tiles have a special place in his heart; an apprentice tiler when he left school, he now owns a highly successful building company, specialising in bathrooms and kitchens.

Nina is looking more exquisite than ever in a pale grey fitted suit with a dark trim, green eyes luminous, white hair tumbling over one shoulder. I give a cheery hello and get a shock-and-horror stare in return.

Yes, it's me and I've found you out. Tough. I grit my teeth and turn to acknowledge Callum.

Today has not been what anyone, however misguided, would have called a picnic and it now slides into heretofore uncharted territory of non-picnicness.

The person opposite Nina is Jackson.

As my brain struggles to compute what is going on, he reaches out across the table and takes her hand, giving it a loving squeeze and effectively stamping on any remaining shreds of doubt.

Jackson is *with* Nina.

They say we are all capable of murder if pushed hard enough and let me now take a second to confirm that this is, in fact, true. Right now, I am ready to kill. Both of them. Preferably before they get to the cute cakes and fizzy drinks.

Who do I kill first?

Nina, definitely Nina. You don't do this to a girlfriend, a best friend. Best friends are sacred.

Or Jackson. Oh God, Jackson, you hypocritical bastard. Sanctimonious and always so fucking righteous, and yet – here we are.

As I am eying up the available implements for violence – a very poor choice involving a Cartier pen that I know Jackson keeps his top pocket or a brooch pinned to Nina's lapel - an unexpected, steely calm washes over me. I grasp that for once, for the first time ever, I am occupying the high ground.

Advantage Stella.

'Jackson, *darling*, Nina, *sweet*heart,' I cry, loud enough to attract the attention of the surrounding tables.

Jackson hates a scene and he glances around, his expression strained; who could be listening? Anyone important?

Point to Stella.

'You naughty people!' My voice reaches an unusual pitch here, not unlike the moment a choir boy's voice unexpectedly breaks. I clear my throat. Need to concentrate, keep the upper hand. 'I've been looking for you all over!'.

'For God's sake, Stella, shut up.' Jackson's head is swivelling left to right, a periscope on the lookout for trouble. 'What's happened to you? Is that a black eye?'

'Like you would care,' I say, glancing around for a spare chair.

'Stella, are you –'

'Cut the crap, Nina!' She recoils as if I have hit her. 'Just shut up and quit with the fake solicitude.'

'Excuse me Madam,' says a stern voice at my left shoulder. 'Is something the matter?' A man in an expensive suit oozes unease, swaying from one foot to the other.

'No, not at all, everything's marvellous.' I coo. 'We're celebrating! We need champagne! And would you mind finding me a chair? You are so kind and that is a truly magnificent tie.'

Jackson opens his mouth to object, but before he can get a word out a waiter sidles up with a bottle of champagne, ice bucket and two glasses.

'That was quick! Such amazing service here and we'll be needing another glass. So fun to celebrate with friends, don't you agree?' I smile sweetly at our stern friend who gives a brisk nod before turning on his heel and striding off to find a worthier recipient of his attention.

We sit in a spiky silence while the waiter does the honours; presenting the bottle politely to Jackson, meticulously unscrewing the little wire mesh, easing out the cork with impressive finesse and finally pouring a measly amount into the two glasses. I look at him with pleading eyes and he disappears before coming back seconds later with a glass for me.

'Don't be shy,' I say, nudging the bottle as he pours.

Jackson is now white with rage and Nina looks like she's just been swindled out of large sum of money.

Ha. Another point for Ms Halfpenny.

'Well, this is nice,' I say, wetting my lips with the pale liquid and feeling the bubbles pop against my tongue. 'What exactly are we celebrating? You're holding hands, which is a bit of a giveaway, so I'm going to hazard a guess and say you're celebrating a fuck-buddy anniversary. Am I right?' Silence. 'The burning question is, which anniversary is it? How long have you two been carrying on like a couple of sleazy, crappy, cheating, fucking lowlifes?' I demand, pleased to have summoned so many good adjectives at such short notice.

They share a long look.

'Stop being flippant, Stella. We were going to speak to you, tonight,' says Jackson, his voice cold.

'Yeah right. You lying fuck, Jackson.' Shock registers on his face and I shiver with pride. He hates swearing and I have been toeing the line to stay in his good books for five years now. 'Where were you last night? Suppose you couldn't drag yourself away from the juicy Swedish meatball on offer, could you? Your thanks are overdue by the way, leaving me to deal with your friend, Callum. You'll enjoy that Nina, all Jackson's bor-ring, arrogant friends.'

On some weird level I am enjoying this. I have never spoken to him like this, never dared. Deciding to award myself another point, I take a big swig of champagne. Damn this stuff is fizzy! A huge burp pops out causing Jackson to tut with disgust and Nina to roll her eyes.

'This is good stuff. What is it?' I lean over to look at the bottle. Damn. Cristal. 'Fuck me, only the best for our little Swedish ice axe.' I have to concede a point to Nina here. 'We only had the house champagne when Jackson brought me,' I say, looking at Nina. 'You must remember, Nina. I was so excited about it. Even *you* were excited. Helped me buy that lovely Whistles suit. Remember?'

She shakes her head looking massively put out. Had she really forgotten Jackson brought me here? First.

Yet another point for Stella.

'Zero marks for originality Jackson,' I gloat, picking up my glass and taking another deep drink. 'This stuff is helping enormously with the general nausea, should be available on prescription. I might write in to the Daily Mail; they love this kind of health scoop.'

'What's that then?' A hand lands delicately on my shoulder and I turn to find Kim taking in the scene with wide-eyed curiosity.

'Champagne, helping with the overall malaise. Cristal too. We only had the cheap stuff when he brought me. Anyway, pull up a chair. We're having a meeting about my boyfriend getting it on with one of our best friends. Ex best-friend. Friend no longer. You'll need a glass.' I give a quick yodel, trying and failing to attract attention of a passing waiter.

'I do love a meeting, especially one with such a meaty agenda. Oooh, and snacks too,' says Kim, as a cake stand arrives groaning with tiny edibles.

'I'm not sitting around listening to you two,' huffs Jackson, standing up.

'Sit down, Jackson, or I will make such a scene you will relive it in your nightmares forever. Everyone will have their phones out in a flash filming it all for posterity.'

'And the front cover of The Mirror,' adds Kim, for good measure. 'Bart's friend, Jeremy, is features editor in the People section.'

He pauses, no doubt weighing up the horrors of appearing on the front page of The Mirror against staying another minute at the table with yours truly. A Catch-22.

He sits. Ha.

Feeling victorious, I take a teeny tart with a strawberry the size of a pea perched aloft a creamy hillock and pop it in. 'Hmmm, paradise on a plate.' I take another, this time with a blackberry surfing a wave of purple froth. 'Dee-vine. Were you planning to eat any of this or was it just for decoration?'

'Shame to let it go to waste,' says Kim, scoffing a mini lemon tart. 'Now, bring me up to date. What have I missed?'

'Nothing. We're just establishing the initial facts. I want to establish how long the *A-ffair* has been going on.' The champagne is bouncing about in my glass I am shaking so hard, but it is worth every second to see their pokey, pissed off faces. 'They claim that they were going to tell me about it tonight, which would mean it is no longer a sleazy affair, but a *relationship.*'

'Riveting,' Kim breathes. 'You know, we should keep a record, make it official. Plus, I need to be able to report back to Bart accurately. He's a stickler for details. So, I'll do the minutes if that's all right with you guys?' Jackson and Nina look on nonplussed as Kim rummages about in her bag. 'Christ, I have a lot of crap in here. Wait, here we go, this will do nicely.' She looks up triumphantly and produces a crumpled receipt from Boots and an old Bic biro.

'Right. Pen and paper, tick. I'll just have one of these sandwiches, oh, perhaps two, then I need a glass of something fizzy and I'm good to go. I'd have a bite to eat if I were you, Nina, you're looking very pale and peaky.' She grabs a passing waiter and begs another glass, adding, 'a big one if there's a choice,' and within seconds he has glided back with a glass.

These guys move as if they're on wheels. Most impressive.

'Right, pour away Stella, the more the merrier.' Kim holds out her glass and I fill it right up to the brim. 'Perfect.' She takes a gulp, slurping nicely. 'I'm ready.'

'Haven't you got a Harvey Nick's receipt or something Kim?' I venture, politely, 'you know Nina doesn't like Boots. Selfridges? Space NK? Harrods would do.'

That pierces the chilly carapace; she never could take a joke. 'Stop it, Stella, stop being so juvenile. We have been trying to find a way to break this to you, kindly, sensibly, gently.'

She stops, trying, I think, to frown disapprovingly as her forehead reluctantly hefts itself into a faint ripple. 'You are making this much more difficult than it needs to be.'

Did she really just say that? Out loud.

'Nina, can we clear something up from the off?' I say, teacher to her idiotic pupil. 'I, we, are not here to make it easy for you, and betraying a lifelong friend by fucking her boyfriend is not filed under *kind* or *sensible* either.'

'Stella!' Jackson barks.

I jump. 'Hello?'

Kim doesn't miss a beat, warbling, 'Helllooo? Love a bit of Lionel.'

A snort of laughter bursts out of me and I swallow down a few more. Must focus.

I clear my throat. 'You, my little Swedish dumpling, do not do *kindly*. You are lost in a Sea of Selfishness.' I stop to nudge Kim. 'Make sure you get that in the minutes, I like that.'

Kim nods. 'I'll put it in bold.'

'Underlined.'

'Got it.'

I turn to Jackson. 'It's all mig mig. That means ME in Swedish, Jackson, m-i-g, you should take note. She uses it a lot.'

'Stella!' His voice is unusually tense.

All the more reason to ignore him and lob in another grenade. 'And you need to get that Botox topped up Nina. Your forehead is showing signs of movement. Put that in the minutes Kim. Move-ment, *such* a good word. Before you know it, you'll have a full-on crease.'

They both register their shock; Jackson because he hates Botox – how could he not have noticed the smooth shiny forehead and lack of frowning potential? – and Nina because we were long ago sworn to secrecy.

Point to Stella. I am way ahead now.

I decide to plough on before they recover. 'Sometimes it's hard to tell what she's thinking, but we have it worked out now, don't we Kim? I could do you a series of photos if you like, to get you started; Nina when she's cross, Nina happy, Nina thinking, *surely you're not going to eat that?*'

'Stella!' Jackson shouts. Heads around us turn, avid, curious.

'I expect you know them all already though don't you. Nina before sex, Nina after sex, Nina -'

'Shut up!'

'Testy,' from Kim, who is loving every second judging by the smirk plastered all over her face.

'Stella, this is not a joke,' Jackson says in a failed whisper. More of a throaty squawk.

'Oh, but it is, my darling. The joke has been on me for some time. You.' I point at him with a shaky finger. 'Are a stinking, lying, repellent, amoebic...' Where am I going with this? Amoebic? 'Pitiful bastard,' I finish quickly.

'How do you spell amoebic? Does bastard have a capital B?' Kim is busy taking notes on her blotched receipt. 'I like the amoebic touch though, original, very primitive and they have, after all, been surrendering to their most basic instincts.'

'I'm leaving.' Jackson stands (again) and puts his hands on his hips. All rather Peter Pan from this angle.

With great restraint, I decide not to mention it.

'*We're* leaving' he corrects himself and nods at Nina who doesn't move. He needs to learn that Nina does not like being told what to do. 'We are finished Stella, as you so correctly surmise. We wanted to be civilised. However, clearly you're not capable of that.'

'I beg to differ. Just how long have you and the Swedish chef been mucking, sorry, fucking around behind my back?' Silence. 'All that working late must have been *so* exhausting for you both.' I flick Nina a filthy look, but she has found something interesting to look at on the ceiling. 'Civilised, my arse.'

A red stain is creeping out of Jackson's shirt collar and stalking up his neck. He could blow at any point.

Dragging a hand through his hair as if composing himself, he intones, 'I'll give you a week to move out, Stella. I'll come by later to collect some clothes, but I want you gone in a week.' He looks at Nina who is applying lipstick with a shaky hand. She is not used to getting so much abuse. I watch as she presses her lips together, carefully, meticulously and a burning rage clutches at my heart. I want to hurt her, make her suffer too, smash that lipstick into her sad, pretty face and hack away until it is a sodden mush.

'SIT RIGHT DOWN, JACKSON,' Kim barks. 'Now! We're not done yet.' Jackson doesn't move. She points at Nina. 'Don't you dare.' She swivels back to Jackson. 'I'd sit if I were you or this will go public and I know how much you loathe the tabloids.'

Jackson sits down slowly. 'Make it quick,' he mutters.

'Ready, Stells?' she asks, gently. I nod, bracing myself. 'We always knew you were a motherfucker, Jackson, but Nina, you've fooled us for a long time. We accepted that you were narcissistic, self-absorbed, running too close to the bone with your *tough love*, but you were our friend and we loved you all the same.' A pause, a sip of champagne, the glass steady. 'However, we could be here all day discussing what a traitorous bitch you are. We need to move on and, as they say, cut to the chase. You both think you are so bloody superior, but expensive tastes and paying a fortune for the hotel room doesn't mask the fact that you're just another cheating pair of fuckers. Excuse the language - when the glove fits and all of that.'

Damn, she is good at this.

'It wasn't -' Jackson tries to get a word in.

Kim shuts him down immediately. 'Shut it, Jackson. You think you're a cut above, both of you, but you're not.' She takes a big gulp of champagne, which seems like a good idea, so I do the same. 'Five weeks, Jackson. Stella needs five weeks to get herself sorted.'

'Absolutely no bloody way. I'll give you two weeks. Not a day more.'

Kim remains calm despite his intransience. 'You're not paying attention. The Mirror. Rich banker cheating on his Mrs with her best friend is just the kind of exclusive they love.' She turns to me. 'I can just see your tear stained face under the headline, Stells.' Back to Jackson. 'Five weeks. It's not as if you've nowhere to live. Nina has acres of spare room.'

Jackson and Nina hold a look together, saying nothing. Bart is a dangerous opponent and they know it.

'Slymann Hodge would love it.' Kim rubs it in a bit further. 'What's the chairman's name, Stells?'

I choose this somewhat taut moment to fall off my chair. I had been slowly drifting sideways like the leaning tower for some minutes, not wanting to interrupt Kim in full majestic flow. Now I hit the floor hard with one leg beached up on the chair, skirt around my waist, M&S pants on full display. Shaken and stirred, I give a nervous chuckle as I try to pull down my skirt and cover my knickers; not wearing my best pair of course and, worse, I can't remember when I last had a bikini wax - not what you want with your cucumber sandwiches.

'Come on lovely, let's get out of here.' Kim somehow gets behind me and with help from an old but surprisingly strong waiter, hauls me to my feet. I sway like an unsteady toddler and giggle quietly to myself.

'Stella!' Kim barks at me and I shut off the hilarity like a tap. Man, she is getting scary and she's on *my* side. 'Five weeks. You can come and get some things, but Stella has five weeks.'

'I don't think so, Kimberley. I'll be round this evening. And don't touch anything.' He points a finger at me accusingly.

I stare at him in shock. 'What do you mean, don't touch anything – I live there, you moron.' I try and sound sure of myself but there is a giveaway wobble creeping in. Time to go before I cave completely. 'He's all yours, Nina. You go together perfectly.'

'You are being so childish, both of you.' Nina's ruffled. 'This is serious. You knew you were never right together, Stella. Right from the beginning, you knew it wouldn't last.' Her expression changes then, and she glances at me slyly. 'One of the first things you said to me when you met him was, *I don't know what he's doing with me.*'

I add a final dash of the good stuff to my glass, a quick sip, one final burp, then I take a step towards her and put my face right into hers. So close I can smell her newly applied lipstick.

'And you Nina, remember what you said?'

She watches me and I know she remembers.

'You said, *he's lucky to have you.*'

CHAPTER 5

Integrity

/ɪnˈtɛɡrɪti/

noun: the quality of being honest and behaving according to strong moral principles

Kim has me installed on the sofa like a chilly Queen of Sheba with a bag of frozen peas on my sore knee and a few ice cubes wrapped in a tea towel for my eye. She has been heroically clearing up the wreckage from last night, spread expansively from living room to kitchen to bedroom to bathroom – the smashed shower eliciting a few heartfelt expletives as she swept the worst of it into the airing cupboard. She appears now holding a large piece of the door.

'We should be suing someone over this. I'm going to ask Bart, he'll know, defective materials or faulty construction, something like that.'

'Unsound owner,' I quip, pleased to be making a joke at Jackson's expense.

'That's my Stella,' she says gently, coming over. 'You'll get over this, you know. It's utter crap right now and it will be for a while, then little-by-little the pain will start to recede. One day we'll laugh about the Hemplewood, you'll see.' I try to give her an evil, disbelieving eye but it won't cooperate and she carries right on, oblivious. 'I'm right, I know I am. And you'll get over Jackson quicker than you'll get over Nina and I'll help you with that. She was my friend too and what she has done to you was indefensible.' She pauses to allow us both to contemplate the indefensibleness of Nina. 'I just hope one day, when she's no longer with Jackson, we'll be able to absolve her -'

'You are fucking kidding me,' I roar. 'If you ever forgive her, I will never forgive you! Have you already forgotten what we just witnessed? Fuck. Get a grip, Kim.'

'Keep your hair on. I'm not talking about now, or even next week, but I believe it will happen at some point. You'll see. So, calm down and let me go and see what I can find to put on that cut. Now that you've taken off all the slap, it looks infected. Where's the first aid stuff?'

'Fuck the first aid. Let me be very clear: I am not ever, ever going to forgive Nina. Ever. Got that? If he dumps her tomorrow, or she dumps him, I don't give a shit. Not. Forgiving. No pardon possible. Ever.'

'OK, sweetie,' she says, cheerfully. 'Now, first aid?'

'Bathroom, second drawer. Jackson has a stash worthy of a military hospital. Snake bite, Ebola virus, malaria, man-flu – all catered for.'

'Bart relies on aspirin and Irn Bru.'

She is dabbing at the cut with kitchen roll and Dettol, Florence N to her very core, when Bart himself rocks up weighed down with bottles of the magic Irn Bru and red wine. With him, carrying two pizza boxes, is a slouching wreck of a man with a beat-up face and a badly fitting brown suit.

I eye him crossly. There is a time and a place for company and this is not it.

'Stella Bella, this is Jeremy. You remember? We share a place in Wandsworth. Near the prison. You meet one time.' A vague memory of Bart's old flat where he lived when he met Kim staggers grudgingly into the light, although I have no memory of this hulking structure.

'Now is not the time, Bart,' I huff. 'I'm not feeling very sociable.' I wave Bart in closer. 'What's he doing here anyway? Just make him go.'

'Now, now,' admonishes Kim. 'He's here for you, Stells. The Mirror, remember? Back-up if Jackson appears and starts telling you to pack your bags again. Besides, he can get some useful background details in case he really does have to write an article. Would be kind of fun, wouldn't it?'

'No, it would not. It will be *my* face in the paper and I'm way too unphotogenic for that. Besides, the whole office will read about it. I don't think so.'

Jeremy steps forward into my line of sight; he looks like he should be writing for Farmers Weekly, not *people* stories for the Mirror. 'Heard you've had a bad day,' he says, gruffly. 'I'm here as a favour to Bart, but I don't want to intrude if I'm in the way.'

'You *are* in the way,' I hiss.

'Stella,' says Kim, her voice firm. 'Jeremy is a friend. He is not the bad guy. He's doing us a favour and we're very grateful and we will treat him accordingly.'

'Speak for yourself.'

'Just imagine Jackson's face if he turns up later. A reporter from one of the lowly *tabloids.* He'll have a heart attack.'

She has a point. And the thought of Jackson having a coronary right now is very appealing. Not a fatal one, obvs, just enough to give him a proper scare. Then I could save his life with some of that chest thumping massage and earn his life-long gratitude. *This is my wife, Stella, she saved me, I owe her my......*

'Are you listening, Stells? He said he could arrange for a photographer to come and take your picture.'

'I just hope he knows how to use photoshop. Have you seen my face?'

'Not now, not today. When you're feeling better,' he says.

'Oh, best make a booking for 2025 then.' The bite of sarcasm feels good.

'She's not usually like this,' says Kim.

'Everyone's entitled to a bad day,' he says, kindly. 'And it sounds like you've had a particularly tough one. I'll do what I can if push comes to shove.'

'I want to push him under a train,' asserts Bart. 'Can I kill him? Please? Then we take care of Nina. I have friends who make her disappear for very low price. Very discreet.'

He looks so sincere I want to cry. I love Bart. He is huge, solid, towering over Kim who secured the coveted position of goal attack in the school netball team because she was a good head taller than anyone else. His already giant head is made larger by a shock of light brown hair that lives in a permanent state of having been pulled through a hedge. His hands are like polar bear paws and just as strong; they could snap the traitorous Nina neck in seconds.

I close my eyes, visualising Bart's giant mitts around her fragile neck.

Sensing my rising emotion, he changes tack. 'First wine, then pizza, then more wine, then vodka! Good Polish vodka. Works on every problem know to man.'

'I probably shouldn't drink too much; it'll make me emotional.' I make a token attempt to hold back the tide.

'Ah, but the emotion must come out. Inside, emotion is poison. Toxic. And, in Poland, they recommend a shot of vodka for everything. You too Jeremy. You very good at Polish.' They share one of those high five type handshakes that all the blokes do nowadays. 'So, can I offer a glass of best Romania red? Very quiffable.'

'Quaffable Bart. A quiff is for your hair, like Elvis.' I make a shape over my head and he nods in understanding, mouthing the word to himself. 'Tonight, though, Jackson is supplying the wine. Go and take whatever you like, top shelf only.'

His eyes light up. 'Top shelf?'

'Whatever takes your fancy, but it has to be from the top shelf.'

And he is off like a shot, banging through to the kitchen, whistling and calling for Jeremy to come and help. It would be fair to say that, from the off, Bart has not been Jackson's greatest supporter. They are chalk and cheese really, one full of spontaneous surprises and the other hell-bent on keeping a lid on everything and maintaining control. The only reason they have been able to rub along is because of Bart's ability to get along with absolutely *anyone*, and this despite what Kim and I like to refer to as *kitchengate.*

A couple of years ago, when Jackson decided to redo the kitchen, Bart gave him a fantastic quote for the work. A quote which, to my embarrassment, was summarily declined. The official line was that he had a better deal from someone else, which was a complete lie. The truth was that he refused to even consider Bart a serious candidate, despite the raft of recommendations I showed him, including an article in a prominent architectural magazine, which had done a feature on a bathroom Bart's company had done. Instead, he paid over three times as much to a cack-handed shark who took over three months to finish the two-week job, with tiles so badly laid that four have since fallen out. Sworn to secrecy, I was terrified of even seeing Kim and Bart in case the truth popped out – which of course it did one day after they plied me with vodka. Now, the first thing Bart does every time he comes around is check out the kitchen, see how it is holding up. Or preferably - not holding up.

'Two more tiles gone!' he shouts from the kitchen now, amid banging noises. 'Three!'

Kim goes to join in the fun and I hear some very inappropriate giggling considering the solemnity of the situation. They take their merry time eventually reappearing with Bart cradling a bottle of.....I wave him over so I can see.....Le Pin, a Pomerol.

'1998,' hums Bart, passing the bottle to Jeremy. 'Very excellent year.'

'Crack it open then, I could die of thirst waiting for you lot.'

Bart does the honours while I direct Jeremy to the cabinet with the posh glasses and Kim gets onto Google. 'About three grand,' she says, sounding disappointed. 'Thought it might be more.'

That makes me sweat.

'How can they charge so much for a bottle of wine?' I ask, peering into the glass to see if it looks any different from the cheap stuff I normally drink.

'Because they can,' replies Bart. 'Exceptional product, low output, high demand and a helping hand from Lady Luck.'

'Bit like Nina,' sniffs Kim, 'She always did have a sense of entitlement.'

This leads to a delicious discussion detailing the shortcomings of our two leading protagonists. I am fully aware that we are pulling to shreds two people who, until a few short hours ago, were two of the most important in my life, but once we have started, we can't seem to stop. It is fun at first, but the longer we go on with the unvarnished truths piling up, my life a barren wasteland beyond, the less I like it.

Then Jeremy, content up to this point to just listen and take a few notes, decides to add his pounds worth too.

'He sounds like your archetypal sociopath,' he muses.

Which does not help.

'Oh, for fuck's sake. Now I've been living with a sociopath for three years? My day just gets better and better.'

'Ah, you see, Stella,' he goes on, 'the flip side to their antisocial behaviour is that they are typically very charismatic, very charming, especially when they first meet you. Pulling you in. Seducing you.'

Still not helping.

'Now, now,' soothes Kim. 'He kept it well hidden when you first met him. That's how these people function.'

'Why did he bother if he was more interested in the goods over in the Swedish aisle?'

She giggles. 'He needed someone to wash and fold all those Calvin Kleins.'

'And iron them,' I sniff, before I've had time to realise what I am admitting to.

There is uproar from Kim and Bart at this additional nugget of information as they demand details on the ins and outs of Jackson and his meticulous wardrobe maintenance, followed by an inspection of the underwear drawer and a head count. Kim then gets busy, hoping to mess with Jackson's head; the offending pants are hidden in various locations around the room, white T-shirts are infiltrated into the blue pile, socks are paired with unfamiliar faces. He will hate it, so I cheer on enthusiastically from the side-lines while Bart carefully switches all the jackets of his suits so that they are no longer with the matching trousers. Jeremy looks on like a proud parent, taking a few photos and asking me whether he has any other fetishes, preferably involving sex toys. I am just contemplating cleaning the loo with his toothbrush or putting my hair remover in his shampoo when there is a noise, a door slamming. The front door.

Jackson.

Abandoning our work, we all charge back to the living room, throwing ourselves onto the sofa and trying to look nonchalant, the jovial atmosphere draining away with his every step up the stairs.

'Well, well. A party.' Jackson leans against the door frame, arms folded. He is the epitome of studied cool, jacket on but not buttoned, tie loosened but not undone. His dark hair, trimmed every two weeks, is immaculate as ever, his beautiful face calm. My heart gives an unhealthy lurch and I know in that instant that despite the hurt and humiliation of this afternoon, despite the fact that he is apparently a *sociopath*, I still love him. I stupidly thought the pain would eradicate the love like a decent stain remover. Instantly.

'Does four friends having a drink constitute a party?' Kim asks, clasping my hand in reassurance. 'I don't think so.'

71

He shrugs, conveying a complete lack of interest, he even starts inspecting his nails just to ram home how much he does not give a shit.

Bart, clearly wanting to puncture his smug insouciance, lifts his glass high. 'Very good vintage. Na Zdrowie!'

That gets his attention.

'How dare you,' he says in a low growl, striding over and grabbing the bottle, the planes of his face visibly sharpening as the anger builds.

'Don't say a word! Just don't,' I shout. 'You care more about your precious fucking wine than me.'

'This wine is irreplaceable,' he hisses, waving the bottle at me.

There is a cold lull at this statement, an uncomfortable stillness, eventually broken by a low rumbling to my left. I look over at Bart who is getting to his feet. At full height, he is a few inches taller than Jackson, broader, and, despite all his hours in the gym, Jackson just doesn't have the same solid presence. Bart puts down his glass and leans across the table, stabbing a meaty finger at Jackson who inches back fractionally.

Bart articulates his words slowly. 'Stella is irreplaceable. There is always more wine, but there is only one Stella.'

Kim applauds loudly. 'Hear, hear.'

'That's a good quote, Bart,' says Jeremy quietly, pulling his notepad out of his back pocket.

'That wine is unique, invaluable,' Jackson blusters, blushing to be caught out on such a cheap point. 'And who are *you,* anyway?'

Jeremy stands up, bulky and somehow dangerous in his shabby suit with his bashed-up nose and heavy brows. He holds out a hand. 'Jeremy Jenson. Daily Mirror.'

For a couple of seconds, the quiet is absolute as Jackson absorbs this information, colour rising in his face again until it is a dark purple hue.

Not very becoming. He suits a paler colour.

Gathering himself, Jackson mutters, 'Kim. Bart. I want a minute. Alone. With Stella. And *you* can leave, Mr Jenson. Now.'

Silence. No one moves, no one speaks.

'Stells?' Kim asks.

I nod, then shake my head. 'OK, but *he* stays.' I indicate Jeremy with my head. Might as well get this over with. Besides, I am buoyed by Bart getting one over Jackson and saying there is only one Stella.

Bart gives me a refill before shuffling off to the kitchen, herding Kim and Jeremy before him like reluctant sheep. Jackson then moves to sit opposite me in one of the armchairs, leaning forward, elbows on his knees, eyes on the floor.

I wait for what feels like half a lifetime before he speaks.

'Stella. This was not the plan.' He raises his head a fraction and looks right at me. He doesn't look contrite, apologetic, sad. No. His expression cold, indifferent. 'This is not how we - '

'Oh, cut the crap. What bloody plan? How to dump Stella without getting your hands dirty?'

'I don't do messy breakups. Once it's over, that is it. There is no point in raking over the coals. And we are over, Stella. Time to admit it.'

'Hay-soos. You are one cold fish Jackson. Five years we've had. Five. That's worth more than this. Surely? Living together, building a life together requires work, compromise. You know all about hard work, so why aren't you willing to work for us?'

He shakes his head. 'Not wasting my energy flogging a dead horse.'

'Always the romantic. You'll have to up your game for Nina,' I scoff. 'She has expectations.'

'We understand each other.'

'Ha,' I force out a bark of laughter. 'You understand each other over snatched evenings, secret meetings, hotel fucks, but will you understand each other when you *live* together? Two ambitious perfectionists jostling for the upper hand, that's going to be a bundle of laughs.' I stop to consider the two of them shacking up together and driving each other crazy. 'What I don't get is the secrecy? If you didn't love me anymore, why didn't you just tell me?'

'I never loved you, Stella.' Ouch, that is a low blow. He has never - and I have not admitted this to anyone, least of all myself - said he loved me, but I had convinced myself he did. 'Stella. It was good for a while, but it's over. Has been for a long time. Admit it. We're not suited, at all, and any pretence has gone on long enough.'

'Bullshit. You would never pretend for anyone. What I don't get is why you didn't just tell me? If it's been so crap for so long. Why all the fucking around?'

'Don't be so crude,' he sighs, looking pained. 'Christ, I don't know how I put up with you for so long. Nina is simply a class above.'

I try to butt in and object to this, but he talks over me.

'We met today at the Hemplewood to celebrate. We got confirmation.'

'Confirmation?' I look at him suspiciously, my chest tight. What now? 'Go on then, do tell. Is she pregnant?' No, they wouldn't celebrate that, both actively interested in *not* procreating and maintaining a life free of constraints.

'God, no.' He looks horrified. 'No, Nina got her promotion and is being transferred.' A weighted pause. 'To New York.'

There is a tiny pulse of time, an emptiness. New York?

'Woo hoo,' I croak. 'You'll have to start having phone sex.'

'And I will be heading up Investment Strategy, for Slymanns. In New York.'

Fuck. 'You're moving to New York?' my voice rises, finishing in a Mickey Mouse squeak. I take a deep breath, searching for the calm. Fail to find it. 'YOU ARE FUCKING MOVING TO NEW YORK? WITH NINA?'

Kim and Bart, clearly glued to the keyhole, burst into the room on their white chargers, demanding to know what is going on.

Jackson explains. Proud as pigging punch.

Kim doesn't flinch though. 'Perfect. The further the better. Wasn't there anything available in Hong Kong, or Tokyo? Auckland? An icecap? Still, New York will have its compensations; the Americans *love* Nina. All those wealthy Wall Street bankers will be all over her and with a loyalty rating as poor as hers, well, I'd watch my back if I were you.' She winks at Jackson and I want to hug her.

Meanwhile, Bart is topping up everyone's glasses and Jeremy is taking discreet snaps of Jackson on his phone. When everyone has more wine, Bart asks Jackson if he would like a drop.

'Keep. Away. From. My. Wine,' he shouts, loss-of-cool making a startling reappearance.

I look at him in disgust. 'I have no idea who you are anymore, you never used to be so stingy and mean.'

He snaps his head round, pouncing on the opening I have given him. 'Exactly, Stella. You have no idea who I am or what is valuable to me. You never have and you never will. You live in your safe little bubble, working that crappy job, seeing your stupid friends, doing nothing with your life, going nowhere. You are nothing. I'm sick of you. *Bored of you.* Nina has life, ambition, spunk.'

'Plenty of that,' I quip, trying for a joke, but his words have hit me like poisoned arrows, each one injecting a toxic mix of self-doubt and self-hate.

Kim moves over to where Jackson is standing. 'Don't you think you've done enough damage for one day, Jackson?' Her voice is soft and all the more powerful for it. 'You can blame

Stella as much as you like, but you're in the wrong this time. Just get some clothes and get out.'

'This is my house, Kim, mine, and I'll tell you now that Stella can have two weeks. After that the house is rented. Thanks for showing Callum around yesterday. He's taking it.' He gives me a satisfied grin. 'So, I suggest you find somewhere quickly. I'm sure your friends here have a spare room. Or ask Angus. You liked him.' He starts to walk away, then stops and turns to fix me with another aggressive stare. 'And don't touch my things. *Anything.* You can move into one of the spare rooms. I don't want you in my bed.' And he strides off.

It doesn't end there of course. There is a roar as he discovers the reorganisation of his wardrobe, another louder roar as he finds his shower in pieces in the airing cupboard – Kim's comment about Jackson being like a cross bear now making perfect sense – a final conniption about the kitchen tiles and, as an encore, he goes into one about the office.

'Do not set foot in my office, do not even *think* about setting foot in my office.' He glares at us, eyes flicking from one to the other. 'In fact, I'm going to lock it, I don't trust you lot.'

CHAPTER 6

Exhume
/eksˈhjuːm/
Verb: restore or revive, especially after a period of neglect

I wonder if I could move in with Kim and Bart? They could adopt me or I could be their housekeeper, or nanny. It is only a matter of time being they start producing baby Barts and there is no way Kim will want to give up work completely, she loves her job. They also have a vast garden so I could live in one of those fancy garden sheds, coming in for showers and the loo, earning my keep by cooking and washing up.

My daydreaming is shattered by a cry from the office. 'I'm in!'

Bart has been picking the lock to Jackson's office. I have lived here for three years with free access to the office and all his papers, as and when, and now he suddenly tells me to keep out: suspicions have understandably been aroused. Kim and I charge through from the kitchen – Jeremy doesn't want to get involved for professional reasons, so he stays put - and we gather in the small office space: a desk, office chair, filing cabinet, leather armchair, book shelves.

'How did you get in so quickly?' I ask Bart.

He shrugs, waving a bunch of weird looking keys at me. 'I keep special keys on me always. One time, I get locked out of a house. The owner is in Portugal, tiles is half finished, paint is open. Cost me a lot of cash and a big fight with the owner. Now, I am always prepare.'

'Let's have a look-see then.' Kim moves around behind the desk and plonks herself in the big chair, enjoying a few swivels while she is at it. 'What are you hiding my crusty little carbuncle?'

She gets busy on a small chest of drawers hidden under the table while Bart starts on the lock of the filing cabinet – something I have never taken the smallest interest in before - and I survey the shelves. People hide things in books, or behind books. Under books. There is always something on the bookshelves in the films, so I start pulling them out, one by one, and flicking through the pages. Waste of time no doubt, but I want to look busy. After a few minutes, there is a grunt of satisfaction from Bart as he masters the lock on the filing cabinet and pulls open the first drawer.

'Oooh, lots of interesting looking files, my karaluch,' he says, failing to mask his excitement.

'What's a karaluch, hon?' asks Kim, picking through the drawers like an extra from NCIS; any minute now she will have snapped on some plastic gloves and called for back-up.

'A cockroach,' he mumbles, brow already furrowed in concentration as he flicks through an orderly queue of matching blue folders.

As for the books, I am already bored. Finance, law, currencies, history of banking, not a novel in sight. Typical. When we went to Tuscany last year, Jackson brought a book called Irrational Exuberance to read, which I foolishly had my eye on, only to find it was an impenetrable look at the financial markets. Who reads that on holiday? In the end, I swopped books with a woman I met by the pool, spending the final three days of the holiday hot and bothered as I read an outrageously naughty (pornographic) book about swingers in Berlin.

There is a long, drawn-out whistle from Bart. I look up and Kim stops, head cocked in anticipation. He waves his hand for us to carry on while pulling out a bulky file, his focus absolute.

'Glad Bart's on my team.' I whisper to Kim.

She smiles in return, winks, and moves on to another drawer, opening it as if it might be booby-trapped. The minutes tick by and eventually I give up, signalling to Kim that I am heading back to the kitchen – no sign of Jeremy - where I slump into a chair, suddenly exhausted. Just the thought of all I have to do over the coming weeks, apart from piecing back together my shattered heart, makes me feel weak. Finding somewhere to live, packing up, making the move, unpacking, changing address, updating phones. And then there is the 'starting over' palaver to be factored in; take up sport, buy new clothes, get radical haircut, fly to New York, make sure ex sees radical haircut, fly back, get new job, become whole new person, write a blog, write a book, adopt a child, run a marathon, row the Atlantic, swim the channel....

Dr-rain-ing.

I vow there and then that there will be no mid-life new-life start-over makeover for me:

1) Hair is radical enough

2) I can't be arsed

3) Kim would kill me first

Wine, I need more wine. Will worry about my liver at a later date, in 2025 sometime, 2026. Or I could order a new one on Amazon; there is nothing you can't buy on Amazon. I am sure if you search hard enough you could find someone willing to flog you a vital organ. Or there is the deep dark web – something I know precisely nothing about but would be willing to learn if necessary. I could ask Jeremy; he should know as a journalist. Probably goes for a wander down there every day, see what's happening and what's not.

A whoop from Kim brings Jeremy back from wherever he has been – talking into a Dictaphone this time - as she stampedes through to the kitchen, fizzing with excitement, grinning so hard her face has gone all lopsided.

'Before you tell us *anything*,' I say, feeling huffy and defensive, 'I want some more wine. I can't imagine you have unearthed anything nice, like a list Stella's attributes or Things I love about Stella? What to buy Stella for Christmas possibly?' She looks at me sadly. 'Didn't think so. Bart,' I shout, slapping my hand on the table. 'Wine! Make it snappy. Top shelf only.'

Bart bustles through with an armload of blue files and gets busy with the top shelf. He comes back looking as if he is carrying an unexploded bomb rather than a bottle of some of France's finest.

'What you got, Bart?'

'Ssshhh, no speak,' he whispers, easing his precious cargo onto the table.

We gather around to inspect the bottle, Kim and I leaning in close to read the label.

'It's a Petrus,' rasps Kim, clapping her hands excitedly. 'Quick Stells, see how much it's worth. Then we can work out how much per glass.'

But I am shaking too hard to do anything useful, terrified of Jackson coming back and finding us, so Kim gets her phone out and does the honours. Frankly, I'm not sure I want to know. Jackson might have left the Stella but the Stella has not yet left the Jackson and his sphere of influence.

'Kim?' Bart is getting impatient.

'Hang on, just doing the calculation. How many glasses per bottle? Six?' She taps away on her phone, puffing out her cheeks in concentration. 'Fuck me. I've gone for an average as there was a range on the prices, so, rounding up to keep it simple, we'll say sixteen grand a bottle, that'll be a mere two thousand seven hundred of the Great British pounds, *per glass.* If you don't mind.'

That shuts us all up. Even Bart, who has the corkscrew half way in, pauses. We all stare at the bottle accusingly: that is outrageous. I knew it would be expensive but not *that* expensive. As reality sinks in, a great surge of joy erupts from deep inside me.

'All the more reason to *get on with it, Bart.* Stop procrastinating and get the corking cork out of the bottle and pour me a large one.' I let rip with a heartfelt cackle. 'Sixteen grand for a bottle of wine! You could buy a car for that. New. I can't believe it. To think he made me pay five hundred quid a month.' Kim mouth opens in protest at this statement, as she has long believed my time here was rent-free. Something I couldn't bring myself to correct.

When Jackson moved me in, he managed to sell me the five hundred quid per month as the *deal of the century,* which, in a way, I suppose it was for prime real estate in Primrose Hill. Except now, in light of bottles of vino at almost three grand *per glass,* it is starting to look less like a deal and more like a massive rip-off, especially given that I bought nearly all the food and household stuff, something Jackson considered beneath him.

'So, how many months have I lived here for? Bart, what's three times twelve?'

'Thirty-six,' he says, easing the cork out of the bottle and taking a hesitant sniff.

'That's thirty-six times five hundred, which is -'

'Eighteen thousand,' snaps Kim. 'You never said, Stells. I can't believe he charged you for staying here. He's loaded and you earn a pittance. He should have been paying *you.* Imagine all that washing and ironing of Calvin Klein's, folding, putting away.'

'Exactly, so I think we can agree that the wine is mine. I've paid for this wine with my hard-earned cash from the House of Clay. Pour away, Bart. Let's do some tasting and then we'll have a photoshoot for Jackson. Then we'll open another.'

Bart pours four glasses and we all gingerly pick one up. I look at the dark red liquid filling about a third of the glass. Three thousand, for *that?* I clutch my glass a little tighter as we all start sniffing and swirling the wine around as if we know what we're doing – which we don't, trust me. Finally, nervously, we tip up our glasses and take a taster of the precious liquid. Ooooh, that is good. My taste buds instantly spring to attention and start begging for more. I take another sip just as Kim holds up her hand, ordering us to stop.

'How many sips have you had, Stells?' I hold up two fingers. 'Jeremy? Right. Keep track. No gulping allowed. Then we can work out how much per sip.'

Jeremy then announces that we need to let it breathe for ten minutes, which seems an impossibly long time to resist having another quaff, but I agree to give it a go on the proviso that we have some pizza in the interim. Pizza and Petrus? Is that a sacrilege or plain common sense? No one argues however and we are soon tucking into cold pizza. Carbohydrate, cheese, grease, salt, it is ticking every box for me and two slices later I feel brave enough to ask Kim what she unearthed in the office.

'So, give, what juicy nugget did you find tucked away in Jackson's drawers?'

A satisfied smile lights her face. 'Oh, you're gonna love this. Hang on.'

She takes another bite of pizza, licking her fingers with satisfaction and then meticulously washing her hands, drying them on a tea-towel. At last, waving her fingers in the air like a surgeon about to start cutting, she walks over to the sideboard where she carefully picks up a folded scrap of paper.

'So, in the most psychotically organised drawer I have ever laid eyes upon, the man has colour coded his paperclips for fuck's sake, I spied a piece of paper sellotaped to the back of said drawer, which attracted my attention. As you can imagine.' She pauses here for some more pizza and then asks Bart if the ten minutes are up as she wants some wine, then has to go back and wash her hands again, faffing about with the tea-towel and generally asking for a slap around the head.

'Just get on with it,' I say, crossly, sitting back and hugging my wine glass close.

'Patience, my little poppet, good things come to those who wait.'

'Don't fucking poppet me, just tell us what's on that piece of paper, as it's clearly not an *Ode to Stella*.'

'No, but Stella is gonna love this a whole lot more than a rubbish ode. God, this wine is good. Why did we ever think it was alright to stick to the bottles at the bottom of the fridge when this stuff was lounging about it the top? Fab-u-lous.'

'Kochanie, tell us now or I go first and tell you my find,' Bart says, trying to get his missus back on track.

'The paper, folded neatly à la Jackson T. Lysander-Perry, is a birth certificate,' she trills.

A birth certificate? Interesting. 'Does it say what the T stands for?' I demand. I have long wondered what the T stood for. Jackson maintains it is simply an initial, something I have never believed.

She puts her fingers to her lips to shush me. 'The T is not important, in fact the T is pure fabrication, as is the rest of his name. Jackson T. Lysander-Perry is not Jackson T. Lysander-Perry at all. Jackson T. Lysander-Perry is a great big fat phony pretender person,' she enunciates with relish.

'What do you mean? Who is he then?'

Kim waves the flimsy piece of paper at me. 'Would the real Jason Percy Lander please stand up.'

'Get out of here.' I snatch the paper from Kim's hand, ripping the corner. Jason Percy Lander. Born 12th March 1981. 'Can't be him. He was born in 1985.' I say dismissively. Duh. 'This probably belongs to the bloke he bought the desk off. I can't see Jackson lowering himself to sellotaping things to the back of a drawer. That's more my territory.'

'Of course, it's him. He's just added a few letters and rearranged the order. A C-K in Jason, a Y-S in Lander and he swopped a C for an R in Percy. If he wasn't such a nob, I'd say it was ingenious. Imagine, he wedgied his favourite pants into his name and transformed it.'

'A wedgie,' I say, starting to giggle.

'Percy,' honks Kim.

And we're off, howling with laughter, stomach muscles weeping in protest, jaws aching, eyes streaming. Every time we try to calm it down one of us squeaks *Percy* or *wedgie* and off we go again. Bart watches with paternal amusement until he is able to ask what a wedgie is. Kim tries to explain, but I think it must be exclusive to a British upbringing and school playground mentality as he fails to get to grips with the idea. Jeremy, who has been busy taking notes, then offers to demonstrate – on Bart - which sets us all off again.

Wiping my eyes on a tea towel, I say, 'I swear he's so proud of that name, the strength of Jackson, the Greek *and* Shakespearian associations of Lysander.'

'He sounds like both a Greek tragedy and a Shakespearian comedy,' says Jeremy and I feel myself warming to him a fraction. 'Where was he born? This Jason bloke.'

Kim looks at the certificate again and tells us he was born in Durham. 'University Hospital. To John Percy Lander and Saffron Lander.'

'He told me he was from Cambridge,' I sigh, the laughter draining away. 'Born and bred. I bet they're not even dead. He told me they died when he was young.'

'I can find out, if you're interested,' says Jeremy. 'If it would help.'

I shrug, not knowing what to think or what would help.

They all take another look at the birth certificate, inspecting it closely for further clues, while I take myself off to the loo for emergency repairs and a break from all the drama. The mountain of revelations today is starting to take its toll. In the bathroom mirror, the sorry face that stares back at me is barely recognisable. Where have I gone? Where is Stella? It doesn't take long to erode away the foundations of who we are, or who we think we are. I rinse my face, enjoying the feel of the cold water on my skin, drying it with the soft towel and rubbing in some of the hand cream in the hope that it will work some much-needed magic.

Back in the kitchen, Kim is on her phone calculating the sips. '....an average of eight sips per glass, I mean you have to be able to *taste* the stuff or there's no point, so, that amounts to.......shit, three hundred and thirty seven pounds per sip.'

'That's obscene,' sighs Jeremy, taking an enormous gulp. 'I should try and drink this slowly because I'm unlikely to ever taste wine like this again, but I've never been good at sipping.'

'Man of my own heart,' I hear myself saying. He is not so bad this Jeremy bloke. 'Fill us up, Bart. No holding back.'

Wine duties over, Bart announces it is time for his revelations, thumping his pile of blue folders onto the kitchen table. What now? What next? A secret child? A Russian spy? Foreign Legion? Anything is possible.

'What you got, Bart? Can you top my birth certificate?' asks Kim.

'Ha!' he cries with confidence. 'An itty-bitty birth certificate? Is nothing. I have a house in Battersea.' He flaps the first folder at us, then puts it down and picks up the next one. 'A house, no, a *villa*, in Mykonos.' He puts that down and grabs the next. 'A house in New York, Green-which Village.' The next file is a paler blue. 'Ah, this is interested. A house in Neville's Cross, County Dur-ham.' He flicks through the pages in the folder. 'Yes, yes, ah, here we is. The house is rented to John Lander. Look.' He turns the page around as if we are not going to believe him, which we don't. Kim snatches the sheaf of papers and lets out a string of juicy swear words.

Rich as Croesus Jason Percy Lander didn't buy a house for his parents, he rents them a house. Were they like Babs? Cruel and uninterested and dismissive. Is this a form of revenge?

'Go on,' says Kim, giving the folder back to Bart. 'What else? There must be more.'

Bart clears this throat. 'He has a small place in Paris and,' he looks at me sadly as he picks up the last of the files, 'a house in Stockholm. Paris, Dur-ham and Battersea is rented. New York, Stockholm and Greece not rented.'

'The bastard has a villa in Mykonos and has never invited us.' Kim is indignant. 'All those holidays. All those missed opportunities by the pool. I bet there's a pool. Is there a pool? How big is it? Who buys a villa in Greece and doesn't share it with their nearest and dearest? Is it sitting empty? Is there a house sitter? He could have given the job to us; we could have moved out to Greece and lived the life of Riley. A house sitter, Bart? We should have this kind of information at our fingertips.' She snaps her fingers impatiently. Then she turns her attention to me. 'Did you know about this Stella? If you've been sneaking off to Mykonos for sneaky weekends without us, it will signal the end of a long and thus-far happy friendship.'

'That doesn't merit an answer,' I say, crossly. 'This is Stella you're speaking to. I am *not* a liar like Jackson, Jason, whatever his stupid name is, nor am I a selfish bitch like Nina. She'd have kept it for herself.' Then I get a horrible thought. 'Oh. My. God. I bet she knows, I bet she has been. Laid out by that pool flaunting her perfect bod and asking Jackson to top up the sun cream every ten minutes. Oh fuck, oh fuck, oh fuck. Remember when she disappeared last summer and tried to fob us off that it was a work trip, then came back nut brown and looking like she'd just stepped out of a Vogue shoot. Remember that?'

'I remember. Said they had meetings on the terrace all the time. Was Jackson away then, too?' asks Kim. 'And she went away with that friend that we'd never even heard of, what was she called? Patricia? Portia?'

'Phoebe,' says Bart.

Kim snaps a finger at him. 'That's her. Who the fuck is Phoebe? Never heard of her since. Has Jackson ever been for a work trip and come back with a suspicious tan?'

'He's always travelling and he has one of those perma-tans so it's hard to say.'

'Guess they're going to be moving into the New York place when they move over there. Christ, I knew he was rich, but not *that* rich. Jason Lander made it good. I wonder why he changed his name? Why he rents to his parents, while pretending they are dead! Which is just not normal. This is turning into some kind of spy thriller, a murder mystery. Do you check the cupboards for bodies on a regular basis, Stells?'

I snort into my wine as Jeremy, who has been taking pics of the Lysander-Perry property portfolio, looks up. 'Maybe he has more than this to hide? He lied about his name, he lied about his age, his parents, he kept a series of very expensive properties hidden from the person sharing his life. I'd be interest to know if Her Majesty's Revenue and Customs know about all this?' He waves a hand over the table. 'That is the question you could ask if he tries to get you to move out before you're ready.'

'After checking for bodies,' adds Kim. 'Is there a cellar here?'

No one speaks for a while then as they all pore through the other files, searching for more hidden treasures and swooning over the infinity pool in Mykonos. It would be fun if it wasn't so *not* funny. All this and I didn't have a clue. What was I in this fraud? A convenient live-in housekeeper who he could also tap for a shag if he felt the urge. Someone to keep the fridge full and the Calvin Klein's topped up. A skivvy. A cook.

It comes to me then, with absolute certainty, that I don't want to live here any longer. Not one more day. The thought of being here on my own, in his space, amongst his lies, feels about as appealing as sharing a small caravan – for life - with Feet-of.

'I want to move,' I blurt. 'Now. Tonight. Tomorrow. Can I come and stay? Or I'll book a hotel. I don't care, but I don't want to be here when he comes back. It'll be like that film, what's it called? With Julia Roberts and her psychopathic husband, the one who straightens the towels all the time?' I look to Kim. She knows this stuff.

'Sleeping with the Enemy?'

'That's the one. I've been sleeping with the enemy. He could bop me off in the night in case I reveal his real name to the world. And that Callum? There are not enough wasabi nuts in the world to make living with him worthwhile.' I start to cry now, big, fat, childish tears. 'Oh, crap, what am I going to do? Where am I going to go?'

PART TWO
BEATRICE AVENUE

CHAPTER 7

Wallow
/wol-oh/
Verb: indulge in something without restraint (usually with
pleasure – although not the case here...)

It has not been an easy seven weeks. Not for me and most certainly not for poor Olive - or anyone else for that matter who has had the misfortune to be in the same airspace as me.

Olive, seventy-two years old, widow, owner of a vast house in London's SW10, is Jeremy's godmother and my fairy godmother. Olive, who, on receiving a loud and incoherent phone call at the very end of what I now like to call *the longest day,* agreed to rent out one of her numerous spare rooms to a sad waif and homeless stray, called Stella Halfpenny. A brave woman. Of course, had she known what she was taking on there is no doubt she would have politely refused and put an extra couple of locks on the front door just to be sure. But she didn't, poor soul, lulled into a sense of security by Jeremy pushing my good points – still breathing, non-smoker – and ignoring the bad points – unhinged, unwanted, depressed, phenomenally grumpy, loser dumpee.

When I announced that I needed to move out tout-de-suite, there was a reassuring voice inside of me saying that Kim and Bart would take me in, giving me a roof over my head complete with in-house, round-the-clock, morale-boosting pep-talks. Only I had forgotten, my memory having been erased by alcohol and stress, that they were in the throes of a major refurb and the whole place was quasi-uninhabitable; they themselves were sleeping in the kitchen. We were contemplating whether I could make a go of it in the loft when

Jeremy had a light bulb moment – Olive - and the rest is recent history.

They all came to help me pack up and move out the next morning, taking a day off work and bowling up, bright eyed and bushy tailed, as if we were going on a jolly outing. They were high on the jinx of smuggling me out when Jackson least expected it and leaving as much mess as possible to ruffle up his perfectionist tendencies. Bart spent some time in the kitchen checking out the loose tiles and a further fifteen had hit the floor by the time we left, along with two cupboard doors and the fridge had developed an irritating wobble that came into play every time you opened it.

I felt unable to share their enthusiasm, overwhelmed by the speed with which my life was falling apart - had fallen apart - coupled with another crippling hangover. Kim threw my stuff into black bin liners, pulling out drawers and emptying them wholesale into the bags, piling in the clothes from the wardrobe complete with hangers and being very cavalier with the toiletries in the bathroom, Jackson having far more than me and all the expensive ones. Jeremy carried everything down to one of Bart's company vans, parked illegally in the street below, and the whole thing was over in less than an hour. One hour to pack up my life and move on.

One measly hour.

Jackson's OCD and meticulous cupboard maintenance had made it easy to find my stuff, but I was still shocked by how little I had and how easy it was to bag it up and – to quote Bart who was, frankly, overexcited – haul ass. I swear I had more when I moved in, but living with a fastidious minimalist leaves no space for hoarding or sentimentality. I also left behind all the things he had given me – not much it turns out - and the photos. I didn't want to look at either of us, ever again; not my idiot gullible face nor his smug phoney one. Only one photo gave me pause for thought; the picture of the three of us in Crete.

'Don't even think about it,' said Kim, snatching it out of my hand. 'We'll leave it for Nina, remind her how much she's lost. Make her engage her brain and think.'

Before they left, Bart carefully laid out all the documents we had found so Jackson would realise that we had unearthed all his sneaky secrets and Kim wrote a rude letter to Nina about not being invited to the Mykonos villa. And then we were done. They all waited for me in the car while I made a final tour; I wanted it to be significant, *to close a door* on my life with Jackson, move on, put it behind me, but it just turned into a sad journey around my crumbling life, tripping over the hopes and dreams I had harboured when I moved in.

The drive to Fulham was depressingly short and of course there was no parking spot within a mile of Olive's house, so Bart stopped in the middle of the road and for a few mad minutes he threw everything out of the van to Jeremy, standing on the pavement outside my new home. Ten minutes later and it was all inside. I was ashamed at my pathetic life, thirty-four years old, a rejected failure with a few bin liners of cheap clothes and a heap of charity shop books. Olive tried to soothe me in the kitchen, while Kim and Bart unpacked my things upstairs and Jeremy fixed the door on my new bedroom.

I wish I could have enjoyed the attention. The love. But I couldn't and in the end, I just wanted them all to leave.

'Please go,' I said plaintively to Kim. 'I need to wallow.'

'I'm not leaving you like this,' she replied, folding her arms and jutting out a hip to make her point.

'I want to wallow and I can only do that alone. And self-pity is so much more effective if there's no one else in the room. Besides, I'm not ready to hear that I am better off without him, I don't to be told to buck-up, brighten-up or, God forbid, look to the future. I want to wallow in my pain, let it wash over me, seep into every pore. I want to cry without sympathy. I want to be sad and pitiful, pathetic. I need to do this alone, get it out of the way and *then* I can get on with my life. Only then.'

'I don't like it.'

'I'm not having much fun either, Kim, but I have to wallow. It's my right as a dumpee.'

Jeremy left first, high fiving Bart and kissing Kim on each cheek. Kim and Bart were harder to dislodge, but I stuck to my story and they eventually agreed, talking to Olive at length before they left, no doubt issuing instructions like a couple of bossy school teachers.

There is a knock on my door. Olive. On schedule.

'Stella dear? I've made some tea. I'll leave it outside the door. There are some Ginger Snaps and a couple of brownies that I made this afternoon.' She waits for me to reply. 'I'll be downstairs.' Another pause. 'Why don't you come down? We can watch The Chase together.'

'Thanks Olive. I'll see how I go.' This is what she says every evening and every evening I say the same thing and every evening I stay in my room and – wallow.

There is no pleasure, but I can't stop. I am caught in a web of *self*: self-pity, self-reflection, self-hate.

What I hate (most) is my gullibility, my naivety and most of all my inability to act when in the heart of my heart, I knew Jackson and I were never going to make it. I knew, but I didn't want to know. Head in the sand like an ostrich.

Which everyone knows is stupid.

And I hate being stupid.

The wallowing has to stop. I know it does. It is just easier right now to indulge than face up to my miserable, empty, life.

Another knock on the door. 'Stella?'

'Still here,' I say, sharply.

If there is one person on this planet who deserves better than I am giving her, it is Olive.

'Bart and Kim are coming around,' she says, cheerfully.

Fuck.

I am deeply ashamed to even think that word in association with my two best, most steadfast, loving, generous, patient friends. But, fuck! They are relentless, endlessly popping around to check on me, chirping away in the kitchen with Olive, trying to coax me out to the pub (and failing), trying to bolster my flagging sense of self (and failing), trying to inject some life into my life (and failing). I am sick of them and tonight I cannot be arsed.

Visits mean conversation, something I have grown very averse to since *the longest day*. I have lost the knack of small talk. Silence is my new friend, preferably a heavy brooding silence, ominous in its intent to allow wallowing. Visits also mean wine – if Kim and Bart are involved – and I have been following a strict no-alcohol regime.

Wine (and other alcoholic beverages but especially wine) = enjoyment and that runs contrary to the rules of wallowing. I could have decided to go the other way and cane it every night, allowing the resulting hangover add some spice to the wallowing, but there would have been too much enjoyment in that first glass, something to look forward to at the end of the day. Also, self-pity can be ratcheted up several degrees if you force yourself to forgo the things you love.

And I love wine.

What I also love, like any self-respecting woman, are sweet things: cakes, muffins, chocolate, biscuits, you name it. However, in contrary to my abstaining from all grape juice products, I have given free rein to my sweet tooth, which I found enhanced the wallowing experience considerably:

1. I have felt sick for, on average, 90% of my waking hours since *the longest day*.
2. Every time I am open my mouth to force in another bite of Banana Fudge something-or-other, I can hear both Jackson and Nina sighing their haughty disapproval.
3. I am the size of a small Pacific island.

4. I have permanent toothache. Dentures probably soon featuring on my 'to do' list.

Olive knocks again and pushes open the door. 'Did you hear me?'

She stands looking at me, tiny frame swamped in a pair of baggy brown trousers with an elasticated waist, a baggy beige shirt tucked in to said elasticated waist and a very Nora Batty style waistcoat. Flattering it is not. And does she know she has got mud on her knees and grass in her hair?

I say nothing though. That would invite conversation.

'You alright, love?'

Duh. As if.

'Kim and Bart are coming around in half an hour and I'm cooking a fish pie. You like that. You ate it when I last made it.'

I look at her crossly. 'Honestly Olive, I'm too tired. Not in the mood. I'll send a text to Kim, tell her not to bother. I'd rather stay here.' I pat my bed where I am slumped in my work clothes, spare tyres at ease, fat arse in repose.

To my annoyance, she pushes the door wider and bustles over to the big bay windows, pulling back the curtains. 'It's only six o'clock, for goodness sake. You can't sit up here with the curtains closed all evening.' She pushes open a window and I get buffeted by a waft of fresh air. 'Again.'

'Olive, I want to sit here, all evening. Again,' I say, pedantically.

She ignores me, picking up the tray with the cooling tea and biscuits. 'Get in the shower and wash off the day. Then put on something comfy and come downstairs.' She stands looking down at me on the bed. 'It's time.'

'I will decide when it is time, thank you for asking. And I was going to eat those,' I whine, pointing at the tray. Those brownies will be heaven-on-earth if Olive's previous efforts are anything to go by. Besides, my rolls need plumping up. Helps with the self-loathing.

'Too late. Anyway, fish pie is much healthier. Now, come on, chop chop. Get in that shower and I'll be expecting you downstairs in fifteen minutes.'

'I said I don't -'

Olive cuts me off. 'I don't want to hear it. Not tonight. Your lovely friends are coming around to see you, *again,* and I for one cannot sit around for another night watching you mope and sulk in this fusty room. It's done. He's gone and she's gone. From what I hear, and I've heard a lot, you are well rid of them,' she says gravely, fixing me with a keen eye. 'So, young lady, it's time to buck up and smell the roses, or, if you're lucky, the rosé wine. I'm having a glass and I suggest you get yourself downstairs and join me. Kim says you used to enjoy a rosé.'

She gives me a sweet smile and I want to hit her. She is like Jekyll and Hyde. That old lady exterior is just a front; behind she is a nasty shrew in beige clothes. She doesn't know what it is like. Bloody Derek, the dead husband, was probably a fucking saint.

'Come on. I'll be waiting. Fifteen minutes and I'm not taking no for an answer this time.' And with that, she is off down the stairs, humming.

By the time I have grumbled off to the shower, grouched on a pair of (grubby) pyjamas and stropped my way downstairs, Olive, Kim and Bart are deep into a bottle of rosé and doing a crossword.

'Eight down. Travel company achieves equilibrium ahead of Tour's arch villain. Anyone?' Bart's head is bent low over the paper. He looks up and sees me. 'Ah, Stella, my grumpy little pumpkin, take a seat, I get you some wine.'

'No wine, thanks Bart, I'll have some water,' I say piously. 'Or that tea I never got a chance to drink earlier.'

'Shut up and list-ten,' says Bart, calmly. 'Tonight, you drink wine like a normal person, like the Stella I know. The real Stella. The Stella I love. We all love.'

Bloody Bart. Trust him to switch on the charm.

'You've had seven weeks, my lovely,' says Kim. 'About five weeks more than I thought you'd need to get over those two selfish pricks.' She pushes a glass of rosé over to me. 'You're letting them get the better of you. Every night of crying and poor me, poor me, eating crap and drinking tea, is another night lost to those two that you will never get back. Enough, as they say, is enough.' She raises her glass to me. 'Drink, Stells, drink to you, and us, and the incomparable Olive.' The three of them raise their glasses and drink deeply.

I look at the pale pink of the wine, pretty and inviting, condensation beading the glass, a lonely drop forming and sedately wending its way down the stem. It feels like breaking a vow if I drink this wine. Plus, I am deep in unchartered territory – it has been a long, long time since I managed seven days without wine let alone seven weeks and I don't know how to end it. Or if I even want to.

'Lovely,' sighs Olive.

'It's rosé o'clock,' sings Kim.

'Fruity,' Bart chirps, winking at me.

They all drink some more, watching me, waiting for me to crack. 'Just get on and leave me alone,' I cry. 'I'll drink when I'm ready. I'll drink if I want to and not before and not to please you lot either.'

'Touchy,' mocks Kim. 'I'll give you five minutes before I force it down your throat. Too much tea isn't good for you.'

'Especially with two teaspoons of sugar,' adds Olive, unnecessarily.

'How many times have we said wine is good for the soul?' Kim says, sotto voce.

'Nectar of the Gods,' rumbles Bart.

'And, don't forget how much Jackson *hated* rosé wine.' Kim looks smug as she hammers another nail into my abstinence.

The first sip is a subtle blend of forgotten flavours, flooding my taste buds and piquing my senses back into life.

Nectar of the Gods indeed. I try to maintain a neutral expression, not wanting them to see how much I enjoyed that one sip.

'Balance!' shouts Olive, making me jump. 'British Airways and Lance Armstrong. Balance.'

'Yes, yes, yes, Olive.' Bart fills in the crossword. 'Now, nine across: Virginia wolf on target to earn after shy start.'

'She's a demon at the crosswords,' says Kim to me, throwing an admiring glance at Olive. 'Match made in heaven with Bart.'

Olive brushes off the compliment and gets up to fuss with the fish pie, fluffing up the mash with a fork and sprinkling it liberally with paprika before putting it into the oven. I get an unexpected buzz of pleasure at the thought of the meal ahead, all at once happy to be here instead of up in my room watching YouTube and replaying events from the Hemplewood over and over, wondering if I missed an important detail that will make it all bearable. Olive made a fish pie a couple of weeks ago that I was persuaded to eat – off a tray in my room – and the resulting empty plate was taken as a sign of hope. In truth, it was a heavenly sensation of smooth buttery mash and three different types of fish in a rich creamy sauce. Not that I told her it was good, that would have involved communication and admitting I liked something when I didn't want to like *anything* – apart from sugar - in keeping with the full wallowing experience.

We are all soon spooning in giant mouthfuls and swigging back large glasses of a Chilean red.

'We have ban all wines from two-hundred-mile radius of Bordeaux,' Bart states. 'To avoid crossing-contamination with Jafuckson. You like my new name? I add 'f-u' to the ck.'

'Stands for fuck you,' says Kim, shoveling in more fish pie. 'Sorry, Olive.'

'Don't mind me. I've been updating my cussing vocabulary since Stella moved in. She's very well versed,' Olive says with a small laugh as a blush of shame creeps up my neck.

'Sorry Olive,' I say. 'I'll tone it down, I promise. And sorry for being such a crap lodger. Crap, is crap a swear word?' I look to Kim for guidance. 'I'll do better, I really will. I think I'm ready to draw a line under the wallowing.' There is a general whoop from around the table.

'Halle-fucking-lujah!' shouts Kim. 'Sorry, Olive! I've missed you so much Stells, you have no idea. I lost Nina too, but I can live without her, at least for the moment.' I want to object, but she is on a roll. 'You though, Stella, I need you, *we* need you. Right, Bart?' She looks over to Bart, who nods. 'Olive needs you.' Olive bobs her head, welling up and wiping her eyes on an oven glove.

'Ok, ok. Enough,' I say, as the tears start gathering in preparation for an outing. 'I'm ready. It's time, I'll admit it, but go gently with me, I'm out of practice.'

'Well, I suggest we give you a few weeks to get back in the swing of things and then we'll have a reunion party with Jeremy. What d'you think Olive?'

'Oh, yes, lovely. I don't see him nearly often enough.'

'It's a done deal,' smiles Kim.

CHAPTER 8

Crush
/krʌʃ/
Noun: a brief but intense infatuation for someone

Olive and I are watching The Chase; my new after work ritual.

Now the wallowing is officially over, I find Olive waiting – dare I say, excitedly – for me when I come home every day, tea and some kind of homemade cake on a tray, The Chase paused and ready-to-go on the television. If you've never seen it, The Chase is a hugely popular quiz show and Olive is its greatest devotee. She never misses it and scrupulously organises her day so as to be poised for the off at 5pm. A schedule she's had to adapt in order to include me as I am still pandering to Clay's every whim until at least 5.30pm, so she pauses the TV as the opening credits roll and waits for me.

The Chase; let me just say that, in a nut shell, I am useless and Olive is a red-hot genius quizzer. Whatever the topic, she is all over it: history, politics, geography, food, Greek mythology, weather patterns, South American dictators. Today she only trips up on a question about Bob Marley which, to my annoyance, I also get wrong.

'You'll get better with practice,' she soothes, without much conviction and without losing focus.

When the doorbell goes, I am ready for a break.

'I'll get it Olive,' I say, standing up. 'You carry on here. No, don't worry about pausing it. I won't be long.'

Any excuse. I am expecting Kim and Bart, possibly a neighbour, local MP or even a Jehovah Witness. The person I am not expecting is Jeremy. I haven't seen him since *the longest day* and I genuinely don't know how I feel about seeing him again. It's hard not to associate him with the shattering events of that day, the humiliations that piled up under his watchful eyes, the careful note taking. There is something exposing about someone you don't know seeing you at your absolute lowest.

His generous frame fills the doorway, housed in a tweed jacket with leather patches on the elbows, frayed green shirt open at the collar, no tie. The bashed nose that I remember looks more skewed than ever, his pale grey eyes are tired, underscored by dark purple smudges. He looks knackered.

'Stella,' he says, with a gentle smile. 'Nice to see you.'

And with that he steps forward and pulls me into a big hug before I have time to decide if I want to be held. Is hugging appropriate? I don't *know* him, despite all he knows about me. My mind flickers about, undecided, but my body is already moulding itself to him, sinking into his gloriously thick, strong arms and melting into his huge chest. He has a wonderful masculine smell, with a faint side of soap. No fancy shower gel or aftershave. Just Jeremy. He feels safe, so reassuringly here-and-now that I don't want to let go, ever, and I cling on a little tighter. He puts a hand gently on the back of my head and kisses my hair as Olive's voice floats out from the living room.

'That's a mandolin,' she cries, confidently.

Jeremy doesn't speak, but I sense his question and murmur, 'The Chase,' feeling his head nodding in understanding.

Tucking my head under his chin, I allow myself to drift a little deeper, my hands pressing into his broad back, the muscles firm beneath my fingers.

Bliss.

A squawk from Olive pops the bubble, 'Jeremy!' She has to peel me off him, climbing ivy to his sturdy oak, to get in for a hug of her own. 'We weren't expecting you until next week! Do get out the way, Stella. Did we get our dates wrong? I'm sure Bart and Kim aren't coming until next Friday.'

'No, you're not wrong, I had an interview in Putney and finished early so I thought I'd pop in. See how you're doing, see how Stella's getting on.' He turns to give me a crocked rugged smile and my heart does a full-on swan dive. 'Nice to see you after all this time. I'm glad you're feeling better.'

'So am I,' adds Olive with feeling. 'Even the plants were starting to wilt. I think it was the low pressure brought on by her depression. Things are much improved, aren't they, love? Come along through, we don't want to miss the show. Bradley's on cracking form today.' She stops in the doorway, staring at the television. 'Oooh, that's a tough one, Franklin D. Roosevelt, now you sit over there Jeremy and Stella will get you a cup for some tea.' She points me towards the kitchen. 'And a side plate, please, matching of course, don't forget the saucer, the ones with the yellow daisies will do nicely. Orangutan!'

I welcome the chance to escape to the kitchen, a space without a Jeremy in it. I need to calm my heart, currently trying punch through my chest and throw itself to the floor at his feet. To say I am surprised at my reaction is an understatement. Until this moment, Jeremy has been nothing more than a bloke who turned up as my life was disintegrating. He has not featured in my weeks of wallowing at all. Now though, I can't think why.

Jeremy is my Knight in Shining Armour.

My hero, who found me somewhere to live, who introduced me to the incomparable Olive, who whisked me out of the ogre's cave. How did I not see this earlier? It could have shortened the period of wallowing by several weeks.

Back in the living room, Olive is on the edge of her seat ready to pounce on the next question.

Bradley Walsh doesn't miss a beat, digging out some ancient word that I have never heard of before.

'The word cacoethes means to have the urge to do something: A, heroic: B, inadvisable: C, with chocolate?'

'Inadvisable!' shouts Olive, springing to her feet.

Crikey. That could be my middle name right now, overwhelmed as I am by the desire to take Jeremy's giant head in my hands and kiss the life out of those bruised lips.

I have got it bad, no doubt suffering from some kind of syndrome. White Knight Syndrome. Hero Worship Disorder. I will look it up when I am alone, safe from prying eyes, but it would definitely be helpful to be able to blame someone or something else for my growing state of infatuation, save me from having to shoulder the full responsibility of a teenage crush alone.

'Stella? Stella?' Olive is standing beside me, waving her hand in front of my eyes. 'She's been so much better, Jeremy, I don't know what's happening this evening. Stella?' She gives my cheek a light slap.

'Easy Olive. I can hear you, I'm just tired. It's been a long week.'

'You went all vague, not paying attention at all and you missed the end of The Chase,' she tuts. 'Now, do you want to make up the spare bed for Jeremy or get a start on dinner? I was planning to make a chicken curry from scratch. I got all the spices from Mr Mukherjee at the Bengali Master Grocer on the Fulham Palace Road. So knowledgeable, there is nothing he doesn't know about herbs and spices. Charming too. What's it to be?'

'I'll go and get the bed made up. Need a quick shower to wash off the office too.' And I need to get changed, I think, feeling my oversize midsection billowing over my over-tight skirt. Not a look I recommend and entirely unsuitable for wooing knights.

There are two spare rooms, both wallpapered to within an inch of decency. One has a riot of pink and blue flowers arranged in columns with a trellis effect in between and the other is a geometric pattern in sludgy greens and yellows repeated ad infinitum with, unbelievably, matching curtains *and* matching cushions on the bed. Makes the head spin but the colours are a good fit for Jeremy today so I make up the bed in that one, carefully pulling the bottom sheet tight, smoothing out the duvet, plumping the pillows and planting a special kiss on one of the clean white pillowcases. I imagine his battered head resting there, my kiss transferring on to his cheek - FUCK! STOP! NOW!

Get out, get out, get out.

I am sick. I shouldn't even be around Jeremy at the moment, cannot be trusted. Inadvisable actions could spring into being at any moment and therein lies toe curling embarrassment and humiliation.

A cold shower is needed, and a hiatus. Like putting myself on the naughty step on a freezing cold day until reason has returned to the roost.

My room, following the general faded 19'70s vibe throughout the house, is painted orange, mercifully paled now to a tame tangerine, with one wall papered with a riot of gold and bronze flowers. They comforted me those flowers during the wallowing, I never tired of looking at them, counting them, running my fingers over the raised flock designs. The bathroom I am less fond of in its homage to the colour green. Avocado green for the matching shower unit, sink, cabinet and loo, with a mismatched fluorescent hue for the loo seat. The walls and ceiling are covered by white tiles, each with a bright green apple in the middle and, here and there, to mix it up and really mess with your mind in the morning, an orange.

After a blisteringly hot shower, I turn the taps to cold for a blast of the artic in the hope that it will douse the flames of my raging lust and restore some calm. It doesn't. What does is a glimpse in the mirror of what looks like a small hippo frolicking in the early morning steam rising off the plains of Africa. What the feck? I had brushed up under Jackson's watchful gaze, taking great pains with my diet and doing my all to ensure that the Halfpenny bod was not letting the side down.

I was disciplined and kept myself under the radar. Not anymore; I am too vast to fit under the radar. I dress quickly in an enormous silk shirt that could house three Royal Marines and a pair of jeans stretchy enough for me to tuck everything in. Not exactly glamorous but general hippo-ness is under wraps.

Downstairs I find Olive cooking up a storm and Jeremy outside checking the garden, something I am ashamed to say I have failed to do in all the weeks I have been living here. Apart from the fact that going outside to benefit from all that nature had to offer would have been detrimental to the wallowing experience, I have never (ever) lived anywhere with a garden and it never occurred to me that there might be something out there to see. Feeling absurdly shy I go and stand by Jeremy, saying nothing, taking in the tidy flower beds, a wash of daffodils at one end of the neat lawn and an abundance of trees and shrubs. He doesn't seem to be inclined to speak either and for a few quiet minutes we walk slowly across the grass, down towards the bottom of the garden where I can see a flush of pink and purple despite the early season.

Does she have help, I can't help but wonder. It is a sizeable garden and it is perfectly maintained. Who mows the lawn? Who clips that orderly hedge? Who weeds all those weed-free flower beds? I want to ask except that I am too embarrassed to be the one living here who doesn't have a clue.

'How d'you like my camelias, Stella?'

Olive has crept up behind us unheard and wedges herself in between Jeremy and I, pointing out the different plants, detailing their life histories and individual personalities. She talks about them as if they are old friends and after a while it becomes clear that her best friends in this well-peopled garden, her most dearly beloved friends, are the azaleas. Once she gets going there is no stopping her as she expounds on the ideal soil conditions, exposure to the sun, moisture levels, most potent fertilisers. You name it, she knows it. She is waffling on about some festival in Japan when I find myself distracted by Jeremy's left ear, a sad affair showing signs of time spent at the bottom of a ruck on the rugby field. Mesmerised, I reach up to tenderly stroke a particularly nobbly bit when Olive's voice penetrates my love-fog and hauls me back from the brink.

'Are you following, Stella? All azaleas belong to the Rhododendron genus, but not all Rhododendrons are azaleas.'

'Olive, how do you know all this stuff?' I ask, breathless from the close encounter with the ear. 'I bet Alan Titchmarsh could learn a thing or two from you. You should have your own TV show. Olive and the Azaleas.'

'Don't mention the Titch,' hisses Jeremy. 'Olive's affections lie firmly with the Monty.'

'Oh, that Monty,' she breathes, going all starry-eyed. 'Taught me everything I know.'

'Monty?' I query.

'Stella! Don't tell me you don't know Monty Don. Gardner's World?'

'Er, no, actually I don't. Never watched it. I've never had a garden. Never even had a terrace. I did have a spider plant when Kim and I lived together in Clapham. Kept it for years, baby spider plants all over the shop. Then I moved in with Jackson and he didn't do plants, so I gave it away.'

Olive tuts at the despicable Jackson before throwing herself into a long and heartfelt eulogy on the great and unparalleled Monty Don, covering his penchant for a blue shirt and uncombed hair as well as his intimate knowledge of the plant kingdom.

'We can watch Gardeners' World together now, if you like,' she says to me, her voice full of hope.

'Book me in, Olive,' I say. 'But be warned, I know precisely nothing about anything to do with everything in a garden.'

'Well, we'll start slowly. I'm sure you'll grow to love him as much as me. Now that there is the Gunnera manicata. Some people mistake it for giant rhubarb, but you don't want to be making a crumble with that unless you want an early meeting with our Maker.' She points a grove of huge leafy plants that do indeed look like giant rhubarb. 'And that is my evening sherry chair in summer, by the hostas. I do like a hosta.'

'And a sherry. Harvey's Bristol Cream only,' states Jeremy. 'Don't even think about inviting a different sherry into the house.'

'And we need to bring another chair down here, Jeremy. Stella might want to join me sometimes.'

'I'm in. A sherry is just what I need after a day at the coalface.'

CHAPTER 9

Clement
/ˈklem.ənt//
Adjective:
1. lenient and forgiving towards someone;
2. mild or pleasant weather

For the first time in an age, I managed to haul my weighty carcass out of bed at an early hour, had the run of a near-empty bus for the journey to work and reported for duty ahead of the crowd. And it feels good. This is what I do, this is how I, Stella Halfpenny, function. A return to normal, although I feel a thousand times better than normal, I feel *alive*. Life is unexpectedly vibrating with possibility again. This is what a crush can do for you; it gives you hope, belief, faith in a better, happier life.

Hail the great, the miraculous, the wonderful, Jeremy.

I might be early, but Marco and Iris are already in situ revving up the coffee machine.

Yes Iris, she of the irrepressible personality and Extra Strong Mints. Still with us and filling the cry for *Help* with aplomb. Noemia, back from Frankfurt after a short-lived romance with the new (now old) boyfriend, has reluctantly had to accept a job at Costa Coffee after failing to dislodge Iris from Marco's protective embrace.

She is worth fifty Noemias anyway.

Somehow, she already knows everyone in the building and is adored by every single one of them. Sharp as a tack on names and coffee preferences, family histories, big work events, nothing escapes her eagle eye or her finely tuned ear. Marco says sales are through the roof as everyone comes by for

109

a daily life-enhancing chat with the little genie, vying for her attention during the peak periods, desperate to update her on little Archie's new tooth or last night's dinner party. Even the boss has even fallen under her spell; I have seen him stop to talk to her on more than one occasion and once I even spotted him smiling.

'Stella! You're in early.' She greets me now, popping out from the Coffee Hut and wrapping her arms around me. Tries to at any rate, her hands don't quite meet. 'We've got a new muffin in. Banana caramel dream. I've had one already and you're going to love it.'

I have a coveted spot as house favourite, though it would be fair to ask why. I did my best to shake her off that first day and have been the Coffee Hut's grumpiest, least communicative – albeit loyal - customer in the weeks (months) ever since. At the peak of my wallowing, I was able to get a coffee without actually speaking. Marco would size up my mood as I came through the front door and silently do the honours, quietly telling Iris to bag me up something tasty and calmly taking my money. No words were exchanged. It was perfect. Yes, I was deeply ashamed but my self-pity took precedence. Besides, it felt safer to say nothing than risk saying something awful.

'I think I need to slow down on the muffins, Iris,' I say, patting my tummy. 'You can't even get your arms around my waist as it is. Marco, I'll have a skinny latté with an extra shot. Please.'

'Rubbish. A girl needs a bit of padding. You don't want to end up like me. I'll be the first to go in a famine.' She nips off to join Marco again and starts warming milk for my latté.

'Here, Ste-lllaa. One latté, skinny, extra shot.' Marco hands me the coffee and I give him a fiver. 'You better today. Eyes bright.' He has a vague notion of just how badly things went wrong, without the finer details. Although, I could be kidding myself - with Clarissa in the building, the finer details are probably public knowledge.

'You do look better,' agrees Iris, handing me a paper bag. 'Shortbread. Just a tiny slice. Don't want you getting dizzy before lunch.' No wonder takings and my weight are on the up.

At my desk, I look around the empty office and what I feel is relief, a return to my comfort zone. First in, getting a grip on the day before the day gets a grip on me.

Bob arrives and gives me a wave, his raised eyebrows revealing his shock at seeing me here already. He fumbles about behind his desk making the daily transfer of hip flask from jacket pocket to bottom drawer, then switching on his computer. I don't know what is in the hip flask, I have never wanted to ask but he does make frequent trips to the toilet when the boss on a bad day, returning with a refreshed sparkle in his eye and a calmer demeanor. I would have tried it during the wallowing weeks except that I was on my alcohol embargo.

I wander over to say hello, undecided if it would be appropriate to give a full-on apology for my recent foul, anti-social behavior.

'You feeling better?' he asks as I get to his desk. 'First time you've been in before me since, since, since,' he stops, flushes, looks at the floor, looks at me, up to the ceiling, back to his feet, before finally finishing with a lame, 'the thing.'

'The thing?' I ask, teasing. 'What thing?'

'You know. The thing. With the banker. Your *ex*.' He looks so embarrassed, I feel sorry for him.

'Yes, well, the thing and the banker are over. History. Relegated to. Stella is back. Get the swear box ready, I feel like letting rip today.'

Clarissa comes in next, bypassing her desk completely and making a beeline for me. 'Well, hello stranger,' she drawls, hands on hips, assessing me.

'Clarissa, I'm here every day. Hardly a bloody stranger,' I protest.

'Here in body, maybe, but your spirit was nowhere to be seen. However, today, not only are you here on time, you have a clean shirt on. You know.' She juts a hip and points a finger. 'Just because a shirt is black doesn't mean you can wear it for three weeks without washing it. Khaki is the best for that and I've never seen you wear khaki. Just as well, wouldn't suit your sallow colouring. Still, nice to have you back and not in black.'

'Fuck off,' I cry, subtly inspecting my pristine white shirt for coffee stains. I have to admit to wearing almost nothing but black since *the longest day,* mainly because it suited my mood and because it didn't need much washing. Or so I thought. Washing anything seemed entirely superfluous to my needs. Olive did sneak into my room from time-to-time while I was at work, changing the sheets, picking up clothes, washing stuff, cleaning the bathroom.....at the time it just annoyed me, an intrusion on my wallowing and associated slovenly lifestyle, but I realise now that I owe her yet another big thank you.

'Fifty p Stella,' cries Bob, rattling the swear box and heading over. 'You told me to be ready and here I am.'

I ignore him, turning back to Clarissa. 'I've been here every day dealing with Feet-of-Clay, which is never a given, especially when you're not at your finest.'

'Ha! Even Mr Clay hardly dared talk to you. That black cloud hovering over your desk was very intimidating.'

'Fuck off.'

'Stella, that's a pound and it is not even nine o'clock,' says Bob happily. 'We'll have enough for an Easter party soon.' He holds out the swear box and waits for me to find some change in my purse. 'She's right though. There is a perceptible lightening of the thundercloud today. Much nicer view. Friendlier.'

'Fuck off, both of you,' I cry, handing over a handful of change to Bob. 'I was in a good mood and now I'm not.'

'You know we're teasing don't you, Stella?' Clarissa asks, looking worried. 'We've missed you. No one dares talk to you

112

these days, except Miles of course.' She gives a lascivious wink, almost losing a false eyelash. Speaking of which.

'Clarissa, why the f-udge are you wearing false eyelashes? In the office?'

'Just trying to raise the morale of the troops.' She flutters her lashes extravagantly and there is a discernable movement of air. 'Now, while you've got your purse out, you owe me two quid for your riders in the Milan San Remo.'

'I'm sure I said I didn't want any riders. And what is the Milan San Remo when it's at home anyway? Is it a horse race?'

'Don't be stupid. It's nearly three hundred kilometers long. Poor nags would be knackered.'

'So, what is it and when is it?'

'It's a bike race and it's this weekend. Ringo's going to bring in the highlights on Monday. Mr Clay is away so we can all watch.'

I look at her in disbelief. 'We're going to watch a load of people peddling along for three hundred kilometers? Watching paint dry would be more exciting.'

She tells me where I can stick it and asks if that is a black cloud she can see on the horizon. Which shuts me up. I hand over two pounds and she hands me two slips of paper with my riders on; Nathan Van Hooydonck and Julian Alaphilippe. Two amateurs no doubt who will be stopping for coffee and doughnuts before they have left Milan.

Piqued by Clarissa and Bob's comments, I am making an effort to be uber-nice to everyone and anyone who comes within spitting distance of my desk. My debt of gratitude to Olive, Kim and Bart was already taking up large amounts of room in the Bank of Life and now I have to factor in half the office as well, although I will draw the line at Feet-of.

It would take more than I possess to be genuinely nice to him.

Across the room I spot Ringo talking to Clarissa, probably

swept in by the unusual air currents around her false eyelashes, and try to figure out what has changed. Something is different about him but I can't place it......trousers! He has new trousers. Since the dawn of man, Ringo has been wearing an ugly pair of brown chinos. They were covered with multiple unidentifiable stains and somehow managed to be tight around the crotch area – an unpleasant sight if it caught your eye – and yet baggy and shapeless everywhere else. On quiet days when the boss was away, we have been known to waste unreasonable amounts of our day discussing whether he ever washed them or was just letting the dirt build up. Clarissa even tried to map the stains once to see if they changed, but it was too boring a task to hold her attention for long. Now, in the place of the repellant chinos, are a pair of slim fit dark grey trousers finishing just above the ankle and revealing a very neat pair of buns and a quantity of thigh that I had no idea he possessed.

'Who'd have thought a change of trousers could make such a difference?' Miles is by my desk, watching me. I close my mouth, feeling the heat rush to my head. 'Me thinks Ringo is enjoying something of a make-over. And you can speak to him face-to-face now without having to hold your breath.'

'No? Really?' I say, glancing back at Ringo who is still talking to Clarissa. It is true; he is bent low over her desk and she is leaning *in* towards him.

'You probably won't have noticed. He hasn't dared approach you lately. Only the brave.' He gives me a cheeky smile. 'Feeling better? You look happier.'

'What is it with you lot? It's like I've got a giant neon sign over my head saying **CRISIS OVER!**' I huff. 'I haven't been *that* bad. Below par, I'll admit, but that is life. Up and down we go and anyone who says otherwise is a big fat liar. The wheel of Fortune they call it and if you are swanking about up at the apex, buffing up your nails and enjoying the view, just get ready for the drop. It's less fun here at the bottom.'

'Ah, there she is. There's the Stella of weeks past. For an awful moment, I thought there was a new Stella in town. Don't want her. Far too cheerful.'

'Fuck off.'

'Better and better. I'm going down to get a coffee. Shall I get you a latté, extra shot? Might take the edge off.' And he's gone before I have a chance to refuse.

So much attention from the office heart throb is always good for morale; the trick is not to let it go to your head. That way lies humiliation and heartbreak and I've had my lifetime's share of both. Plus, he is nice to everyone and that's not normal. He is no doubt hiding some terrible depraved secret; we just haven't uncovered it yet. It is always the nice friendly neighbour who feeds your cat while you're away on holiday that turns out to be the serial killer in the films.

While he is gone, I turn my attention to more important matters: Jeremy.

I found his telephone number in Olive's address book, one of those old-fashioned ones with alphabetical divider tabs. The urge to speak to him again is overwhelming, the only thing holding me back is that I haven't yet come up with a decent enough excuse for calling him. After he had gone, I spent the rest of the weekend poring over the Google Earth map of Streatham, where he resides, and trying to divine where his house might be through willpower and obsession alone.

Olive. That's my ticket to Jeremy. Jeremy loves Olive, so if I show enough love to Olive, who I am starting to love anyway, it is impossible not to, then Jeremy will start to love me.

Simple.

Using the office phone, I dial, turning my back to Clarissa and her powers of intuition.

'Hello? Hello? Oh, is that you Jeremy? It's me, Stella, how are you?' My hands are trembling, my voice is wobbling and there's a frisson somewhere under my heart that could be

115

cause for concern. 'Stella, it's Stella.' A frisky giggle escapes me as he asks if everything's OK, if I am OK. 'No, I'm fine, Olive's fine, I just wanted to say how lovely it was -,' I stop myself just in time: stay on track, Stells. 'I just wanted say how lovely Olive is, you know that, she's been so amazing and I wanted to treat her, do something special, for you too actually.' Another nervous whinny. 'Er, to say thank you, for everything, I don't know where I'd be without you, probably on a park bench somewhere, plastic bags at my feet, can of Special Brew, you get the picture, honestly Jeremy, I owe you *so much*.....' I peter out, aware that I am straying off subject, a horrid gushy tone creeping in to my voice.

Keep it cool.

I press the back of my hand to my forehead, now slick with sweat, as I listen to his gorgeous deep voice rumbling away. I close my eyes, leaning back in my chair and letting the words wash over me, his low tone thrumming through my chest. It is only when he has finished talking that I realise I haven't taken in anything he has said. Nothing. A blank.

'Er, Jeremy, the line went fuzzy for a second there, I lost you, could you just repeat that last bit? Oh, something for the garden, of course.' Duh. 'I'll get down the garden center.' Somewhere I have never been before in my life. 'Right, I've got to go too, see you Friday then. Jeremy. Saturday? Right, lovely, I'll tell Olive.' A tiny pause and, before I can button up my lip and shut the fuck up, I whisper, 'I can't wait.'

I drop my head into my hands, wishing I hadn't been so obvious.

'Who is Jeremy?'

Miles. I levitate about a foot off of my chair, spinning around to find him standing there with my coffee. He looks quizzical, interested, curious and I feel exposed, unmasked, embarrassed.

'Er, no one,' I stammer, feeling my face ignite. 'A friend.'

'A friend?' A small smile snags at the corner of his mouth. 'Have I got competition already?'

I don't know how to reply to that, so I don't. Instead, I hold out my hand for the coffee and take it, raising it high in an unspoken thank you.

He hovers for a minute, waiting for more, but with my mouth full of coffee and my head full of Jeremy, I am incapable of further communication for the time being. Finally, he salutes, swivels on his heel and ambles back to his desk mumbling, 'Stella, Stella, Stella.' I watch him go. He resides in proper toy boy territory and I don't have the energy, let alone the confidence or the body, to start living as a *cougar*. What I need – and have found, ha! – is someone safe; a sensible age, reasonable (undemanding) physique, not too good-looking, on a par with me basically.

Safe.

Nina told me to aim for the stars and look where it got me.

Much safer to aim for Streatham.

'Are you staring at that wall for a reason or day-dreaming?'

Feet-of's piggy eyes are boring holes into me from across the desk. There should be an early warning system in this office to alert us to his presence. For someone so large and ungainly, he manages to waddle from the lift to his office without making a sound and is constantly sneaking up and scaring the hell out of me.

'Morning, Mr Clay, just, er, wondering, er, whether to ask maintenance to put up a white board here. Might be useful.'

'Useful for what?'

'Um, well, you know, lists, keeping track, travel plans.'

He looks at me shrewdly. 'Would that mean the end of all the piles of paper on your desk and their various *meaningful* labels?' He says *meaningful* with so much sarcasm it can hardly get out of his mouth.

117

'No, of course not,' I say, horrified. My piles of paper are the backbone of the fail-safe Stella Halfpenny system. 'It would be a visual tracker of the day.'

'So, the Himalayas on your desk are not visual enough?' We both take a second to inspect the mountain range of paper spread around me. 'Go ahead, it might be useful. I can see what you're up to even if you're not at your desk.'

I dug that hole, threw myself in, then dug some more.

What is it about Mondays that mean they go on *forever?* The boss has been in and out of his office so many times the door will need new hinges by home time. How he thinks I can do any work when he interrupts every five minutes with some new urgent task, more urgent than the last urgent task given to me five minutes ago, I can only guess. It also means that I've had precious little time in which to think about the *man-of-the-moment*, so I decide to escape to the loos for a mini-break.

In the Ladies, I take the end cubicle and settle in for a small snooze and some light fantasising about Jeremy.

I am enjoying a scenario where we are indulging in some light petting on the beach – with me positively sylphlike in comparison to Jeremy's magnitude – when someone comes in, taking the cubicle next to me. It is impossible to hold on to my fantasy while listening to someone else doing their business, so I wait. Patiently. They finish, exit the cubicle, wash their hands and then....nothing. They don't leave. What are they doing? Inspecting their nose for blackheads? Reapplying mascara? Whatever they are up to, it makes any meaningful day-dreaming impossible and after a few minutes I am forced to give up. I push out a small wee, flush and open the door to find Robyn standing there, arms folded in a display of both studied patience and impatience.

'Stella?' she says, eyebrows high. 'I wondered who it was. Tummy trouble?'

She is like a forgotten member of the Stasi, hunting down potential dissenters and skivers.

'Just been doing my five-minute meditation as recommended by Dr Asher Manufandali on the TV. Works wonders for concentration and productivity. I imagine you do yours in your office when the door's closed?'

She hesitates, her eyes flicking back and forth as she tries to assess if I am serious. In the end, not wanting to risk me being one up, she says perkily, 'I do! Isn't it marvellous? What's the name of your man? I'm thinking of rolling it out across the company, going to speak to Malcolm during our next one-on-one.'

'I'll email it to you. It's difficult to spell.'

So now I am now frantically googling YouTube meditation gurus, when what I would really like to be doing is sitting at home with Jeremy, *on* Jeremy, kissing Jeremy, ravishing Jeremy and occasionally sipping a glass of cold champagne to celebrate our mutual love for each other.

Got. It. Bad.

CHAPTER 10

Crush

/krʌʃ/

Verb: to press or squeeze with a force that destroys

Tried and failed to get into a pair of jeans that I used to wear in my Primrose Hill days; not even close. Too much gelatinous thigh in the mix by far. And I have been diligent this week; skinny lattés and *small* edibles only from Iris, no muffins, vegetarian wraps for lunch with nothing much more than a lettuce leaf inside *and* I have resisted seeing Kim and Bart in order to avoid the temptation of something fruity. All that for no discernable impact on my curves. I have put on more weight than I realised and it is not a good look on me: the fat. Clarissa carries her extra pounds with ease and grace whereas I just look lumpy – feel bumpy - and I can't bring myself to even think about my bottom. You will remember the hippo I recently spotted frolicking about in my bathroom? Well, another sighting has revealed the *back-side* of said hippo in the form of a vast white orb.

Dimpled, like the moon.

Only bigger.

Primrose Hill jeans being a no-go, I was obliged to stuff said orb into the super-stretchy jeans again and throw on a new purchase from Primark, a purchase that clearly enjoyed a former life as a wigwam. My hair has been blow-dried into sleek submission, my freckles and age spots have been painstakingly painted out and my sallow yellow colouring – as pointed out by Clarissa – has been pepped into a healthy glow with the addition of ludicrous amounts of make-up.

Quick question: how do you differentiate an age spot from a freckle? Answers on a postcard please.

One last squirt of perfume and I am done. I trot downstairs to check on my chocolate mousse. My contribution to the evening's festivities is a highly sophisticated creation involving melted Toblerone and whipped cream. That's it. This wonder recipe has been on the receiving end of some pointed critique from Olive, repeatedly trying to impose the use of eggs.

'Put the egg down, Olive. I'm in charge of pudding.' It wasn't easy holding firm, especially as she is such a whizz in the kitchen.

Giving my wigwam a final tweak, I head downstairs to find I am not the only one to have upped her game tonight. Olive is dazzling in a sky-blue cardigan, pearls and newly styled hair – a fact I know because there are two curlers still stuck in the back. As I gently ease them out of her hair, the doorbell goes.

Jeremy!

Determined to beat Olive to it, I thunder down to the front door, hauling it open with a flourish, a warm welcoming smile on my face.

'Oh.'

'What d'you mean, oh?' demands Kim. 'Who were you hoping it'd be?'

'No one!' I stutter. 'We aren't quite ready and I wanted to be ready and I haven't had time to test my pudding and Olive is - '

'Right here! You're blocking the front door, Stella. How can they get in with you in the way?' She shoves me to one side, preening a tad in her pearls and pouffed hair, before leaning in to collect her due in kisses.

'Olive!' squawks Kim. 'Don't you look lovely.'

'Oh, don't be silly,' she demurs, giving her curls a pat and failing to hide her delight.

'Which is more than I can say for your house guest. What *is* that thing you're wearing Stells? It looks like a tarpaulin or an old Scout tent or -'

'Just shut it, Kim. It's about the only thing I can wear without exposing my extensive collection of stomachs to the world.'

'If you say so,' she says, giving me a disbelieving look before turning her attention back to Olive. 'And this is for you, for taking care of our lovely Stella and generally being a top-notch person.'

Olive beams. 'Now you're being silly, but, oooh, that's a Munstead Wood English Rose, isn't it? One of my absolute favourites. What a treat, we'll plant it tomorrow, won't we Stella? You're all very naughty, it's not even my birthday. Stella got me an Olea Europaea in a beautiful terracotta pot. I've put it right outside the kitchen window so I can look at it every day and keep an eye on it.'

'What is an olly Europa?' asks Bart, staggering in with three bags of food and another from Majestic Wine, the giveaway clanking heralding the arrival of tonight's selection of wines.

'An olive tree,' she says with delight, clutching my arm.

And for that alone it was worth making that phone call to Jeremy. I splashed out on a decent one too and had it delivered to the house, distracting Olive in the back garden when it arrived and hiding it in the cupboard under the stairs until this morning.

We all settle into the kitchen where Bart gets busy unpacking all his purchases and telling Olive to sit down every ten seconds. He is cooking tonight and she is meant to be doing nothing – not something that comes easily to her and eventually he has to give her some onions to chop to shut her up and keep her in one place. Meanwhile, I am multi-tasking by opening some wine and keeping an all-important ear open for the doorbell; you have to be quick in this house, Olive moves like a whippet if someone is at the door.

When the already familiar ding-dong sounds, I am up and out of the traps before Olive's had time to register what is happening. A deep breath, tummy in, a silent prayer and I pull open the front door. There he is in all his wonderful, scruffy glory.

'Stella,' he breathes.

For a second, I can do nothing, mute and overwhelmed, desperate to throw myself into his arms yet frozen to the spot, yearning for him to step forward and take me into his powerful, life-affirming hold. I ready myself, heart racing, as reaches behind him. Flowers? Roses? *Red* roses?

'Stella, I want you to meet Julia.'

He pulls forward a girl as small as he is tall. I say girl because she cannot be more than eighteen or nineteen. Daughter? Half-sister? Niece? Neighbour?

'Hello, Stella,' she says. 'I've been looking forward to meeting you. I've heard so much about you.'

Which is worrying.

She steps forward and reaches up to give me a peck on the cheek and I am forced to bend down so she can reach. She smells of youth and patchouli and up close I can see that she has a mass of different coloured diamond studs all around her ear and what looks like a miniature dream catcher dangling from the lobe. We both stand back and I can't help but stare at her, a vision with short brown hair, tanned face clear of make-up, the white of her eyes startling in contrast. She is wearing a long Indian style patchwork skirt that hangs perfectly off her prominent hip bones - the likes of which haven't been seen on the Halfpenny since the early '90s when I got tonsillitis and couldn't eat for ten days - and a tight, dark pink vest.

I immediately feel like a badly dressed horse in comparison, envying her casual hippy chic and funky cropped hair. She looks as if she's just stepped off the beach in Goa and an unwanted image of Julia frolicking in the waves flashes into my mind, Julia with -

'Stella?' says Jeremy quietly, interrupting my reverie.

'Yes! Sorry, busy day. Lovely to see you, er, Julia and you of course, Jeremy.' I give him a kiss and take the opportunity to press my considerable cleavage to his mighty chest for a second. 'Come right through. Bart's cooking up a storm with Olive as acting commie chef and I've just handed over sommelier duties to Kim.'

Julia is greeted like a long-lost friend in the kitchen, not only by Olive, but Kim and Bart as well - both giving unnecessarily enthusiastic whoops and big hugs. An extra tight squeeze from Bart and she'll snap like a twig.

Go on, I think uncharitably, as he carefully envelops her, give it your all, squeeeeeeeeeze.

'What's with the big love-in? How come you already know each other?' I ask Kim in an undertone as we both watch Bart handling Julia like a priceless Ming vase, totally failing on the tight *squeeze* front.

'We've met a couple of times. Once up in town and once here. Don't look at me like that. *You* declined to leave your room. It wasn't long after you'd moved in and you were in full wallow.'

'You should have made me come down. Anyway, who is she?'

'Don't you listen at all,' she hisses. 'That's Jeremy's fiancée. The wedding's next year and if you play your cards right, you'll get an invite as Olive's plus-one.'

Fiancée? The room starts to spin and I grab the back of a chair for balance, dipping my head in a feeble attempt to hide my face from Kim. How the hell am I going to put the brakes on my crush, now an out-of-control juggernaut on a steep hill?

'Stells? Anyone home?' Kim clicks her fingers by my left ear.

'Bit dizzy. Back in a sec,' I wimper, making a beeline for the door and the stairs.

Five minutes. That's how much time I've got to rearrange my thoughts, hopes and dreams into a configuration that includes Julia. And excludes Jeremy. Or Jeremy and I to be exact. How did I not know he was engaged? Where was I when this information was made available? How have I stumbled from one shattered heart to another in a matter of days? Why is my life such a fucking mess? Again.

'Stell?' Kim is at the door. 'What are you doing? We're waiting for you to have a toast to the Re-emergence of Stella. Olive came up with that.' She approaches me cautiously, as if I might bite or make a run for it. 'Stells, what's wrong? You know she loves sharing her house with you. Said she didn't realise how lonely she was until you got here. She is thrilled that you've finally come out of your room and we need to celebrate that. For her, if not for you.'

Olive. I need to do this for Olive.

I clear my throat, stuffing my sadness down. Out of sight. 'I panicked. Sorry. All these people, all this bonhomie. Julia.' There, I have said it, said her name. 'Not used to it.'

'Come on.' She tows me towards the door. 'Time to get back on the horse or whatever that saying is. No more hiding. And you're going to love Julia, she's a hoot.'

A hoot? Not just tiny and svelte and gorgeous, not just a perky pixy-haired goddess, she is also a hoot.

'How old is she anyway? She looks about fifteen,' I moan as we make our way back downstairs.

'Don't be daft. She's the same age as us. Drinks like a fish too for someone so petite.'

I should like her for drinking like the rest of us but I can't. Not yet. Besides, she shouldn't be allowed to drink *and* remain so youthful. It's unfair.

Back in the kitchen, they are all waiting with full glasses to drink to me and my re-emergence. They shout it loud, clanking glasses with so much gusto and gaiety they are in danger of breaking, and then everyone drinks. I glance around the room, feeling like a fool, my eyes resting for a second too long on Jeremy who catches me looking. He winks and my heart gives a feeble, dying flutter.

Where would I be without him? Without them all? Without sweet Olive?

I raise my glass high and thank them all, one after the other, including Julia, and then I blow everyone a kiss - privately giving Julia's kiss to Jeremy – because I don't know what to say without sounding like a trite, over-grateful guest on an American talk-show.

Bart serves up a Coq au Vin worthy of a top London restaurant, steamed broccoli, snow peas and a mountain of buttery mash. All washed down with heroic quantities of Chilean Malbec. It is a feast and I fight a short, losing battle with myself before having seconds. Of everything. Under my voluminous top there is plenty of room for expansion, it would be rude not to make use it.

'It's refreshing to see a woman who loves to eat,' says Jeremy.

My fork, piled high with mash and thick gravy, stops half way to my mouth.

'Julia eats like a bird.'

I lower the fork back to my plate.

'Ah,' sighs Kim. 'But she drinks like a fish. We can forgive her tiny waist because she enjoys wine like the rest of us, right Stells? Our friend, sorry, ex-friend, Nina -'

'Is that the one that went off with Jackson whats-his-face?' interrupts (tiny-waisted) Julia.

'That's the one. Well, she didn't eat *or* drink. Not much at any rate. A glass of bone-dry white could last her all evening.'

'She liked to watch it evaporate,' I add, relieved that we are talking about someone other than me and wondering how to keep it like that. 'Less calories that way.'

'And less fun,' states Julia, taking another gulp of her Malbec and I feel my resentment weaken fractionally.

'I haven't put you off, have I?' Jeremy asks, looking at my unfinished plate. 'I shouldn't have said anything. Julia's always telling me to get my foot out of my mouth.'

'No, no,' I mumble. 'Eyes bigger than my stomach.'

This provokes a snort from Kim and although she refrains from making the obvious comment, I can see that she is gearing up to say something maybe less pointed but equally embarrassing.

I decide to get in first. 'I know, I know.' I hold up my hand. 'Comfort eating. It helps. Helped. It'll be celery and cucumber only from Monday morning, I promise.'

'Absolute rubbish, no one wants a stick insect.' says Olive-the-stick-insect. 'You should stay exactly as you are, Stella. Men like an extra pound or two to get hold of. Right, Jeremy?'

Jeremy delays replying by stuffing in forkful of my discarded mash, alternately nodding and shaking his head, clearly searching for a diplomatic answer. 'Stella is beautiful as she is,' he starts, as Olive nods in agreement, then goes on, 'but if she would prefer to lose some weight then she should do what makes her comfortable.'

That's it. Water and fresh air from here on. Jeremy obviously thinks I'm a complete porker.

'A little exercise is all you need,' says Julia, kindly. 'Nothing drastic.'

'Why don't you come to the gym with me?' Kim asks. 'I'm thinking of starting CrossFit. Everyone says it's amazing and the poster in the gym says beginners are welcome. We should go. Come with me, please, I'm dying to try it.'

'CrossFit? Are you mad? Didn't you hear Julia? Nothing drastic, she said, and she knows, look at the size of her. I'm not attempting CrossFit. I get puffed on the stairs these days.'

'All the more reason. It'll be fun, we'll go together,' she urges.

'No,' I say, digging in my heels.

'Come on, we both need to do this. We need to up our game, so to speak. I'm as unfit as you are.'

'But not as fat,' I sigh. I cannot believe I am having this conversation in front of Jeremy and Julia.

'I come also,' says Bart. 'With popcorn and beer. I support. Is there seats or I bring my camping chair?'

'Fuck off, Bart. Sorry, Olive. Anyway, what do you wear to CrossFit? I'm not buying any special clothing, except possibly a small tent. Or I could wear this,' I say, plucking at my green top. 'But I'm not wearing Lycra.'

'Just wear your gym clothes, if you've got any. A T-shirt and a pair of shorts will be fine.'

Everyone is watching me, waiting, and out of the corner of my eye I can see, or rather feel, the shrimp-sized Julia and that is enough to decide me.

'OK. We start week after next. I need to prepare, mentally. What day is it?'

'Wednesday,' she says, coming around the table to give me a high-five and finding another curler in Olive's hair on the way past.

That leaves me precisely ten days to shape up and size down before easing the baby hippo into some gym clothes. I cannot show up for CrossFit looking like this, I just can't. I could fast. All the health and weight loss magazines drone on about it these days; it not only transforms the physical, it works wonders for mind and spirit as well and, let's be honest, all three could do with a decent spring clean in the House of Stella. Plus, think of the money I will save. I can use it to buy a new gym outfit, one that highlights my high points (I will let you know when I have located them) and lowlights my low points (a challenge worthy of Stella McCartney herself).

I'll be back in those jeans before you can say Toblerone.

Which reminds me; it is time for the *great unveiling*. I retrieve it from the fridge, Olive eying the pale mousse with suspicion.

'It doesn't look very chocolatey, dear,' she sniffs.

'Withhold judgement until you have tasted,' I say, giving her a giant dollop of the gorgeous stuff and sticking a teaspoon into the top to make up for the lack of decoration. It looks supremely light and fluffy and that is surely half the battle with a mousse. Who cares about the colour? Bart is meanwhile uncorking a French Muscat to go with my creation, although pairing sweet wine with a sweet pud is what you might call *over-egging*, despite the fact that none are involved.

'Now my little Olive tree, eat and weep.'

She takes a dainty taste, about enough to feed a small ant on a restricted diet, and closes her eyes. We all stop to watch. A small frown. Slight wrinkle of the nose. Chewing motion.

'Oh, come on!' I burst out. 'For fu -, for Gordon Bennett's sake, what do you think? Like? No like?'

'Well, I suppose it's not too bad,' she concedes. 'Considering the unusual recipe.' She takes another miniscule blob on the tip of her spoon and nibbles it off. 'Quite nice.'

'Quite nice! That's as good as saying you hate it,' I cry hotly. 'It's Toblerone and cream. What's not to like?'

'I'm only joking,' she twinkles. 'It's delicious. Well done, Stella.'

And I promptly burst into tears.

Everyone goes into panic mode and I am soon buried under a hillock of tissues, wine glass full to the brim and repeated slaps from Kim.

'Stop being such a drama queen. It's only a bloody mousse.'

'I know, I know. But it's an emotional day,' I sniff. 'My re-emergence.'

And my crush being comprehensively crushed in its infancy, I think sadly to myself.

'I've felt so useless lately that I think I have *become* useless. You are what you think, something like that, and as I think I am useless, ergo I am useless. Even at work, I keep checking and double checking everything, convinced I must have made a mistake and if I can't find a mistake then I'd better check again as there is bound to be one in there somewhere. It's exhausting. I doubt everything I do. I've been dealing with Malcolm Feet-of-Clay for years and yet since the Jackson,' sniff sniff, 'and Nina,' sniff, '*thing*, I don't know how to deal with him anymore. Everyone says I am the mainstay of the office, but it's bollocks. Right now, I'm hanging on by my fingernails and they will out me any minute and then it'll be curtains. I'll be out. Unwanted goods.'

'Stella,' Kim says. 'Look at me. You run that place, have done for years. You're the only person who can handle Malcolm Clay, for what it's worth, and he'd be lost without you. He knows it, the office knows it, I know it, everyone knows it.'

'I know it,' adds Bart, thumping a fist on the table.

'Lack of confidence is normal after the knock you took, but it'll come back. You're not long back from the Land of Wallow, it was bound to take you a while to get back to normal service. Like coming back after an amazing holiday, only ten times worse cos you had a shit time, not a great time. Does that make sense?'

We all nod. It does make sense. Weirdly.

'That's all right then.' She rubs her hands together. 'Let's get back to this Toblerone fluff. I for one am having thirds. We'll soon burn it all off in CrossFit.'

CHAPTER 11

Negligence
/nɛɡlɪdʒ(ə)ns/
Noun: failure to give necessary care or attention which leads to damage

'Stella? Stella? Are you alright, love?'

I am face down in the hallway, nose planted into the scrubby carpet, and I intend to stay here for as long as possible.

Today has been challenging, both physically and mentally. Hard to say which tried me more, the physical – I cannot move – or the mental, as humiliation once again came knocking. Although *knocking* does not do justice to the scale of the mortification I suffered this evening; more of a thundering, destroying all the self-esteem I had been so painstakingly piecing together.

Pumped up by Kim's words last week, I've been attacking work with renewed vim and vigour, buoyed by a reassuring return to belief in myself, my abilities. This, I admit, has been made significantly easier by the absence of Feet-of who has been away on an impromptu visit to Japan to assess the investment opportunities. Malcolm Clay in Japan. Is there anyone less suited to the polite Japanese culture? So, before he left, in keeping with my new *I-am-so-on-this* persona and fearing for the sensibilities of the local population, I made him a crib sheet of simple pointers on how to behave and impress; bowing when you greet someone, not blowing your nose in public, offering a business card with two hands, elementary things that even he should be able to manage. His response? *Don't be ridiculous Stella, I'm not bowing to anyone.*

Making friends and influencing people? I think not.

Today, sadly, he was back. He flew in yesterday – Easter Monday - for a family party. It was not what could be called a success, mainly because he flew back just as the inappropriately named Storm Fifi was ramping up the chaos. I had tried to warn him about parties and bank holidays and the inevitable bad weather, but he chose to ignore me and thus spent the day clinging to the hired pagoda to stop it blowing into next week. As a result, he has been in a foul mood all day and determined to get his worker bees flying around to his every beck and buzz. I didn't even have time to put my *super-light skinny* latté – a newly developed version that Marco has been refining for me - down on my desk before I was summoned to his hive for a bollocking.

'How many times have I told you to book me the *front window* seat, Stella? How many? And, where was I? Right at the back, on the aisle, which is exactly where you do not want to be when flying in a storm.'

'We booked so late we were lucky to get a seat at all. That was the only one left.' I said, stoutly. Then, taking my courage with both hands added, 'And the back of Business class is hardly the back of the plane.'

If looks could kill, I would have been done and dusted.

'Book earlier next time. In time to get the right seat,' he snapped.

I stood with my mouth open at this moronic statement, stunned into silence before rallying and saying hotly, 'I booked as soon as you told me you wanted to go. I can't book earlier than that because I have yet to develop any telepathic powers.'

He looked at me crossly. 'Well, work on them. And in future, Stella, please advise me in advance of adverse weather conditions when you know I am planning a family lunch. I would never have organised such a large party if I'd known there was a veritable hurricane on the way. The pagoda is beyond repair and they are demanding full payment.'

'I booked that pagoda three weeks ago when Fifi had not yet been conceived. I did warn you that a bank holiday weekend was bound to be a washout.'

'Rain I could have managed but a full-on hurricane is a big ask. Now, go and get me a coffee and pay more attention next time.'

That was at approximately 8.12am this morning and it went downhill from there. I had added three pounds to the swear box before 10am and Clarissa wore a trench between her desk and mine, coming over to empathise every ten minutes and discuss ways to wind him up. Her preferred idea is putting a daily weather forecast up on the notice board that will be systematically wrong. Especially on a Friday. There was one small ray of light when Miles turned up for a meeting and had to wait for over half an hour, time he spent lounging on the edge of my desk looking disconcertingly like Ryan Gosling. Only better looking, with bluer eyes and darker hair. Slightly darker skin too. Broader shoulders. Not really like Ryan Gosling at all in fact. I blame the lack of food; I had not yet eaten and was existing on coffee alone. Not quite the fast I was promising, but you can't work an eight-hour day with no fuel on board and if you google *coffee*, you will find it is good for all sorts of things, including giving the brain a right old boost.

And I need all brain boosting I can lay my hands on, including clairvoyant abilities and an enhanced weather forecasting function. Anyway, it would be rude not to drink any coffee with Marco downstairs and I like to think I contribute to the Iris paycheck too.

Mid-afternoon, when Clay was safely occupied by a conference call, I escaped downstairs to get a tea. Iris was still in situ polishing anything that wasn't moving and a few things that were, including Ringo's new specs, ending him on his way in a dazzle of unimpaired vision. Over the weeks, Iris has gradually been staying longer and longer, a tiny satellite orbiting around Marco, dispensing goodwill and cheer freely to anyone who has the good fortune to step into her sightline.

'Hello, Stella, did you see Barry's new glasses? Aren't they smart? I said he should have changed them years ago and you know what he told me?' I looked at Iris, waiting for the answer, more interested than I would have thought possible. The Ringo / Barry make-over is becoming a hot topic of conversation upstairs as each new phase is unveiled. 'He said he didn't have to please anyone except himself before, but that is no longer the case!'

'Ooooh, hot gossip, Ringo has a girlfriend,' I said, intrigued.

'Exactly!' Iris squeaked, excitement mounting. 'Wouldn't tell me who it is, so I'm working it out by process of elimination.'

'And how are you doing that? It could be anyone!'

'I have my methods,' she said coyly.

'Stella, dear? Speak to me.' Olive gets down on her hands and knees in the hallway, peering at me nervously.

No idea how I even got this far; it was a long walk from the taxi to the front door, an eternity as I scrabbled in my bag for my keys, an extended agony to lift my arm up to lock only to find I couldn't turn the key. I was finished. Batteries comprehensively flat, steamrollered into oblivion. In the end, I managed to ring the doorbell and toppled through into the hallway as Olive pulled open the door.

So much for Cross-fucking-Fit. There is not one cell in my body currently not begging to be put out of its misery.

Note to self: Never speak to Kim again. Ever.

'Stella? Shall I call an ambulance?'

'I am broken, Olive. It was hell on earth. Don't ever let Kim back in the house.'

'What's Kim done? She's a lovely girl.'

'Took me to CrossFit.'

'Those training classes? How did it go?'

I try and give her a scathing look, but my face muscles have gone on strike. 'Have a guess, Olive. How do you think it went given my current state? I might have to sleep down here. Can't move.'

'Bit much for me do you think? I was keen to give it a go.'

'Olive, I don't think CrossFit is the right fit for you.'

'Shall I try the Pilates then? There's a lady called Rhonda who does classes and she offers a discount for pensioners.'

'Olive, sweetie?'

'Yes, pet?'

'Could we discuss your fitness regime another time?'

'Yes, perhaps you're right. How about a hot bath?'

Only problem is the bath is upstairs. I get up on all fours and start to inch forward while Olive nimbly side steps around me and nips up to get busy with the taps and bubble bath. Each stair causes me to break out in a monsoon of sweat and it takes a full ten minutes to negotiate the full set, plus an interminable stretch of landing.

'I'll leave you to get in and then I'll bring you a drink,' she says gently.

'It has to have alcohol in. No water. No tea. No juice.'

'Righty-ho. I'll get us a nice soothing sherry.'

In the bath, I lower myself into the scalding water and let the heat relieve my battered body, bubbles coming up over my head.

Who has tried CrossFit? No? Let me give you some pointers. STAY AWAY. DO NOT ATTEMPT UNDER ANY CIRCUMSTANCES. It is a fucking nightmare. With acronyms. Like a sadistic army training camp designed to inflict maximum pain, humiliation and total submission.

We trooped in, Kim looking absurdly trim by-the-way, to join a cluster of fit looking people with proper muscles, all jogging about on the spot, arms wheeling, necks cricking under repeated heads rolls. Then there was me, the blobby one, regretting I hadn't gone for the tent after all. Kim kept waffling on that beginners were welcome; so, I kept myself occupied by praying fervently that I wouldn't be the only one.

Then Cliff arrived.

My prayers had been answered, I thought, as a vast heft of a man waddled in, squeezing himself through the doorway. *Another beginner and he is even fatter than me! Hooray!* I gave myself a mini pat on the back, delighted that I wouldn't be the worst, haha! Or the fattest, double haha!

Only Cliff wasn't a beginner. Yes, he was fat but this was not his first CrossFit; everyone knew him and greeted him like a rock star. *Cliff! Great to see you! Looking good, Cliff! Ready for more pain, Cliff! You're the main man!* On and on it went, the high fives, handshakes and back-slaps never ending as everyone got in line to have a go. It might have gone on even longer – people were going to the back of the queue for a second go - had a man built like a tank not arrived, his head swivelling around on broad shoulders as he barked orders to his troops.

'Get in line, at the double, that is NOT fast enough, MOVE IT!'.

Everyone jostled into a scraggy line in front of a white board covered in ACRONYMS and nasty looking lists of what I feared were exercises.

'What's the WOD, people?' yelled the Sergeant Major.

'BAMBI,' everyone cried. It was written at the top of the board in caps, so not too hard to find, although I had no idea what a WOD was, or BAMBI for that matter.

'I can't hear you,' sang the Sergeant Major.

'BAMBI!' everyone screamed, pumping their arms and upping the on-the-spot jogging.

'Is it gonna hurt? Will there be pain?'

'Yes! More pain, more gain,' they all roared.

For fuck's sake.

I had positioned myself next to Cliff, the only one fat enough for me to hide behind effectively and I was already edging out of the sadistic meathead's eye line. He was striding up and down, sticking his beefy face into people's very personal space, eyeball-to-eyeball. Not my thing at all.

'Bambi,' he sneered, 'is because we have some beginners with us today and we need to break them gently.' They all booed as I slid in right behind Cliff. 'But we all know that CrossFit doesn't do *gentle.'* Cue the whoops and cheers – including, I might add, Kim, already showing her true colours. 'So, don't be fooled by BAM.' He slammed one hand into the other. 'BI!' Double fist punch. 'BAM first. *Bad and Mad.* Then BI – that's *Brutal Intensity* people.' Everyone groaned in ecstasy. 'Every exercise in BAM is AMRAP. All those in BI are EMOTM. List is here.' He rapped a knuckle on the whiteboard.

'What the fuck is AMRAP?' I whispered to myself, tucking closer in behind Cliff, who smelt soothingly of lemons.

For those of you who have never endured a CrossFit session, let me explain the alphabet of pain that you need to become acquainted with:

WOD = workout of the day

AMRAP = as many reps as possible

EMOTM = every minute on the minute

Never have I seen so many people in such a small space actively seeking pain and self-abasement. I was in trouble early on when we started the warm-up. Surely a warm-up should include little leg bends and knee lifts like they do in your average village-hall keep-fit class, grapevines, a few arm twirls for good measure. Not in CrossFit, no no no, we were brow beaten into squats and lunges and press-ups – press-ups!!! By the time we got to star jumps I needed a lie down and we hadn't even started our first AMRAP.

Two minutes later, as I was busy trying to summon a major gynaecological problem that would get me out of there,

I was flattened by a low flying medicine ball thrown at me by the dickhead Sergeant Major – do I look like I can catch a fucking medicine ball? I think not.

'Wakey, wakey, Stella! Is anyone home? Come on, MOVE IT! I want twenty, RIGHT NOW!'

As if. I consoled myself by giving him the finger as he strode off to fondle Cliff, giving him a shoulder massage and cooing, 'Cliff, you're a legend, way-to-go, my man.'

More horror followed and for each AMRAP I aimed for an AFRAP (as few reps as possible), continual WBCs (without being caught), multiple MLFERs (mini lie-downs for essential recovery) and unsuccessfully tried to stay out of sight.

And then it was my turn on the pull-up bar.

Oh, the pull-up bar.

Let's be perfectly honest and admit that the average human body is not designed to do a pull-up, it's one of the reasons we came down from the trees. Even if you've been keeping off the doughnuts, which I of course haven't due to my recent AMOMEM diet (a muffin on the minute every minute). Predictably, I couldn't even work out how to get up to the bar to get started pulling-up. I had a vague notion that if I could just get up there, I could dangle for a bit and have a small rest, stretch out my aching back. So, when the bloody Sergeant Major helpfully pointed out a giant elastic band cunningly designed to help the weaklings like me to get up to the bar, I was game.

It went like this; I managed to get my foot into the loop, no small feat, then hopped around for a while wondering what the hell you were supposed to do next. How do you go from here, to there? I was working out how I could get my foot back out of the bloody band when the Sergeant Major came over, got a good grasp of my lardy arse, and launched me into the air. I made a grab for the bar, but my sweaty hands had no grip and over I went, feet up, tits down, head hitting the floor with a hollow knock before I bobbed back up again, trapped in the clutches of the giant elastic band. Momentum, coupled with the increased gravitational pull of such a heavy muffin-laden mass, kept me bouncing up and down for a very long minute before I slowed to a halt, dangling like a carcass of beef at the local butchers.

The entire class had stopped by this point, transfixed and silent, until a loud snort – a snort I recognised, a snort I have grown up with - set them all off and the room roared with belly laughs and guffaws. Even the Sergeant Major allowed himself a throaty guffaw, while doing precisely nothing to come and help.

I should sue for negligence. Damage to my shattered ego, not to mention my private parts - badly burned in a moment of high friction with fast moving rubber. I genuinely do not know how long I would have stayed suspended if the one good Samaritan in the room, an angel descended from the heavens, hadn't come to my rescue, untangling me, and laying me gently on the mat like a corpse.

It was one of the worst hours of my life and it was pride alone that kept me in that room, that and not wanting to give in to the taunts of the Sergeant Major. As we were finally (officially) allowed to lie down for some relaxation, he started bellowing again.

'Awesome people, breathe now, you've earned it, pull in that oxygen, what a great bunch you are, love you guys.'

There were about two seconds of calm before everyone sprang up and started whooping and high fiving. Including Kim. Pretending to be unfit and then rushing around the place like a Ninja contestant. Disloyalty of the lowest kind.

And she was smiling at me. Thrilled. 'God, that was mental, I'm in agony, but it was brilliant wasn't it, we should come twice a week, be fit as in no time. Gotta run my sweet, Bart's broken down on the M4.'

I didn't shower. Too much effort. Even the thought of all that running water made me break out in a new sweat. I pulled on my coat over my sodden clothes and tried to negotiate the stairs, but my legs had already seized up, so I was forced to sidle over to the disabled lift. Downstairs you have to exit through the small club bar, smoothies and juices, spinach and kale gulpies, berk, that kind of thing – I was nearly through, swinging my legs a little to the side to avoid any unnecessary bending at the knee, when a voice called my name.

'Stella?'

I didn't stop. Not while I had some momentum going.

'Stella!' More insistent this time.

I turned, painfully, even my neck had given up, and saw the guy, the angel who rescued me from the pull-up bar.

'Hey, I owe you a big thank you,' I said, with feeling.

'Let me get you a drink,' he called, 'you've earned it.'

'No, thanks, I should get going, it's going to take me forever to get home as it is.'

'It's on me. Take a break. Juice? A smoothie?' He stood up and approached.

I gazed longingly over at the bar. Juice? Are you kidding me? I needed alcohol, nothing more, nothing less. Preferably wine.

'Do they do wine?' I asked, my eyes still fixed on the bar, searching forlornly for a sign of vino. 'Rosé wine?'

He laughed, 'I've never asked. Let's find out.'

He ambled over to the bar and I took a second to check him out; tall, rangy, hair halfway to a full-on afro, black skin beautiful against a pale blue shirt. Hmmm, I liked and, better and better, he came back holding two large glasses of rosé wine.

'D'you think you could ask for a straw?'

'A straw?'

'I can't lift that. My arms.' I flapped a hand at the glass. 'Toast.'

And he got me a straw, good man, popping it into my glass. 'Your first CrossFit I take it?'

'And my last.'

He laughed indulgently. 'Come on now, it will get easier, you'll be in shape in no time.'

'I'm happy with my shape, thanks.' Total bare-faced lie.

'Touché. You'll be fitter in no time.' He lifted his glass in a gesture of cheers and took a deep gulp. 'Wine after workout. Could be the way forward.'

'The only way. Cheers.' I took a few long sips. Lovely. The world is always a better place when wine is on the table. 'And you are?'

'James.'

'Thank you, James, for wading in to my humiliation and saving me from an indecent incident with a giant rubber band. I hope you didn't put your back out.'

He waved me away. 'You handled it well.'

'My Book of Mortification is full to bursting.'

'You'll come back though?'

'No chance. It's not my *thang*, and I can't deal with that Sergeant Major shouting at me. I need to be coaxed and encouraged.'

'He's tough, has to be, it's his job. He needs to push us.'

'Right. He was all over me like a bad case of eczema but Cliff, Cliff got cheered if he managed one sit-up, Cliff didn't even have to attempt a pull-up. Cliff got a bloody shoulder massage after like one press-up.'

'Cliff is special. We all love Cliff.'

I sniffed dismissively. What's so special about Cliff? If I go back, will I be special and loved? For being a gloopy, unfit lardy-arse?

'Come again on Friday, Leroy's on, I'll have a word and he'll sort you out.'

'Ha! You're kidding. Tell me you're not serious. I am not ending my week in that torture chamber.'

'Well, I occasionally come in on Sunday, late afternoon. If you like, we can do a gentle session in the gym, I'll show you round the machines. No CrossFit. No Sergeant Major.'

'Um, I'm not sure.' Hedging, I drank some more wine. I would definitely like to see James on Sunday, but the gym? On a weekend?

'Say yes. I'll buy you wine afterwards.'

'Rosé?'

He laughed. 'Sure. Maybe not here though. We can find better rosé elsewhere.'

And, based on the fact that he is willing to buy me rosé, in public, and drink it with me, I agreed.

My phone rings making me jump, water sloshing out of the bath, and before I have time to engage my brain, I pick up.

It's Kim.

'I'm not speaking to you Kim. Ever again. Go away.' And I hang up.

It rings again two seconds later.

'Why?' she asks, giggling, knowing full damn well.

'You're a liar and a cheat. You are about as unfit as Jessica Ennis, you did pull-ups, sit-ups, stand-ups, lots of ups, ups all over the fucking shop. And you snorted when I was trussed up like a dead pig, I heard you, and you whooped. You actually whooped like a fucking cheerleader.' I pause for a quick review. What have I missed? Oh, yes. 'And you had gloves.'

'Gloves?'

'Those cycling gloves. Like a pro. You never mentioned gloves to me. Let me turn up like a bloody learner driver and what happens? Head-on collision. All. Your. Fault.'

'Stella -'

'Leave me alone. And stop talking, my ears hurt. There is not one part of me that doesn't hurt.'

'Why do your ears hurt?'

'I think I pulled an ear muscle when hanging upside down with all the blood rushing to my head. There's only so much blood that can fit in the average head and I clearly had too much so my ear had to give way to make more room.' I hear a muffled grunt. 'Was that a snort?' Another honk teeters down the line. 'Kim, this is the end, finito. Now fuck off.'

'Sorry sweetheart, you're making me laugh and I'll never forgive myself for snorting when you fell off that bar, honestly I didn't want to. I crossed my legs and held my breath but a tiny toot got out. I did a little wee too, couldn't help it.'

'I made you wet yourself? Good. I feel a bit better. I did a wee too but mine was down to sheer effort. Too much straining. Going to have to start pelvic floor squeezes soon or invest in some incontinence pads.'

Another honk comes down the phone and before I can control it, a burst of laughter escapes from behind my battered rib cage.

'Stella?'

And we're off, howling and cackling down the phone until we're interrupted by a knock on the door.

'Come on in!' I wheeze, unable to stop.

'Who's that?' Kim squeaks.

'Olive's come with supplies.'

'Sherry?'

'And biscuits. I've got to stay off the biscuits. The sight of myself in those shorts. Fuck.'

'Rubbish. You're gorgeous as ever.'

'I know what I looked like. Don't be nice for the sake of it. I do have a date though. For Sunday.'

'How? I only saw you a couple of hours ago.'

'Not a proper date. A workout date. James. The guy that picked me up off the floor.'

'Idris Elba, you mean?'

I giggle happily. 'He does look a bit like him. He's going to show me round the gym machines and take me for wine after. Rosé wine.'

'He knows the way to a girl's heart.'

CHAPTER 12

Fickle

/ˈfɪk(ə)l/

Adjective: changing frequently, especially as regards one's loyalties or affections

'Stella? Well, well, well.'

For fuck's sake, it's my very own private dementor. The Sergeant Major himself.

'Disappointed not to see you in yesterday's class. We missed you,' he says, a distinct smile in his voice. 'Cliff was asking after you. He put in another good session.'

'Oh, here we go. Just let me get my prayer mat for some in-depth Cliff-worship,' I say, pondering the advantages of dropping a dumbbell on his foot.

'He's earned it.'

'He does like five measly seconds in the plank and you applaud him!' I grunt. Flat on my back with a hefty weight in each hand pinning me to the bench, I am at a disadvantage.

'Stella,' he says, taking the dumbbells and hauling me upright. 'Listen. When Cliff started CrossFit, he was carrying thirty-five pounds more than he is now. He couldn't even get into a plank, but it didn't stop him trying. Can you imagine how hard it is to hold all that weight off the ground for five seconds? To do a press-up? Think about it before you criticise. It's not easy turning up for a CrossFit class in his condition, all those sleek fit people staring at you, but Cliff is there, religiously, twice a week. And always with good humour, with humility, with determination. That's why he gets special treatment.'

'Bully for Cliff,' I say, feeling about an inch high.

'Bully for Cliff is right. He doesn't give up. I'll be expecting you Wednesday. Firm up some of that slack flesh.' He grabs a handful of blubber on my upper arm.

'Rather my flabby bod that your ridiculous Popeye look. You should ease up on the bicep curls. Getting out of hand.'

'That's more like it. Now, you going to show me what you can do with those bells or they just for decoration?' he asks.

'Testing them out for my Christmas tree,' I whip back.

He cracks a half smile and I feel absurdly pleased.

'Ah, Jimmy, look who I've found. Our very own circus performer. She's coming back on Wednesday for another go. Got to work on her dismount.'

James looks at me with what could be admiration but is more likely disbelief. 'Really?' I nod, reluctantly. 'Great stuff. I'll be there to help.'

'No help, Jimmy,' he asserts, Sergeant Major traits returning to the fore. 'You know the rules. It's every man for himself.'

'Here, well done, you deserve this.'

James hands me a delicious glass of pale pink liquid, so cold the glass is beading with condensation already. We are in a small wine bar down the road from the gym and I have to admit I'm buzzing, a hoard of endorphins surfing around my body, distributing general pep and vigour.

'Thank you. Not the recommended reward but I'll take it tonight. I'm going to try a liquid diet to allow for wine and coffee.'

'You need to eat if you're exercising. Get some good protein in you.'

'A protein shake will do the job nicely while remaining in the liquid remit. Anyway, thanks for this evening. Appreciate it. Cheers.' I raise my glass.

Hail to the rosé. Crisp, fresh, fruity. Perfect.

'So, Stella, what do you do in life?'

'Do? Work you mean? I'm a PA.'

'Who for?'

'You won't have heard of them. I work for Claybourne Estates.'

'Jesus, do you work for Malcolm Clay?'

'Also known as Feet-of. The very same.'

'Feet of?'

'Feet of Clay.'

He laughs out loud and a shiver of pleasure ripples over my body. 'Feet of. Very good. He has quite a reputation.'

'For being a prize arse?'

'Well, yes, he's not what you would call popular. However, he is clever. Those warehouse apartments, quite the coup.' I look at him blankly. 'You don't know? Back in the late '70s, he bought a ramshackle pile of warehouses out east of the Docklands for a song, peanuts. No one else was interested then in the derelict buildings from the deserted port area. He sat on it for years until the area started picking up in the late '80s, early '90s and there he was sitting pretty on a huge piece of land and numerous old buildings.'

Fascinating. Who knew Clay had it in him to be so entrepreneurial?

'He started renovating the old warehouses into luxury flats, some of the most expensive in the area. His genius was using the old buildings, the fixtures and fittings, and incorporating them into the modern flats. A wall of the original red brickwork forming the main feature in a living room or a freight elevator converted into a bathroom. He used the old discarded factory machines and renovated them into stunningly original lamps and feature pieces. The Warehouse Lofts are more sought-after than ever as the area has developed, not to mention the Olympic factor a few years ago that gave the whole district another massive lift.'

I am gobsmacked. Feet-of-Clay? I thought he was just a lucky bastard who'd made good by chance and pure luck.

146

'I had no idea. Most of the time, he's so busy being a pain in the arse, it's difficult to see beyond the void where his personality or genius might be hidden, let alone a bunch of luxury warehouses.'

'He sold all them all years ago when his wife went off with one the builders. I think she was responsible for a lot of the interior design, not that he has ever given her credit. She just walked out one day.'

'Did she?' I perk up at all this juicy gossip. 'I never even knew he'd been married. He's a classic bachelor now, crumpled shirts and stained ties. He once asked me how to work his washing machine. Had to make him up a simple guide. How is it that so many successful businessmen can't work out how to use a simple household appliance?'

James himself is clearly in full control of his white goods judging by the pristine nature of the striped shirt he is wearing, complete with sharp crease down the arms. That or he pays a fortune for dry cleaning. Or, shudder, he has a girlfriend / wife at home doing them for him. I try to get a look at his left hand, but it is tucked out of sight.

'What?' he asks.

'Nothing,' I say, straightening up. 'What about you? Why do you know so much about my boss? Do you work in property?'

'Investment banking,' he replies.

Oh, fuck, not again.

'I have clients who invest in a lot of property. And anyway, when someone pulls of a deal like Clay with the warehouses, word gets around and it slowly filters into legend. Even now, people are on the lookout for another opportunity like that.'

'Who do you work for?' My turn to ask. I'm hoping to hell he doesn't work for Slymann Hodge or I am out of here.

'JP Morgan.'

'Not Slymann Hodge then, that's a relief.'

147

'Not a fan? What do you know about Slymann Hodge? Or who do you know? They're big players in the city.' He drinks some wine, studying me.

In an instant I can feel my skin prickling with unease as memories float to the surface like scum on a pond. 'No one important. Anyway, he's buggered off to New York now with someone else unimportant.' His inquisitive face asks for more details and, restraint loosened by the fast-disappearing rosé, I go on. 'Jackson T. Lysander-Perry, don't forget the T please. He works at Slymann's and he's hoofed it off to New York with a ho by the name of Nina Bergdahl.'

'Lysander-Perry?' he asks. 'Rings a vague bell, but I don't think I've ever met him. I'm just back from a few years abroad so I'm out of touch with much of the London crowd.'

'Whereabouts?'

'Singapore mostly, with a short spell in Cape Town. My dad's from there and I'd never even been so I engineered a move. Africa is an interesting, if volatile, prospect.'

'Nice gig if you can get it,' I say with envy.

He drinks some wine. 'Tell me about this Lysander man and, what's her name? Nina? Why have they gone to New York?'

'They were *promoted*, if you can believe that. I have my doubts. Probably paid their way or offered other insalubrious services. They say the casting couch is alive and thriving,' I say crossly.

'Ouch. Not a fan, then. What've they done to upset you?'

There's no way to answer that without giving too much away, so I shrug non-committedly. Can't have Jackson and Nina hijacking the evening all the way from New York.

He watches me for a while as I fidget, playing with my wine glass. Then he says, 'I'm a good listener. Especially with a glass of wine in my hand.'

That's all it takes. The prospect of venting about Jackson and Nina to a new and sympathetic listener, one who doesn't know them and will therefore be one hundred percent on my side, is too strong and I launch into an unrestrained account of my sorry tale.

'So, they're in the City of Dreams together? How's that going, I wonder? Want me to check up on them if I can, see what happening? I'm going next week.'

'To New York?'

He gives me a slow smile and says, 'I'll have a dig, if you like. See what the word is on the grapevine. Jackson whatshisname, you said he works at Slymann Hodge so I can check him out no problem. How about this Nina? Where's she working now?'

A pause. I am reluctant to admit where she works, how brilliant she is. But having my own spy, a *mole* on the ground in New York, helps loosen my reserve.

'Goldman Sachs,' I say, softly.

He whistles in appreciation and I almost regret telling him. Then I imagine him finding a ton of juicy dirt? Unpopular, crap at her job, fat and spotty with the stress.

'Foreign currency,' I elaborate.

'Right then. Let's see if I can dig up some dirt.'

'Take a shovel and I'll buy you rosé when you get back.'

'It's a deal.'

On the bus now, I am puffed with positive energy and trying to push away the thought that I am also a craven, fickle woman. A short week ago I was mentally planning a life with Jeremy and now I am only interested in more rosé with James. CrossFit will have to become a staple if he is going to be there, keeping an eye on me - even if there is way too much of me to keep an eye on. An image of that hippo in the mist seeps uninvited into my mind's eye and I vow to redouble my efforts to shed the excess.

Then, there is Nina.

Does it make me a bad person to want her to be unhappy

in New York? Because when I wrote the words, *unpopular, crap at her job, fat and spotty with stress,* I meant them with all my heart. And they are just the start of a long and painful list of horrors that I am hoping will befall Nina. Disturbed, I fire off a text to Kim.

She texts me back immediately.

Kim: *Not bad person*

Kim: *Wounded animal will strike out*

Kim: *She hurt u and u want to hurt back*

Kim: *Difference is that u only think it*

Kim: *Wouldnt actually do it*

Which, I am forced to admit, is up for debate.

CHAPTER 13

Plethora

/ˈplɛθ(ə)rə/

Adjective: a large or excessive amount of something, more than you can deal with

'We're going for drinks after work. Third Thursday of the month we always go to the Chopper Lump. How about it? You want to join us?' Clarissa is standing in front of my desk, handily blocking the view as Feet-of stumps in. 'Morning, Mr Clay,' she chirps over her shoulder.

He doesn't reply.

'I've never been to the Chopper Lump,' I say.

'No, well, you didn't do evening drinks when you were with the wanker banker and then post-wanker banker you were in your sulky phase,' she says this in a loud whisper. 'And we wouldn't have dared ask you then even if we'd wanted to, which, to be honest, we didn't. Had enough of you by home time back then and I don't think we'd have fitted your black cloud into the Chopper, it's a tight fit down there.'

Fucking cheek. I open my mouth to protest, then close it again because she is right.

'Today though I thought you might like to join us, given the change in your circumstances. And mood. Lack of cloud.'

'Good of you, thanks.'

'We did ask you, Stella, ages ago and more than once, but you were not interested. Made it quite clear. You never did anything with us after work so I stopped asking in the end.'

Jackson only met Clarissa once and that was it; all of my colleagues were deemed loud, uncouth and common. And fat.

151

A heinous crime. He made his thoughts on my mixing with the after-works drink crowd very clear.

'So?'

I pretend to be engrossed by an email for a minute, wanting time to ponder if I really want to spend all day *and* all evening with this lot. Yes, I like them, but that much?

'I'm taking that silence as a yes. It's not much different from our lunchtime tipples in the Bunch, only more fun and way more to drink. Everyone lets their hair down. And what happens in the Chopper, stays in the Chopper. It's the law.' She smiles and I think what a great smile she has: plump cheeks, fabulous teeth, dimples. She is really rather gorgeous and I wonder if I should ask her for some style tips on how to make my extra pounds work for me.

Instead I ask, 'So, who will be there?'

'The usual crowd, mostly from this floor, except Clay of course. He's not invited.'

'Not invited where?' Clay materialises at Clarissa's shoulder. Where the fuck did he pop up from? He's like a silent assassin, creeping up for the kill. Clarissa doesn't miss a beat though. 'The new referencing system for the Wellford Estate Farm. You don't need to join us, admin stuff.'

He grunts and stomps back into his office.

'So, we'll be about fifteen, I guess.' She pauses. 'And Miles is coming. He doesn't always come, but he is tonight. Can't think what made him change his mind, although I did mention that you were coming. We leave at 5.30pm. On the dot.'

At gone 5.45pm, I finally manage to make my escape. The lobby is quiet as I come out of the lift, the Coffee Hut locked up for the night, Marco no doubt making the long evening commute out to Clacton where he lives with his wife Ana and their five children. Clicking my way across the expanse of floor towards the swing doors out into the street, I spot a familiar beret behind the Security desk.

She cannot still be here.

'Iris? There's only one person I know who can rock an orange beret like that. What are you still doing here? It's way past your home time.'

'Oh, hello Stella. Just clearing up after Devon.' She waves a blue cloth at me. 'So many crumbs, you wouldn't believe it. I like to get it spick-and-span ready for the morrow.'

She won't look at me, just fiddles about polishing the immaculate shiny desktop, and that is when it hits me – finally, I get it - Iris doesn't want to go home. All the cleaning and wiping and chatting and dusting, all the other little tricks in the Iris handbook are delay tactics. I have no idea where she lives or why she doesn't want to go home, although educated guess would be that she's lonely, a horrible thought that makes my heart creak.

'Iris,' I say, gently. 'Leave that now, it's already spotless. Look, a few of us from the office are meeting for a drink. Why don't you join us? You've earned a drink after all your hard work. Really, Clay should have you on a monthly wage by now for everything you do here.'

'Don't be silly. I'm just happy to help out. And anyway, Marco pays me.' Her eyes go misty as she mentions Marco's name. Can't blame her. The man is a saint.

'Well, join us for a drink then.'

'You don't really want me hanging about,' she demurs, sounding uncertain.

'I'd love to have you hanging about. Come on. I'm buying you a drink. I insist.'

Any doubts Iris might have had about being unwanted are comprehensively dispelled when we get to the Chopper Lump and she is mobbed by an avalanche of welcoming cries, followed by a scrum to get to the bar first to buy her a drink – port and lemonade, she says, her cheeks going pink from all the attention. Soon she is installed in a corner table involved in an in-depth discussion on the merits of Sgt Pepper's versus Abbey Road with three of the Beatles - George couldn't make it - and berating Ringo for his lack of knowledge on the Fab Four's music.

'Really Ringo, if you're going to go by that *alias,*' she says, a little scornfully, 'you need to brush up on your musical knowledge. At a very minimum you should know that he, Mr Starr, wrote Octopus's Garden *and* Don't Pass Me By, less well known but wonderful all the same. And I don't suppose you can name me a song he sang lead vocals on?' She looks expectantly at poor Ringo, clearly regretting that anyone ever had the stupid idea to name the accounts team The Beatles. 'There's several to choose from you know.'

'Er,' says Ringo, trying to climb inside his pint glass to get away from the Iris glare. 'Hello Jude?'

He shoots him an incredulous look. 'Everyone knows Paul wrote that,' she sniffs. 'And you do know it's Hey Jude, not Hello Jude. He wrote it for John Lennon's boy, Julian.'

Which gets her a round of applause from Mr McCartney himself.

When Clarissa said drinks, what she meant was a river.

The quantity of alcohol being consumed is colossal. I am thinking of calling Guinness, no pun intended, for greatest quantity of booze consumed on a post-work drinks outing on a Thursday. I am on the white wine, a mistake as it is large glasses only and a large glass is, gulp, 250ml, which is a third of a bottle.

And I'm on my third glass. You don't have to be good at maths to figure out that I am headed for trouble.

'White is it, Stella?' Ringo is muscling his way to the bar.

Note use of the word *muscle*. Weedy Ringo has not only changed his style, he has bulked up. That increased quantity of thigh that I spotted a few weeks back has now spread to a pair of very respectably muscled arms, a noticeably broader chest and an appreciably flat stomach. The transformation would be startling if it hadn't been so gradual. Clarissa, who I suspect of having a hand in the metamorphosis, has been throwing indiscreet admiring glances all evening. Me thinks it is time for an intensive Q&A but first I have to get to Ringo and tell him to get me a glass of water, tea, air, I don't care as long as it's not wine.

Before I can catch his attention, Miles slides in next to me, one arm resting on the bar.

Fuck, he is a dish, I think, admiring his end-of-day look; tie off, top button undone, sleeves rolled, hint of five o'clock shadow. And those eyes, those startling blue eyes.

Lush. Plain lush.

'Good to see you out and about, Stella.' He holds up his pint and I gently tap it with my wine glass. 'Nice move bringing Iris. She's currently putting Nathaniel in his place so the queue to buy her a drink just got even longer. You doing OK?'

'I can't keep up. Do they always drink this much?'

'They're just warming up. I don't usually make it. Thursdays are Krav Maga but on special occasions I give it a miss.'

I don't want to read too much into that comment, so I focus on the Krav thing instead. 'What is Krav Maga? Is it a martial art?'

'Kind of. It's a self-defence system from Israel based on the best parts of karate, aikido, wrestling, judo. All sorts. I can't do the gym thing, I get bored, and I hate running, especially around London with all the traffic, so I was looking for something to get me fit and keep me interested.' He flexes an arm in demonstration and I can't resist a little squeeze, my hand clinging on to the rock-solid bicep longer than is polite. 'Krav Maga ticks all the boxes. You should come along one day, give it a try.'

My hand finally lets go of his arm, allowing me to take a

a step back, putting some distance between us. He is mesmerising and it feels reckless after so much wine to be in such close proximity.

'You can come with me next Thursday if you like,' he goes on.

'Fuck, no. Why does everyone want to get me into a fitness class,' I say, trying to suck in my belly. 'Maybe, just maybe, I am happy with my surplus. As a modern woman, I should be allowed to embrace my rolls, sit on my fat arse with pride and gobble up another piece of cake if I want to. Only people keep inviting me to the gym, therefore *implying* that I need to get off the fat arse and do something about it.' I slap my hand on the bar, making Miles flinch. 'First it was Kim, then Jeremy, then James, the sarcastic Sergeant Major and now you. Just leave me be.'

I look over to see what's keeping Ringo with the refills, abandoning any thoughts of water or tea.

'Are you done?' Miles asks.

I nod, too sulky now to speak.

'Feeling better?'

I nod again.

'I was going to say, *feeling lighter*, as in, weight off your chest all that. Then I realised you might take it to heart.'

He is laughing at me now, so I decide not to nod again.

'What you need is some food after all that wine. Makes you emotional drinking on an empty stomach. All they've got here is crisps and peanuts. How about I take you for some proper food, somewhere else?'

I freeze.

Dinner with Golden Boy. You have to be kidding; we would never hear the end of it, not with the whole office here to wave us off. Half of them would probably insist on coming. And Miles. Eating in the face of such divine beauty would be impossible. Just a slice of bread, perhaps, to soak up the longing....

'Stella.' Miles is clicking a finger by my ear, trying to get my attention.

'Best if I don't eat,' I stammer, 'trying to cut down.'

For a second, I look up, caught instantly in the glare of those lethal blue beamers. Insanity lies beyond.....look away, Stella, now.....

'How about some peanuts then? Crisps?'

I shake my head.

'You do know you're lovely, just the way you are.'

'Oh, fuck off, you big fat cliché!' I cry. He can't think I am going to fall for that old chestnut. 'Just the way you are. As if.'

'You're not fat.'

'I most certainly am,' I say, indignantly.

That gets me a laugh, easing the tension a fraction. 'I'm serious. You got way too thin a while back. Just my opinion of course, but I honestly prefer women, you know, with the edges rounded off.'

'Per-lease. Stop being so fucking PC about it all. A fatty is a fatty. Call me out. Denying my rolls helps no one.' I grab a handful of tummy to make my point.

He laughs. 'Nothing wrong with that, I don't mind a bit of belly. It's soft. Sexy.'

'Says the man with the rock-solid abs.' I poke a finger at him and fake a wince. 'Could break a finger on that.' Then, unable to stop myself, I place my hand flat against his stomach and feel the strength and tension in the muscles behind that white shirt.

'I've got good genes,' he says modestly. 'Look, if it would make you feel better, lose a couple of pounds, but you really don't need to. It's just nice seeing you looking so much happier. You are very, very pretty when you smile. Anyway, more importantly, *who* is James?'

My cheeks are instantly alive. Burning. He thinks I am pretty. Jackson used to tell me I was pretty, a long time ago, in the dark and distant past. Then he started in with the criticism; a comment here, a remark there, and before you know it, doubt is everywhere.

'James?' Miles prompts.

What to say about James? There is no intrigue, no salacious update since our last meeting. We have been for wine twice, he has untangled me from the most unedifying situation imaginable once, he has kissed me goodbye on the cheek in the same way that he would his old granny once. That, to date, is it. Do I want more? Well, duh. The man is gorgeous, kind and chatty, not to mention offering to go spy on my nemesis in the Big Apple. Above and beyond. Yet I don't want to say any of this to Miles. While I rebuff his ridiculous compliments at every turn, find the continued attention inexplicable and even faintly embarrassing - I don't want it to stop. Yet. He is an excellent tonic for my weary self-esteem and makes the office that much more bearable; when he saunters up to my desk, fresh coffee in hand, the world becomes a better place for a few minutes.

As I don't know how to reply, I try to distract him with humour and tell him about the incident with the elastic band, adding as a vague afterthought that it was James who untangled me.

'A knight in shining armour.'

And before I can think straight and zip up my big mouth, I say, 'No, that was Jeremy.'

'Oh, Christ. *Him.* The friend who is not any old friend but a knight in shining armour to boot.'

The real world then comes crashing back in with the arrival of Clarissa. 'Guys, I can't believe you're both here, at the same time, I am ma-hu-sive-ly overexcited.' She steps in between us, arms around our waists. 'Miles darling, can you believe we have our Stells out at last? Office drinks are finally complete.'

'Is everyone here?' I ask, looking around the packed bar. 'Why isn't Robyn here? Not that I want her to come, just wondering.'

'I don't invite her anymore. She's in the Clay pocket,' she says, scathingly. 'You know that time when you were in the loos having a nap?' I nod uncertainly. 'Pretended you were meditating? Googled all those online gurus and sent them through to her. She only went and squawked to Clay.'

'She did not!' Damn, how was I had so easily? 'And how the hell do you know that anyway?'

'She told me too. She was pissed because Clay told her to leave you alone.' Her eyes sparkle. She is loving this.

Gobsmacked, I stare, open-mouthed until Miles puts a finger under my chin and gently closes it. 'Feet-of Clay has a heart after all,' he says. 'Go figure.'

Miles gets kidnapped by the Beatles for a game of darts and I take my opportunity. Now is a good time to investigate the Clarissa / Ringo intrigue further, while her defences are soaked in gin and thus breachable. I take our drinks and pull her over to a small table.

'Right, I want the lowdown, spare me nothing. Ringo. Barry. What is going on?' She takes a sip of G&T and looks at me, unusually mute. 'That man has had the make-over of the century. He is unrecognisable,' I say, watching her closely for a reaction. 'Debugged.'

Ha! I spy a flinch.

'Debugged?'

'The bugs have been removed. The nerd specs, horrible T-shirts, stained trousers.' I see a hint of smirk. 'Come on. I'm not blind. The air quivers every time he walks past your desk, which is like every two minutes these days, he's wearing out the carpet, for fuck's sake.'

Clarissa searches for Ringo over by the dartboard, clocks him, checks no one around us is listening and turns back to me. 'Oh Stella, who'd have thought, Barry from Accounts, Ringo, a Beatle!' She gives a nervous giggle.

'A Beatle, indeed. Can we establish the basic facts first? Are you a couple? And if so, how the hell did you two get together? I did not see this one coming.'

'Neither did I. It was with the gods really.'

'Right, so, the gods. How?' I demand.

'Well, and this remains strictly between us.' She fixes me with a firm stare.

'Hand on heart.' What is coming now? And do I really want to know?

'Ok, so, well, you see -'

'Spit it out. Tell your Auntie Stella all about it.'

'You won't tell?'

'No! You've got me worried now.' *What is coming?*

'Bounteous,' she whispers to me.

'What? Did you say bounteous? I don't get it.'

'Dating site for larger ladies.'

'Oh.' I wasn't expecting that. 'Where does Ringo fit in at Bounteous? Oh fuck, I think I've got it! Really?'

'Yep.'

'No!'

'Oh yes. Barry likes something to get hold of. And how!' She gives a dirty little cackle and I shiver uneasily. 'I didn't know it was him at first, we swopped emails for a week before meeting. He was very naughty by email.'

Well, I did ask.

'Where did you meet? I mean, you didn't know who it was, it could have been anyone, an axe murderer.'

'I always meet at the Punch and Judy in Covent Garden. Plenty of people around.'

'Always?'

'Well, he's not the first.'

'Oh, and how many have you met with?'

'Twelve, although I've only slept with eight of them.'

160

'Twelve! Eight! Fuck.'

'Exactly! Why are you so shocked? Just because I'm fat you think no one wants to sleep with me?'

'No! God, no. You're gorgeous. But twelve! Eight! Is that a lot in the internet dating world or average? Is that a lot for Bounteous?'

'We are much in demand you know. Men are sick of sticks with no flesh.'

'Really? I thought it was *in* to be a stick.'

'Women like sticks but most men crave a curve. Miles likes a curve too; I can tell by the way he looks at you now, since you plumped up a bit. The hard bit is weeding out the tourists. They don't deserve my luscious body.'

'Tourists?'

'Tourists just want to try it out, fat, visit for a while before going back to skinnyville. They don't really love us.'

'Right. Good for you. Tourists. This is quite an education. But, when Ringo, Barry, who is not a tourist, turned up at the Punch, didn't you want to run a mile? This was *old Barry,* I assume. No offence, it's just that before turning into a butterfly, he was a caterpillar. Not a very good-looking one either. With bad breath. And orange socks.'

'Oh, he was very eloquent. I was half way out the door, mortified, but he talked me round quick enough.'

'Like Cyrano de Bergerac?'

'Who's he?'

'A poet with a long nose.'

'What's he got to do with it?'

'Roxanne?'

'The Police song? You've lost me.'

'Not to worry. Back to Barry. So, he sweet talked you into staying.'

'Yep. And we ended up talking until closing time. He turned out to be a-mazing company.'

'A dark horse.' Very dark, midnight black more like. I have known Barry for over six years and, to date, he has singularly failed to slay me with his wit and repartee.

'And red hot in bed.'

'Waaaay too much information. No more sex talk. Tell me about the make-over, the man is transformed.'

'Yeah, he looks good right? A gentle tweak here and a personal shopper there.'

'No!'

'His birthday present. He loved it. We've been revealing the purchases bit-by-bit in the office so that people wouldn't notice.'

'That's not really worked out, has it? The alterations are too radical. And the, um, halitosis?'

'Still working on that. It's better but not perfect. I sent him off to the dentist. He's had four sessions, with two more to go. They are doing some industrial descaling, using a hammer and chisel by the sounds of it and he has to scrape his tongue.'

'Fuck.'

'I could do with one, it's been days.'

Did she just say that? I feel like I've opened Pandora's box here. Much more and I'm going to have to try and stuff it all back in, close the lid, padlock it shut.

'I told you. No more sex talk. How about the bulking up? There are real live muscles hidden beneath his new, personal-shopped, rags.'

'He's in the gym every morning before work. Gets up at the crack of dawn. And he's started going to that Krav Maga thing that Miles does. He's on a mission now and it means he can toss me about in bed. Doesn't want me to join him though, which is a relief. Exercise and I have never seen eye-to-eye.'

'I hear you,' I say, with feeling.

162

CHAPTER 14

Hangover

/ˈhaŋəʊvə/

Noun: a severe headache, stomach upset or other after-effects caused by drinking too much alcohol

Just to say that I am never, ever, *ever,* going for office drinks again.

Ever.

CHAPTER 15

Dirt

/dəːt/

Noun: (informal) gossip, especially of a malicious, lurid, or scandalous nature

'People, quiet people, I have an important announcement to make before we start today's workout.' The Sergeant Major is sporting a new pair of tiny red shorts, the likes of which would not be out of place on Love Island. 'Cliff.' There is a roar of approval at the mention of the great man's name. 'Cliff has now lost a total of fifty pounds since he joined us here at CrossFit. Fifty, people. Five oh.' The class erupts, everyone rushing to congratulate Cliff and pat him on his immense back.

Yes, me too.

It didn't take me long. I love Cliff as much as everyone else. His quiet determination, his humility, his lemony smell. When I did my first press-up, it was Cliff who came over to give me a discreet high five. Everyone else was too busy focusing on themselves to hear the Sergeant Major's congratulations but Cliff picked it up, abandoned his medicine ball and made the trip over to where I was face-down on the mat to salute me. He notices things. He sees other people, looks beyond himself and deserves every bit of his popularity.

I wait until everyone has had their say and the Sergeant Major is busy telling us how much we are all going to suffer in the next hour, then slip an arm around his waist and whisper a sincere, 'Cliff, you legend.'

'Thanks, Stella. You?' he whispers back'

'Five pounds!'

His face lights up with genuine happiness. 'Hey, that's great.'

'Stella, this is not a social club.' Oh, crap. 'What was I saying about tonight's WOD? How is Cliff going to know what's required of him tonight if you're bending his ear? Now shut it.'

I give a cheeky salute and stand to attention. 'Yes, Sir!'

'For that, young lady, you can start with fifty mountain climbers. And if I see your arse in the air, I'll get Cliff to come and sit on it. Get to it!'

It never pays to put yourself in the firing line before we have even started. He is on my case every two minutes, alternating between cooing at Cliff and shouting at me; no one else in the class gets a look-in. By the end of the hour, half the class comes back to thank me for taking the heat as I sit slumped in a sweaty heap.

'Would a glass of rosé help?' A deep voice behind me says.

'James! You're back!' I had been disappointed not to see him in class today. I was expecting him and have been desperate to know what happened in New York. Did he get the dirt? If so, how much? Shed load? Lorry load? Landfill? 'Let me get changed quickly and I'll meet you downstairs,' I say, curiosity restoring energy to my flagging legs.

He is waiting at the gym bar with two glasses of wine; rosé for me and red for him. He gives me an update as I sip the pale nectar; he has been working late, catching up after his trip to New York, business is booming and he is struggling to manage it all. Boogie for you my man, I think, but when do we get to the important stuff. The nitty gritty. DID YOU GET THE DIRT?

Maximus dirtius, please.

'How was the Sergeant Major today?' he asks.

'Hell on earth. Caught me talking to Cliff during his intro and that was it, wouldn't leave me alone. I was only congratulating him on his half century; the man has lost fifty pounds. It was the bloody Sergeant Major who gave us the big news then bollocked me for patting Cliff on his cliff-face of a back.'

'It's a sign of affection you know. All the attention. He loves you really. He loves that you are here, trying.'

'Against all the odds?'

He laughs and takes a drink of wine to avoid agreeing with me.

'So, tell me about New York? How was it?'

'New York was exhausting. You land at dawn after no sleep, taxi to the hotel, shower, change and then head off for twelve hours of meetings. You do that for five days, trying to adjust to the time difference, fighting the jetlag, then just as you are about sorted you fly back and have to re-adjust to the time here.'

'That sounds less fun than a trip to New York should be. So, er, I suppose you didn't have time to dig the dirt on Jackson and Nina then?'

'Not much and there wasn't much to dig, I'm afraid.'

My face sags with disappointment. I had an entire scenario playing out in my mind where Jackson had been demoted and now has to report to a female intern half his (real) age and at Goldman's everyone hates Nina. Plus, she is crap at her job, her looks have fallen apart, bloated by the American super-sized portions (as if) and for some reason her hair has fallen out too.

'Hey, I know I promised, but I really didn't have time and, to be honest, I forgot all about it for the first couple of days. I did go for a drink with an old friend from Goldman's though and that's when I remembered.'

'Goldman's? He must have had some dirt?'

'Not exactly, no.'

'Did he say anything about her?'

He gives me a sad look.

'What?'

'They like her.'

'Noooooo,' I wail. 'She's sucked them all in, hypnotising them with those green eyes until they can't see the wood for the trees.' I pause here because I'm not sure that I have chosen the right idiom and James is looking confused too. 'Beguiling those around her with the siren call of the thingybob, enticing them to the shore where they will be crushed upon the rocks and killed.'

'A mermaid? I think that's too poetic for Wall Street.' James is smiling at me and shaking his head at the same time. I should shut-up. I am ranting, coming across as the unhinged, revengeful, saddo ex-girlfriend. Something no self-respecting man wants a part of. Besides, I should have known they would love her. Everyone loves her. They can't see the black-hearted harpy that lies within that glossy exterior.

'Sorry,' I say, summoning my contrite face. 'Got a bit carried away. Maybe next time there'll be some dirt. Some of her rotten core might have seeped out.'

'Or not. Wouldn't it be better to leave it?'

'How so?'

'Well, what if there is no dirt? Work is clearly going well so far, her colleagues like her, not always a given in that male-dominated environment. And what if she's perfectly happy at home too? With him. The guy.'

That makes me think. When he said he would dig for dirt, I immediately thought there would be dirt to dig for. Only what if there is no dirt, just a happy, immaculately clean and successful life. Do I want to know that?

'Remember, curiosity sometimes kills the cat,' he adds. 'Anyway, I'm off to Cancun next week for a conference and I honestly don't know when I'll be back in New York.'

'Cancun? Sounds like a massive jolly to me.'

'Financial crime. It should be interesting. There are some good speakers and a forum on money laundering. An ex-Mafia accountant is coming, although we're not allowed to see him. He'll speak from behind a screen and his voice will be distorted. Protection.'

'I wish Feet-of would stay behind a screen. Make my day much more bearable.'

CHAPTER 16

Chary

/ˈtʃɛːri/

Adjective: cautiously or suspiciously reluctant to do something

An email pings into my inbox marked *personal.*

From Miles.

Ridiculously, I look around to see if anyone is watching before opening it. The email is short and to the point: *Would you let me take you out for a drink?*

The short answer is, *no.* The long answer is, *you have to be kidding.*

I risk a quick peek around my computer screen and spy Miles slouched in his chair, relaxed, eyes on his laptop, waiting. He can't be serious. Why me? What if he's identified me as easy prey, the Golden Boy act being a cover-up for a psychotic personality? When I first met Jackson, he was all charm and what-can-I get-you Stella? Solicitous. We met at a black-tie fund-raiser event for charity. I was only there because Nina had asked me to come as the plus-one of a colleague, Algernon Rhys-Davis, regretfully reduced to Al for short after I had spent two weeks practicing saying Algernon instead of Algebra. It took me all of two minutes to realise why Algernon didn't have his own plus-one – he was not just a nob, he was a nobhead, oblivious to the fact that his every word, his every action, was offensive in some way. I would have defied any sane person to have spent five minutes in his company without wanting to throw him under the nearest passing bus. Consequently, I took the only reasonable option available and beat a swift retreat to the champagne bar - *free* champagne bar – where I set up residence for the night, monitoring consumption and dispensing advice on a diverse range of subjects from wardrobe malfunctions to partner suitability (based entirely on looks and chosen outfits). If I wasn't making many friends, I was keeping the cute barman, Rod, entertained and he in turn was keeping my glass topped up.

Thus it was that Jackson found me, counselling a man on his long-term prospects with a girlfriend dressed inadvertently as Little Bo Peep; with more peep than advisable for someone of her stature. My filter was off, dissolved by the unprecedented quantities of champagne, and Jackson was quick to show his appreciation. In black tie, he looked like a well-groomed Henry Cavill and I strived to keep him amused and interested. Every now and then Algernon would swim by, his sloped forehead and lack of chin giving him the look of a basking shark, and I would coyly take cover behind Jackson until the danger had passed. His plus-one? I never found out but it was me he left with and me he installed in one of the many spare rooms at the Primrose Hill flat that night. And the next.

'Stella?'

Crap, he is here. At my desk.

'Miles.' I plaster on a grimace.

'Did you get my email?'

'You sent me an email? I'm way behind this morning. Is it urgent?' I must be the colour of Clarissa's skirt; a vermillion mini, as dazzling as it is short.

'I'll just wait while you read it then. It's not long.'

Why didn't I just email back a quick, *thanks, but no thanks.* Short, polite, to-the-point and thus avoiding any awkward face-to-face refusals. I pretend to scroll through a hundred emails, my mind frantically searching for the right diplomatic words. Why is this so difficult? I am a grown woman, in charge of my own destiny, and if I don't want to go out for drinks then, dammit, I don't have to. Obviously, there is part of me that desperately wants to go out for a drink with Miles, you'd have to be dead not to, but self-preservation is more important.

Clearing my throat, I force myself to look at him, fixing my gaze on his nose to avoid getting lasered into submission by those blue, blue eyes.

'Ah, Miles. Thank you. You're so kind. I do appreciate it, I really do, but you don't have to. I'm sure you'd rather be out with someone your own age. And I'm so much better, happy even.' I give a quick burst of 'Happy' by Pharrell Williams to mark my point, which causes Miles to look at me with such incredulity that my embarrassment quickly turns to panic. What if he's not even asking me on a date? It could just be a work drink. Maybe he wants to pick my brains about how to deal with Feet-of when he's on an off-day or how to put together a decent PowerPoint?

Fuck.

'Is it a PowerPoint? Have you got a presentation?'

'What?'

'We could have a session this afternoon if you like, or you could just send me through your notes and I'll put together a first draft.'

'PowerPoint?'

'I've a new template if it's for an overseas client. We could - '

'Stella, I've asked you out for a -'

'Miles.' It's the boss, doing that thing where he materialises out of the carpet. 'Just the person I wanted to see. Come into my office would you.'

'Tomorrow,' Miles says over his shoulder. 'I'll text you.'

I shake my head but he has already turned his back and is heading into the Feet-of lair.

Relieved to be nearly home, I turn into Beatrice Avenue and pick up my pace. For once I am back in good time and it's a beautiful evening. I might tempt Olive out to the hostas for a cheeky glass of something cool. Approaching our gate, I spy a flash of colour at the front door. Who is it now? This house is like Grand Central half the time, the doorbell's wonky chimes ringing on an almost daily basis. Last week was *book week*. First up was the local school who were collecting for the summer fête; Olive gave them a truck load of Mills & Boon and a whole bookcase of some of Derek's old reference books. Then the library came around asking for unreturned books, something Olive denied all knowledge of before finding three under her bed after they'd gone. And to round it all off, Janice from next door came to ask if we had anything she could read as the library had just suspended her membership for not returning twenty-two books. How did she get hold of twenty-two books? Did she smuggle them out in her handbag or has she got a pile of library cards under a series of false names? She was so traumatised when she heard about the Mills & Boon collection that Olive had to take her for a sherry in the garden.

Opening the gate, I see it's Olive at the front door, hunting about under the various flowerpots for a key. Not one to usually hide a key, it is obvious why she has to do so now – she has no pocket to put one in; Olive is dressed in a pair of bright blue woolly tights over which she has pulled some waist-high stripy orange pants, with a purple long-sleeved thermal vest on the top.

My first thought is that she is in the grip of an *episode*. The first stages of dementia or, please-dear-God-no, Alzheimer's. Olive, forever swamped in over-sized gardening gear or buttoned-up in one of a thousand neat cardies, would never go out looking like this. I hustle up the path, keen to get her inside before too many of the neighbours realise what is happening and come out to gawp.

'Olive? Hello sweetheart, it's Stella, gently does it now,' I say slowly, putting on my most reassuring voice.

'I can see it's you, Stella. Why are you talking in that strange voice? Are you alright?' She peers at me, concern scrunching up her well-wrinkled brow.

'Olive, what are you doing? You haven't been out anywhere, have you?' It comes out harsher than I planned but the thought of Olive, dressed as she is, in the dairy aisle of Waitrose, sniggering school kids following behind, has made me tense up all over.

'I've been to Pilates. With Colin,' she says, calmly, picking up another flowerpot.

'Colin? *Who* is Colin?'

'Mr Denby, from number ten.' She points down the road.

'I didn't know you knew Mr Denby from number ten,' I huff, put out. 'Who is he?'

'Do pay attention, Stella. His name is Colin. We met this afternoon. Had a lovely chat on the bus.'

'You've been on the bus? Dressed like this?'

'Really you are quite hysterical tonight. Shall we go in and have a cup of tea? I've got a thirst on after all that exercise.'

I open the door with my key and bundle her inside. She has been out in public, on a bus, dressed like this? The men in white coats will be round in no time. 'So, where did you go on the bus? Where was the Pilates class?'

'The Pandora Leisure Centre.'

'That's miles away!'

'It was easy on the bus. Really quite fun sitting on the top deck in amongst the school kids. Might as well make use of my bus pass, it is free you know.'

'Were they laughing at you?'

'Who?'

'The school kids.'

'They were very friendly as it happens. Asked for a group photo and everything. I met Colin at the bus stop. He stopped to admire my outfit and asked where I was going, then decided to come along.'

Am lost for words.

'He's really very charming. And awfully supple. Got his leg almost up over his head.'

Still lost for words.

'I based my look on Jane Fonda. Derek got me her book years ago for Christmas. I've never actually tried it but dug it out to see what I should wear.'

I shake my head in an effort to relocate my voice. 'Jane Fonda, eh? Colin must have been dazzled.'

'Oh, he was. Particularly liked my stripy pants.'

'I bet he bloody did. Right, you get the tea on and I'll get my iPad. We're going shopping. I'm not letting you out like that again and it's time we got you a mobile phone.'

The mobile phone has been a hot topic between us since I re-emerged from the wallowing. She is adamant that she doesn't need one, has managed this far without one, blah blah, usual excuses. I am adamant that she should have one so that she can always get hold of me and I can get hold of her, even if she is out of the house, at the bottom of the garden, or on a bus with a load of school kids and an unknown man, wearing a pair of stripy pants and not much else.

'I've told you, Stella, I do not need one of those mobile phones. I've managed seventy years without one.'

'I know you have, but I'm still getting you one. Imagine if something had happened on the bus and you'd needed help?'

'Colin was there, wasn't he? All those lovely children. The bus driver. What good would you have been, miles away in your office with Feet-of-Clay? How would you have even found the bus?'

She had a point. Not that I was going to admit it.

'Anyway, I was quite the sensation in the class. Attracted a lot of appreciative comments.'

'That's just it. You're giving away too much for free. Discretion is the way forward, make them work a bit. Imagination is everything, Olive.'

We spend some time perusing the John Lewis app on my iPad. She is new to internet shopping and the phrase *kid in a sweetie shop* would not be inappropriate. I take her for a spin through the different departments, explaining how you select what you want, choose a colour if necessary and a size, adding it to your basket.

'Basket?' she queries.

'A virtual basket that you put your shopping in.'

She doesn't look convinced. 'And how do you pay for your virtual basket? With virtual money I suppose. Although when you think about it, the money we have in the bank is virtual. I mean you never see it, do you? That's why Derek and I always preferred cash. It felt safer.'

'You pay with a credit card. You do have a credit card?'

She shakes her head. 'No, I've never had one. Derek didn't like the idea. Someone could steal it and then where would you be? All his hard-earned money. Gone. All those hours and days and weeks and months and years, hunched over a desk. Gone.'

This is interesting. I have always wondered what Derek did. I know he died soon after a delayed retirement after a brief battle with prostate cancer but whatever he did, he must have been good at it because he left Olive well-cared for financially.

'What did he do, Derek?'

'He was an actuary,' says Olive, not elaborating further. Which leaves me no better informed as I don't actually know what an actuary does. 'I can't see where you'd put a credit card in.' She picks up the iPad and inspects it closely.

'You don't put it in, you just put your card numbers in.'

We then get into a heated debate about what to buy. Olive wants to go full-on Fonda: leotard, shiny tights, leg warmers, while I want to get her into a decent, covering, yoga outfit. However, it is her money and her Pilates class and anything has to be better than the superwoman stripy pants, so we go all out '80s spangle. Then I click onto the electronics department and order her a basic mobile phone, one of those ones that you can snap shut; she'll like that.

Before I pay with my card – refusing a fist full of cash from Olive, the woman pays for everything as it is – she tries to get me to buy myself a new outfit for CrossFit. I can just see the Sergeant Major's face if I turned up *à la Fonda;* he would laugh himself into an early grave. Anyway, I am buying no new workout clothes until I have lost some of my rolls, rolls that are going nowhere fast; I got on the scales this morning full of hope and all l I got was a, *Suc-ker! Still a fatty!*

Shopping done and tea drunk, Olive moves into position for The Chase, but I decide to head out for a turn around the garden. I have been trying to show a keen interest in Olive's masterpiece, keeping track of the plant life out there, what's new, what's blooming, what's not; I just wish it wasn't a full-time job as I have one of those already.

Down by the hostas, I slump into Olive's favourite chair, closing my eyes and listening to the hum of central London living; traffic and trains mainly, interspersed with the high drone of the planes coming in to Heathrow and the odd toot from an impatient driver's car horn. It is peaceful enough though here, despite the background noise and as the day slowly seeps away, I realise that for the first time in a very long time, I feel content. Was I happy before? With Jackson? Yes and no. Yes, on the good days, no, on the bad.

Of course, the bad days out-numbered the good ten-to-one.

At the beginning, when we met, there were plenty of good days; Jackson was attentive, solicitous, in charge - and how I loved having someone in charge, he did it so much better than me. We pottered along, him in Primrose Hill and me in my flat in Clapham with Kim, seeing each other two or three times a week. Kim had not long met Bart, so the timing was perfect. Then after a couple of years, Kim moved out to live with Bart and I had to either find somewhere less expensive to live or find a new flatmate, something I dreaded. How do you move from living with your best friend in harmonious complicity to living with someone you have never met? Then I thought I could move in with Nina, who, lights years ahead of me in terms of career, earnings and ambition, had bought her vast loft out in the Docklands, only she was helping out a colleague for a couple of months and refused – inconceivably - to move them out to make room for me.

And that is when Jackson suggested I move in with him. I had not been expecting him to offer and couldn't quite believe my luck; that amazing flat, in Primrose Hill, with Jackson, together, the two of us. Where do I sign? I admit, I got carried away, imagining we would be holed up like two peas in a luxurious pod, cooing at each other over the risotto I had thrown together, a chilled glass of wine selected by Jackson from his cellar, candles flickering in the evening light....

Fucking candles. Dream on, Stella.

Two weeks after I moved in, I planned a surprise thank you dinner (see above). Did not go well. Jackson, unaware, came home late to an overcooked, gloopy risotto, a wilted salad and the flat in near darkness as the candles had burnt themselves out.

'Stella,' he said, angrily flicking on the lights. 'If I want dinner, I will let you know in advance. Tonight, thankfully, I do not, which is just as well, as that,' he jerked his head at the pan of grey sludge, 'is inedible. Also, and you know this, I never touch white wine.' A nod at the (very well) chilled Pinot Gris. 'Finally, and I will not repeat this, never ever light another candle in this house. Apart from the fire risk, they are a *bohemian,'* he spat out the word as if it was toxic, 'indulgence that I abhor and they cover the walls with grubby soot. I paid a lot of money on a lot of expensive paint to get this place as I want it and I have no intention of doing it again because *you* think candles are it.'

Life with Jackson went downhill from there.

And now, here I am, alone on a Friday evening, nowhere to go, no one to play with. Thirty-four, friendly, lucid, *nice* (fuck you, Nina), fun and yet still a Norma (no-mates).

Pre-Jackson I had friends. There were never masses, I spent too much time with Kim and Nina for that, but there were enough before Jackson's hostile disinterest sent them running for the hills. Only Kim and Nina survived the cull, and Bart because he came as part of the package and was non-negotiable.

Pathetic. I know.

Love is a strange beast. The problem being that once you have fallen in love, it can be incredibly difficult to climb back out again. Even if, or perhaps especially if, that person turns out to be a frequently unpleasant control freak. As Jackson tried to mould me into the person he thought I should be – and one that suited him and his lifestyle (not to mention maintaining the weekly supply of Calvin Kleins) – I lost all sense of Stella, buried under the daily avalanche of pointed critiques and general dissatisfaction.

All in the name of so-called *love.*

There is no logic. There is no reason. There is no dignity.

You have no pride. Self-esteem is something you knew back in a distant past along with your discarded friends.

Every day becomes an assault course to be completed in order to keep him happy, and that becomes your life's ambition; keeping him happy, making it work, doing what it takes.

I shake my head in disbelief. Enough reminiscing about the bad times, let's focus on the positives, the here and now.

Kim and Bart. Solid as.

Olive.

Clarissa and the gang.

James.

Miles. He said he would text and knowing Miles he'll be good to his word. And I know we would have a good time; he is too nice not to make it a good time. But what happens then? A second date, maybe, or – horror – no second date, Miles having decided that he has been there, done that, declined the T-shirt and moved on. Or, a second date and – double horror - he wants some, you know, *action.* There is no way, *no way on earth,* I could allow my white hippo-ness under the sheets with his golden gloriousness. Some things are just not meant to be enjoyed together, like chocolate and beer or radishes and milk.

No. A date with Miles is fraught with danger.

I need someone altogether less risky. *Safe* is my watchword.

CHAPTER 17

Gentleman
/ dʒentəlmən/
Noun: a educated, sensitive, or well-mannered man

Miles texted this morning as promised and suggested dinner. I politely declined. Said I was busy. Which was a lie. Of course, I wasn't busy, diary was empty, queue of people waiting to take me out totalled precisely zero. Even Kim and Bart are away, in Poland, meaning I was on my own.

Except, I am not on my own.

Olive was thrilled when I suggested we go to the cinema. Her last visit was in 1982 when she and Derek went see ET at the Odeon in Leicester Square. There was apparently an *altercation* when Derek went to the loo during the film and mistakenly ended up in the Ladies. Details remain sketchy but suffice to say that they never went to the cinema again. She has even agreed to change out of her habitual grubby gardener's garb and is upstairs selecting a pair of trousers and a cardie from the world's largest collection of cardies. She has hundreds. I've seen them lined up on their hangers, in a range of colours and styles, never veering away from the *cardigan* remit.

She eventually appears in a pair of navy-blue trousers with a pale blue cardigan buttoned up to the top, over which sails a vast expanse of navy-blue collar.

We decide to go to the Curzon on the Kings Road. This is a beautiful old music hall, which was converted into a cinema back in the 1930s and, despite living up the road, Olive has never been (see above). Jackson brought me here more than once, charmed by the history of the place and the worn faded glamour. There was, I admit, a short but sharp internal debate listing the pros and cons of coming here before we left until, thankfully, the desire to treat Olive proved greater than the self-defeating desire to avoid every place associated with Jackson until the end of time.

And that, people, is what you call progress.

Olive's eyes grow large as we approach the Curzon and she goes off for a mosey while I get in line for tickets for the new Wonder Woman film. It is a perfect choice for Olive who I consider to be something of a wonder woman herself. And who needs a cape when you have a collar like hers – one strong gust and she'll be airborne; it is like a built-in hand glider. The walls of the lobby are lined with framed posters of classic films from across the years and she is soon nose-to-nose with Marilyn Monroe, Jack Lemmon and Tony Curtis in Some Like It Hot before moving on to Alfred Hitchcock's Psycho. *A new and altogether different screen excitement!!!* screams the headline across the top of the poster, somehow underselling the fact that Janet Leigh is going to get hacked to pieces in a shower.

'Here's your ticket,' I say, peering over her shoulder. 'Have you seen this film? Bloody terrifying.'

'Don't be stupid, Stella,' she says, dismissively. 'I don't enjoy being terrified. The Maltese Falcon was enough for me.'

'Who's in that?' I ask.

'Bogart, of course,' she sniffs.

'Was he your favourite?'

'No, not Bogart. Cary Grant is my all-time favourite,' she flutters, going all gooey-eyed and showing that there is no age limit to being a super fan. 'Oh, I loved Cary Grant. Went to all his early films. He was a profoundly moving actor.' She is getting into her stride here. 'You know, back then, there wasn't all of the fancy special effects that they have now. You couldn't rely on fake dinosaurs rushing around to enhance your film, the actors had to do it themselves. Oh, he was a marvellous

actor, so handsome of course but he expressed such *emotion*.'
There is a tear now in the Olive eye. 'An Affair to Remember,
that's the absolute best. My favourite film of all time. I can't
think how many times I've seen it. Cary Grant plays this *very*
handsome playboy character who is crossing the Atlantic on a
liner, like the Titanic, only it doesn't sink, thank goodness. Can
you imagine? Wouldn't be the same film at all. Anyway, they're
happily afloat when he meets Deborah Kerr, she's also on the
boat, only she is with someone else and, without wanting to give
away all the plot, he is with someone too, so -'

'Olive, I don't need the whole story now and it won't be a
surprise when I watch it if you reveal the plot to me now.'

'You've never seen it? Oh, Stella. *Really*. It's a classic. I'll
keep an eye out for it on the television. We could watch it
together.' She looks at me hopefully and I nod.

'We'll hire the DVD. It might not be shown on the TV
for months, years even. Now, how about some nibbles? What
do you fancy? I'm buying.'

Olive takes her time scrutinising the large choice available
before making her selection. Maltesers, Liquorice Allsorts,
Jelly Babies.

'Olive,' I say. 'You're on your own with that lot. I'm
sticking to the popcorn. Salted. Less calories.' I think.

'Derek and I only ever used to have a Cornetto in the
interval,' she replies by way of explanation, adding a bag of
homemade fudge to the pile.

'Well, go for it then, but I can't guarantee an interval.
They tend to run straight through nowadays.'

'That's a shame,' she says, eying up the ice cream display
and no doubt wondering if she should get the Cornetto now.

'Why don't you go and find a table. I'll pay for these and
then I'll get us some drinks. How about a G&T for a change?'

'You do know, Stella, that tonic is full of sugar. If you're
serious about calorie intake, you should have a gin on ice, dash
of soda maybe.' I scowl, but she is not done yet. 'Sugary drinks

are packed to the hilt with fructose and that is linked to the fat around your middle.'

Why does she have to be such an expert on absolutely everything?

Waving her away to get a table, I head off to the bar, relieved to be wearing my new tunic from Primark, cleverly cut to disguise all that fructose induced fat around my middle. The bar is busy and I discreetly elbow my way past a couple of less experienced punters, waving a tenner around to attract the barman.

'I think you'll find that I was here before you,' says a voice to my left.

I whip my head around to remonstrate and find myself looking up into the friendly face of....

'Angus! What are you doing here?'

'What a lovely surprise, I've been worried about you.' He gives me a quick one-armed squeeze, not wanting to lose his place at the bar. He is also holding a fifty-pound note, which is bound to attract more attention than my weedy tenner. 'Two glasses of merlot please,' he instructs a passing barman, 'and what are you having, Stella?'

'Two G&Ts please. I'm with someone,' I add hastily, in case he thinks I want two for myself. 'Olive.'

He raises a bushy eyebrow and turns back to the barman. 'And two large G&Ts please. Bombay Sapphire if you've got it, Hendricks, anything but Gordon's. Thanks.'

As we wait for the drinks, I feel strangely vulnerable. He knows Jackson well, he was intimate with Nina, he is *in the know*. Makes me feel exposed.

'You alright, Stella?' he asks, gently.

'Never better, thanks,' I say, hoping to put an end to any further questions.

'I should have been in touch, checked you were OK.'

'Rubbish. I had Kim and Bart and the incomparable Olive. You must come over and say hello.'

'Incomparable, is she? Then I would be honoured.'

We track down Olive in the busy lobby, finding her engrossed in a group of young girls on the next table, her chair angled towards them, not the slightest effort being made to disguise the fact that she is listening in. I try to catch her attention but she waves me away, edging her chair a little closer.

'Olive,' I hiss. 'Get over here. Stop being such a nosey parker.'

It is another few minutes before she can drag herself away, pink with excitement. 'The things these modern girls get up to, Stella, you wouldn't believe.'

'I think I probably would, I've been there and done most of them myself. Now, here's your gin, bought and paid for by Angus.'

She notices Angus for the first time and the pink colour in her cheeks deepens.

'Olive, what an absolute pleasure,' he says, smooth as silk, taking her hand and brushing it with his lips as she lets rip with a whinny of delight. 'I am pleased to see Stella's keeping such good company nowadays.' A low bow before he switches his attention back to me. 'It's clearly doing you the world of good. You look ravishing.'

Bloody charmer, now it is my turn to blush while frantically trying to hold down the tunic, billowing up in the breeze from the door and threatening to reveal my less-than-ravishing mid-section.

'So Olive, where do you fit in with Stella? Are you related? Tell me all.'

Olive is giving Angus a potted history of how I ended up living with her when a statuesque blond, built like a blade of grass, stalks up (see what I did there!) and taps him on the shoulder.

'I was waiting by the door,' she huffs. 'At least you can get some air over there. It's so stuffy in here. Where did all these *people* come from.' This is not a question, it's an accusation.

She then, and I am secretly impressed, stands with her hand out, waiting for Angus to lift that heavy glass for her, while, a) saying nothing, and b) looking elsewhere. Angus is well trained though and dutifully hands her the glass with an exaggerated wink to Olive, who visibly trembles with glee.

She is smitten.

Meanwhile, the blade of grass takes an impressively big gulp of red wine and then promptly spits it back into the glass. 'Christ, don't they have anything better than this?'

'Just drink it, Louisa,' sighs Angus. 'It's perfectly quaffable. We don't need to drink a Premier Cru every night.'

There is a glorious silence of one, two, three seconds as she takes in the fact that Angus has just rebuked her, in front of two members of the *great unwashed* no less, before she marches off towards the entrance (glass of wine firmly in hand, crap wine being better than no wine), sky scraper heels clicking on the hard floor.

'Christ, that's my fault. I've been spoiling her. Mainly because the only way I can deal with her is to soften the edges with some decent wine. I really need to get rid of her but she's like double sided Sellotape: impossible to dislodge.' He leans forward to help himself to a handful of popcorn. 'Love this stuff. Did you get the sweet or salted? I like a mix.' He pops in about ten pieces one after the other, then dips in his hand for more.

I am about to propose a toast when Olive asks Angus how we know each other.

'Oh, I used to go out with the enemy. Nina and I were an item a while back.'

'You were not,' says Olive, scandalised. 'That jezebel.'

'I'm afraid so,' he says, helping himself to more popcorn. 'I called it a day in the end. Far too much like hard work, which,' with a glance over his shoulder, 'could also be said of the latest model. You should get some sweet mixed in with this,

Stella. It's very salty. Makes you drink more.' And he takes a swig of merlot to prove his point.

I, however, am not interested in the popcorn. 'Hang on Angus, *you* called it a day? With Nina?'

'I did. She started getting very demanding. I prefer an altogether simpler life.'

I gulp my gin, riveted. 'She told us *she* had dumped *you*.'

'That doesn't surprise me. I think it was her first experience of being dumped. She didn't know how to handle it, so it was easier to change the story line. She did ask me to stay away from you all for a while. Said you were *her* friends and I didn't belong anymore.'

'Ha! And now it's Nina that doesn't belong,' I assert with feeling.

'She has lost out there too. Mad decision. Now, I'd better go and find Louisa before she has a full-on tantrum. It wouldn't be the first time.' He stands up, finishing his glass of wine. 'Shall we have a drink next week and catch up properly now that we're allowed? How about lunch?'

'Lunch would be lovely,' I simper, foolishly pleased. I might get a photo, heavily edited to ensure that I look about twenty-five and slim as a whippet, to send to Nina. And Jackson. *Angus says, hi.* I could be kissing his cheek, one hand on his knee.

'And you Olive? Why don't you come into town and join us?'

Which takes the edge off both the invitation and the photo op - until I see Olive's happy face.

'I think that's a brilliant idea. You can come up to town on the bus. I'll show you around my office and then we'll meet up with Angus. What do you say?'

Olive looks from Angus to me, unable to speak.

'I think that's a yes, Angus. Thank you,' I say.

'Thursday week alright for you both? You still working for Malcolm Clay?'

I nod, a pulse of delight that he remembers where I work.

'Lovely. I'll come and pick you both up. 12.30. Got to dash.'

And he's gone.

CHAPTER 18

Candid
/ˈkandɪd/
Adjective: frank, outspoken, truthful and straightforward

Since the cinema trip and the invitation to lunch with Angus, Olive has talked of little else. The idea of a lunch, *in town,* has generated so much excitement you would think we had been invited to tea with the Queen. There have been endless (and I mean *without end*) discussions about what it will be like, the weather forecast, how to get there and what she should wear. She has googled the Shard (the venue) so often we must be listed as stalkers.

And now the day is here. The weather has come up trumps, the taxi has been booked and an outfit selected from amongst the other identikit outfits (navy blue trousers, as per, with a pastel green cardie – buttoned up to the top, as per – and a flowered shirt with another of those fabulous wing-like collars). I agreed to set the alarm an hour earlier than usual to set Olive's hair in curlers. Although, had I known how difficult it is to get short fine hair onto a curler, I would never have offered.

Respect for hairdressers across the land.

I had primed the gang at work to shower Olive with attention and they don't let me down. Marco is first in, making her a coffee in a (never seen before) china cup and generally making an enormous fuss. Iris, hesitant at first, soon finds her habitual spark and gives her a private tour of the Coffee Hut and the entrance lobby, including Devon, finishing with an all too detailed description of the state I was in when we first met on the bus. Devon then takes over and presents her with a special (never seen before) visitor's badge. Upstairs, Clarissa is poised for action and I find myself tagging along, a spare part in my own tour. She is introduced to everyone, given a brief glimpse of the kitchen and an in-depth lesson on how the photocopier works before being invited to join the sweepstake for Roland Garros. This causes a low hum of anxiety to percolate through the room because no-one has yet been allowed to dip into the hat and everyone wants first dibs in the hope of getting Rafa Nadal. I decide to leave them to it and get on with a few emails, while keeping an ear out for general topics of conversation.

Foolishly, I was hoping they might talk me up a bit.

Ha! As if; they run true to form, gleefully recounting my every blunder and showing her the swear box, shaking it to demonstrate how full it is.

'So, that is Olive of Fulham?' Miles wanders into view.

'That is Olive.'

'She's making friends.'

'It's impossible not to like her,' I confirm.

'Although she did pick out the Fed, which has ruffled a few feathers.'

'She got Federer? Typical.'

'Beginner's luck.'

We look over to where the lucky beginner has been cornered by Robyn, probably slagging me off or hoping for a scrap of something crusty she can use against me.

'She is completely overexcited. Spent all weekend deciding which cardie to wear. She has even put on some lipstick. Pulling out all the stops.'

'As are you,' says Miles, with what could be appreciation. This sends the heat rushing to my head, as I have indeed pulled out all the stops. On the back of an unprecedented few days of self-control, three pounds to the wind, *three,* I spent an unreasonable amount of money on a full-body Spanx thing (other brands are available) which is working wonders on the

Halfpenny silhouette, although I have yet to master peeing so have refrained from drinking anything at all today. Over the top I am wearing a wraparound, bottle green dress so flattering I might have to buy another couple and wear nothing else until the end of time.

'Special occasion?' he asks.

'No, no, no,' I shake my head emphatically. 'Just lunch with Angus.'

Miles is watching me like a hawk and I fidget uncomfortably.

'Angus?'

'Old friend.'

He sighs dramatically. 'An old friend who merits a new outfit.'

'This old thing,' I say with a lack of conviction.

'Yet more competition. There's James, Jeremy and now Angus. I'm going to have to up my game.'

'Stella, you've gone all red. Are you alright, dear?' Olive appears at my desk. 'She's barely eaten this week in preparation for this lunch.'

'Rubbish,' I object, ostentatiously looking at my watch. 'Is that the time already?'

'Face masks every night, green tea in the morning and that new dress,' goes on Olive, oblivious. 'Looks very fetching, don't you think?'

'Very,' nods Miles.

'She even went to Cross training twice. In one week!'

'Time to go, Olive. We're late!' I cry, leaping to my feet and towing her towards the door.

'I'll see you both down,' says Miles, tagging along. 'Need to see what I'm up against.'

We are thus given an unnecessarily elaborate send-off by Marco, Iris, Devon and Miles. Angus looks the part in a beautifully cut suit, pale blue shirt and yellow tie. His neat hair is perfectly parted and brushed over to one side in a manner not unlike a small boy on his first day at school. Beside him, Miles's ruffled hair and open jacket are infinitely more appealing. Sexy even, the way his –

Focus, Stella.

Angus. Lunch with Angus.

He kisses us both on the cheek, gives Olive a rose – thus sealing her devotion until the end of time - and ushers us out of the door and into a waiting cab.

The Oblix is up on the thirty-second floor of the Shard, London seemingly at our feet, an indigo sky decorated with fluffy white clouds providing the perfect backdrop. We were seated by a superbly deferential Maître d' who cottoned on in an instant that all the attention was to be directed towards Olive first, me second, Angus a distant third. Olive, overwhelmed, didn't say a word for the first five minutes, eyes flitting from left to right and hanging on to my hand for dear life. It belatedly occured to me that she might be simply paralysed by a fear of heights, but a whispered exchange while Angus was busy choosing wine confirmed that this was not the case.

'It's very smart. My mauve jacket would have been more appropriate, don't you think? With my black evening trousers? And a scarf, perhaps? My pearls. Why didn't I wear my pearls? Oh, Stella.' She paused, fingering her pearl-free neck. 'Will we be having a drink, do you think? A small Harvey's? I know you two have to go back to work so perhaps you're not allowed to drink, although I do find a Harvey's enhances one's mental capacity. The Chase always seems much easier after a sherry.'

'Calm down, Olive. You look fabulous and Angus is ordering wine now.'

Not just wine either. The Maître d' himself hefted an absurdly large free-standing ice bucket over and expertly opened a bottle of Dom Pérignon, pouring a drop for Olive to taste before filling up her glass and then personally handing it back to her with a discreet bow.

What can I say?

We ate, we drank, Angus conquered.

It was almost 3 o'clock when Angus poured Olive into a taxi, handing the driver a fistful of cash, before securing a second taxi for me and sending me on my way with a kiss and a promise to call soon.

Now, at my desk, happily tipsy and keeping a squinty eye out for Robyn, I am trying very hard to keep things in perspective and not let another crush in the door. Especially an ex-of-Nina crush. The humiliation, even if it was Angus who did the dumping. She'll think it is a pathetic attempt to even things up, which it is not.

Is it?

I ponder this for a few minutes, allowing the thought to wash around along with the wine and champagne and just a teeny tot of dessert wine.

What I like about Angus is that he is so reassuringly down-to-earth, despite the wealth, the privilege, the vast mansion in Cadogan Square, the family seat in the country and the top job. And nice, an underrated quality, as previously mentioned. And attentive, making sure that he talks to everyone, showing an interest in everything and anything. When he was with Nina, he would happily talk plot, cast and bloopers about the latest rom com with Kim and me before going on to discuss winter rendering techniques with Bart and tossing out invaluable tips for his business model. At lunch, he discussed gardens at length with Olive – inviting her, and me by association, to visit the family estate in Cambridgeshire to see the Italian inspired gardens – and has promised faithfully to start watching The Chase.

He also asked me to dinner – just the two of us – next week. As a friend? As a maybe-more-than-friend? I have no clue and am trying not to look for clues in case I misinterpret them.

Of course, my extended lunch has not gone unnoticed. Clarissa has been by three times already, antennae on full alert for gossip, Bob has given me a fine on the basis of it being a *virtual* fuck-you to the boss and even Sonia came over to ask me where we went. Oh, and here comes Robyn, smug face showing that she knows she has caught me out and intends to make me pay.

'Stella,' she announces.

'That's me.'

'If I'm not mistaken, you left for lunch at 12 o'clock and returned some three hours later. Taking advantage of the absence of Mr Clay is completely unacceptable. As his personal assistant, you are in a position of *great* responsibility and should be leading by example, not profiteering.'

Insulated from her threats by the level of alcohol in my blood stream, I decide the best defense is attack. Standing, I push back my chair back and step adroitly to my left where I can lean against the wall and reduce the risk of toppling over.

'What exactly is the problem, Robyn?' I want her to spell it out. 'I am up-to-date with my work.'

'The problem is you taking a three-hour lunch break. As you well know, the permitted time for lunch is an hour. One hour. Would you like me to print you out a new copy of the office rules and regulations?'

'I would actually, that would be most useful. And one for the boss please, if you don't mind. Because if you're going to get picky about hours worked, and you came over here to get very fucking picky indeed, then it is time you and our esteemed leader figured out how to compensate me for my overtime. If I can't even take the odd long lunch break when Mr Clay is away then we're going to have to look again. Aren't we?'

Robyn glares at me, chewing her lip and finding herself on the back foot when she thought she was leading from the front.

'You see, when the boss is here, and you should be fully aware of this in your highly responsible position as head of HR, I end up either working through my lunch hour or staying late almost every day. Sometimes both. It's amazing how often the urgent letters need doing right at the end of the day. And because I am so bloody responsible in my position as the top dog's perpetually assisting PA person, I stay and do them. Every time. Not to mention the phone calls at home in the evening, usually requiring me to spend valuable *me-time* changing a flight. All in all, we're looking at one to two hours overtime a day on average, more if he is overseas when I have to factor in the time difference. That makes, say, six hours of overtime a week. Times that by forty-eight weeks to allow for the paltry four weeks holiday we get and we should have an idea. Hang on, where's my calculator?'

'Two hundred and eighty-eight,' shouts Clarissa from her desk.

'Holy crap. Two hundred and eighty-eight.' Even I am taken back by how quickly it all adds up. 'Well, let's say two hundred and eighty-five to make up for my ludicrously long lunch break today. Now, what's the hourly rate? Anyone?'

'I'm on it,' shouts back Clarissa.

'We'll check it out and get back to you, then you can have a word with Mr Clay on his return. I'll accept a one-off payment or a simple pay rise would also be acceptable. I'll talk to Roger from Legal if you like. He's good at this kind of thing.'

She keeps trying to shoe-horn in a word of her own but I am reluctant to let her in.

'Better still, you should install one of those clocking-in systems. That way you can easily keep track.' I know that the very last thing Robyn wants is to clock in and clock out as she herself adheres to the highly popular *arrive late / leave early* system.

Behind us the office has ground to a halt.

Robyn, white with indignation, is searching for a suitably withering reply. Except there isn't one. Everything I have said, perhaps a little too plainly and a lot too loudly, is true.

'Is there anything else?' I ask.

She takes a step forward and hunches over the desk. 'Very clever, Ms Halfpenny. You think you run this place but you don't. In Mr Clay's absence, I am the most senior -'

'- person in HR, Robyn. In Mr Clay's absence the CFO would be the most senior person and I don't believe that the company finances are included in the HR job description. Next in line would be Roger. I took a long lunch break, Robyn, get over it. Sneak to the boss when he's back, I don't give a fuck. Tomorrow, I'll be here at 8am, which is about an hour earlier than you. And I'm willing to bet I'll get a phone call this weekend from the boss and I'll pick up. I always do because I'm a sucker.'

'I wouldn't put up with the shit Stella deals with daily,' says Clarissa, coming up behind Robyn and laying an arm across her shoulders. 'Although I couldn't say that I'm not a sucker.' This is said with a straight face and a glance to the accounts room. 'I am. Just not in the office.'

Robyn's face goes from pasty white to purple as her brain catches up with Clarissa's meaning and I almost feel sorry for her.

Almost.

She fights to disengage herself from Clarissa who has worked the arm around her neck into a light headlock, brushing down her skirt and trying to look unruffled.

'You can rest assured,' she huffs, 'that I will be speaking to Mr Clay about the level of disrespect in this office.'

'Rock on,' I say.

And she is gone, speed walking through the silent office and tripping by the automatic doors where the carpet has come unstuck.

Miles shows up five minutes before home time. I haven't seen him at all this afternoon which has left me feeling relieved and disappointed in equal measures. He perches on the end of my desk, his body language for once indicating that energy levels might be low. In fact, he looks as worn out as I have ever seen him.

'How was lunch? Have a good time?' He asks this nicely, as if he hopes that I really did have a good time. 'Where did you go?'

'The Shard,' I mumble. Then, wanting to distract from my lunch and Angus, I tell him about Robyn. 'Robyn came by to have a go because I was late back and I had a pop.'

'So I heard,' he murmurs.

'Did you? Who? Clarissa?' He nods. 'Do you think I'll get in trouble?' The alcohol is wearing off and a hangover is creeping in, along with doubt. Miles, last to join the office, has already, discretely and without fanfare, leapfrogged his way past all other pretenders and is nibbling at a privileged position as *right-hand man* to Feet-of-Clay. I therefore trust his opinion above all others.

'Don't be daft,' he says. 'Robyn has no sway over Mr Clay, much as she likes to think she does. He knows exactly what goes on in this office and I'll bet he is fully aware of the hours you work, even if he does take it for granted. He also knows that Robyn is usually last in and first out. Don't sweat it. You did good. Just wish I'd been there to cheer you on.' He gives me a wolfish grin and everything feels brighter again. 'Now, how about lunch with me next week?'

'Don't be soft.'

'Why not? Why does Angus get a lunch and not me?'

It's a fair question and not one that I have an answer to.

'Stella?'

'He's an old friend.'

'And I'm a new friend.'

I stop to consider this. Is Miles a friend? Would being friends with Miles be safe? Or would I be opening a door better left shut? Besides, I have dinner with Angus to look forward to and James will be back from Cancun next week.

'We'll see,' I say, fudging it.

'We will,' he says.

CHAPTER 19

Inhibition
/ in-i-bish-uh n/
Noun: fear of acting or expressing oneself freely

So in demand, and yet not.

Angus has cancelled.

James has disappeared.

Miles has postponed.

Angus has dashed up to the country estate to deal with a sick cow, James has not been seen or heard of since Cancun and Miles has been forced to postpone because I am too scared to agree to a one-on-one meet. The nicer he is, the further and faster I want to run.

Kim suggested I do some internet dating to open up my prospects, but I had a sneaky peak last night and oh, my sainted Aunt Nora. You have to be fucking kidding. All that pouting and posturing and flirting and putting-yourself-out-there. It's not me. Added to that, I am something of a social media dinosaur these days having forsaken all things online during the Jackson days. Pre-Jackson, I dabbled with Facebook, Instagram and Twitter because everyone else did but frequently found myself asking, what is the bloody point? I had fled Palmerton as soon as I possibly could and there was absolutely no one there I wanted to keep in touch with, except Kim and Nina whom I saw every day as it was. Plus, that whole *liking* business is disastrous for someone with as little self-esteem as me, a fast-track to sorry episodes of why-did-they-get-1230-likes-and-I-only-got-four? What's she got that I haven't? Is that photo-shopped or does she really look that good? Then I met Jackson and he was savagely anti-anything-to-do-with-social-media. It was an early condition of us getting together that I should not only never ever, *ever* publish a photo of him, or, on pain of immediate termination, mention his name but that I should delete my Facebook and Twitter accounts – thus avoiding any possibility of a late-night drunken slip-up. It makes complete sense of course now that I know all about his former life as boring old Jason Percy; Facebook would have outed him years ago.

Before dismissing the idea completely though, I did some research via the only place any of us ever do any research today....... Google. Initial findings were positive as I read that an impressive 20% of people in committed relationships met online. One-in-five. My antipathy unpadlocked the door and allowed for the possibility of opening it. Those were good odds. I read on. More positive news followed when I read that on average there are more men than women on the dating sites and over 70% drink (alcohol) which is, frankly, a relief. Imagine meeting up and not even being able to have a glass of the good stuff to calm the nerves. I was almost ready to crack open the door and let opportunity in when I read that on Tinder only 54% of the people are actually single. The rest? Well, you don't have to be Sherlock Holmes to figure out what they are looking for. Oh, and get this; an average of 53% of people online tell porkies, giving false information about height and weight, age and income, with an old or heavily photo-shopped picture.

Now, I know I am naïve, but **WHY?** Why the fuck would you do that? It's not as if they – the clicker, the swiper, the interested party – are not going to find out all too soon that you don't look like Brad Pitt in real life or that you are in fact fifty-four, not thirty-four, or, or, or.....

I got the padlock ready and read on.

Crap. You have to be different and interesting and engaged (politically, socially and on occasion spiritually) and cute (but not too cute) and witty – all at once – to stand out from the crowd.

Imagine trying to cram that lot into a first date.

Then I found something I could do, hooray, or rather not do; we are advised NEVER to put up a photo of ourselves doing yoga or climbing a mountain – far too common apparently – which is fine by me as I have never done either. I should have got James to have snapped a photo of me killing that carcass-look in CrossFit before he untangled me; original, standout, funny (for some).

Finally, and this confirmed all I have been worrying about re Miles, men of every age are most attracted to women younger than themselves, the most popular age being twenty-two. Read that and weep. Twenty-fucking-two. That puts me twelve years past my prime. Our desirability to men – I don't know the stats for our desirability to other women – drops off from this age onwards, while they themselves become more attractive to us, the women, as they get older.

Too depressing for words.

I put the padlock firmly back on the door, add a couple of deadbolts and an alarm.

So, here I am facing another Saturday night at home not-quite-alone with Olive. And Colin, who has been round all afternoon helping us clear out under the stairs – a greater, dustier, job than either of us bargained for - and is now drinking sherry with Olive in the usual spot. Kim is out with Bart on some company do and is out-of-town tomorrow on a jaunt to visit her cousin, Peter, in Brighton. She did ask me along, but I turned her down, didn't want to feel like a hanger-on, which is plain stupid as I *am* a hanger-on. These past weeks and months I have been hanging on to Kim – and Bart – for all I am worth.

My phone beeps.

Clarissa: *WAYD?*

Anyone? I have not the faintest idea what that means.

Me: *In English pl*

Clarissa: *What are you doing? Doh*

Clarissa: *GNO! CTFO + join us*

Wish she'd write things out like a normal person.

Me: *??*

Clarissa: *Girls night out*

Clarissa: *Chill the fuck out*

I hesitate before replying, wanting to make it seem like I'm busy but not too busy - should I want to go out. Dare to go out.

Me: *Late lunch with friends*

Which is not a lie. I did share a sandwich with Olive and Colin about 3pm.

Clarissa: *So? Fun starts 2nite*

Clarissa: *Son coming*

Me: *What time r u meeting?*

Clarissa: *AEAP!*

Not a clue.

Me: *??*

Clarissa: *As early as possible*

Clarissa: *Get yr butt over here. Soho. Uncorked*

Clarissa: *Its time*

The Uncorked is a wine bar under the Prickly Thistle pub in Soho and, as any self-respecting Londoner will know, Saturday nights in Soho can swiftly end up in the territory known as *pear-shaped.* I don't know if I am up to this. Clarissa is a handful in the office or during lunchtime drinks, so I am under no illusion that we are going to sit sipping an apple juice for a couple of hours and discussing the latest Brexit developments. Olive makes me eat a slice of toast to line my stomach before having a dig about my chosen outfit.

'You're not going out wearing that, are you?' she says, looking at my orange silk shirt and ripped *boyfriend* jeans.

'Absolutely. Why? What's wrong?' I ask, miffed. For the first time in a long time, I'm not wearing a tunic or a scout tent.

201

'I just thought you might make more of an effort, that's all. Back in my day, we'd never go out looking like that. Why don't you put on a nice dress?'

'With all due respect, Olive, fashion has moved on since your heyday and this will do fine for a night out with Clarissa. A dress would be too dressy. Besides, I'm comfortable and that is key.'

'All the same, those jeans are very scruffy, full of holes. I'll have a go at repairing them if you like. Won't take me a jiffy on the Bernina.'

'I paid for these holes, Olive. They are the very height of fashion. I am *in*.'

'In what?'

'In fashion. With it.'

'And they're awfully baggy.'

'These are boyfriend jeans, Olive. Meant to be baggy.'

'But you don't have a boyfriend.'

'The irony is not lost on me either.'

She gives me a small smile. 'At least put on some nice shoes.'

Anything for a quiet life, so I put on some heels and then tuck her up with Ant and Dec, another sherry and a packet of Ready Salted. I have also promised a debrief tomorrow morning over coffee.

It is only just after 8pm when I arrive, but the place is packed, upstairs and down. How the hell am I going to find them in here, I think, as I squeeze myself down the stairs, regretting with every step that I agreed to come and wishing I was home with Olive and Saturday Night Takeaway. I fight my way through the crowd, ducking down to avoid bottles of beer and glasses of wine. It is not until I have battled my way to the far side of the room that I spy Clarissa, crammed into a tiny booth with a brooding, dark eyed Goth. No sign of Sonia. The booth is one of six or seven lining the back wall, half-moons lined with shiny red leather seats and art deco swan-neck lamps that look as if they got lost on the way to a more salubrious establishment.

'We managed to bag a table!' she shouts, her eyes abnormally big and her mascara already smudged. 'Later, there's dancing on the tables and we've got our own!' She thunders her hands on the table making a bottle of wine wobble dangerously. 'We've got a bottle of Pinot Grigio, alright for you?' She holds up an empty glass.

I nod and she pours.

'Where's Sonia?' I ask, eying up the Goth and wondering if I should introduce myself.

Clarissa lets out an almighty cackle and points a finger at the red-lipped glamour puss.

'Sonia?' I simply do not recognise her, even now that I know it's her, I can find nothing that resembles the dormouse from the office.

Clarissa is beaming like a proud mum. 'Knock-out, isn't she?'

I nod again, searching frantically for a sign of the old Sonia. Nope. Nothing. Porcelain white skin, killer eyes thick with kohl, black glossy hair with a fringe so razor sharp you could cut cheese on it, and two long plaits with purple ribbon woven in. Then there are the lips. In a break from the overall blackish theme, the plump lips – when and how Sonia obtained said lips is a mystery I intend to get to the bottom of – are deep red and so shiny I can see my own reflection.

Clarissa nudges me. 'Give it up. It's Son!' she hoots. 'Give us a wave, Son.'

The Goth obliges with a restrained royal wave, fingers tipped with long black nails, mouth pulling to one side in a half smile. There she is! I found her! There is just enough of office Sonia in that half smile to convince me.

We finish the bottle and Clarissa bulldozes her way to the bar for another, coming back with an ice bucket under one arm as well. I want to kiss her; this place is like a sauna and I am fast overheating. My orange silk shirt is starting to stick to parts of me, principally the sticky-out parts, rebelling against my badly fitting black bra.

'How's Ringo?' I ask, clinking glasses with Clarissa. 'Having a night in?'

'I'm going round later,' she says. 'He's having a Game of Thrones night with the lads, so he'll be revved up à la Jon Snow and ready for action.' She gives a lascivious grin.

'Woah, woah, enough already!' I say, recoiling. 'I have to work with you guys and unwanted images of the two of you at it like a King's Landing orgy will be disturbing on a Monday morning. Anyway, what is a Game of Thrones night?'

'They re-enact scenes from the series, costumes and everything. He's very sexy after a night as Jon Snow, as you can imagine and,' she leans in close, 'massively turned on.'

'Stop!' I screech. 'You need to find the line between information and too much information.'

She sniggers, happy. 'There's a big scene now in Game of Thrones role play. Personally, I have tried to interest him in a bit of ER with him playing Dr Ross from the early days and me as Nurse Hathaway. He says he needs a month or so to get into the role, watch the DVDs, work on the character, that kind of thing, but he should be good to Dr Ross by the end of summer.'

The mind boggles. Recent makeover aside, Ringo is no George Clooney, although Miles could work it; he would cut a dash in a white coat and stethoscope, life and death decisions – fuck! I jump as a soft voice says in my ear, 'Well, this is an unexpected bonus.'

I turn to see Miles looking down at me, handsome in a loose, pale grey shirt, one button undone: discreet, enough.

'Miles!' shouts Clarissa, arms in the air. 'You made it!'

'Hey,' he says, unperturbed. 'Wasn't sure I was going to find you in this mad house. Bob bottled it on the way in. Sends his apologies. Hey, Son.'

Sonia, who has yet to say a word, gives a sly nod of the head and moves her hand in a slow arc. Who is this cool diva? And who invited Miles?

I give Clarissa a kick under the table and she gives an exaggerated shrug, managing to look both delighted and sheepish.

My mind immediately spins into overdrive; why is he here? Is it for me? How should I play it? Why did I drink so much wine already?

As the questions pile up with no answers in sight, a minxy redhead emerges out of the crowd, sliding an arm possessively around Miles's neck and assessing us through seductive almond-shaped eyes. She is very beautiful, hair gleaming under the bright artificial lights, long legs lithe in a dress so short and clingy it makes Clarissa's own dress (and she is the queen of short and clingy) look positively staid by comparison.

Miles makes the introductions. 'Janey, this is Clarissa, Sonia and Stella. We all work together.'

Janey, radiating displeasure, stares at us as if sizing up the opposition, decides there is nothing to concern her and lifts a hand in hello, not bothering to say it. Perhaps we should put her next to Sonia and they can compete for the evening's *most silent* accolade.

'Wasn't expecting her.' says Clarissa softly in my ear, shuffling along the seat. 'Budge up Son, we've got company.'

'Wasn't expecting him,' I mumble, as Miles slides in next to me, his fresh firm body pressing up against my damp slackness. Too close for comfort and with nowhere to hide, I fix my gaze on Janey who is grumpily settling in opposite us. Who she is she and how often does she go to the gym? The expanse of thigh on display is showing distinct signs of muscle and the bottom under the tiny dress is pert. Decidedly pert.

'Miles, before you get comfy, we need another couple of glasses for you and Janey. Unless you want something else?' Clarissa waves the bottle and waits for their approval.

'Miles, darling, I'll have a vodka tonic. Make it a large while you're at it.'

We all turn to look at Janey, then whip back to see how Miles will react to this demand.

Not well, is the answer. 'I'm not buying you large vodkas all night,' he says. 'Wine will do, unless you want a beer?'

Janey, looking intensely put out, flaps a hand, which could mean wine or beer but is probably code for, *get me the fucking vodka!*

When he returns with an empty glass and a bottle of beer, I am stunned to see her refusing the wine as she holds out for the vodka. This woman has will. Determination. No wonder she has such strong thighs. We all fill up our glasses and silently wonder how long she will hold out. With Miles ignoring her and the rest of us quaffing with gusto, I sense a weakening; she is tracking the wine bottle the way a shipwrecked sailor eyeballs an approaching raincloud. Finally, she cracks, ungraciously holding out her glass and leaving Clarissa free to finish the bottle, filling it to the brim. Realising we are already out of wine again, Miles sighs, tells me not to move, and clambers back out into the fray.

'So, where'd you and Miles meet?' Clarissa doesn't waste a second. 'We didn't know he had a girlfriend.'

'He's my ex.'

Clarissa, sensing gossip, leans in a little closer. 'Do go on. Are you getting back together?'

She glances over at the bar, eyes searching, then purrs, 'Maybe. We'll see.'

'Oh, Stells, I wasn't expecting this,' mutters Clarissa, as I concentrate very hard on not moving my facial muscles at all, determined not to let my consternation show.

I don't want to be with Miles so I shouldn't care, I have turned him down repeatedly and he has a right to do what he likes, when he likes, with whom he likes. Free world and all of that. Only, I *do* care. Right now, feeling old and fat and inadequate, right now I care. I care that Miles, who pays me more than my fair share of attention in the office, is gallivanting about with a cute redhead with killer thighs at the weekend. I care that there is someone else who is also the object of his attention. I care because, right now, I am consumed with jealousy.

None of which is reasonable. Or justifiable. Or even legitimate.

It just is.

Self-protective instincts leaping to the fore, I wonder if I should make a dash for it now while Miles is at the bar; I could tell Clarissa I'm going to the loo and creep out via the back wall. They would never see me in this crowd, they wouldn't realise I'd even gone for ten minutes, fifteen, by which time I would be safely on the tube nursing my exhausted ego.

Undecided, I hesitate and the moment is gone as Miles comes back, loaded up with wine, beer and a teetering stack of bar snacks. We all fall on the food as if we haven't eaten for weeks, even Sonia who delicately picks up the olives with her long black nails, popping them in one after the other. Janey is the only one who doesn't eat, making up for it by necking her wine and pouring herself another large glass.

The evening is starting to slide.

Let me try that again: the evening has slid. Another bottle of wine has come and gone, possibly two, more beers for Miles and an untold quantity of nibbles.

Janey, out-drinking Clarissa, is totally plastered and has decided that the snacks are worthy of her attention after all. She has meticulously put an olive on the end of each finger and is waving them in time to the music, occasionally licking one and then trying to feed it to Miles, who – thankfully – doesn't want to play.

Sonia, silent and deadly as an assassin, is being chatted up by a fit bearded man in a red Jaws T-shirt, his ears pierced with those giant black studs that stretch the lobe. With no room around the table, he is leaning over the back of the booth and giving her his undivided.

Seeing Janey fully occupied, Clarissa decides it's time to get the nitty gritty.

'What's the deal with you and Janey then?'

'She's a friend.' He looks at me as he says this. Can't think why. 'An *old* friend. She was lonely and invited herself along.'

'Right. She said she was your ex and she might be getting back together with you.'

Miles laughs. 'Trust you to have wheedled that information out of her already.'

'Well?' Clarissa demands.

'I'm not getting back with her. We weren't suited then and we're not suited now.'

We all glance across to where Janey is now chasing a peanut around the table with her straw. She finally corners it up against the wine bottle, sucking it on to the tip of her straw before trying to transfer it to her mouth. The peanut drops and it's back to the chase. It hurts to watch and I look away, embarrassed for her.

Miles sighs deeply. 'Christ, I'd better get her home. She'll fall asleep soon and then she'll be impossible to move.' He turns to me. 'I'll put her in a cab, but wait for me. Promise?'

I feel more than see Clarissa watching us, so I nod quickly and he scoots around the table to Janey, talking to her gently, pulling down her dress and collecting her bag from the floor. He pulls her up and, with his arms protecting her, guides her through the beery Saturday night drinkers.

I watch them go, wondering if he'll come back and undecided if I want him to or not.

'Just relax and go with the flow, Stells.' Clarissa shuffles around to me. She has lost her sheen; sweat beads her forehead, her mascara is half way down her cheek and her hair a straggly mess. She looks wrecked.

'Why don't you pop to the loos and have a tidy up.'

'My make-up fallen off?' She runs her fingers under her eyes, smearing the black mess further.

Heaving herself to her feet, she signs something to Sonia and wriggles out from the table. Alone now, Sonia being engrossed elsewhere, I play with my wineglass, smeared with greasy fingerprints, trying to sift through my muddled emotions.

A hand lights on the back of my neck and I know he's come back. Miles. He slides in next to me, somehow still as fresh looking as when he first arrived.

'Stella, Stella, Stella,' he says, so softly I can hardly hear him in the noisy bar.

'What?' I squeak.

'I like you,' he says simply, pointing a single finger at me. 'You.'

My heart does a double thump, then another and I feel hot and yet freezing cold. Did he really say that?

'What did you say?'

'You heard me. I said, *I like you*.'

He really said it and just like that, my barriers rear up, solid and inpenetrable. 'Fuck off.'

'I'm serious.'

'Fuck right off.'

'I'm *serious*, Stella. Why won't you give me a chance? I'm one of the good guys.'

I look away for a minute, gathering my thoughts. How to express this so that he gets it? Clearing my throat, I say, 'I am thirty-four years old, thirty-five next year. Middle age is but a short hop, skip and another spare tyre away. I'm too old for you, Miles.'

'Jesus, get over yourself. I'm twenty-seven.'

Crap. Seven years! 'You need a younger model. Lighter, in mind *and* body.'

'You have no idea what I need because you won't open up to me, talk to me. Besides, seven years is nothing.'

'It's a lifetime for a possum.'

'You do talk a load of old crap, and how do you know that anyway?'

'Olive told me. It came up on The Chase.' I look away, unable to hold his gaze.

'Stella? Stella, look at me.' I reluctantly squint over at him. Beautiful Miles. I should get out of here; I am drunk and vulnerable. 'I've liked you since my first day at work. I remember Robyn was messing about trying to show me how to switch on a computer as if I'd never seen one before, Clarissa was managing an argument about who got first pick for the Wimbledon sweep stake, Bob was fussing about putting up the prices for the swear box, Nathaniel was searching for a new car on the internet, and you, you were ignoring everyone and everything around you, composed, focused, buttoned up tight. The Miss Moneypenny of the office, holding it all together. I remember you were wearing a black dress with your hair up, a pencil stuck into it, dark eyes flashing as you tutted and sighed at whatever you were working on. You looked exquisite, yet unattainable.'

'That doesn't sound like me at all. I'm never composed. Or focused. I'm doggy-paddling frantically trying to keep my head above water.' I pause to check I have covered everything. 'And I think that calling me exquisite is overdoing it.'

He ignores me. 'Beauty is in the eye of the beholder and I'm drawn to you, especially now that the horrible banker is out of your life. There's a new twinkle in your eye and you're starting to let go, to live a little. Letting people back in and I plan on being one of them. We'd be good together, you and I.'

This is too much. Where is my safety net? 'Please don't mess with me,' I beg, tears threatening.

'Stella, I'm not messing with you. It's very simple: I like you. Always have.'

I don't say a word. What is there to say? Anything, everything, feels too dangerous.

'Give me a chance,' he says, leaning into me.

'I don't know how.'

'Why? Tell me. Give me a hint.'

'You're not safe and I need safe. Reliable. Like an old Toyota or a Volvo.'

'I reckon I'm as safe as they come and my Dad drives a Volvo, if that helps.'

I shake my head.

'You don't trust me?'

More head shaking. 'I don't trust anyone right now.'

'That's not fair. You haven't even given me a chance to prove myself. I know you're scared, but you can't go through life saying no to everything on the off-chance it doesn't work out. I'm scared too. Right now, I'm scared you're never going to say yes to me.'

Clarissa comes back then, face repaired, holding five bottles of beer. 'Cheer up people, it's Saturday night and I've brought supplies,' she shouts, handing out drinks. We all take a beer and drink deeply; ice-cold, hoppy, quenching. Heaven.

How much have I drunk tonight?

Best not to think about it. Just hope Olive's not sitting up waiting for me to come home. She has seen me sad, sullen and monumentally sulky but never drunk and, for a reason I cannot name, I don't want her to. There is a lack of dignity about getting drunk after a certain age and if there is one thing Olive has in spades, it's dignity. Even in her Pilates regalia the woman maintains a certain poise.

Supping our beers, our all-too-intimate talk having been silenced by the arrival of Clarissa, we watch the Saturday night drinkers for a few minutes. A raucous, restless energy fills the room, as if everyone is trying to squeeze as much loud fun as they can before the last order bell rings. There is a girl near us in a completely see-through dress, red bra and panties on display. Does she realise, I wonder? She must do, in which case, why bother? Why not save on the laundry and leave the dress at home?

Miles puts his finger under my chin and gently closes my mouth, whispering into my ear, 'I prefer having to use my imagination a little more.' He moves his hand to my back as he says this, where my orange shirt is now glued to me like a second skin and leaving nothing whatsoever to anyone's imagination.

More's the shame.

I drag my eyes away, looking at my watch and noting that this is the latest I've been up for years, with the exception of the disastrous night when Callum came around and Jackson didn't. I don't know exactly what time I went to bed that night but repeated flash-backs would indicate that it was early morning, not early evening. As I'm about to suggest making a move, there is a deafening cry over the sound system.

'Taaaable tiiiiiime...' a distorted voice screeches.

Oh, crap. Clarissa said something about dancing on the tables and I thought she was joking.

'Table time!' shrieks Clarissa, as *Pump Up the Volume* comes blasting out in an '80s throwback, initiating a frantic scramble to secure a spot on the tables.

Moving with a speed I didn't think possible for someone her size, Clarissa is first up.

'Come on Stells, get your cutesy ass up here,' she cries, already starting to shimmy.

I shake my head, pushing myself back into the seat and edging closer to Sonia. The uber-cool Goth doesn't have to get up on a table and I'm with her. My dancing-on-table days are over, especially with a lake of wine sloshing around inside me. Thankfully, an oaf in long shorts and a sleeveless T-shirt elbows his way through the crowds, leaps onto the table and starts getting jiggy with Clarissa. Never one to be averse to a bit of jiggy, she switches her attention immediately, sticking her impressive bottom into his crotch and grinding with unrestrained joy. I lean back against the booth, relieved to be out of it and happy to observe, just as Miles gets other ideas. Nudging me, he stands, pulling me with him as Pink exhorts us to, *Get the Party Started.*

I can't remember the last time I went dancing, it not being an activity that interested Jackson. In fact, in was a pastime he actively disapproved of – including night clubs in general – so I gave it up. Easier not to. Tonight though, with Miles by my side, his arm tight around my waist to keep me close, I feel a tug of joy. The music is so loud I can physically feel it pulsing through my body, a long-forgotten, thrilling resonance. How I used to love dancing! Restraint falls from me, I feel loose and supple, yielding to the sounds, aware yet unaware. It is joyously liberating and I find myself belting out the words as Pink segues into INXS, *Need You Tonight.* Miles draws me closer still and the temperature skyrockets as, his mouth at my ear, he sings, low and vital, sending an electric current shooting through my body, all the way down to my toes with the briefest of stops en route to tweak my most intimate parts. Exhilarated and breathless, I cling on to him, partly to avoid being sucked into the vortex around us, partly because – well, the man is insanely gorgeous and I would be a fool to turn down the opportunity to handle such fine goods, it might never happen again and at this precise moment in time I no longer care. I, Stella Halfpenny, don't care, I –

Fuck!

Clarissa is down! A flash of thigh, a grasping hand, a glimpse of red undies and off she goes, tumbling onto the leather seat of the booth and, with a remarkable double bounce, disappearing under the table. Miles and I stop, frozen, an unforgiveable giggle stuck in our throats, until we rally ourselves and go to fish her out.

'Holy cow, that was awesome, like the Big Dipper!' she cries, pulling me into a sweaty hug. Her dress is ripped and one leg of her tights seem to have disappeared completely, she has a blob of something unidentifiable in her hair, but she remains unbowed; triumphant as ever. We brush her down, hug some more and then, by unspoken agreement, start to gather our things to go. Clarissa leans over to dig Sonia out of Shark T-shirt's embrace, taking his number and tucking it into her bra with a promise to pass it on.

'I'm not leaving without her,' she tells him.

It is a relief to get outside, ears ringing in the relative quiet, the city air miraculously fresh as we all start sucking in lungfuls of air as if emerging from a shift in the mines, clearing out the stale smog of so many bodies enclosed in such a small space. Sonia is smoothing down Clarissa's hair and picking out the unidentifiable blob when a taxi – miraculously free – pulls up beside us. Within seconds, Clarissa has hustled Sonia in, clasped both Miles and me to her damp breasts and shouted instructions to the impatient driver.

That leaves me and Miles, Miles and me, alone together on the pavement. Out of the bar, away from the music, the cool night air clearing my head, reality comes crowding back in.

'Come on, let's walk, I'll find you a cab, get you home.' Miles says, as if sensing the rising panic. He takes my hand, drawing me to his side and we head off towards Regent Street.

My mind is a chaotic tumult, every step ramping up the misgivings. If we had been in the bar another half an hour, I don't know what would have happened. Holy crap, I was falling fast, for Miles, a whole possum-life younger than me, a toy boy. PUT THE YOUNGSTER DOWN – NOW.

'Stella?' Miles stops, pulling me into a dark shop doorway. 'Hey, stop thinking, overthinking, analysing.' What's with Mr Mind-reader? 'Just relax a little, not everyone is out to hurt you, life doesn't always bite. You got burnt, we've all been burnt, doesn't mean it will happen again and if it does, time heals, slowly but surely every time and we move on.' He pushes me gently back against the shop door. 'And as a marker of my good faith and to prove to you just how serious I am, I'm going to kiss you.'

And he does. I try to resist (honest) but he holds me firm, bringing his hands up to my face, his thumbs caressing my cheeks. Against all my best efforts, I feel myself giving, sagging, revelling. Damn, this is a good kiss. Fucking Miles, trust him be a good kisser, his tongue easing gently into my mouth, teasing me, so damn sexy I can feel it everywhere, fluttering across my belly and snaking down *there*, crap, my knees are giving way, oh-my-heart this is sensational, don't ever stop, this is the best kiss in the history of kisses, I push my hands into his thick hair, tugging on it, pulling him closer, his torso holding me up now, his hands still on my face, I can feel his thighs, his groin pushing at me, he groans, I groan, fuck, I have to stop this, I know I know, oh-just-one-minute-more, is that a harp I can hear, an angelic chorus, his lips, my lips, his tongue probing, please don't stop, please, I have never in my life been kissed like this....

After what feels like an hour – or was it no more than a minute - Miles pulls slowly back, eyes black and unreadable.

'Jesus, Stella, that was some kiss,' he whispers, hoarsely.

'You talking to me or Jesus?' I try for humour, to break the spell. He leans in, his forehead resting on mine, I can smell him, he smells good and then he is kissing me again, more urgently, his tongue strong and insistent in my mouth, my heart galloping, surely he can feel it through my flimsy shirt, fuck, I am so turned on, I can't remember feeling like this, *wanting* someone this badly, I am in lust, can you be in lust, is lust good? Don't stop, please don't stop.

This has to stop.

It's Miles. Golden Boy!

I push against him. 'Miles, I have to go.'

He holds for a beat, then lets go, backing off, his arms straight against the door on either side of me. At once I feel protected, yet hemmed in. Rattled, I duck under his arm and out into the road, scanning the traffic. When I see a flash of a yellow light fly past, I am off, clattering up the road, screeching after the cab. Miles quickly passes me, hand held high, yelling for the taxi as it pulls up ahead. I come panting up as he waits, hand on the door staking possession.

'Thanks,' I gasp.

'Anything for Cinder-Stella.'

'Very funny. I have to go.'

'Can I see you tomorrow?'

'No!'

'Why?'

'Just because. I need some space.'

'Don't push me away, Stella, I'm serious about you. Let's give it a go. What have we got to lose?' And he pulls me in, one hand on the door, one hand behind my neck, and kisses me. Soft and sensual this time, damn this is soooo – the cab blasts his horn and I leap back.

'Get in or get away.' One unhappy Saturday night driver.

Miles open the door and I fall in as if I've been shot. He leans across, hands some money to the driver, kisses me on the cheek, says, 'I'll see you Monday. And stop panicking. We're good.'

I swivel round and look back as we drive away, watching him watching me, until we turn a corner and he disappears from sight.

CHAPTER 20

Lepidopterophobia
/ˌlɛpɪˈdɒptərəfəʊ.bi.ə/
Noun: fear of butterflies or moths

'You look like shit, Stells. Sorry to be so brutal first thing on a Sunday, but have you slept at all?' Kim tells it like it is.

Worse. She is right. I look like shit. I also feel like shit. Tired, hungover, seeping Pinot Grigio from every pore, I have barely slept, my mind and body buzzing with the lost beat of INXS and that kiss with Miles.

Miles, Miles, Miles.

That is why I am here, on a train with Kim, heading down to Brighton.

Around 6am I gave up any pretence of getting to sleep and gently carried my fragile head downstairs to make some tea. I made a pot and took a mug out to the garden, down to the hostas, where I sat listening to the London day waking up. There were birds singing, actual birds tweeting their hearts out in the trees at the bottom of the garden. When did I last hear a bird sing? When did I stop long enough to listen? The garden was heaven: quiet, green, fragrant. Balm for my troubled soul and my hungover body. Olive was not long in joining me, thrilled to have company so early in the day, chirping away like the feathered friends around us. I gave her an abbreviated version of the night before, omitting the bit in the shop doorway on Regent Street. Not that it stopped her picking up on the fundamental concern: Miles.

'And this Miles man, how does he fit in? What about Angus? Aren't you courting?' she enquired, an edge to her voice.

'I'm not *courting* anyone, Olive. Not Angus, not Miles, not James.'

'James?' her voice wobbled with worry.

'From the gym, you know, we've had drinks a couple of times, except now he seems to have vanished.' She nodded uncertainly. 'Anyway, they are all just friends,' I said, adding, sotto voce, 'for the moment.'

'Well, I like Angus a lot,' she stated, as if I was in any doubt.

'I got that, yes. He is a nice man. And he seduced us with that lunch, champagne and all the trimmings. He's like that. Default behaviour for Angus.'

'*Such* a gentleman,' she cooed. 'You couldn't find a kinder man, Stella.'

'I know, Olive. But Angus and I, we're friends. More than that, I just don't know. Besides, he has a girlfriend: Louisa.'

Despite her efforts, I couldn't shake Miles from my head so I sent an emergency WhatsApp to Kim asking if I could join her in Brighton today after all. Consultation required ASAP.

I got to Victoria at 9.19am, which left me just enough time to grab the all-important coffee and a blueberry muffin. And a flapjack - diet be damned, a girl cannot live on wine and mixed nuts alone – then had to run for the train. Running is not something that comes naturally to me at the best of times and this morning found me far from my best. Every wine-soaked cell in my body shrieked in protest at my ungainly sprint, the guard watching me unmoved, a whistle clenched between his yellow teeth. He let me get to a couple of metres away before shrieking the off and I had to leap, literally leap, to get in before the doors hissed shut and the train lurched into life. Kim was thankfully only two carriages further down, holding four seats around a table, the Sunday Telegraph – a paper she has faithfully read since they launched the Stella Magazine years ago - open in front of her.

'Thanks for the upbeat welcome,' I deadpan, struggling to get into the window seat opposite her without letting go of my drink. The only thing between me and total decline right now is my coffee, the biggest size available with two extra shots, and I cannot risk the jolting train upending it. I sigh dramatically as I finally get settled, putting my head back against the seat and closing my eyes, which just makes my head spin so I open them again.

'Sorry,' she says. 'But you do look like shit. Now, tell me all. What's the urgency? What couldn't wait?'

I take a second to regroup, gulping the coffee then choking as the rough bitterness hits the back of my throat. Maybe two shots extra was one too many.

'Miles,' I summarise, unable to hold her interested gaze, looking out of the window instead as we head over the River Thames.

'Ooo eer, this sounds interesting. Welcome aboard my little friend,' she says, gleefully, rubbing her hands together. She looks impossibly bright eyed and bushy tailed, red hair tamed and glossy, no-make-up make-up in place, pristine T-shirt dazzling in its whiteness and immaculately filed nails featuring a discreet pearly sheen.

'Why are you so perky anyway? Dressed up to the nines for a visit to Peter. No Bart. Should I be worried?'

'Don't be soft and stop changing the subject. Now, tell me all about it. What has the boy wonder done to get you in such a tizzy?'

I hesitate, not sure where to start or how. 'He kissed me.'

'That's a good start, I approve. Wholeheartedly. Being kissed by the office hottie is definitely on the to-do list. Did you get a pic? A selfie? We could send it to Jackson and Nina,' she cackles. 'You kissed a boy. You liked it. What's that song?'

'I kissed a girl. Katy Perry.'

'That's the one. I was close. Kissed a girl, kissed a boy. The important things is......did you like it?'

'I did like it. A lot. More than I am comfortable with. More than is healthy. He's wearing me down with his *niceness* and positivity, telling me to let go, to stop analyzing everything, to stop *over*-analysing, live a little,' I say with as much scorn as I can manage on no sleep.

'Sounds like a clever lad, this Miles. I like him more and more,' she says, leaning over to take a swig of my coffee. 'Christ, that's strong. How many shots have you got in there?'

'Three. One normal one and two extra. I didn't sleep a tiddly-wink. Lay awake glassy eyed all night long, awash with wine and misgiving.' I put my fists in my eyes, trying to rub away the fog, hoping for clarity. 'I just don't know what to do.'

'For a start, and to quote the *sujet du jour,* stop over-analysing. You kissed a guy. A hot guy, no less. Girls kiss guys every minute of every hour of every day. You're not getting married, or living together, or pregnant – are you? How far did this kiss go?' I shake my head. 'Right, so calm the fuck down. Now, where did you go? Where did the kiss take place? I need all the details. Spare me nothing.'

'I wasn't even out with *him*, with Miles. I went out with Clarissa – total lunatic by the way, should carry a warning sign around her neck – and Sonia, the office dormouse, who is in fact anything but. Outside of the office she is a uber-glamourous Goth. I didn't even recognise her. She got chatted up by a handsome beard in a Jaws T-shirt.' I stop for some coffee.

'And you got chatted up by Miles?'

'Kind of. He turned up by chance, accompanied by a cross redhead with spectacular thighs wearing not-very-much-at-all who tried to get him to buy her large vodka tonics all night. He refused, so she drank all the wine instead. Now we all know wine is the very nectar of the Gods, the ambrosia that feeds the tormented soul, the bridge over troubled water.' I pause in honour of the virtues of wine and Kim nods in agreement. 'But, as we all know, you can have too much of a good thing and Janey had way too much and was poured into a taxi by Miles. I don't like to think how bad she feels this morning, given my current condition.'

'So, this Miles turns up by chance, does he? Or by secret planning? Are you sure Clarissa didn't set you up?'

'I did. She was expecting Miles but not his side-kick, an ex who fancied her chances getting back with him, but he wasn't interested. So he said.'

'His interests lie elsewhere.'

I sigh. 'I don't know. I can't think straight. Bloody Uncorked. Have you ever been?'

'Dancing on the tables? God yes, once, a couple of years ago. Never again. Bart invited all his staff for a night out, a thank you for all the hard work. Took me about three weeks to recover.'

'Then you will empathise with my fragile state. And why my defences were down.'

'You're going to have to explain yourself a little better. From what you've told me, Miles is a younger, totally gorgeous, intelligent guy who has recently been paying you a ton of attention, looking after you in the office, bringing you a coffee every ten minutes and deferring to your every whim. Shall I go on? He is endlessly indicating how much he likes you, has fluffed up your flattened ego and generally been a top-notch bloke.'

I have to agree, albeit reluctantly, at this succinct - and accurate - resumé.

'So, sweetpea, why is it such a drama if you've finally let him near enough to kiss you? And I assume it was a good kiss?'

'The best,' I affirm. 'Never better.'

'Butterflies?'

'Hundreds of the buggers. A group, a herd, a swarm. What do you call an enormous gathering of butterflies?'

'I've no idea, but I get the gist.'

'I'll ask Olive, she's bound to know.'

221

Kim smiles and puts out her hand for more coffee. 'Funny how that's worked out, you living with Olive. Jeremy coming to take notes and saving the day.'

'My hero,' I say, feeling the gentle rush of gratitude that sweeps through whenever his name is mentioned. 'And now I can't imagine living anywhere else. I'm *so* much happier than, you know, when I was living with Jackson.' That is the first time I have allowed myself to express that, out loud.

The train pulls into Clapham Junction, doors humming open and announcements blaring. The station is busy, more than you would expect at this time on a Sunday, but with a forecast of sun, sun and blue skies, Brighton beach beckons. There are couples with cooler boxes and blankets, families with little ones and bags of food, loners with books and an apple. We watch as they climb onboard, shuffling and manoeuvring all their gear down the narrow aisles. I pray that no one will come and sit with us, but we soon have two lads with no luggage, no bags, no water. Just phones and earplugs.

The freedom of unencumbered youth.

'How many times did we catch a train here, Stells?' Kim asks, gazing out at the station platform.

'Too many to get nostalgic about,' I say. We stay silent for a few minutes longer as the train pulls out, lost in memories of all those years we lived here.

'We had fun though, didn't we?'

'The best. I loved that little flat, our sofa from DFS for twenty-five quid and that armchair you found in the road one night.'

'I tried to take that chair to Bart's but he wasn't having it.'

'It was totally manky.'

'It had spirit!'

'Only because you spilt your gin and tonic over it on a weekly basis.'

We share a smile. 'You were never going to find happiness with that man, Stells. It's like he was trying to stamp out all the good, fun bits, the Stellabrations that we loved so much.'

Stellabrations. Spontaneous Stellabrations, to give them their full name, covered any fun, unplanned, uninhibited, no-holds barred activity. We were specialists for a while, Kim and I, and even Nina before she got serious, in our free and unencumbered youth. Then I gave them up for a more regimented lifestyle in Primrose Hill.

'I know that now, Kim, and I accept it. But in the early days, before we lived together, he was lovely. Even you were impressed when you first met him. You said he was, *quite a catch.*'

'Well, he did fool us for a while, putting on the charm and splashing the cash, unleashing small doses of charisma when absolutely necessary. It was later on that he started showing his true colours.'

'Took me a long time to see those true colours, Kim. You're colour blind when you're trapped in the headlights of *love,* or what you think is love. Which brings me back to Miles.' I stop, wanting to be sure I get this right. 'Life's too short to waste it all being dazzled by ultimately unsuitable men.'

'Oh, for fuck's sake. Life's too bloody short *not* to, Stella. Wake up and smell the coffee, and then keep smelling it until you find your perfect brew. Unleash your inner Stellabrations again. What are you going to do? Settle for an unattractive, unappealing, unwanted bloke on the off-chance that he might not cheat on you or leave you, because no one else would touch him with a barge-pole? Jackson was an arse. Is an arse. Probably becoming more of an arse with every single passing minute and every new dollar that drops into his bank account.' She stops, grabbing my coffee again and draining it. 'You should have got two of those, bit moreish. Did you get anything to eat? I'm starving.' I pull out the paper bag and we rip into the muffin. 'You know,' Kim goes on, spraying crumbs. 'And I know you won't like this, but I think about Nina sometimes,

223

worry about Nina.' I open my mouth to protest, but she raises her hand. 'Stop. Let me finish. We've known Nina since she was knee high. Yes, she has changed, yes, she has ambition, maybe too much, but it's not a crime, and yes, she is very selfish. *But.*' She points a finger at me, fixing me with a steely green eye. 'Under all of that, she is our friend. And where is she now? Somewhere in New York City where she knows precisely no one, bar the Arse, and for all her beauty and all her confidence, Nina was never good at making new friends.'

'Don't - '

'Nope, I haven't finished. Just listen. *You* were taken in by the Jackson charm offensive. I was. Bart for a week or so, not long in his case, he's got some kind of x-ray vision that sees straight into the heart of people. But what if Nina was floored by a heavy dose of charisma one day and got sucked in, same as everyone else? Same as you? She doesn't know about his secrets, name changes, hidden family and all that. The more I think about that the more uncomfortable I get, worried that she might be miserable as sin and realising she made a massive, life-changing mistake.'

'Boo-fucking-hoo,' I say, unmoved.

'We all make mistakes, Stella.'

'Have you gone soft in the head? Maybe she is actually happy as fucking Larry and thinks the sun shines right out of Jackson's arse?' My voice cracks, betraying the tears that are prepping for another outing. 'How is it that Nina betrays one of her best friends in the most appalling fucking way, buggers off with her boyfriend and then gets to hoover up all the sympathy too? Get with the programme Kim. She's the villain not the victim.'

'Calm down. That's not what I - '

'It's exactly what you're saying, Kim. Fuck.' There is a short surge of emotion and a couple of tears make a bid for freedom. 'We have no idea who turned on the charm, who seduced who. It could have been Nina that turned her hypnotic blue eyes on Jackson and made the play.' She shakes her head at me, making me even more frustrated. Why won't she understand? 'OK. Look. Imagine it was Bart and Nina.'

'He wouldn't,' she says, sure of herself.

'Maybe, but I need you to imagine that he could. We didn't think self-righteous Jackson would either. To really understand *me, you* have to stand in my shoes and walk around for a while.' I pause to give her time to go for a stroll. 'Then tell me how you feel about Nina? Still want to be friends? Worried that she's finding it hard to meet people?'

She looks at me stonily. Says nothing.

'Not feeling so charitable, are you?'

Kim shakes her head looking sad.

'Me neither. I hope she's miserable as fucking sin. Call me small minded, call me shallow, I don't care, I'm not ready to forgive Nina and I don't think I ever will be. She and that fucker Jackson are the reason I've lost my mojo, why I'm terrified of trusting anyone, looking under every gesture for some sign of treachery, inspecting every word for a hint of deceit. It's bloody exhausting, but it is the only way I can feel safe.'

'I get it, Stells,' she says, softly. 'I really do. And I get the safeguards you're putting in place. However, you also need to remember than not every man is Jackson. In fact, most men are decent and loyal and kind. Like Bart.' She smiles. 'Or Miles? He seems decent and loyal and kind.'

'What d'you know, Kim? You've never even met the guy.'

'Something we need to put right. Bet Olive's dying to meet him too.'

'Olive can see no further than Angus at the moment.'

'So, you've got Angus and Miles gnashing at the bit. How about James? What's the latest? He ever dig for dirt on Nina?'

'Didn't find so much as a crumb. Reported back that they like her in New York, which was not what I wanted to hear.

Then he flew off to Cancun for some financial knees-up and I've not heard from him since.'

'Haven't seen him in CrossFit for a while.'

'Probably shacked up with some beach babe in Mexico.'

'Forget James. He was a passing moral-boost. Let's get back to Miles. Just what are you afraid of? Lovely guy making it clear he likes you and, what? Failing to see the issue.'

'He's anything except safe. On the back of your idea to try internet dating – not gonna happen by the way – I did a load of research and the stats are clear, men of every age like a younger woman. At a weighty thirty-four, I am, at a push, if there's nothing younger available, a possibility for men in their fifties or sixties, or older. God forbid. Now that I think about it, Colin could ask me out at any moment.'

Kim snorts dismissively. 'God, you do talk a load of crap sometimes, Stella, and stop generalizing. It's getting boring. Anyway, how old is Miles? Twenty-seven, twenty-eight? It's hardly a dramatic difference. Imagine he's the *one,* gorgeous Miles, and you let him slip through your fingers cos you were too scared. Think about it.'

'You'll have to pick up the pieces when he dumps me. And think of Olive! It wouldn't be fair to have me moping around again. And I'd get even fatter.'

'Then you could sign on with Bounteous,' she says with a wink. 'Worked for Clarissa.'

CHAPTER 21

Lament
/lə'ment/
Verb: to mourn or to deeply grieve

Have I made a special effort today?

Olive thought so and called me out before I'd got as far as the kettle this morning.

I told her she was talking rubbish, at which point she said, pointedly, 'I've never seen you wearing lipstick before and you've blow dried your hair.'

Iris then pounced on me before I was half way across the lobby.

'Stella! So smart! Are we expecting someone important today?' She has made herself the building's official VIP welcoming committee, licking boots and buffing-up egos before they even get to the lifts.

Then Marco gets in on the act.

'Ste-lllaa, veeery preeetty. Extra shot for luck.'

There is the smallest possibility that I might have made a teeny tiny effort but *only* because I still looked like shit this morning despite twelve and a half hours of shuteye and an absence of anything alcoholic yesterday. Obviously, I will be seeing Miles and it would be a shame if he thought, *Holy crap, what the hell was I thinking?*

So, I may have made the smallest whisper of an effort to ensure that I looked my Moneypenny-best rather than my Halfpenny-worst.

As I take the lift up though, catching sight of myself in the mirror, the doubts start creeping in. Clarissa is not one to miss changes in appearance, however subtle, and I am starting to realise that my Moneypenny-best is way too indiscreet for a Monday. I need to take the edges off. Veering left as I come out of the lift, I hoof it down to the Ladies loos and get to work. Wetting my hair, I put a swift end to twenty minutes of painstaking blow-drying this morning, then I damp some loo paper and carefully remove most of the make-up. Now for the dress. How to dress-down a little black dress that, in the cold light of the office loos, is not only ludicrous, it makes me look like a well-fed sheep trying to pass itself off as a trim leg of lamb? I go back to my desk and consider my options. If I am quick, I could pop to the M&S around the corner and buy something less LBD and more BBD, or a baggy cardigan. A bin liner.

'Morning, Stella.' Crap. Feet-of is here. Early. 'I need twenty copies of this. Meeting at nine. Strutt and Bull.' He lobs a hefty looking file at me, which slides across my desk and solves my little black dress in one full, hot cup of coffee.

Leaping to my feet, I hold my sodden dress away from my legs. 'Fuck, that's hot.'

'Language, Stella! Asking for trouble leaving your coffee there. Go and get cleaned up and I need those copies, ASAP.'

Bastard then marches into his office and slams the door.

Wait, here he is back again. What fun. 'And I'll have a coffee too when you go and get a refill.'

I try and clean off the worst of the coffee but with only hand towels to work with, I soon end up with thousands of tiny shreds of paper which do little to hide the coffee stains. On the bright side, I can no longer be accused of having made an effort as confirmed when I go and get the coffees, putting mine on the Feet-of tab to cheer myself up and adding a shortbread while I'm at it.

'Stella?' Iris looks at me with incredulity.

'Mr Clay threw coffee all over me,' I summarise.

'But your hair?'

'Splashed it cleaning my dress.' Which does take a stretch of the imagination, something I am certain Iris is not short of.

The workers bees are muted this Monday morning and my appearance goes largely unnoticed, except Clarissa who saunters by to remark, 'Stella? Is there something I should know?'

I shake my head.

'Miles is coming in late this morning.'

'And?'

'Anything to do with you?'

I shake my head, throwing out a few ripe expletives which get me my first fine of the week from Bob. Disappointment and relief flood me in equal measures. After I left Kim at Brighton, going straight back to London without even getting off the train, I tried not to think about him at all, which of course meant that I did nothing else but. I am terrified, excited and horrified all at once and have no idea what to do, how to act, what to say. He has sent me two texts since the taxi drove me off into the night; one late Saturday asking if I got home safely, to which I replied, yes; one Sunday morning asking if I was OK, to which I replied with an honest, no. Verbose I was not. Part of me knows that Kim is right, that I should run with this for as long as I can, squeezing out every ounce of pleasure until he decides he's had enough – except the thought of getting dumped again, healing my wounded heart, makes me want to rebuild the wallowing wall and consider becoming a nun.

Strutt & Bull live up to their name, even giving the boss a run for his money as they settle into his office. Ironically, given how the day started, I am not considered *acceptable* to meet / greet / cater-to-every-unreasonable-whim and Sonia is drafted in as a reluctant replacement. This allows me to keep a wary eye out for Miles who wanders in just before 10am. As I am expecting him to make a beeline for my desk, I keep my head down and try to look busy. He doesn't come by though. After fifteen minutes, I peer around my computer and see him gathering papers on his desk, focused. His face, as he strides across the office, is blank. Only when he gets to my desk, with his back to the rest of the office, does he break out one of his panty-wrecking smiles.

'Hey,' he says, softly.

'Hey.'

'You alright? You look worn out already.'

'That's what happens when Feet-of arrives early on a Monday morning and throws coffee all over you.'

'I've got to go into this meeting. Grab a sandwich with me at lunch?'

'No!'

'Why?'

'I don't know.'

'Relax, it's only a sandwich. I'll come by later.'

However, any decision on lunchtime sandwiches with Golden Boy is comprehensively taken out of my hands when Kim messages me later:

Kim: *Stells, can you take a week off? 2?*

Me: *What's up? We going to the beach?*

Kim: *Mum's died*

Me: *Kim?*

Kim: *Dont call me. Cant speak*

Me: *What can I do?*

Kim: *Come home with me*

Me: *Course*

Kim: *Cant do it alone. I need you. Bart away*

Me: *I'm coming. When?*

Kim: *Asap*

Me: *Will see boss, go home, pack, text u. meet kingsX*

CHAPTER 22

Catatonic
/katə'tɒnɪk/
Adjective: as in an immobile or unresponsive stupor

It has been a brutal few days; Kim and her dad, Reg, are in meltdown.

The heart attack was sudden, ferocious and fatal. I swing between feeling utterly useless as there is nothing I can do to alleviate the grief, and completely indispensable as they are both incapable of doing anything. Even making a cup of tea is beyond them let alone making a decision and there are hundreds of those, queueing up down the road and all demanding attention: death certificates, funeral arrangements, announcement, flowers, readings, music, hymns, transportation, reception, drinks, food, the list is endless.

As the more immediate tasks are pushed deep into the fog that has descended over the house, I keep busy cooking, cleaning, making incessant pots of tea, hot toddies and running baths that stand steaming into the empty bathroom air as they cool to cold and I eventually let the water run out. Yesterday, I filled up a watering can for the houseplants before letting the bath drain, overcome by the shame of waste. I have tried to lead them gently through the hell of the first disbelieving days, coaxing them out of their pyjamas every morning and into the light of acceptance. And every morning they sit taut with fatigue, faces grey, eyes pouchy, ignoring the slices of toast and marmalade I prepare – comfort food par excellence, surely – and forcing down a few sips of tea.

Yesterday I hit the panic button and called the local doctor who miraculously came around within the hour. A

231

family friend, he knows both Reg and Kim well and was reassuringly calm, firm and in charge. Never have I been so relieved to pass over responsibility, even if it was just for a few minutes. He prescribed some tranquilisers that I gave them last night with a hot toddy – *do not do this at home* – in the hope that it would at least knock them out and they could get a few hours of rest. It worked on Kim anyway. I know as I am sharing her old bedroom, sleeping on the pull-out bed where I spent many nights back in our school days. She won't talk to me, can't talk to me, so I have taken to talking to her, soothing stories about her mum, Pam, reminiscing with heart about her legendary school packed lunches complete with three courses, notes of encouragement and sneaky treats for break time, her embarrassingly vocal support on the side lines at Kim's netball matches, lazy days on the beach in summer with a guarantee of chips on the pier at the end of the day. We never minded spending time with Pam; she was a fun mum, a cool mum, a steadying handhold as we navigated the treacherous teenage years. Along with Hilma, Nina's mum, she was a mother to me from the age of seven on. I owe her so much but my grief cannot be theirs.

Try as I can to help, they are falling apart before my eyes and I don't know what to do next, which is I why I am counting down the minutes until Bart arrives. If anyone can breathe some life back into Kim it is Bart, and if anyone can breathe life back into Reg it is Kim. Bart has been visiting his family in Poland, caught up in some urgent legal stuff for his Dad who has been falsely accused of fraud by a jealous cousin, but he is on his way now. I have been calling him on an almost hourly basis, giving updates and seeking advice. Support.

He thankfully rolls up just after four with a surprise in the front seat.

Olive.

My first uncharitable thought is that Olive is just going to be another person to look after. Why I should even think that defeats me as Olive has been looking after me since the day I moved in. And she maintains standards here. Within minutes she has assessed the situation and is busy getting organised in the kitchen, kettle on, teapot at the ready, milk jug filled. A milk jug! Cups and saucers, not a mug in sight. She moves around the kitchen with an ease that is eerie in its precision, unearthing everything she needs for a curative afternoon tea. As the teapot is warming, she starts unloading cakes, biscuits, flapjacks, sherry – two bottles - and God knows what else from her suitcase; it is like watching Mary Poppins. The table is soon covered with home-cooked delights, immediately relegating my toast and marmalade to inadequacy.

Bart is already in the sitting room, a hulk of reassurance, flitting between Kim and Reg, dispensing soothing platitudes and comforting words without effort. I clear the coffee table of undrunk mugs of cold tea, bundles of used tissues and various books of poetry that I have been encouraging them to look at for readings for the funeral, then head back to the kitchen to help Olive bring in the tea things.

'Kim,' I say brightly, buckling under the loaded tea tray, 'look who's here. Reg, this is Olive. I live with her in Fulham now. You remember, when I moved earlier this year?'

Reg raises his head and looks at us with unfocused eyes. He says nothing, just lowers his head again and slumps a little further into his chair.

'Hello, lovey,' says Olive, dropping a kiss on the top of Kim's head. 'Hello Reg,' she gives his hand a gentle squeeze. 'I'm so sorry for your loss.'

Coming from Olive, that overused, stock phrase, sounds sincere and appropriate. Bustling about with the tea things, she emanates compassion and understanding and it reminds me that only a couple of years ago she lost her Derek. She has been here and dealt with this kind of loss.

'Now, Reg, will you have a slice of coffee and walnut or perhaps a homemade custard cream?' He looks at her blankly.

'They are a treat, I promise, so much better than the supermarket ones. However, I think, a small slice of the coffee walnut is just the ticket today. I know you don't feel like eating, but you simply have to keep your strength up. You cannot fight the sadness with nothing inside you. I'll put the tea here, careful, it's hot, and we'll put the cake on the table here.'

Olive, bless her, draws up a foot stool and sets herself up next to Reg, cutting a tiny piece of cake and passing it to him. Relief washes over me as he obediently pops it into his mouth and slowly starts to chew. Now, I have eaten that cake and it is impossible to remain unmoved by the moist coffee sponge and heavenly mocha filling. Watching him closely, I see a tiny flush of life on the pasty cheek. Olive cuts him another morsel and he gobbles it up. I exchange a glance with Bart who has an arm around Kim, a plate of Olive's finest in the other hand, and for the first time since Kim's text came through on Monday, I believe it is going to be OK. Not easy, not fun, but OK.

I have left Kim and Reg in the capable embrace of Bart and Olive and I am going for a walk. It has been over three days since I stepped outside and I need some air before cabin fever sets in definitively. The evening is mild, the sun still bright in the clear summer sky and there is a long forgotten but instantly familiar scent in the air. What is that? The smell of my youth? Is it the trees, the proximity to the sea or simply a different brand of tarmac?

With no conscious thought, I end up outside the school gates of Palmerton Grammar where Kim, Nina and I spent five long years of our life. The school is deserted at this hour, so I am free to gaze without reproach or suspicion. Little has changed, outwardly at least. The main part of the school is an older building, the main front entrance leading directly into the staff room, dated windows in impractical wooden frames, which let in the icy chill of a windy winter's day yet somehow refused to let in so much as a breath of fresh air in the summer months. Around to the right is the pupil's entrance, up two steps and through a heavy swing door. I can see myself rushing up those steps, my arm outstretched to push the door, a weighty bag of books banging against my hip. How many times did I do that? Hundreds? Thousands? Enough to remember the feel of the door against my hand, the resistance of the seal brushing against the floor, the thump as it slammed back into position behind you. There is a chain looped across the door now, something they didn't bother with in our day.

Far to the right is the sports hall. It looks the same, unbelievably; it wasn't what could be described as modern in our day and that was sixteen years ago now. Beyond the hall are the sports fields: football, hockey, netball, basketball. A well-equipped school for a small town. Hanging on to the bars of the high gates, I get a rush of nostalgia for the comparative simplicity of those days. Bolstered by the strength of being part of a solid trio, I got through the usual heartaches of unrequited love and failed tests with relative ease. Being with Kim and Nina gave me status, an invaluable currency in those fragile adolescent years. Kim was strong, opinionated, sporty, while Nina grew, seemingly with every passing day, into a stunningly beautiful girl who went against the perceived conventions by also being fiercely intelligent, acing every test and walking off with the Maths prize four years in a row. And me? I was Miss Average. I made the second-tier hockey team by the skin of my teeth and the broken leg of Mandy Miller. I passed my exams without exciting anyone with my grades and my looks were ordinary rather than extraordinary; there were good days and bad, good haircuts and regrettable disasters.

From the school, it seems a natural progression to make a tour of our old hangouts, except that none of them are there anymore. The teashop is a newsagent, the chippie is a wine bar, the sweetshop is a bookshop and the tiny Spar supermarket where we were sometimes able to blag our age to buy a bottle of wine before the school disco, is an estate agent. And so, on I walk.

I know where I am going, I just don't want to get there.

No. 5, Fitzwilliam Road.

Once my home and last known address of the mother known as Babs.

To delay arriving, I take a detour past Nina's old house, a lump forming in my throat as I stare up at the top floor window: Nina's bedroom. There is no sign of life, no indication of who lives there now; Edvin and Hilma moved back to Sweden years ago, not long after we all left school. I have only seen them once since when Nina, Kim and I went for a long weekend. They live a quiet life in Malmo and were as sweet as ever, but the intimacy that I felt throughout my school years when I spent so much time with them had gone.

When I finally get to Fitzwilliam Road, the house is unrecognisable. Gone is the flaky off-white paint, stained with damp and neglect. Gone is the brown door, paint permanently chipped near the bottom right corner where Babs would kick it when she couldn't find her key, or could find it but couldn't get it in the lock. If I was home, I would wait for that low thud, quick to hop out of bed and down the stairs to avoid the inevitable shouting if I delayed. Once, when I first started staying at Kim or Nina's, she got locked out. Unable to open our front door, she went on the rampage at the Smith's next door, a sweet elderly couple who were completely out of their depth with the lunatic stamping on their carefully planted borders and hurling abuse. They called the police in the end and Babs spent the night at the local constabulary.

After that, I would pop home every night after supper and unlock the front door. There was nothing worth stealing anyway.

Now the house is painted a pale green colour, with a neat dark green door. No dents. No chipped paint. The downstairs windows have a light frosting to keep out the nosy neighbours and brightly patterned curtains held back by red sashes. There is a small tree in a terracotta pot by the front door and actual real live flowers in the beds of the tiny front garden.

Makes me think what could have been.

Then the front door opens and a cross looking woman in a pink dress comes out. 'Can I help you?' she asks, not sounding as if she means it.

'Oh, sorry, I just......I was......so rude of me, really sorry,' I blather, caught out and inexplicably tongue tied.

'Is there something wrong? Are you from the agency? You're from the agency, I can tell. Poking your nose in where it doesn't belong. We've paid the rent, we pay every month and you can tell that woman in Spain that if she puts up the rent one more time, we're out of here. We're only staying because we've done so much work on the place. Work *we* have paid for and if we move, you can bet that we'll take it all with us. Don't put it past me to scrape the paint off the walls.'

This outburst stops me in my tracks. 'Spain,' I say, weakly. 'Woman in Spain?'

'The owner. That Halfpenny woman. Lives in Spain. *You* know that, you must be in touch with the cow. No doubt sitting with her feet up by the pool living off our hard-earned rent money.'

I put up my hand as if fending her off, trying to silence her. I need a second to regroup.

Babs *owns* this place?

How the hell? Babs had no money. Babs spent all her money at the bookies or at the pub. And when did she buy this place? I haven't heard a word from her in over ten years and haven't seen her in twelve. She would occasionally track me down via Pam to ask for money. I never replied and I certainly never sent any money, so how did she manage to buy a house? Admittedly a tiny house, in a small town in the middle of the sticks, but a house all the same.

'I'm not from the agency, I'm not from anywhere, I was just wandering around town,' I say.

'If you're wandering around town, why are you staring at my house? What is so special about my house?' She is getting belligerent, aggressive.

'I used to live here,' I admit eventually.

'Live here? Are you related to that woman? If you are, then you can tell her that she owes us for the work we've done on this place. It was a shithole when we took it over. Disgusting.' She looks at me accusingly as I say silent. 'So? Who are you?'

I realise that I'm getting into something I haven't the heart or the means to sort out. I wouldn't know where to even start looking for Babs; Spain is a big country. Thank fuck.

'I must have lived here before she bought the place. Sorry, I don't know her. Didn't mean to bother you. Hope you get it sorted out. Get your money back. The place looks great anyway. Bye now.'

And with that, I hurry off down the street before she can see the guilt in my eyes and demand a refund. Unsettled but determined to finish my impromptu tour, I walk with purpose to the Beer Tap. The chances of Eric still being in situ are remote, but it feels like a logical conclusion before I head back to Kim's.

Like everywhere else in town, the Beer Tap is no longer the Beer Tap, although it is still a pub, now called The Wheatsheaf. Inside, despite the new name, little has changed. The bar area is middle back with clusters of tables and chairs to the left and right, old-fashioned juke box and one-armed bandits against the back wall. The furniture, incredibly, looks to be the same and even the smell is unchanged, an uncomfortably nostalgic British pub odour of stale beer and a lingering tang of cigarettes, even though smoking has been banned for years. In the far-right corner of the bar is the high stool where Babs used to rule the roost. *Her* seat, where she could keep tabs on everyone in the house. I walk over and run my hand over the worn leather, recognising the black hole where she liked to put out her cigarette.

It literally is *her* seat.

I sit down, tucking my feet on to the metal bar, taking in the view from up here. There are a few customers scattered around, but it's too early for much of a crowd and I have to wait a few minutes for any sign of life behind the bar, time I spend digging around in the dusty corners of my brain for memories, details. I can see her pint, Stella Artois, her pack of cigarettes, B&H, with the Zippo lighter stacked on top, the ashtray by her left hand studded with butts smoked right down to the filter. I hear her raucous throaty laugh, her loud voice slicing easily through the background noise of a busy pub, a steady stream of cutting comments, her loyal band of hangers-on dutifully laughing.

When an old man emerges from the back into the serving area, I am relieved to be distracted from my reminiscing. Tall, stooped, wide shoulders now curving around a sunken chest, tufts of white fluffy hair sprouting at seemingly random spots over his head, specs perched precariously on the end of a beaky nose. I wave to catch his eye and he shuffles over, peering at me over the top of his glasses. Is this Eric? It can't be; Eric was short with a pot-belly, wasn't he? He would give me frequent hugs, squashing me against his tummy.

'What can I get yer?'

'Do you have rosé?' I ask, feeling absurdly timid.

'We're a pub, aren't we? Course we 'ave rosé. White 'n red too. All mod cons,' he replies, brusquely, but not unkindly. 'Large?'

'No, a small one please.'

There is good reason for declining the large glass; too close to, *chip off the old block, apples don't fall far from the tree, etc etc.*

'Small one, eh?' He allows himself a wry smile and goes off to pour me a generous measure in a beautiful crystal glass that he retrieves from the back room. He puts the glass carefully down in front of me, then goes back to get the bottle, showing me the label. 'There you go. Italian. Luvly stuff.'

Leaning in to look at the bottle, I shudder when I see the name, *Il Conte, Stella Pink*. Without moving my head, I raise my eyes to look up at him.

'Awright, 'alf Pint? Wondered if I'd ever see you again. Given up, I 'ad,' he says, "opin'.'

'Eric?'

'Still 'ere. They'll 'ave to carry me out in a box,' he wheezes, choking out a cough that seems to come from deep inside that collapsed chest. 'Lil' Stella. Well I never.'

'I didn't recognise you,' I stammer, embarrassed. Even now I can't see the Eric I remember in this ancient wreck.

'No kiddin'. Ain't seen you for, what? Twenny years?'

'Sixteen.'

'Is that right? I'm an old man now, 'alf Pint. Seventy-nine if I make it to my next birthday. I'd like to get to eighty. Decent age, eighty.' He gives another rattling cough, pushing out a tear at the same time that disappears into the deep furrows around his eyes.

Completely tongue-tied, I don't know what to say. I came here hoping to find Eric, not expecting to find him but hoping all the same, and now that he is here my mind has gone blank. Instead I take a sip of the wine, which is cool and vaguely peachy, with a tart acidic bite at the end.

'Good, innit?' He looks at me expectantly and I nod. 'So, what you doin' back 'ere, sittin' in yer ma's old seat. Trip down memory lane?' He gives a rough disbelieving laugh.

'Kind of. I'm here for a friend, Kim Fisher, her mum died couple of days ago.'

'Pam? 'eard about that. Sad business. I'll be there Monday, see 'er off.'

'You know them?' This surprises me. I can't see Pam and Reg drinking here, despite the name change and absence of Babs.

'I known 'em a while now. Got interested in wine, see. Sick o' beer. Can't stand the smell of it. There's a nice wine bar on the 'igh street and on a night off, that's where I go. Often shared a game of Scrabble and a bottle a red with Reg 'n Pam in there. Didn't know 'em at first, then I 'eard them talking one night about their girl Kim. I 'ad to ask 'em if they knew my 'alf Pint.'

'They never said,' I say, immediately regretting how rude it sounds.

'Nah, didn't want to bother you. Was just glad to 'ear that you was doing alright. Didn't 'ave it easy, did you, with Babs. Mother'ood weren't really 'er bag.'

I hack out a tinny laugh at that understatement, relieved to have an excuse to cover my rising emotion. It's not Babs. I am long over her. What is causing a tightening under my ears, a pressure behind the eyes, is Eric. Eric wondering how I was doing. Eric being glad that I was doing OK, bothering to ask. He cared. And just like that the hazy memories of evenings spent out back watching musicals together are washed with a tender new sheen.

'Thanks Eric,' I mumble, my voice betraying me with a wobble. 'For caring back then. For the musicals. Crisps and stuff.'

''alf Pint,' he sighs. 'The whole pub cared 'bout you. Cute little mite you was. Didn't like the way Babs talked to you, realised it was best to keep you out the way.'

He goes off to serve another customer and I drink some wine, trying to summon some of the old show tunes from those evenings out back, enjoying for perhaps the first time ever recollecting those distant times. So much so, that when Eric comes back, I dare to voice a question that has long haunted me.

241

'What was she like Eric? What did she have that you all liked so much, were willing to put up with her bullshit, let her treat me like that?'

He doesn't answer for the longest time. So long that I think he may not have heard. Then he goes and gets himself a glass and pours himself a small amount of the rosé. He drinks, sighs, drinks again.

'Like might be too strong a word. She was,' he stops, searching, 'seductive. Such a good-looking woman, such charisma, she could charm the birds from the trees if she wanted, but she 'ad a nasty mean streak. Most selfish woman I ever met. She cared for no one but 'erself. And 'er drink. Christ she could put it away. Always pints of Stella, with a shot of vodka if she could afford it. Or if she could persuade someone else to afford it. Never knew 'ow she kept 'er figure with all that booze, then again I never saw 'er eat.' He sighs. 'Then you came along and she named you after her favourite beer. Thought it was hilarious she did, but Stella's a nice enough name so you did OK.' He pauses to take a drink, taking a brief second to appreciate the wine before swallowing. 'Look, I knew 'er long before she got pregnant wi' you. They swarmed around 'er, the men. Those blue eyes, that blond hair, dressed to impress, unafraid of putting it out there was your Babs.'

'Not my Babs,' I say.

He nods in understanding before going on. 'She was steadfast, a regular, became part of the furniture really and it was 'ard to turn her away. She was in 'ere every single night of the year. There, on that stool. She was loyal, drank a lot, brought business in.' He sighs, taking another sip of wine. 'Then she got pregnant. She 'ated being pregnant. Couldn't stand being told not to drink so much. She did drink 'course, less though.' He looks at my shocked face. 'Don't sweat it. You're OK 'alf Pint. More than OK.'

Neither of us speak for a couple of minutes. Me, contemplating my cerebral shortcomings because bloody Babs couldn't keep off the beer when I was in vitro and Eric lost in some unarticulated reverie.

Out of the blue, it occurs to me that Eric must know my dad. There has never been anyone to ask. Reg and Pam didn't even know Babs let alone one of the many men that passed through her life. Edvin and Hilma only moved here long after he had gone. And of course, Babs wouldn't talk about him. Gave me a right clout if I asked and I soon learnt not to.

Feeling bold, with nothing to lose, I say, 'And my dad? Did you know my dad?'

He is toying with his glass as I ask this, twisting it around by the long stem, swirling the wine. He looks up at my question, a small smile tugging at one corner of his mouth and I briefly wonder if he had some kind of stroke at some point. His face appears lopsided; one cheek sagging lower than the other, one side of his mouth moving as if reluctant.

''e was a good bloke, Stella. You look just like 'im now. Or like the Mike I remember. Think so any rate. My memory is not always reliable these days. Could be imagining it.'

My eyes are fixed on him.

He knows my dad. I look like him.

He puts up a hand as if to stop me getting carried away. 'I didn't know 'im well, mind. 'e only started coming in when 'e met your Babs. He came from....' He stops, trying to summon the information. 'Christ, I can't remember. Not from 'ere anyways. Was 'ere on business or summit, met Babs, got sucked in like so many before 'im. Decent bloke. Didn't live 'ere so wasn't always around. Then Babs was expectin', that shocked us all.' He stops again, picks up the bottle. 'You alright 'earing this, 'alf Pint? Not really what you came 'ere for is it? Let's 'ave some more wine. Don't usually drink 'ere, but I'll make an exception for my 'alf Pint.' He gives me another crocked smile and I find myself grinning back. My Half Pint,

243

he said. A great bubble of love for this old man balloons into life inside my chest and I hope and pray that little Stella realised how much he cared back then. 'Stuck around did Mike for a while, coming and goin' a bit for work like, pretty much took care of you for the first year or so. Babs went back to 'er job at the bookies and spent 'er evenings in 'ere. Mike couldn't stand it. 'e would try and get 'er to go 'ome, take care of you but she weren't interested and she 'ated him for giving more attention to you then to 'er. Then one day 'e left. Walked in with you in a carry cot, put yer down and walked out.'

'He walked out? Put me down and walked out?' I swallow down a wave of nausea.

Eric sighs. 'I think 'e must've 'ad a job or summit. 'ad to go.' I stare at him, willing him to go on. 'That's it, 'alf Pint. Never saw 'im again.

'What do you mean?' I splutter. 'Never? He didn't come back?' Tears well, bulge and dribble down my cheeks in an instant.

'Now, now, 'alf Pint.' He reaches over the counter and takes my hand. His grip is strong, belying his withered appearance. 'It was a long time ago now. I dunno what 'appened. I tried to find out, believe me, we all did. Thing is, we din even know 'is surname. Stupid I know, but, 'e was just Mike.'

'Didn't you ask Babs?'

'Course I did. She wouldn't talk about 'im. Refused to 'ear 'is name. And back then, remember, there was no innernet, no mobile phones, nuffink like that. I wasn't family so the police wasn't interested. Time passed and gradually we all stepped in to keep an eye on you. Din want the social services gettin' involved.'

'What do you think happened? To Mike?'

'Accident. Gotta be. 'e loved you alright.'

My heart squeezes so tight hearing those words, I'm afraid it might actually stop beating altogether.

Watching me, he says softly, 'Ah, Stella, we weren't much, but we did our best.'

'Thank you. I remember watching the musicals with you. I enjoyed that. Felt safe with you.'

Now it's Eric's turn to look emotional. He blinks a few times then says gruffly, 'We all tried to keep you safe.'

'Who is *we?*' I ask, needing to hear more of the good bits, the people who cared.

'Crikey girl, there was a queue some days to look after yer. Dave 'n Sandra, Arthur, mad Bella, Bill. All did their bit. We did alright, eh? Look at yer. Beautiful, 'alf Pint. Mike would be proud.'

When I get home, three sheets to the wind in a strong gale after so much rosé, there is a perceptible improvement in the general state of affairs. The meltdown has passed its zenith.

Kim is in the bath with Bart popping out every now and then for refreshments.

Olive is drinking sherry with Reg in the sitting room. She has dragged an armchair over to his and is encouraging him to talk about Pam as if she is the most fascinating person she has ever heard about.

'Really Reg, she must have been a complete marvel in the garden judging by those dahlias I saw when I arrived. So hard to get them to grow like that in a north facing bed. Did she like watching Gardner's World? With Monty Don?'

I leave them to it, making myself some beans on toast to soak up the wine while I go over everything that Eric said to me, carefully inspecting every piece of information for further signs of affection, care and attention. Love. It had never occurred to me to go to the Beer Tap. The pub was like a toxic wasteland for me, infested by Babs. Now though, I wish I could remember more about all those kind people who looked out for me back then...I will leave the door wide open and hope that some more positive memories waft slowly in and I have promised to keep in touch with Eric.

CHAPTER 23

Roller coaster

/ ˈrəʊ.lə ˌkəʊ.stər/

Noun: a situation of persistent ups and downs, emotions fluctuating between elation and despair

The lobby of Claybourne House is quiet when I get there and I breathe a sigh of relief; this is my first day back since Kim's text two weeks ago and I need some time to myself to ease back into office life. The funeral on Monday was a sober, dignified affair. Reg and Kim, while a thousand times better, were not yet up to a festive celebration of Pam's life, so we kept it simple. There was, however, a very decent turnout from the local community in testament to her popularity, which was a comfort to Reg. To see so many people around him, supporting him, was also hugely reassuring for Kim who had been wondering whether to bring him back to Clapham to live with her and Bart.

'We're out all day though. Not ideal is it?'

'Not,' I agreed. 'But look at all these people. He's lived here for over fifty years Kim, he has friends here, community. He knows no one in London.'

There was also an unexpected guest. While Miles had texted and offered to come in support, a shoulder to cry on if needed – I thanked him but turned him down, feeling like he'd be an unnecessary distraction – Angus rocked up at the church with no prior warning, coming directly over to Kim and giving her a gentle hug before taking a seat behind us.

'How sweet, but what's he doing here?' whispered Kim. 'Did you ask him to come?'

'Of course not. I don't know how he even knew there was a funeral to come to.'

Later it turned out that Angus had contacted Bart about some work that needs doing on his house and the whole sorry story had been discussed.

'We always go and support our friends when a close member of their family dies. It's traditional for the Calthorpes,' he explained afterwards.

It was touching and I know how pleased Kim was. Me, rather less so, only because I had put Miles off and then felt bad when Angus turned up and spent the day glued to my side, a pressed handkerchief at the ready to mop any leaky eyes. Bart cried as much as Kim and I was a close third, especially when Eric came over and gave me a whiskery hug. Reg, well-supported by all his friends – with Olive on hand just in case – held up better than we could have hoped.

'Hello Devon, how are you today?' I call, walking past his desk and heading for the Coffee Hut. He stands tall as ever, imposing and immaculate in his uniform, not a hair out of place.

'I's good mon,' he says, waving me over. We all love it when he puts on a Jamaican accent. Brings a tiny ray of sunshine to Claybourne House every time. 'You irie, Stella mon?'

'I'm here, Devon, that's the best I can do this morning.'

He gives a half-hearted smile and I know in an instant something is wrong. Devon has a smile that travels from one ear to the other, strong white teeth lined up in perfect order. He could earn a fortune advertising toothpaste, I have told him more than once, but he's not interested. As well as working here, he is doing an Open University degree in Economics. This will be followed by a Management Financial Advisory Course, Level 4, a stint as an Intern in some kind of financial institution, before finally nailing a plaque to the door reading, *Devon Powell, Financial Consultant / Wealth Management.*

Devon has plans and will go far. I just wish I had enough money for him to manage when the time comes.

'Everything alright, Devon?' I ask.

'No, Stella, it's not.' I raise my eyebrows, enquiring. 'Iris,' he whispers.

'What about Iris?' I look around me wildly, searching for a brightly coloured beret. 'Has something happened? Where is she?'

He nods his head over towards the Coffee Hut. 'I don't know what happened for sure, she says it's a cupboard, but everyone says it's a cupboard.'

'Cupboard? Did she get locked in?'

'No, no, she *says* she *walked* into a cupboard. She's got a nasty black eye. I don't like it. Doesn't ring right. And she won't talk to me.' His usually open face is tight with worry. 'She always talks to me.'

'She does like a chat and you are her favourite person to chat to. I'm sure it's nothing serious. I'll go and find her. Get some ice maybe.' I go over to the Coffee Hut, greeting Marco and looking around for Iris.

'Is Iris about, Marco?' I ask.

He shakes his head at me sadly, pointing at something at his feet. I peer over and see the back end of Iris who has her head deep inside a cupboard. No pun intended.

'Iris?' I call.

Nothing.

'Iris? It's Stella, just wanted to say hello.'

There is a muffled sound, but she doesn't come out.

'Iris? I need your advice. Shall I have the Sicilian Lemon muffin or the Tuscan Orange? You are the oracle on all things edible around here and I will bow to your superior wisdom.' Nothing. I go around and ease Marco out of the way. 'Iris,' I say gently, putting a hand on her back. 'Iris, come out of there. You can't hide all day. Marco needs you. Devon needs you. We all need you.'

Gone in a puff of compassion for *her.*

Later that night, in bed, alone, I carried out an in-depth search for sympathy. For Nina. To have both Kim and Angus expressing concern for her had me in a right lather. I scoured my conscience, had a thorough rummage around in my heart, examined my psyche, all to no avail. There was no sympathy, empathy or compassion of any kind for Nina in the house. Abso-bloody-lutely devoid of the smallest scrap. Then I went back in, double checked, swept away the cobwebs in the darkest corners of my conscience / heart / psyche in the hunt for concern.

Na-fucking-da.

CHAPTER 25

Deep End
/ (di:p ɛnd)/
Noun: to describe starting a new and difficult activity when
not fully prepared or ready to do it

Miles is waiting for me at Fenchurch Street Station looking like
a Levi's Ad in washed-out jeans and a faded red T-shirt with
the familiar logo highlighting his. I, on the other hand, have on
a long dress covering all sins, even if, hallelujah, I was another
three pounds lighter this morning, probably in part because I
ate nothing at all yesterday. Too nervous. Miles has not spotted
me yet, so I take a couple of minutes to admire the aesthetics
and brace myself for a day of one-on-one.

He refuses to tell me where we are going, but I hear it on
the station announcements as we board: Walton-on-the-Naze.
The seaside! When did I last go to the beach? Too long ago,
that's for sure. The closest I have been recently is when I got
the train to Brighton with Kim, despite not actually leaving the
station.

Miles guides me into First Class and I look at him in
astonishment. Luxury treats from Angus is one thing, but Miles
is on a mingy Claybourne Estates salary and that cannot be
much, even with his position as Most Favoured Employee.

'You nutter,' I say happily, sinking into the comfy leather
seat.

He grins and stretches out his legs. 'Got a deal. And we
deserve it. Besides, if we're lucky, we'll have more space and
privacy.'

The privacy remark makes me quiver and I cross my legs
to stop my knees jiggling up and down. Sitting here, just the two

of us, sober and without the comforting distractions of the office or a busy bar, is unsettling me. Unable to look at him, I gaze out of the window to watch the passing houses, back gardens littered with swing sets, paddling pools, bikes and sun loungers, some manicured to within an inch of their lives, others a rambling tangle of long grass, overgrown weeds and abandoned apple trees. We pass apartment blocks backed up against the tracks, windows closed and curtains drawn and once again I think how lucky I am to be living with Olive.

When we get to Basildon, a few people join us in first class, including a young couple who sit across the aisle from us and waste no time in wrapping themselves around each other; arms, legs, tongues, all entwined. They appear unaware of their surroundings, sinking deeper into their embrace, his hand roaming freely on the extensive amounts of exposed flesh. Her dress, modest in quantity and immodest in reach, reveals way more than it covers.

Miles kicks my foot and I realise I'm staring.

He wags his finger in rebuke, then, like a magician performing a trick, digs deep into his pack and pulls out a half bottle of champagne in a cooler pouch and two plastic glasses.

'Thought this might help you relax,' he says calmly. 'I don't want to lose you to your negative thinking. Today, the champagne glass is half full.' He smiles, ripping off the foil wrapping and little wire cage. He expertly eases out the cork and pours a frothy glass of pale pink ambrosia. 'Agreed?' he says, handing me a glass.

I nod, taking a sip of the icy cold champagne.

'Good?'

'Lovely,' I say. 'Thank you.'

We tap our plastic glasses together and, tongues loosened by the fizz, we start talking. I want to know why we are going to Walton-on-the-Naze. I have heard of it, seen the pictures of the pretty, brightly coloured beach huts, although I have never been. Miles tells me that he grew up there and has an aunt who still lives there now who we might, or might not – *I don't know if I want to share you today* - pop in and visit. We talk about work, Clarissa and Ringo, the makeover, and we discuss Iris for a long time, how you can work with someone five days a week and yet know nothing about them. The real them. Where does Iris live? Who with? On her own? Why does she spend all day, every day, at Claybourne House? How old is she? We know nothing. Except that she came in every day last week in body but her spirit was nowhere to be seen. The Iris we all know and love was missing. From there, it feels like a natural progression to talk about Olive, which leads to how exactly I ended up living with her.

'Tell me about Nina. I don't know the whole story, just bits and bobs that have floated about the office. It will help me to understand.'

So, I do. I recount the whole sorry story, including all the juicy stuff we found hidden in Jackson's office, which is important for added context. He listens carefully, nodding occasionally, shakes his head in the right places and generally makes all the correct noises.

'And you know,' I say, wagging a finger. 'Two people, *friends,* have said to me recently that they worry about Nina living all the way over there in New York, all on her little lonesome with only the nasty Jackson for company. I mean, what the fuck! 'My voice finishes on a shrill squeak. 'Poor little rich girl stumbling about New York. She has the job, the man, the money, the looks. Worry? I don't fucking think so.'

He shushes me with his hands. 'Ssshh, each to their own. You're never going to agree with everyone all the time. Even friends. She's living her life, in New York, and now it's time for you to live yours.'

'Very philosophical. But she can crawl back, her life weighed down with regret and I won't care. She's not having another minute of my time. Or my sympathy, obviously.'

'You know, I think you should try and speak to her.'

I look at him in shock. 'Et tu, Brute?'

And he laughs. 'You're still so bitter. It would be therapeutic for you to get it all out, vent your hurt.'

'Stab her eyes out you mean?'

He shakes his head. 'Listen, having your say can be very healing. I'm just saying that it could be useful to speak to her, not only to have your say, but hear what she has to say. You don't have to agree, just listen. It could help and you might learn something that changes the way you feel.'

My well-trained hackles shoot up. 'Well, she's in New York now, where, may I remind you, she decamped in the company of *my* boyfriend, so we are - thank fuck - unlikely to bump into each other.'

It is a very cool day. Cool as in relaxed and happy, no reference to the temperature, which is scorching. From time to time, I try not to enjoy myself so much, but (happily) fail. It is a day lived through rose-tinted specs, all that is missing is a cute soundtrack and my rom com would be complete. We spend much of the day on the beach, taking a break for a late lunch in a backstreet pub with an impressive selection of craft beers and a deconstructed Ploughman's that deserves a place in the pub food Hall of Fame. It is so hot that we regret not having bought our swimming things, or Miles does and I pretend. The thought of exposing my white wobbly body brings me out in goosebumps despite the heat. He has spent most of the time with his T-shirt off, tucked into a back pocket of his jeans, and it's about as good as it could get in terms of the view. Only when we come out of the pub, tipsy after two large beers each, he ducks into a shop selling all things 'beach' and suggests buying some trunks and a bikini so we can go for a dip. A bikini!

Oh-my-sweet-mother-of-all-things-out-of-the-fucking-question.

He starts flicking through a rail of swimwear as a nervous guffaw escapes me.

Bikini, my arse.

Or my arse in a bikini – *not gonna happen.*

'What?' he says, showing me a blue and white number that would fail to cover any of the bits it is designed to cover.

My laughter edges up a notch and teeters towards the line which, if crossed, will see it topple noisily into full-on hysteria.

'What?' he says again, putting the blue snippet back on the rail and pulling out some yellow bikini bottoms that consists of two miniscule - no, microscopic - triangles about the size of postage stamps that are meant to cover my bum and bush.

Not gonna happen.

'You are fucking kidding,' I say, finally finding my voice. 'I wouldn't wear that in the privacy of my own home. In the dark. Under the duvet. Alone. Not to mention the deforestation work that would need to be carried out first.'

His eyes light up. 'Don't do that,' he begs. 'Don't go Brazilian and cut the rain forest. It's sexy on a gorgeous woman, a bush. Natural.'

There is so much tied up in that short sentence that I can't even look at him, let alone speak. My body, a second before covered in goosebumps, breaks out in a sweat as a wildfire rushes from my toes to my face, making a scorching visit to the *rain forest* on the way up. I walk quickly away from the shop, no idea where I am going but it's not into a bikini.

He jogs up behind me and puts an arm around my shoulders. 'Stella, Stella, Stella. You're very pretty when you blush, you know.'

'I have to work with you!' I say, stupidly, all a fluster.

'I know, Moneypenny, lucky me.' He pulls me to him, forcing me to stop. 'Look at me, Stella.'

Not possible. Rain forest. Brazilian. Nudity!

'Hey, look at me.' He gently turns me around so we are face-to-face. 'Does nakedness and sex embarrass you?'

'Of course not,' I splutter, embarrassed as I've ever been in my life.

'You're blushing again,' he says, happily. 'I like that. There's something very appealing about a woman who is naturally demure.' I am just enjoying being called demure, a first, when he goes on, 'and unwaxed. Then gradually dismantling that shy demeanor and letting out the inner - '

'Do not say *cougar!*' I shout, scaring an old man so much he drops his Ninety-Nine.

Sex.

Sex has recently turned into the scariest word in the dictionary for me. It has of course a lot to do with being dumped from a great height and the resulting disintegration of all known self-esteem in the Stella Halfpenny mind, body and spirit. It has a lot to do with the self-indulgent wallowing when self-reproach and self-pity fought for space. It has a lot to do with Nina's perfect body – something that had never bothered me before, I had simply admired and accepted. Not so now. Now, just thinking about her sleek streamlined physique next to Jackson's sleek streamlined physique, not a single gram of surplus between them, makes me want to hit out at the unfairness of it all. The thought of my anything-but-sleek-or-streamlined body lying next to another, naked, flesh on flesh, touching and exploring......where do I sign for a life of abstention?

All of this was momentarily forgotten when Golden Boy kissed the life out of me in a dingy shop doorway somewhere on Regent Street. My body sprang into life and said, *MORE please, I don't care, I don't mind, just GIVE ME MORE OF THE SAME and ramp it up a notch while you're at it....*

All of this was however NOT momentarily forgotten when demi-God Miles pulled out a bikini that I wouldn't wear if you paid me very large sums of money and promised me I would never have to see Feet-of-Clay again in my life.

(I would consider it though).

I look over at Miles, busy buying the old man a new ice-cream – with sprinkles and a flake – to check he is not watching and thus reading my mind. Sex. I think this is as good a time as any to bring a little-known fact out into the light of day. And I have never admitted this to anyone, not Kim, not Nina (more's the pity) and rarely myself.....drumroll please......

Sex with Jackson was rubbish. Fifty Shades it was not.

More like five shades.

Four would cover it.

For someone who is a perfectionist in so many other areas of his life, he has omitted to brush up on his lovemaking skills. When we were together, I didn't care. Yes, I would have enjoyed a more adventurous sex life, but I was usually so relieved that he still wanted to get it on with me that technique and passion were unimportant extras. The butterflies made an appearance early on, a distinct fluttering in the midriff area whenever we were together, but they didn't last the course; couldn't even manage a single flap of those fragile wings by the end.

As a single woman though, with a hot guy openly flirting with me, those years of elementary congress feel like a stone around my neck. Miles thinks I am demure and he can think away as the real truth is that I am completely terrified, not just because of my lack of muscle tone but because of my lack of expertise. I have been party to some more interesting sexual encounters in my dim and distant past, in particular with a bike courier called Billy with whom I enjoyed a wild time and a host of butterflies before Nina persuaded me he was not a good bet, but it's too long ago to be of any use to me now.

We are in the train heading back to London, slumped back in our seats, quiet, sleepy. First class is busy tonight, the hordes heading back from a day by the sea, sandy, sun-burned, thankfully mute with exhaustion. It is true what they say about sea-air, it invigorates and it burns you out at the same time. I watch the Essex countryside, washed out in the evening sun, thankful for the day while resolutely not thinking about what is going to happen when we get to Fenchurch Street. Glancing up, I find Miles's eyes on me, unblinking, bluer than ever in his tanned face. He moves his feet and takes one of mine between his, a touch I feel right in my solar plexus, as a slow sexy smile lights his face, his gaze so penetrating I have to look away. He always sees so much more than I want to show.

'I had the best day,' he says simply.

'Me too,' I say, hoarsely. 'Me too.'

CHAPTER 26

Disclosure
/dɪˈskloʊ.ʒɚ/
Adjective: the act of making something known, revealing information

'We should start measuring this, keep track of your belly fat. Come see me after the class and I'll take a reading with the callipers.'

The Sergeant Major, galaxies beyond his remit, has a hold of one of my tummy rolls. As he has just put an absurdly heavy weightlifting bar across my shoulders, thus pinning me to the spot, there is little I can do to shake him off.

'I've lost nine pounds in total,' I puff, giving him the evil eye. Has no impact; given that he is the devil incarnate, he just sucks it up as extra fuel.

'I can't see it yet.' He pinches another few inches. 'We need to work on this. I'll give you some nutritional pointers when we tally up after the class.'

'Can't,' I pant, willing him with my eyes to take the bar from me. 'Going out.'

'Out?'

'For much needed, arrgh, this is too heavy.....wine.'

'That'll be one of the first things you'll be cutting out.'

'Which is why I won't be staying after class for any unwanted tallying.' It hurts to say such a long sentence. How can I be so out of breath without actually moving? 'Take the bar, it's too heavy. Please?'

He looks at me in disgust. 'Just get on with it, Halfpenny. When it hurts is when you have to dig deep and you have plenty to dig into.' And he struts off, extended thigh muscles meaning he has to waddle, which gives me a brief lift. However, in danger of another Stella spectacular, I inch sideways, crab-like, until I can rest one end of the bar on a futuristic pommel horse – a piece of equipment the likes of Cliff and I are not allowed near. Lowering it carefully to the floor, I roll my shoulders, releasing the tension while I survey the class; Kim is focused on her burpees, Cliff is doing press-ups on his knees encouraged by the Sergeant Major, James is looking cool with two enormous kettlebells, one above his head, the other held out at a right angle to his body. His dark skin is glowing and his hair is shorter. He looks good.

And he *needs* to see me, which is both exciting and not. What does need imply? Has he news on Nina or has he been missing me so much that he is in need of a Stella fix? It's impossible to know; he hasn't said more than a brief, *Hi, how are you?*

Not exactly the words of a man crippled by longing.

Later, in a wine bar called Piaf's, chilled glass of rosé for me and a small beer for him, James is unusually pensive, watching a trickle of froth slide slowly down the glass and pooling onto the beer mat. Silent and enigmatic is not his usual style so something is amiss.

He has something to say but clearly doesn't want to say it. Which means it's either bad or awkward. His demeanour is not that of a man bursting with good news.

No dirt on Nina then.

I study his face and he looks...he looks....I know, he looks self-conscious. Oh, crap, I think. DO NOT let him be about to declare his undying love. Not now. Not when I have just cracked open the door to Miles. I was born with a dominant monogamous gene and multi-tasking is simply not an option. Besides, I would feel very uncomfortable turning down a man of his calibre.

'Stella?'

267

'Yes! No! What?'

'Cheers,' he says, with a weary smile.

'Cheers,' I say, taking a welcome sip of my favourite recovery drink and preparing for him to cut to the chase. But, no. He says nothing, just looks at the floor and toys with his glass for so long that I am forced to fill up the space with words. 'So, how are you? Haven't seen you since you left for Cancun and that was weeks ago. How did it go?'

He shrugs. 'It was tough, to be honest. Didn't exactly go as planned'

'Oh. That's a shame. I've been imagining you frolicking about in the Mexican waves,' I say, stupidly, immediately regretting it. Makes me sound creepy and someone like James is hardly likely to *frolic*. 'Was it the people, the conference or the resort you didn't like?'

He shifts in his seat, glancing at me and then focusing back on his beer. 'A conference is just a conference wherever you are.'

Which doesn't answer my question, so I plough on. 'Ah, but a five-star hotel in one of Mexico's top resorts must be a better bet than a week at the Holiday Inn in, say, Croydon. Right?'

'I think that Croydon might have been preferable this time around. I wish I could have enjoyed it more but it didn't turn out that way.' I watch him, waiting for more and he eventually complies. 'The hotel was alright for one of those mega-complexes and there were some beautiful beaches.'

'Ah, so you did get to the beach. See? It wasn't all bad. And the Mafia man? How was he? Spilling scintillating inside info on the Mob's creative accounting?'

'He never made it.'

'What? His flight was cancelled or his past associates found him and called in his number?'

'We heard he didn't turn up for the flight, but we don't know why.'

'Highly suspicious,' I hum, intrigued.

He dredges up a tired smile and we sit for a while, sipping our drinks, not speaking. Crap, why does this feel so awkward? Say something, Stells! I drink some more wine hoping for inspiration and before I know what I'm doing, I've said:

'I've been seeing a guy from work.'

Like the sun coming out on a cloudy day, his face brightens, tension I hadn't noticed was there visibly draining away. 'Really?' he says – more surprised than is polite. 'That's good news. Hope he is worthy of you.'

'Yes, well, more the other way around really and we're not, you know, officially, you know, *going out*, but we have seen each other a couple of times and, yes, kind of.....'

'Good, good,' he says. 'Bravo, that's great news.'

Which it is. All the same, he is acting very strangely and the use of the word *bravo* is cause for concern. I drain my glass and hope he will notice because I need a refill.

'After all you've been through, that's just what you need, what you deserve. Happiness.'

'Let's not get carried away. It's early days.' And then because if feels rude not to, I ask, 'How about you?'

He shakes his head, tuts a few times, then says, 'No, no, just me. Easier that way.'

Couldn't have put it better myself, except that now I need to factor in room for Miles....for the time being, anyway.

'Look, Stella, I really am happy for you and what I wanted to tell you, what I wanted to say, was that I've enjoyed our drinks together. For a while, I even thought that you and I......you know...I thought we could have had something, and then......well......' He trails off, giving a deep sigh while I enjoy a deep internal sigh because in a weird way, it's a compliment. Lovely James thought we could have had something together.

He looks pained though, so I say, kindly, 'Don't sweat it. You're still my hero for saving me.'

He smiles, a proper smile this time. 'You're funny and honest and I've genuinely enjoyed our drinks together. I wanted to see you to tell you that I'm moving. Back to Singapore. Things here are not working out for me here. Wanted to wish you well before I went and to tell you to hang in there with CrossFit. I've told the Sergeant Major to look out for you.'

O-kay. A brief resumé of the situation; it appears I am being dumped by a man that I am not actually going out with. Nicely, softened by a vague compliment, but it's a dumping all the same.

A new low.

CHAPTER 27

Waterloo
/ wȯ-tər-ˈlü/
Noun: ...a decisive contest

With Robyn on the prowl when a text comes in from Kim, I decide a strategic visit to the Ladies would be prudent so I can answer in peace.

Kim : *Drink? Bart in town*

Me : *Course*

Me : *Duh*

Kim : *6pm Peter Pan's*

Kim : *Bring Miles*

Kim : *Bart wants to vet him*

In fairness to Bart – aka Sherlock - this is not a bad idea. The only hiccup is that involves me asking Miles for a drink instead of the other way around. It feels safer to reluctantly be persuaded, supposedly against my will, to go for a drink.

Not very grown up, I know, for someone so obsessed with being the grown-up.

Worse, I have hardly seen Miles since our day out, Feet-of having sent him on an impromptu wild-goose chase to Hong Kong for a week. He flew back last night and, as if we needed any further proof of his elevated position as court favourite, he has been granted a day off to get over his jet lag. I pluck up the courage and send him a short text asking if he wants to meet for a drink tonight, then leave my phone on my desk and go downstairs to see Iris. She is still a pale imitation of her former self, distinctly lacking in verve, pep and sparkle; her previous calling cards. I had never appreciated before that you literally *can* have the living daylights knocked out of you. I order a tea,

271

accept a slice of Bakewell tart because now is not the time to say no to Iris, then head back upstairs to my desk. And my phone.

Miles has replied in the affirmative, with three smiley faces. He is coming to pick me up at 5.30pm, which will provoke way too much office gossip, so I push him back to 5.45pm when I can be sure that everyone will have left. No one lingers a minute after 5.30pm, so 5.45pm will leave me time to tart myself up without Clarissa noticing.

It is just after 4pm when Devon calls to say that an enormous bunch of flowers has arrived for me and that he has sent it up with Sonia. Before I have even hung up the phone, there is a rustling of awareness around the office, a sure indication that something interesting, out-of-the-ordinary, is happening. Sonia, barely visible behind a ridiculously large bouquet, is making her way with limited fanfare across the office to my desk. Ever grateful for a distraction, Clarissa, Ringo, Bob and Nathaniel are soon clustered around me demanding to know who, what, why and how much?

'Just give me a second. I expect they're from Kim, to cheer me up,' I say, modesty incarnate, as I open the tiny envelope stapled to the clear wrapping.

'Rubbish,' says Clarissa. 'These are from an admirer. Give it to me and I'll open it.'

'Nice try, Clarissa,' I say, whipping the card out of her reach just in time. They must be from Miles, which is going to send this lot into a feeding frenzy. We will never hear the end of it. A smile pulls at the corner of my mouth and I try and haul it back in. Best not to look too pleased. Pleasantly surprised would be better.

Thinking of you. A.

Angus? Unnecessarily over-the-fucking-top or what? I haven't heard from him since our dinner a couple of weeks ago and now this? In the office.

Clarissa takes advantage of my stupefaction to slip the card from my fingers. 'A is for.....? Oh, I know. And there's me thinking you were getting it on with Miles. Keeping all your options open, eh, Stells?'

'Don't be stupid,' I huff. 'He's a friend.'

'Who's a friend?'

Oh, for fuck's sake. The last person I need to complete this happy circle is Feet-of.

'Well, well, well. Who'd have thought? Stella has an admirer,' he says, hoisting his paunch on to the desk and flapping his knitted tie about. Bastard. Bet he has never been given any flowers, except possibly a posy of deadly nightshade and hemlock.

'They're from Angus,' adds Clarissa, helpfully.

'Are they indeed? And who is Angus?'

'A friend!' I shout.

But no one is listening. They are all inspecting the flowers as if further clues re Angus might be hidden within and taking guesses as to how much they cost. Eventually Clarissa digs her phone out of somewhere – genuinely no idea, given she is wearing a tight sheath dress with no visible pockets – and starts googling. Even Feet-of is taking an interest, which is not normal and, worse, is keeping him loitering by my desk. Usually, he just bollocks us all for wasting time and gossiping, yet here he is spelling out the name of the florist to Clarissa.

This is what happens in our office, especially on a Thursday, which has long been the official start of the weekend. Any excuse, however flimsy, is exploited to avoid doing any work and it is nearly 5 o'clock before the floral diversion loses its appeal and they start drifting back to their desks. I am able to enjoy a two-minute respite before more trouble arrives.

Miles.

He makes a beeline for me, perching on my desk next to the Chelsea Flower Show and, within seconds, the whole office has stampeded back again. Miles, looking good enough to stop traffic in the sexy Levi's with a blue checked shirt over a white T-shirt, glances around in surprise.

Clarissa opens proceedings. 'We weren't expecting you today,' she says, before moving on to the far more interesting topic of the day. 'Did you see Stella's flowers?'

As if he could miss them.

'Impressive, aren't they?'

'They're from Angus,' Bob clarifies.

Then everyone is talking at once, about Hong Kong, Angus, flowers, cost and I start to wonder if we might just get away with it...... until Clarissa, her voice carrying above the rabble, asks, 'Why are you here anyway? You've got the day off.'

That is my cue. I wrestle my way past Ringo and sprint for the loos. It is a weary face that looks back at me and it takes a while to repair the damages of the day. Then I watch ten minutes of Game of Thrones on my phone until it is gone 5.40pm and I can be sure they've all gone for the day. Edging out into the corridor, I find Miles slouched against the wall waiting for me.

'How long have you been there?'

'Only a couple of minutes. I was going to give you until quarter to and then I was going to storm the citadel and carry you out over my shoulder.' He leans in and gives me a light peck on the lips. 'Come on. Let's get out of here.' He grabs me by the hand and we head for the lifts through a deserted office. As the doors hiss close behind us, he is on me, pinning me up against the back wall, hard body pressed against mine, his face inches away. My heart starts hammering so hard, I am sure he must be able to feel it.

'Stella, Stella, Stella, I can feel your heart thumping.'

I shrug, willing my heart to regain a little composure.

'I missed you,' he says, softly. 'Did you miss me?'

I nod.

'You haven't thrown me over for Angus?'

I shake my head.

'That monstrosity on your desk had me worried,' he says it lightly, but I feel guilty all the same and slowly shake my head again. 'So, to make you forget the flowers, I'm going to kiss you.'

His lips have barely made contact with mine when the bell pings to announce a stop. We spring apart as if electrocuted as three solicitors from Beasley, Farnham pack into the lift. One, a striking brunette in a tight pinstriped suit, eyes up Miles.

'Well, he-llo,' she says breathily, edging across the tiny floor space. 'Who are *you?*'

Miles, God love him forever, puts an arm around me and says smoothly, 'Miles.' He then nods at me and adds, 'Stella.'

Which thankfully is enough to shut her up, although she tries to catch his eye a few times on the way down. At the lobby, we let the others out first and make our way towards the exit. My attention is on Miles so it takes me a while to register that someone is calling my name.

Oh, fuck. This is awkward.

'Angus! What are you doing here?'

'I was in the area. Did you get my flowers? Thought I might have missed you.' He takes my hand and pulls me towards him for a peck on the cheek.

'Well, actually......I was.....we are....that is to say.....this is, er, Miles, he works with me.'

'Miles,' Angus murmurs, holding out a hand. Then, ignoring the hint, he ploughs on. 'You're not heading straight home, are you? Time for a swift one?'

'Well, actually, *we,* Miles and I, are meeting Kim and Bart at Peter Pan's.'

'Gosh, haven't seen them for ages. How wonderful. Mind if I join you?'

I honestly don't know if he is being purposefully disingenuous or not. I turn to look at Miles who gives one of his nonchalant shrugs and tells Angus he is welcome to join us. Then, taking a step towards me, he puts a hand gently on the back of my neck, staking a claim and sending my body temperature through the ceiling.

We are nearly at the door when I hear my name, again, and wonder what else is in store for me this evening. I turn to see Devon hurrying across the lobby towards me.

'Stella, can I have a minute?' He jogs up to me, registering Miles at the same time. 'Hey, Miles.'

'Devon,' he says. 'What's up? You look worried.'

Devon puts a finger to his lips and murmurs, 'Come with me. Both of you.'

I apologise to Angus and we set off across the empty hallway. By the Coffee Hut, I am surprised to see Marco is still here; he is usually long gone by this time. We go out through the service doors at the back and into one of the huge storage rooms. The first room is cleaning stuff, masses of it for the whole building, teetering stacks of loo roll, huge drums of cleaning fluids and ungainly machines lying dormant like sleeping giants. Off the back of this room, and I have been once or twice to hunt down something for the boss, is a storage room for Claybourne Estates. It's a windowless room, filing cabinets mainly, general office junk, boxes of out-of-date investment brochures and rolls of architectural blueprints, and it's here that Devon heads, stopping in front of the door. Miles and I exchange a worried look as he gently knocks. I hold my breath as we stand motionless, listening: nothing. He knocks again and then slowly pushes open the door, just a fraction, and puts his head to the crack to peer in.

'Devon, what the hell is going on?' I say, trying to see over his shoulder.

He pushes back the door as far as it will go and we all troop in. I don't know what I was expecting to see but it was not Iris on a makeshift bed of paper towels, knitting.

She looks up at us with big eyes, one still discoloured from the *cupboard* incident, her mass of wrinkles looking sad and droopy as her hands gradually slow to a stop. There is a breathless pause, my heart aching as I take in the scene before me.

'Iris, in the cleaning cupboard, with the knitting needles,' I say breezily, hoping to diffuse the tension. Doesn't work; Iris and Devon look confused, only Miles cracks a half smile. I lower myself to the floor next to her. 'Iris, poppet, what on earth are you doing? Wait, forget that, stupid question, you are camping out in the storeroom, even I can see that. What I mean to say is, well, what on earth are you doing?'

'I'm knitting some fingerless gloves for Marco. Do you think he'll like this colour? It's called mustard and he's partial to a bit of Dijon.'

'I'm sure he will love them Iris. It's very sweet of you. I'm just not sure quite why you are knitting them in here, in a storeroom. On a mattress of paper towels. What's happened? Why can't you go home, Iris? We're here to help, not to judge or get cross or anything like that. We're your friends.'

Her little face is visibly distressed in the harsh fluorescent lighting as a thousand uneasy thoughts tumble through my head.

Finally, she says quietly, 'It was just for a night or two, while I get myself sorted. I wasn't going to make any mess, I promise.'

'Crikey, we're not worried about mess, we're worried about *you*. We can't possibly let you sleep here though, Iris. You're coming home with me.' I try to sound kind and reassuring, but my voice is so strangled by fear that it comes out sharp and severe. I take a second and try again, softly. 'What I mean to say is that I'd really like you to come home with me for a few nights. We have a lovely spare bed and a bathroom. We can't have you sleeping here.'

'You don't have to do that,' she whispers. 'I just needed a day or two away. I'll find somewhere else. Don't like to be a bother.'

'You're not a bother. I can't think of anyone who is less of a bother than you, Iris. You couldn't be a bother if you tried. Right, Devon? Has Iris ever, *ever*, been a bother?'

'No, mon,' he rumbles.

'Miles?'

'Impossible.'

'Hear that? You're coming home with me and that is that. Olive will be thrilled. She loves visitors.'

'Olive?'

'You met her the other week. Remember? We live together. She's my landlord, kind of.' She bobs her head, remembering. 'I insist. We've buckets of room. And much softer beds.' I give her a wink, hoping to elicit a smile.

What I get is a couple of tears, dribbling out and disappearing into the deep folds of her face.

'If you're sure. I'd very much appreciate it, just for tonight though, while I,' she pauses, searching for the right words. 'While I get organised. And I would be grateful if you didn't tell Mr Clay about me, sleeping here.'

'Ha! As if. You secret is safe with us. Why don't you go with Miles and Devon and I'll get your things together?'

There isn't much. A blue beret, an old coat that she is using as a pillow, a plastic bag with two pairs of tights and a pair of pants, a toothbrush and a miniature tube of toothpaste propped up in a cardboard coffee cup, and a well-thumbed book; *The Purple Plain, by H.E. Bates.*

Out in the lobby, Iris is installed in one of the armchairs being fussed over by Miles, Devon and Marco, who rushes over when he sees me.

'Obrigado, obrigado, obrigado,' he cries, kissing me repeatedly on both cheeks.

Overwhelmed, I try and focus. I have to call Olive, text Kim, get rid of Angus, decide what to do with Miles and find a cab.

Leaving Iris in Marco's capable hands, I make my apologies to Angus who wants to help and refuses to leave, ask Devon to find us a cab, somehow, anyhow, and take myself off a distance to call Olive. Miles follows me, laying an arm across my shoulder as I dial.

She picks up immediately. 'Hello, this is Olive Armitage, who may I ask is speaking?' she intones in her Jeeves voice.

'Olive, it's me, you can see it's me if you look at your phone. My photo should appear.'

'Yes, I can see it's you.'

'Then why did you ask who was speaking?'

'I always ask who's speaking.'

'But if you can see it's me, why ask?' Miles nudges me to get on with it, his head touching mine so he can hear. 'Look, Olive, can you make up the spare room? A friend from the office is going to come and stay for a night or two. If that's alright with you.'

There is silence for five seconds. Ten. 'What kind of friend?' she asks, suspiciously. 'A male friend? Is that Miles coming? Won't he want to sleep with you, in your room?'

I blush so hard so fast my hair is in danger of catching fire. I do not look at Miles, cannot look at Miles, but I can feel the contented smirk.

'No, it's not Miles, it's Iris. You met her when you came the other week. Works with Marco in the Coffee Hut. Is that OK? We'll be there in about half an hour depending on traffic. And she'll probably be with us a few nights. Maybe more.'

I ping off a quick text to Kim who pings back to say they are coming too and will pick up a take-away and a couple of bottles on the way. I haven't got time to argue and anyway, Kim and Bart are always good for morale and we could all do with some tonight.

Devon finally flags down a free cab, fighting off a man with a briefcase who tries to nab it. Miles and I clamber into the back with Iris and Angus hops into the front, taking over and issuing instructions to the driver.

At home, we find Olive in her leotard and legwarmers putting the finishing touches to a homemade Swiss Roll.

'Hello Olive, you're dressy today,' I say, giving her a peck on the cheek.

'Colin and I tried a new Pilates class this afternoon with that Rhonda, in her front room in Tregenna Avenue. Awfully good and terrific value. Hello Iris, do come in and.....' she stops, mid-flow, as her eyes settle on Miles.

'Miles,' says Miles, putting out a hand for her to shake. 'We met, when you came to visit Stella.'

'If you say so,' mutters Olive, giving Miles her fingers tips and unashamedly raking her eyes up-and-down. Then she spots Angus coming in behind him, transforming from dubious to delighted in an instant. 'Oh, Angus, what a treat! I wasn't expecting you. Naughty Stella didn't say you were coming.'

'Naughty Stella also forgot to add that Kim and Bart are on their way too,' I say. 'With a take-away. And wine.'

'Shall I pop around the corner and get a bottle too?' asks Angus. 'Don't like to come empty handed.'

'Good idea. Give us a chance to get Iris installed in her room. Olive? Anyone home?'

Olive is stuck, caught between Miles and Angus and not knowing who to look at. I chivvy her on and she springs into action, grandly escorting Iris upstairs, giving her the full guided tour on the way (cupboard under-the-stairs, stairs, photo of Broadstairs in 1972, African Violet, Stella's room, etc etc. I was surprised that she didn't personally introduce a moth flitting about by the light on the landing). There are four bedrooms and she has prepared the one next to hers, overlooking the Graham's next door. The room, long neglected, has been transformed by Olive into a haven of loveliness in the time it has taken us to get here from the office. The bed is covered in a dusty pink bedspread with four carefully positioned cushions that I know come from Olive's own room. There are flowers from the garden on the dressing table and a single rose in a slim vase beside the bed, along with a jug of water and a glass. She has rolled up three matching dark pink towels in descending sizes on the end of the bed and laid another rose over the top. It is worthy of five stars and I go over and give her a quick hug, whispering my thanks.

Iris, seemingly spellbound, takes in the room. Inspecting the rose on the end of the bed, she suddenly cracks, stifling a sob and popping out a couple of tears.

Olive rushes over, panicking. 'Don't you like it? I did worry there was too much pink, but I could change the bedspread. I've a green one if that would suit you better?' She looks to me in distress. 'Shall I get the green one? I'll get the green one.'

'No, Olive, it's absolutely perfect. Thank you. I think Iris is just very tired and very grateful. Isn't that right, Iris?'

Iris says nothing, perching tentatively on the edge of the bed, one hand still clutching the rose. She is so tiny that her feet only just touch the ground, making her look young and old at the same time. I have no idea how old she actually is; it has never occurred to me to find out. And just like that, a sickening spasm of fear wriggles into my chest; what have I taken on? Who have I invited into Olive's home? What if she is having some kind of breakdown? Or the onset of dementia? Maybe she really did walk into a cupboard and maybe she was holed up in the storeroom at work because she can't remember where she lives.

What if she steals all the silver?

Has Olive got any silver?

Oh, crap, crap, crap.

Miles sticks his head around the door, breaking the silence. 'This looks better, Iris. You're very kind, Olive.'

281

This gets him nothing but a stony glare before she turns her attention back to Iris. 'Now, if you would like to follow me, I'll show you the bathroom.' She leads Iris across the hall. 'This will be your own private bathroom as Stella and I have our own. I hope you don't mind crossing the hallway. I've put a spare dressing gown here on the back of the door so you can use that, only if you want to of course, we don't mind if you don't. Stella is always wandering about in her knickers looking for some shirt or other in the washing basket.'

Miles leans in close. 'Now that, I would like to see.'

'You really wouldn't,' I say, a light sweat breaking out on my forehead at the thought of Miles seeing me in my granny pants. 'It's not a pretty sight.'

'I beg to differ,' he mutters, 'and I'm not alone clearly. You're making me - '

'Miles?' calls Olive, cutting him off.

Making me - WHAT?

'Could you try and get that spider? Don't squash it. You know what they say. Something Stella stubbornly refuses to heed; she hoovers them up with my Black & Decker, just inviting disaster.'

'Leave him,' Iris says in a small voice. 'I like a spider. Friendly fellows if you talk to them nicely and they eat the flies.'

Olive gives me a knowing look at this statement before continuing the tour. 'Over here I have put a selection of toiletries. I wasn't sure if you had anything with you. Stella wasn't very explicit on the telephone when she called earlier. You've got your towels on the end of the bed, there's plenty more if that's not enough, and here's a shower cap. I like a shower these days, really most invigorating if you put it on cold.'

A memory flutters into being. Iris on the bus. Cold showers.

'Ooh, you like a cold shower too, don't you, Iris? Keeps you young and perky. You told me that when we first met.'

This gets me a hint of a smile and I feel like I've won the lottery.

'There's plenty of hot water,' goes on Olive. 'And I've put some bubble bath there in case you'd rather have a bath. Stella likes a bath after her CrossFit, otherwise she can't walk the next day,' she elaborates. 'I've decided to stick to Pilates, more adapted to my age group, and I'm thinking of trying yoga if I can find a class. Perhaps you could come with us one day? I go on the bus with Colin from two doors up. I could put together an outfit for you, if you like.' She pauses, stroking her leotard fondly and giving me a defiant stare. 'I've got some spare tights and adaptable pants that were much admired when I first wore them. Just ignore Stella if she makes any derogatory comments. She has pants envy.'

'Bloody cheek. Let's leave the pants and Pilates outfit for now, although I wonder if we might dig out a couple of tops from your extensive wardrobe for Iris to borrow as she didn't have time to pack. And a nightie.' Poor Iris is looking shell shocked so I go over and give her a cuddle. 'Let's do that later. Right now, I think we should go downstairs and have a quick sherry while we wait for Kim and Bart. And Angus. What do you say, Iris?'

'I like a sherry,' she whispers, taking some loo roll to wipe her eyes.

'You'll fit right in then.'

We all have sherry, two very generous glasses each, with Miles earnestly discussing the subtle flavours of Harvey's finest with Olive, which helps initiate a thaw of the permafrost. Angus, unaware his position as *preferred suitor* is under threat, focuses on me, asking about my day and generally being nice.

When the doorbell rings, Olive jumps to her feet with an excited squawk. There is nothing she likes more than the doorbell and the possibilities it brings.

I push her back down. 'That'll be Kim and Bart. I'll go.' I pull open the front door with a flourish, about to berate them for taking so long, when I find that the person standing there is not Kim. Or Bart. I slam the door shut, leaning against the wall for support.

Fucking Nina.

Now is not the time.

The doorbell rings again and I ignore it, duh, fucking harlot. Thinks she can turn up like a bad smell and get invited in. Not in this house, Olive's house. She doesn't belong. I squat down and shout through the letterbox. 'Fuck off. Get away from the door. Your evil aura is bleeding in and polluting the house. Just go away and lie in the road.'

She tries to talk back to me through the flap in the door, something so ridiculous I try to enjoy it. Savour it.

'Stella? What's going on?' It's Miles. 'Stella? Who is it?'

I look at him, a giggle, that could also be a sob, building in my chest. 'Stupid cow is talking through the letterbox.'

'Is it Nina?'

I decline to reply. I know exactly what he's going to say and I don't want to hear it.

Instead he takes my face in his hands, leaning in, his gorgeous face inches from mine. 'Stella,' he whispers. 'Now is your chance. Talk to her, *tell her,* make her listen to how you feel, what you went through, then you can put it behind you. This is your moment, not hers. Make it *yours.*' His voice is low, sure and confident.

Do I want to do this?

What will I say?

What if Miles takes one look at her and thinks, *OK, now I get it.*

What if she takes one look at Miles and thinks, *I like the look of him.*

'Stella? Shall I let her in?'

I don't answer because I have no idea what to do and he takes my lack of response as agreement, opening the door and stepping aside to let in the ice queen. I smell her before she even gets over the threshold: Jo Malone. Always Jo Malone. Lime Basil and Mandarin. The familiar smell makes me nauseous as she passes me, Miles showing her into the living room and then coming back to get me.

'I'm here until you tell me to go,' he says, as we stand side-by-side, facing Nina. And right now, I want him to go, don't want him near me. Sticking his nose in and foisting Nina on me.

Then I see the curiosity writ clear across her face as she watches us and that, and that alone, decides me to let him stay.

Eat your heart out, sweetfuckingpea.

For a minute, no one says a word. 'What?' I snap, eventually. 'You've come here uninvited, unwanted and you've ruined what was a very important evening for *someone else*, someone who is not *you*. What do you want?'

'I - ' she starts, but I cut her off.

'And don't even think about saying, *I'm sorry.* Don't say those words. I know you don't mean it.' I feel as if I am on a precipice, teetering, dizzy. A pressure around my waist as Miles puts his arm around me.

'I - '

'I should also warn you that if you dare to say you regret it, I'll kill you right here, right now. Your rights to regret have been irrevocably revoked.'

'I don't - '

'And,' I shout. 'Don't even think about telling me you didn't mean to hurt me. You *knew* exactly what you were doing and you knew exactly how much it would hurt. Clever, clever Nina, never does anything accidently.' I put as much derision into my voice as my fragile state will muster. 'You were fucking your best friend's boyfriend. End of. There's nothing else to say.'

'Stella, let me - '

'Why should I let you say anything?' I am on a roll here and can't seem to stop. 'There is nothing, but *nothing*, you can

285

say that will make any difference, alleviate my pain, my humiliation. You're a tramp, a cheap whore. Oh, so beautiful, I know, but for the first time here in this room, standing opposite you, I'm starting to understand the concept of inner beauty, because I'd rather walk this earth looking like me than have the rotten core that you carry around inside that lovely shell.'

She recoils visibly. 'Stella!'

'Oh, please.' I hold up a hand. 'Don't pretend you have a heart. Listen. You have a tiny window of opportunity here, teeny tiny. I don't want to even hear your voice, but you're here and he,' I jerk a thumb at Miles, 'seems to think I should hear you out. BUT,' I cry, as the dam holding back a reservoir of tears starts to groan and creak under the pressure, 'choose your words carefully because there is precious little you can say that will not make me want to hit you.'

'St-ella,' she stammers, unsure.

Ha! I have cracked that carapace of confidence. We all have a weak spot, even Nina.

'Make it good,' I warn.

'I'm - '

'Don't say sorry.' I don't seem to be able to shut up.

'Stella, let her speak now,' Miles tells me quietly. I look at him, loving him and hating him at the same time.

'Stella,' she sighs. 'Oh, Stella, I miss you so much. I miss Kim. I don't know how to express how sorry I am without saying sorry.' I can feel the heat of her gaze willing me to look at her, but I can't. 'I do feel guilty, of course I do, I felt guilty from the first day, I don't even know how it happened, how it started, I didn't plan it, I promise. The whole thing made me hate myself, I tried...'

I launch myself at her, grunting with the effort to get away from Miles, holding me in a vice-like grip. 'Hate yourself? Don't make me laugh, I'm not in the mood. You betrayed one of your oldest friends. Who does that?'

She doesn't speak, her face pinched.

'A big fat fucking ho, that's who.' A big fat fucking ho? Is that the best I can do? I'm losing my touch. And I had the high ground, I had it, and yet here I am slipping, losing (correction: having lost) my cool and throwing pathetic insults.

'You weren't happy with him, Stella. I know you want to think you were, but I've known you since you were seven years old. You were always a free spirit, you - '

'Don't you dare call me a free fucking spirit.' Cue new bout of *spirited* wriggling to get away from Miles.

'I'm sorry that it was you in the crossfire, Stella. It got away from me. I'm so sorry. Please, please forgive me.' She takes a hesitant step towards me. 'I'll go now. I didn't want to upset you. I came to say how sorry I am. One day, I hope we can be friends again. I miss you so much. I want to leave you with this thought. You know in your heart-of-hearts that Jackson didn't make you happy, you were too different, he was too demanding, too critical. He suffocated you, snuffed out the Stellabrations. I know it was all wrong, but I freed you by taking him away. I wanted to tell you so badly, so much, but he wouldn't let me. He was so - '

'You are so full of shit,' I pant, exhausted by the struggle against Miles. 'Trying to justify what you did. You were my friend. You ruined my life, ruined me!'

And with that pitiful outbreak of martyrdom, Miles relinquishes his hold, spinning me away from Nina to face him.

'Come on, Stella. It's time to turn the page. Your life isn't ruined. You're free now. Happier. I can see it. We all can.'

I look at him in horror. 'Whose side are you on?'

'There's no sides, Stella. This is about you reclaiming your life.'

'That's not the point,' I cry.

'What is the point?'

'You don't get it, you don't get me.'

'I don't, no. Tell me.'

287

His hands are gripping my arms hard, digging into my flesh.

'You can't be the victim forever, Stella.'

'But I *am* the victim.'

'Not any more. You've rediscovered yourself, got your life back. You should be thanking Nina for taking him away.'

My reaction is immediate, visceral.

A punch. To the head.

There follows a micro-second of stunned disbelief, the shocked sound of fist connecting with face suspended in the air around us, before Miles, with one final searing burst of the baby blues, turns on his heel and leaves.

What happens next is a blur, lived through the righteous indignation of the forever victim.

Kim and Bart arrive.

Kim cries, 'Nina!'

Nina cries, 'Kim!'

Kim hugs Nina. Hate Kim.

Angus strides in and joins the hugging. Hate Angus.

Bart ignores Nina, hugs Stella. Love Bart.

Olive and Iris join the party.

Iris shuffles over to put an arm around my waist. Love Iris.

Olive puts on her Jeeves voice to tell Nina to leave. Love Olive.

Departure committee of Kim and Angus escort her out.

Olive asks where Miles is.

Bart asks where Miles is.

Iris asks where Miles is.

Stella explains.

Everyone goggles at Stella.

Bart takes Stella to the kitchen.

Bart pours wine.

Stella drinks wine.

And everyone keeps asking, again and again, 'Why, Stella? Why?'

CHAPTER 28

Sequel
/ˈsiː.kwəl/
Noun: an event that follows and is the result of an earlier event

'Stella!' barks Feet-of. The numpty has sneaked up behind me. 'When you've finished with your social media commitments, perhaps you would be good enough to get on with some work.' Sarcastic arse. I was texting Miles, have been texting Miles since dawn.

He has chosen not to reply.

And not to come to work either. So far.

None of which bodes well.

'Of course, Mr Clay. Just reassuring my grandmother that the electricity won't be cut off. She's most concerned. Received a red reminder.' I summon my most sincere face and look him right in the piggy eye.

'Well, that's most unfortunate, I'm sure,' he blusters, before rallying and coming back for another attack. 'I didn't know you had a grandmother,' he sniffs.

'Of course, I have a grandmother.' I just don't know where. 'She's in quite a state. I'm sure you understand. Now, shall I get on with the Shaw House minutes?'

I see him hesitate, unsure whether to back off or persist. Finally, he hitches up his trousers and beats a retreat.

'Fucker,' I say. Quietly I thought, but Bob's on to me.

'Fifty p, Stella. Box is on my desk. There was something in the air when I came in this morning, there was a blue aura around your desk and I wasn't wrong.'

Clarissa comes over then, curious. 'What's this about a grandmother? You said you didn't have any real family.'

'Does anyone do any work around here, or do you all just sit listening to what's going on over at Auntie Stella's?' I huff.

'Tetchy,' she mocks. 'Just keeping tabs. Besides, I can't see what's going on behind the wall of flowers.' And she sashays back to her desk. Today, she has on a pair of black hot pants over shiny black tights and black over-the-knee boots. Apart from the fact that it is about a hundred degrees outside, it's a bit racy for the office. Not that that has ever put Clarissa off, although since the hook-up with Ringo everything has gone up a degree: shorter, blacker, tighter, sexier.

She is right about the flowers though. What am I thinking? Here I am, praying Miles will arrive, while the bouquet from Angus is hogging the limelight, giant blooms sucking up all the oxygen. I try and stuff the flowers into the way-too-small bin, provoking a shower of leaves, petals and pollen and leaving me an armful of naked but resilient stems.

It is gone 10am when Miles arrives, striding through the office, past my desk – without so much as a nod of recognition – straight to Feet-of's office, where he goes in without knocking. A sackable offence if attempted by me. Across the room, I can see Clarissa sniffing the air like a hungry fox on the scent of an isolated chicken as my imagination accelerates from idling to overdrive. There was nothing about that stride across the office that inspired hope.

The minutes drag by as I try to get on with some work, a task made infinitely harder by the fact that every two seconds I move my eyes from the screen to the door of the boss's office, willing Miles to come through it and slay me with a forgiving smile. Eventually I get distracted by an article on the Cosmo website called, *Get Him to Forgive You*. Not recommended is saying *sorry* and then taking your clothes off and initiating sex, which is a relief. However, what they do recommend is -

'Stella?'

I jump a mile.

'Miles,' I say, scrutinizing his face for clues.

There is a tiny cut above his top lip where I must have caught him with my ring. Evidence. I was hoping there would be no trace.

'I'm going away for a while,' he says, eyes on the floor, the wall, the desk. My phone. Anywhere but me.

'Going away? Where?'

'Hong Kong.'

'Hong Kong?' I yelp. 'Does this have something to do with last night?'

'It's work.'

'That's not really why, is it? You want to get away from me. Not that I can blame - '

He shakes his head, eyes meeting mine before sliding away. 'Not everything revolves around you, Stella.'

Ouch.

'Mr Clay needs a representative out there for a big project. He's asked me to go and I've accepted.'

'Yeah, right,' I say, with disbelief.

'Whatever.' He shrugs. 'How about a, *Miles, that's amazing, what an opportunity, good for you.*' He looks up from the floor for a second, pierces me with an angry stare, looks away again.

Fuck. I'm getting this all wrong. Concentrate, Stella.

'Look, Miles, I'm....that is....tremendous....well done, really, so...can I.... look, about last - '

He cuts me off, his voice bitter. 'This kind of break doesn't come along very often. I'd be a fool to turn it down and I'm done being a fool.'

'You're not a fool,' I whisper, pathetically.

'Then why do I feel like one?'

There's no answer to that. Instead, I gather all my courage and say what's in my heart. 'I'll miss you.'

'Sure, you will. You've been merrily soaking up all the attention for months now, with no perceptible appreciation. It's a two-way street, you know. You can't keep taking and taking without giving anything back.'

'It's not like that,' I protest. 'I've been recovering, finding myself.'

'Oh, here we go again. Poor little Stella, got dumped. We've all been dumped and without exception we are all better off for it. Who wants to be with someone that wants to be with someone else?'

'It wasn't like that.'

'Of course, it was. Open your bloody eyes, Stella. Why can't you accept that ultimately Nina did you a favour. You were trapped and she released you.'

'That's not the point and you know it.' I withhold the *duh,* which shows immense restraint on my part if you ask me.

'You're like a stuck record. I don't want to listen to it any longer. I'm done.'

'Done?'

'Done.'

And he strides off.

If I thought *the longest day* was the longest day, I was wrong. It is not even close to the never-ending, grinding, misery of this day. With every second of every minute that crawls by, the realisation that I have made a complete and utter cock-up of my life becomes dazzling clear. Clarissa tries to cheer me up by announcing that she is doing the draw for the US Open next week.

'Not interested,' I say, sulky as sin. 'My one hot pick last time, that Greek fella, went out in the first round at Wimbledon. Even Olive didn't win with her one entry and she had the Fed. Waste of my time and money.'

'Well, you're playing. It's the rules,' she says.

I exhale an indignant huff.

'We don't always win, Stella, that's life. You've got to learn to roll with it. Highs and lows. Wins and losses. Ups and downs.'

Now I'm being lectured by Clarissa and I know she is no longer talking about tennis.

'The ebb and flow,' says Bob, coming over. 'Wax and wane. When we walk the valleys, we must continue to strive for the peaks.'

'That's a corker, Bob,' cheers Clarissa. 'Who said that?'

'All my own work,' he says, looking pleased. 'The view is so much better from the top.'

'Not if you have vertigo' I say, pedantically. 'Can we just get back to the tennis.'

By home time, I am so blinded by my own stupidity, I can hardly see. I had a stab at something good and I blew it. It is only the thought of Iris, waiting for me in the lobby, that spurs me on to make a move towards home, Miles's words, *not everything revolves around you, Stella*, having etched themselves deep into my psyche.

'Oh, you're here, at last, come on in Iris.' Olive is out on the doorstep before we are half way up the path. 'I've made a carrot cake with a tot of brandy and I've paused The Chase. We can watch it together.' She ceremoniously leads Iris through to the sitting room where a tray is packed with the wherewithal for a proper afternoon tea, the teapot wearing a jaunty knitted tea cosy that I have never seen before. 'Have you ever watched The Chase?' she asks, guiding Iris to a chair. 'I never miss it and even Stella likes it now, despite almost never getting an answer right.'

She drags a small side table over to Iris, giving her a dainty cup of tea along with a giant slab of cake.

'We'll watch this first and then I'll get us a sherry and we can have a chat about *you know who.*' She eyes me meaningfully.

'Olive,' I say, drawing her out of the sitting room and down towards the kitchen. 'Not tonight, Olive, please. I don't want to talk about the Swedish strumpet. Or Miles. Tonight is for Iris and Iris alone. Let's have a nice, normal evening, no hysterics, no punching, no nothing. Let's make her feel safe and comfortable.' Olive is nodding attentively. 'Normal.'

'Right,' she says, subdued. 'Normal. Got you. No strumpet. No punching. Normal.'

Emma Henry

PART THREE
ENDGAME

Emma Henry

CHAPTER 29

Karma

/ˈkaːmə/

Noun: about the cycle of cause and effect. According to the theory of Karma, your actions now influence what happens later or in a future life

Olive has been deep in preparations since dawn, seconded by an enthusiastic Iris who is proving very handy with the ancient KitchenAid mixer. Whatever you ask her to do, she stuffs it in the cracked bowl, adds the sharpest blade available and fires it up. The result of all this activity is a series of puffy cakes, so light they almost need to be tied down to stop them floating away, cheese straws thick with cheddar, mini quiches in a variety of flavours, prawn vol-au-vents, devilled eggs and cheese on toothpicks stuck into a couple of orange halves.

This retro buffet is in honour of the inaugural meeting of The Beatrice Avenue Book Club.

Created by Olive and Iris after they watched the Jane Austen Book Club one night, we are finally ready for the off. Enlisted are; me, Kim and Bart, Colin, Angus, Clarissa and, wait for it – the result of a long and tortuous negotiation - Nina. Although negotiation is perhaps not the right word; effectively I was beaten into submission by Kim's reconciliation campaign - top of her agenda since the hussy had the nerve to ring our doorbell that fateful night. Olive has also been chipping away at my resistance, waffling on about friendship being like a marriage, in sickness and in health, the good and the bad, blah-di-blah. I was tempted to put her in touch with Bob so they could philosophize together. I suspect an ulterior motive though as she is clearly dying to get up-close-and-personal with the Swedish Strumpet - now elevated to near celebrity status in this house.

Even Iris is interested; still with us and now a permanent resident of Beatrice Ave after Olive caught her applying for housing benefit one night. She, Olive, got very upset, asking if her home wasn't good enough, which in turn upset Iris. It was the closest these two giving and forgiving people could get to an argument without actually having one. Step in Stella Halfpenny, pensioner-housing-negotiator extraordinaire.

'Olive, do you want Iris to stay and live here permanently?' I asked.

A nod, followed by what sounded like a faint *duh.*

I contented myself with a disapproving look and turned to Iris. 'Now, Iris, would you like to stay here with Olive?'

She bestowed us with a series of wary nods.

'And me.'

Another nod.

'That is if I'm allowed to stay too, Olive?' Which got me another *duh.* 'Case closed,' I announced, pleased with myself. 'We should arrange to go and collect your things Iris. I'll come and help. And we should let people have your new address, friends, family and the bank. Who else?'

These blithely made comments brought on such a long bout of head shaking I was worried something had become disconnected somewhere. Iris had been reticent to discuss her situation and what had brought her to bed down in the storeroom at Claybourne House and I had been reluctant to interfere. Now, though, she was ready to open up. I gently probed, Olive sitting stock-still beside me as if any movement might stop the flow......not that there was exactly a *flow* of information, more a few carefully released droplets:

1. Iris had been living in a shelter near Marylebone before an altercation led her to hide out for a few days elsewhere (the office). This prompted Olive to recount

Derek's altercation in the Ladies at the cinema and the fact that they never went back. 'So, I understand,' she said, gravely.

2. Before that she had been living with a sister (Mavis) and her (Mavis's) husband (Gavin) and, no, she does not want them to know where she is now *under any circumstances.*

3. And before that she lived with her husband, Frank, who died of a heart attack sixteen years ago. 'God rest his sweet soul,' she whispered. They had a daughter, Pearl, who was anything but sweet and thankfully emigrated to Canada a long, long time ago. She misses Frank every day but not Pearl. 'I sometimes wonder if they gave me the wrong baby in the hospital. She never liked me and I didn't like her much either.'

4. She is not interested in retrieving any of her old belongings – why would she, with everything that Olive has given her, she needs for nothing and the clothes are much nicer anyway (cue Olive extracting a tissue from up her sleeve).

5. She doesn't have a bank account and no one she needs to inform of her whereabouts except possibly Edith, her old neighbour, and maybe Ron, from Ron's Café.

6. She worked for thirty-eight years as a dinner lady in a boy's school in the East End before being let go when the catering was outsourced. 'I miss my boys, but now I have you, and Marco, and Devon. And everyone else. And the coffee is much better.'

7. Before she joined us at Claybourne House, she used to like riding the bus, sometimes all day, with her free bus pass.

Olive then pertinently asked about her pension and Iris produced a payment card from a hidden pocket that she said she carried with her everywhere. After a lecture from Olive, she agreed that she would have to let them know about a change of address, something she had been reluctant to do in case Gavin found out where she was.

'He'll want a piece of the pie,' she said, which had us fidgeting with unease.

Every revelation felt like a stab to the heart and I was aware that she had given us but a few snippets from a much longer story. How did we not even know she had been married? That she was a mother to a not-very-nice-sounding, Pearl? What she left untold, the detail around those snippets, hardly bears thinking about. Little Iris, who, unlike the Halfpenny, has faced up to her life's demons with an indisputably sunny disposition, instead of a thunderous (and self-pitying, while we're at it) black cloud, who brings life-affirming joy to all those around her just by being herself.

And here's a thought.

If Jackson and Nina hadn't hooked up, if Jackson had turned up that night to welcome Callum home, I would never have drunk all the good wine and passed out on the sofa until long past my getting-up-time. I wouldn't have been on that later bus, smelly and hungover, to be rescued by Iris and her Extra Strong Mints. She wouldn't have escorted me to safe port at Claybourne House and met her coffee mentor and friend-for-life, Marco. Iris, when she was forced to leave her home, would not have been able to seek shelter in Feet-of-Clay's back room. We wouldn't have been able to offer her a soft bed and a home, here, in Fulham. Olive would still be living alone, waiting for Jeremy to visit. She might never have taken herself off to Pilates and met Colin.

If Jackson and Nina hadn't hooked up, I myself wouldn't be living here.

So much to be grateful for.

It was in light of this new perspective that I was able to accept that Nina should come tonight. Plus, I know Miles would approve, which feels relevant for some stupid reason. Stupid because we are not even in touch. Well, we are in touch because I have to send him stuff from the boss all the time and Miles, polite to a T, always replies with a succinct, *thanks.* Just that one word. End of. And, while we are on the subject of Miles, in the five weeks since he put 9640 miles between us, there has not been a day that I have not thought about him, sometimes I can't get through an hour without thinking about him and wondering how he is getting on, where he lives, who he lives with, where he goes out, who he goes out with (gulp), and a thousand other useless ponderings.

In short, I am, predictably for some (Kim), suffering a severe case of *you-don't-know-what-you've-got-til-it's-gone-itis.*

There is a knock on my door.

'Stella?'

'Come on in, Olive. I'm nearly ready.'

Olive, resplendent in a pale-yellow jumper over navy cords, glides into the room.

'Crikey, Olive. You're cutting a dash. Adding some sunshine to the proceedings. Now, what can I do for you?'

'I was wondering; do we need to take notes, you know, about the book? Because I haven't got enough note pads for everyone. If necessary, I thought you and I could share.'

'Olive, no one is going to be taking notes. It's just a discussion about the book, what we liked, what we didn't, that kind of thing.'

'I did think we might keep score though. Everyone has to mark the book out of ten and at the end of the season, when everyone has hosted a meeting, we have a winning book. What do you think?'

'I think it's a brilliant idea,' I say, sincerely. 'Adds another dimension.'

It was decided that Olive would choose the first book as it's her house and Iris gets to choose the second book as one of the Book Club's founding directors. After that we will decamp to various other venues around London once a month, finishing back in Beatrice Ave with my book. All-in-all, it is going to take us eight months to finish. A long *season*, as Olive likes to call it.

Nina, as a *guest attendee*, does not get to choose a book. Ever, if I get my way.

Tonight, we will be discussing the finer nuances of Olive's favourite book – The Promise, by Danielle Steele. Never having read a Danielle Steele, I was sceptical beyond all reason, thought myself above such a trashy romantic novel and even went so far as to cover my book with a page from the Evening Standard – sports page - so that no one on the bus could see what I was reading. Only to find, two pages in, that it was unputdownable. I had to start going to the loo at work with my handbag so that I could sneak a few extra pages between bollockings from the boss. Predictably, Clarissa was on to me in a flash, demanding to know why I kept disappearing to the loo for long periods with my handbag.

'Are you tarting yourself up?'

As if. And who for?

Colin is the first to arrive with a very decent Chardonnay and a large bag of cheesy puffs (the kind that get stuck in your teeth), cheeks flushed with excitement, head swathed in a halo of fluffy hair. Iris does the honours with the coat and whisks his offerings off to the kitchen, while Olive escorts him into the living room like a Maître d' in a Michelin starred restaurant, seating him in the corner of the sofa. Next up are Kim and Bart, boisterous as ever, clutching four bottles of wine and enough bags of Kettle Chips to see me comfortably through to Christmas. Hot on their heels is Clarissa, raising the temperature in black leather trousers, so tight they were surely sprayed on earlier by Ringo, and a black lace top cut daringly low, so low, in fact, any sudden movement might result in our very own *Nipplegate.* Although nipple fails to adequately describe the danger. Last – excluding Nina who doesn't count – is Angus. You would think the Aga Khan had arrived judging by the welcome he is given by Olive, walking backwards into the living room in front of him, sweeping her hand dramatically to the best chair in the room, *her* chair, and then dashing over to sweep off any dastardly specks of dust that had had the nerve to alight there in the last ten seconds. Angus sucks it all up amiably, handing Olive two bottles of chilled Veuve Clicquot and stopping to admire Clarissa and shake hands with a star-struck Colin.

Just waiting for Nina, then.

Probably waiting around the corner until we have all settled down so she can make an entrance. I go over to the window and scan the garden. No sign, although that doesn't mean she's not ducked down behind the hedge, counting to a hundred.

Olive and Iris are rotating around the room, plying us with ever greater quantities of nibbles – and at what quantity, pray tell, do nibbles cease to be nibbles and become a three-course meal? Angus is splashing the Veuve and with no one showing the slightest inclination to move onto the wine, he pulls out his phone.

'I'll get Claude to put some in a taxi,' he says. 'I've a fridge full of the stuff.'

'Don't be mad, we've tons of wine,' I say. 'And anyway, who's Claude?'

'My live-in housekeeper,' he says nonchalantly, as if we all have live-in housekeepers.

Although, come to think of it, I *do* have a live-in housekeeper in the form of Olive, now ably abetted by Iris. Since I moved in here, I have done no housework, no washing, almost no ironing and barely any shopping. I used to be able to pick up bits and bobs from Waitrose on the way home, but since Olive got going on the internet, a delivery arrives almost daily. We must be their best customers by far. I keep trying to give her handfuls of money and she keeps giving it back to me, so I have started sneaking twenty-pound notes into her purse when she is not looking and putting folded up tenners into her coat pocket – something I might need to knock on the head since she said to me last week, and I quote, 'I'm losing my marbles, Stella. I keep finding ten-pound notes in my pocket.'

'It's on the way,' says Angus, putting his phone away. 'Four more bottles, just to be on the safe side. It won't take five minutes, it's not far.'

'We're never going to get on to the book at this rate,' says Kim. 'I was up until 2am last night finishing it.'

'She leave it very late,' sighs Bart. 'I finish two weeks ago *and* I see the film.'

Typical.

Such a goodie-two-shoes. I bet he was a right swot at school.

'Well, I have to admit that I wasn't expecting much.' I turn to Olive who has just come back from the kitchen with a fresh plate of cheese straws. 'Then I got hooked. Couldn't put it down. Which is a good thing as there are apparently another one hundred and forty to go.'

'She's written one hundred and forty books?' asks Angus.

'One hundred and forty-one. According to Wikipedia.'

'What is Wikipedia?' asks Olive, looking interested.

'A free online encyclopedia. Written by the people. Anyone can write a Wikipedia page.'

Speak for yourself Angus, I think.

Olive, however, is keen as mustard. 'Oh, I like the sound of that. Could I write a page? What shall I write it about? Something in the garden maybe. Stella, what do you think?'

'Azaleas?' I suggest.

'Technically you can do it but realistically it is a little harder and I think you'll find many pages already written about azaleas.' Angus puts the brakes on our enthusiasm. 'There's a host of guidelines and everything has to be verifiable from third-party sources. What you could do, Olive, is look at the azalea pages and see if there are any mistakes. Anyone can edit a Wikipedia page.'

'Really?' sighs Olive, eyes glowing.

'Absolutely. And you could then call yourself a Wikipedian too.'

Angus is very well-versed on Wikipedia. I'm about to ask how he knows so much about it when the doorbell goes.

Veuve or Nina?

Either way, Olive and Iris are off like terriers after a fox, having a brief tussle in the doorway to be first out. We hear them pulling open the front door and then nothing, an ominous silence. A tiny bubble of insecurity springs into being in my chest, growing exponentially with every passing second until I feel that I might burst. I look at Kim, who looks at Bart, who looks at Angus, who is looking at Clarissa, who is exchanging worried eyebrow lifts with Colin.

'Kim?' a voice warbles from the front hall.

Kim and Bart jump to their feet and disappear. Mumbling voices are heard before Kim comes rushing back to where I am sitting on the Grand Ol' Poof; an ancient, raggedy footrest.

'Stella,' she says in a low, firm voice. 'Calm is your watchword. Time to welcome Nina back into the fold. Now, surrounded by friends and buoyed by buckets of Veuve, is the perfect time.'

Angus then gets up from his throne, comes over and gives me a quick peck on the cheek. 'Remember, Stella, *forgiveness is the attribute of the strong,*' he whispers. 'Mahatma Gandhi.'

Pompous git. I've gone right off him. Again.

There is a hum of hushed murmuring from the hall, a squeak from Olive, a nervous giggle from Iris and here she comes. Nina. Dazzlingly gorgeous, she pauses in the doorway, Olive and Iris hovering behind her like a couple of attending Oompa Loompas, before floating across the room in a cloud of lime and basil and throwing herself at my feet.

A performance worthy of an Oscar.

Bafta at the very least.

Except that a tiny puff of pleasure, no more substantial than a single snowflake, sighs into life at the sight of Nina being so *submissive.* I shake myself, trying to dislodge this

307

compassion before it takes root. I look around the room for help. Someone? Anyone?

Olive.

'That's enough now,' she says firmly, coming over and pulling her upright. 'No point in over doing it. Come along and sit over here with Colin and Clarissa.' She steers Nina towards the sofa, away from where I am sitting. 'We're drinking champagne, kindly supplied by Angus, and Claudio's bringing some more because we've drunk the lot. That's his *butler*, you know. I'll get you a glass.'

She shakes her head. Probably the only part she can still move, so tightly is she wedged between Colin and Clarissa.

'No, thank you. Just a glass of water would be lovely.'

'Oh, for fuck's sake,' I cry. 'Put the halo away and have a glass. It might not be Cris-*tal,* but it's good enough.'

Nina blushes – not something I have been witness to before. 'Er, no, really, just water, thank you, Olive. Lemonade. Anything.'

Something's not right. An elephant has lumbered into the room and everyone is peering around it, pretending it's not there. Nina likes a drink. OK, she doesn't quaff it back like Kim and me, but she would never turn down a glass of champagne.

'What's going on?' I demand. 'Why aren't you drinking?'

'Stella, leave the poor girl alone,' says Kim. 'She doesn't have to drink if she doesn't want to.'

'Yes, she does. And she loves champagne. Go on, Nina, spill. What's with the, *glass of water for me, please.* You're not pregnant, are you?'

Now, I said that out of spite, not out of any belief that she might actually be pregnant, which is why it takes a minute for me to register that Nina's skin has gone from an alabaster lustre to pasty lacklustre. With hint of grey.

Holy crap.

Nina is pregnant.

If you dropped a pin on the carpet right down, I swear you would hear it in Bali. Which is unfortunate. Some general background noise would be useful because there is no avoiding the fact that I am about to laugh, my heart swelling with the righteous justice of this news, bubbles of hilarity fighting to get to the surface. I gulp some champagne, privately celebrating that Nina and Jackson are getting exactly what they have never wanted. A child.

This is what is known as a comeuppance. Isn't that a wonderful word? Comeuppance.

Although, I should really spare a thought for the poor bairn. Desperately unfair having those two as parents.

I take another gulp of celebratory champagne. Jackson, who prides himself on controlling every situation, has failed spectacularly on one of the modern world's most fundamental practices: contraception. Most unlike him. Did he forget? Did she forget? Who forgot what? Then again, what if no one forgot anything and they *planned* this? Wanted this.

'Does Jackson know?' I demand.

'Of course,' she says, looking at her belly – flat as a pancake by-the-way.

Her face gives nothing away. Euphoric. Petrified. Bewildered. Take your pick. Not. A. Clue. She wanted us to know though, because you *do not* come for a night out with us and then refuse a drink without a decent – prepared in advance – excuse. She knows us, she knew we would be on the vino and yet she had the nerve to rock up, turn down the Veuve and then act all coy when we ask, *what-the-fuck?*

'Leave her be, Stells,' says Kim, getting up and going over to her. 'We'll discuss this another time. We're here for book club.' She leans down to give Nina a hug. 'We're here for you,' she adds, in a low voice.

We are so *not*, I think.

'And we're here for you, Stells,' says Clarissa, hoicking up her boobs and giving Nina a dirty look. I blow her a kiss.

Emma Henry

'Olive? Something non-alcoholic?' prompts Kim.

Dumbfounded by the latest Strumpet Show amateur dramatics, it takes Olive a second to gather her wits and find her place again.

'Non-alcoholic. Let me think. Water, of course, tea, or I suppose, if you ask nicely, Iris might let you have some of her Cranberry juice. She had a bout of cystitis last week and we've gallons of the stuff. Sales must have gone through the roof. I even considered buying shares.'

Olive. Legend.

'Do budge up a bit Clarissa,' she goes on, getting into the swing of things. 'A pregnant lady needs a little extra space, though I can't see much of a bump. How far along are you, dear?'

Another pin drop moment.

'Er, fourteen weeks. Give or take.'

We all look up and inspect the ceiling, frantically counting backwards in our heads. Fourteen weeks. Early July. A good few months after they left to start their new life then. A Big Apple baby. A baby apple. I do a quick tour of my psyche, the bit where the emotions are stored. How am I doing? This news should be stirring up a poisonous broth of anger and envy, a pinch of grief, a teaspoon of scorn – but, incredibly, the only thing I feel is relief.

When the doorbell goes again, there is a palpable easing of tensions as we are all given a new focus – more Veuve. Angus tours the room filling glasses, while Olive and Iris press yet more food on everyone, both insisting Nina have seconds as she is eating for two now. They are hard to refuse and she soon has her hands full of quiche and vol au vents, while Colin holds her juice and gets stuck in with some pertinent questions about the father. He immediately realises he has ventured into a mine-field - Jackson is remaining in New York while Nina is moving back to London - his face is a picture as he digests the news and tries to work out if it is good or bad.

'Silence, please.' Kim calls the room to order. 'Quiet, everyone. You too, Colin, you can talk to Nina another time. We all have drinks, we've eaten enough to last us a week, it's time to discuss the book, otherwise we'll never get past the first page. Olive, over to you. Perhaps you'd like to give a brief synopsis to Nina. She hasn't read this month's book, but she'll be on board for the next meet.'

'Maybe she's read it, already. It is a classic after all,' enthuses Olive, grabbing her well-thumbed copy and brandishing it under Nina's nose. 'No? Lucky you, you are in for a treat. Briefly, it's about a couple who fall in love, a trauma, a great deception and a move to New York.'

CHAPTER 30

Black bile
Noun: one of the four humours of ancient and medieval
physiology that was believed to be secreted by the kidneys
and spleen causing melancholy

After a long day in the trenches, I get home to find Olive and
Iris in their Pilates gear - Iris with the addition of her orange
beret - fine tuning the downward dog pose in the living room.
The TV is on and a series of lithe bodies are pretzelling on
yoga mats beside a pool, somewhere hot judging by the blue
sky and the fancy villa in the background. I glance down to the
floor and spot an empty DVD case: *Geri Yoga.*

'Yoga with a Spice girl, is it?' I comment.

'I found it in the Red Cross shop for 50p,' cheeps Iris,
randomly lifting a leg. 'What's a spice girl?'

'You know, that pop group called the Spice Girls. In the
'90s. Posh Spice, Baby Spice, Scary Spice?'

'Oh, yes, I remember them. She's a Spice, is she? Which
one? Yogi Spice?'

I laugh. 'No, Ginger Spice.'

'Ginger is part of the Zingiberaceae family,' puffs Olive,
head now almost touching the floor under her sagging arms.
'I've always hoped that would come up in The Chase.'

'Or Scrabble. You'd win in one go with that.'

'Too long. Thirteen letters,' she pants. 'Do you think you
could help me down. My hip is stuck.'

I ease Olive down. 'I'm not sure that taking up yoga with
a pop star is a sensible idea. You'd be better starting slowly,
with a proper teacher.'

'We were doing well, weren't we, Iris? It's our first session, I'm sure it'll get easier with practice. Are in you tonight? Iris is making fish finger sandwiches, with mushy peas. I've never had a mushy pea.'

'That sounds like my perfect meal, but I'm going to the cinema with Angus. New Jack Reacher film. It premiered last night. Tom Cruise was there doing his usual round of selfies and phone calls to mums around the country. And guess who was there, in the front row?'

'Clarissa!' cries Iris. 'She bought supplies from us before she went.'

'Too right. She took the afternoon off work and camped out.'

'Did she get a good selfie with the Cruise man?' Olive asks. She has been practicing her selfies but has only managed to capture an ear or half an eyebrow to date.

'Of course. She'd have tackled him to the floor if necessary. She didn't drink for two days to make sure she wouldn't need to go the loo and lose her spot. Right, I'd better go and get changed. I've got about five minutes.'

I discard my muted office wear and flick unenthusiastically through my wardrobe for something to wear, a decision made harder by a total lack of inspiration; which about summarises my relationship with Angus. After the giddy highs I enjoyed in my short time with Miles, time with Angus is failing to reach the same elevations. He is kind and generous, undemanding, and I have been more than happy to have him wine me, dine me and boost the flagging ego. But, the other stuff......

Passion?

Kissing?

Desire?

All absent.

Passionate kissing in a dingy shop doorway, aflame with desire? Not gonna happen. And it's not just me. Thus far,

Angus has shown no sign whatsoever of wanting to unleash his inner Miles as we have walked the streets of London.

Bloody Miles. Kim has taken to channelling her inner Kylie at every opportunity and singing, 'Can't get you out of my head.' Which does little to help. Mainly because it is true. I can't dislodge him, those killer eyes haunting me night and day, and it's unlikely to get better over the coming weeks either; because he is back.

The wanderer has returned. He has yet to honour us with his presence in the office though, having been awarded time off for good behaviour. Pure, unadulterated favouritism, if you ask me. Clarissa and Ringo met him for a drink earlier in the week – no, I wasn't invited – and reported back that he looked great, Hong Kong was great, work was great, every-fucking-thing was great, although he is relieved to be back on home soil. I chose to take that as a positive until Clarissa added a pointed, 'I mean, fuck, you really pissed him off, eh, Stells!'

'Hello?' Iris taps on the door. 'Angus is here. Are you coming down?' She peers in to find me still procrastinating in bra and pants.

'Can't decide what to wear, Iris.' I flop onto the bed, hugging a pillow to me.

She tuts at me. 'You've plenty to choose from in here.' She disappears into my wardrobe, flicking through hangers and saying quietly, no, no, no, no, no, no....... 'Oh, this is lovely. Wear this.' She pulls out a turquoise tie-die beach kaftan, designed to wear over a swimsuit to cover up.

'That's for the beach, Iris. I can't wear it in Leicester Square, on a Friday night. I'll be the laughing stock. It's only the cinema; jeans will be fine. I'll let you choose the top.'

She grumps a bit and reluctantly returns to the wardrobe, humming, no, no, no, no, no, until, with a triumphant cry, she emerges with a dark red fitted shirt with ruffles down the front and on the cuffs. I love it but have never worn it. Never dared. Far too bright, far too, *Here I am!*

Which is not something the Halfpenny is comfortable with.

However, I said she could choose and we are running out of time so I agree to give it a go.

Angus is gamely drinking sherry with Olive and Iris when I come down, hair neatly combed into its usual submissive side parting, freshly shaved, pristine shirt, tie and blazer completing the picture. Taking him in, I get a sharp pang for faded jeans, an untucked shirt and a hint of five o'clock shadow. A pang I have to stuff away out-of-sight before it gets a grip on the evening. There is an appreciative buzz of approval for my red shirt, Iris proudly informing everyone that she picked it out. Personally, I feel over-dressed despite the jeans and more than a little *mutton.*

'Quick sherry, Stella?' asks Olive. 'Is that a new shirt? You've not worn that before.'

'I'm not sure if we've got time,' I say, ignoring the comment about my shirt. I have a whole wardrobe of clothes that Olive has never seen and never will. Like most women, indeed Olive herself, I only wear a fraction of the clothes that I have handed over my hard-earned cash for. 'Hadn't we better get going?' I look to Angus who shakes his head.

'Loads of time. I'll call a cab to pick us up. That way we can drink sherry with these two lovely ladies until it arrives.'

Angus has reserved tickets up in the royal circle of the cinema, three rows back from the front. He apologises profusely for having failed to get the first row, but I have no complaints. This is my first time up here and the seats are so comfy I would happily stay for a week. We settle in, passing a plate of greasy nachos back and forth, sipping diet Cokes and watching the seats fill up around us with a healthy cross-section of London society. Power to Jack Reacher for his broad appeal, or maybe it's just Tom Cruise. No one can resist Tom Cruise these days. The lights go down and we are blasted by sound as the vast screen bursts into life and it looks as if I have the perfect place with two empty seats in front of me for an uninterrupted view. I settle down for the trailers; one of the best things about watching a film on the big screen, even if I have been to see more than one film based entirely on the riveting trailer, only to find that the trailer *is* the film or the only bits of the film worth watching.

We are half way through a preview for a Second World War film called Hacksaw Ridge when two silhouettes make their way along the row in front of us provoking a salvo of sighs from the people already seated. Grieving the loss of the empty seats in front of me, I pray silently that I get a David and not a Goliath. As they search about in the dark for the pull-down seats, I realise that a clear view is the least of my worries.

It is Miles.

Miles and a perky young blond. At least that is what I can make out in the flickering light of the screen as Andrew Garfield staggers along with another bloody body on his back.

I don't watch any of the film. Can't watch the film. There is a far more compelling storyline playing out here, live, in the audience. Their heads come together repeatedly in whispered exchanges, Miles's mouth against her ear, her mouth against his, a lingering kiss on his cheek, back to the film, another murmured sweet-fucking-nothing that cannot possibly wait until THE END OF THE FILM.......

Breathe, Stella, breathe. I glance sideways to see if Angus has noticed my agitation, but his gaze is firmly on the big screen. Eyes back to the loving couple, now wedged together as if seeking maximum contact. They'll need a private booth soon, if such a thing exists, and I have to bite back from shouting, *Get a room!*

I need air.

Standing up abruptly, I push past Angus, barreling my way along the row, knocking knees, treading on handbags and, ooops, there goes someone's drink.

The harsh artificial light in the toilets is unforgiving, highlighting every anguished furrow and groove. My face seems to have aged ten years and is now the embodiment of *distraught*. Or possibly overwrought. Both. I wet a paper towel and dab at my forehead, the back of my neck, between my sweaty breasts, which are heaving up and down as if I have just done a shift with the Sergeant Major, heart hammering at double speed.

Is this a panic attack?

A heart attack?

A broken-heart attack?

Whatever it is, I am not enjoying it. Dizzy with anguish, I start circling the small space as the present and the past meet; namely, me watching the *love-of* canoodling with someone else. Someone who is not me. How can I be back here, again? Have I made no progress at all? Why am I pining for a man who doesn't want me? What is it about the human condition that makes us fall in love with people who don't fall in love with us?

Or, for that matter, why do we throw away golden opportunities with the likes of Golden Boy when handed to us on a plate?

The return to my seat is a more refined affair, mainly because I really don't want Miles to be alerted to my presence. Stealthy as a cat after an unsuspecting mouse, I slide into my seat, taking care to calm my breathing before allowing my eyes to focus on the action. I see immediately that the plot has moved on without me. The hero now has his arm around the lithesome heroine, holding her close, her head upon his shoulder. I then watch, hynotised (horrified), as she puts her hand to his face and pulls him towards her, giving him a lingering kiss. There is tongue involved, I am certain of it. I can feel it.

When the credits finally roll, I don't even attempt to disguise my relief, jumping to my feet before the lights are up.

Now we can get a drink and mine's a double. Repeat many times until unconscious.

'Stella?' says a surprised Angus, his cut-glass accent carrying easily over the continuing soundtrack.

I shush at him to keep it down.

'Stella?' he all but bellows.

Damn and blast. Subtle as a blood foghorn and, predictably, Miles swivels around in his seat, swearing under his breath as he clocks who it is and quickly returning his gaze to the closing credits. Desperation building, I try a light shoulder charge.

Angus looks at me in confusion. 'What is it? What's wrong?'

'Nothing,' I hiss, peering over his shoulder at the traffic jam between me and the stairway to freedom.

'You're standing on my foot now. Ow. Oh, hello, Miles, didn't see you there. What a coincidence.' Angus stretches past me to shake hands. 'Look who it is, Stella.' Then he turns his attention to Blondie. 'Hello, are you with Miles? Angus. And this is Stella.' He physically turns me about. 'Did you enjoy the film?'

'Not much to be honest,' says Miles, shrugging dismissively.

'It's hard to enjoy a film when your attention is elsewhere,' I snip, unsure whether I am talking about Miles or myself.

'I'm Chloe,' says Blondie, not wanting to be left out.

I take the opportunity to study her for a second and see instantly that Blondie is the wrong name; she is a Babe. Babeness is coming off her in waves. She is standing as if posing, her head tilted to one side in a blatantly coquettish move that deserves a swift kick to the shins. Her long hair is pulled over one shoulder in a wavy mass that falls invitingly over her luscious boobs. My hair never *falls* like that; it springs, expands, fluffs, except when greasy when it flops and sags, but it never falls.

'Shall we all go for a drink?' asks Angus, stunningly oblivious to the treacherous undercurrents swirling around us.

Miles, catching my appalled expression, decides to turn the screw. 'Yeah, why not.'

Babe claps her hands in delight. 'Oooh, goodie,' she simpers, clutching at Miles.

'Great. I know a fantastic wine bar just a couple of streets away. A refreshing glass of rosé is just what the doctor ordered, right, Stella?'

'That film has wiped me out, Angus. Enough excitement for one night. I'm going to head home.'

'Come on, Stella. It's not like you to turn down a glass of wine Is it Miles?'

He shrugs. Not bothered. 'Go home, if you're tired. Chloe and I will take Angus for a drink.'

I look at him gazing fondly down at Chloe and something rebels inside of me.

'Actually, a glass of wine is a great idea,' I say to Angus, brushing a non-existent speck of dust off his shoulder. 'Wouldn't be fair to leave you on your own, sweetie pie.' I keep my voice a flat neutral, with just an edge of saccharin.

We go to Vendange in Frith Street, a five-minute walk, which feels more like a marathon with my racing heart and wobbly legs. How should I play this? Cool and aloof? Hot and flirty (with Angus, duh)? Bored? Life and soul? I simply have no clue and am no closer to a clue when we get to the wine bar and Angus instructs us all to wait outside, while he goes in to see if there is a free table.

Which leaves me alone with Miles and Babe. Not something I had bargained for. She still has her hand tucked in to his arm as if she doesn't want to let go. Not that I can blame her; with the benefit of hindsight, I can appreciate that you should hang on for all you are worth. To distract myself, I take out my phone and hunt about for something that needs my immediate attention. With no messages or WhatsApps, I open up a new anagram app I have been using to challenge Olive and type in *milesandchloe.*

Ha! You couldn't make it up.

Melancholies.

A loud bark of ironic laughter escapes me before I have any hope of catching it and I look up to find the Melancholies looking at me with that annoyed expression people adopt when someone else is laughing - and you don't know why.

'Care to share?' Miles asks.

I wave him away. 'Inside joke. Wouldn't make sense.'

'Nothing ever does with you,' he mumbles, his voice so low I hardly catch it.

Flailing about for a suitably stinging reply, I am saved by the reappearance of Angus announcing that we have a table and we need to get a shuffle on before someone else nabs it.

Turns out shuffle is the right word because the place is packed and any movement faster than a shuffle would be inadvisable. Our table is in the back corner, up against a giant wine rack that covers the entire wall, top to bottom, left to right, hundreds of bottles of vino inches from my out-of-joint nose. As we settle in, Angus opposite Miles, me facing Chloe, a striking woman wends her way gracefully between the crowds to our table. She puts an arm around Angus, dropping a kiss onto his head, as I take a minute to admire. Her face is tanned and deeply lined, her skin free of make-up bar a sweep of mascara framing her dark eyes, her hair is a salt and pepper mix and tied up in a messy bun. She is wearing a loose-fitting silk shirt tucked into tight jeans and cowboy boots. She looks amazing, I think, wondering if I could get away with those cowboy boots.

'What can I get you guys?' she asks, her accent more Newquay than Nashville despite the boots. 'I've a superb new Syrah from Washington State if you're happy with a red. And a cheese platter? That suit you?'

'Shauna, you always know best, so, if that suits you guys?' Angus looks to us for approval.

'Perfect,' from Miles.

A nod and a thumbs-up from me.

We all look at Chloe, expecting her approval. But no. Babe has to be different.

'I'll have a white please. Red gives me a terrible headache. Full of sulphates, you know,' she says confidently and I enjoy a tiny window of reprieve from her perfection as I am pretty sure it is white wine that packs a higher sulphate count.

'What kind of white would you like, Chlo?' asks Miles. *Chlo.*

'Dry please. As a bone. Have you got a Sauvignon Blanc from New Zealand? Cloudy Bay, Dog Point, Greywacke? Any of those would be super. I was there, you know, backpacking,' she kindly reveals to the table at large. 'Drank gallons of the stuff.'

Backpacking? For fuck's sake, not a *gap year student?*

'Or Chile?' She isn't done yet. 'How about a Montes Outer Limits? We went for a tasting when I was in Santiago. Only two hours or so by car. Have you been?' This was addressed to Shauna who declined to reply, contenting herself with a withering, bone dry, glare instead.

An ex-gap year student, I have discovered. In fact, there is little I know don't know about the Chlo. She is one of life's sharers.

At twenty-four she is officially ten years younger than me and only two years past the magical "twenty-two" that appeals to all age groups of the opposite sex. And while I should be enjoying a satisfying, *I told you so,* to all and sundry who refused to listen when I said I was too old for Miles, all I feel is physically sick and in desperate need of a cup of tea, preferably while sitting quietly on Olive's moth-eaten sofa. Half a wheel of cheddar and a kilo of brie might well have contributed to the general nausea but most of it can be attributed to the *Chlo.* She

321

has been painfully cloying and annoying all night, but I am the only one at the table with enough wits about me to appreciate it. Both Miles and Angus abandoned theirs some time ago and are reverently sipping from the youthful elixir of the *Chlo*.

I expected nothing different from Miles, having anticipated such an eventuality from the off, but Angus?

First there was the wine, which she made such a song and dance about I thought I had stumbled into an episode of Strictly. All the while pretending to be a wine buff with an extensive knowledge of all things Sauvignon, especially if they were Blanc, only to reveal her complete ignorance when she turned down the Sancerre recommended by Shauna.

'Lovely, I'm sure, but I'd really like to stick to a Sauvignon,' she said.

Duh. Even I know that Sancerre is a world-famous Sauvignon Blanc and I don't know a lot; it was one of the few whites Jackson would allow across the threshold.

Then there was the food. Instead of hovering up the most heavenly selection of cheese this side of Paris, she announced, proudly, that she was vegan. A gluten-free vegan. Which put paid to the feast of bread and cheese on offer. Shauna gamely offered a variety of delicacies – all an anathema to our Chlo - before finally settling on a selection of raw vegetables and an olive tapenade.

I considered doing everybody a favour and stabbing her with a cheese knife. Only the thought of both Miles and Angus pulling out all the stops to save her held me back.

At one point, I tried to share a sarcastic eye-roll with Angus, seeking an ally, but he was out-of-reach, mesmerised by her peachy skin and sparkling eyes, oblivious to the artifice. He even outed a new laugh, one I had never heard before, a fake sounding guffaw more suited to a spotty teen than a forty-plus landowner. We were forced to endure an endless monologue about her travels, no one else being able to get a word in edgeways, travels that had clearly involved less backpacking than your average gap year student and more – by a considerable margin –*Abercrombie & Kent* style luxury. There is now little point me going to New Zealand, or Cambodia, or Vietnam, or South America, I know everything there is to know about them and I have been forced to look at a hundred photos. Any future joy I might have had discovering these places, amongst others, has been obliterated under the flood of detail and minutia that she inflicted upon us.

Then we got to her studies at the London School of Economics – 'I got a First,' she giggled, with zero shame - her post-grad diploma at Oxford and her sky-rocketing career in Marine Insurance, where she somehow cleverly combines making vast amounts of money with saving the dolphin. No one loves a dolphin more than Chloe, she has a connection (yes, really), an affinity that few (if any) share. She swam with them so often on her travels, it's a miracle she didn't grow a couple of fins.

It was ex-cru-ti-fucking-ating.

To avoid making a scene with the cheese knife, I ate. In fact, I gorged. No one else was eating much anyway, too busy hanging on to her every word, and it would have been rude not to finish all that di-vine cheese and rapturous bread. I washed it all down with industrial quantities of Syrah, sending up a prayer every now and then for the earth to open and swallow me whole.

'And how did you two meet?' Angus enquired benevolently. A lecherous uncle to his favourite niece.

A question I was dying to ask but you would have had to have pulled out my fingernails before I said the words.

'On the plane home,' she drawled, gazing at Miles. 'Daddy treated me to business class.'

'Of course, he did,' I snapped, a spikey edge to my voice. I tried to soften it by asking if they had a nice Sauvignon Blanc on the wine list, which got me nothing but a terse, 'Stella, leave it,' from Miles.

So, I did.

I left.

I didn't storm out as that would have given way too much ammunition to the Chlo and she already had enough in her arsenal. I pleaded gross fatigue, which wasn't far from the truth given the amount of food I had shipped, declined Angus's half-hearted offer to accompany me, accepted his offer of a taxi, pointedly left fifty quid on the table as no one was going to pay for my night of misery except me, and stepped out gratefully into the cold November night to wait for Neil, my Uber driver.

CHAPTER 31

Injudicious
/ˌɪn.dʒuːˈdɪʃ.əs/
Adjective: showing lack of judgment; imprudent; indiscreet

Not for the first time, I consider asking Bob for a swig of whatever it is he has in that hip flask. Miles is back in today and we can expect a welcome fit for Hollywood royalty, all that is missing is a red carpet. Even the boss has arrived early – the last thing I need this morning – sporting a new, badly fitting, waistcoat, complete with a watch on a chain. Every time he squelches out of his office to ask if the globetrotter has arrived yet, he makes a point of taking out the watch and polishing it. I am certain he is hoping I will comment on it, something I have not the slightest intention of doing.

Looking at my empty coffee cup, I decide now would be a good time to get a refill. I'll take the stairs, all twelve floors, and with luck miss the whole caboodle. Six floors down, I start regretting my decision. I had forgotten how tiresome walking down stairs in heels is. The only time I have done them before was during a fire drill, when, knowing it wasn't for real, I took my leisurely time only to be given a rudely sarcastic welcome by the fireman in charge.

'Were we toasting marshmallows and singing Kumbaya, Madam?' he asked, as I wandered into the deserted lobby.

When I get back with a new coffee and a flapjack from Iris, the entire office is clustered around Miles's desk. Deciding it best to keep my head down and not court the pain and humiliation that will no doubt be tracking me down at some point, I decide to stay at my desk, ploughing through the never-

325

ending emails. Once today is over, it will get easier, slowly but surely, day-by-day, it will get better.

'Stells?'

'Hey, Clarissa.' I look up reluctantly. I don't want to know. Whatever it is.

'You coming for a drink after work?' she asks, carefully. Just a quickie. For Miles. Celebrate his return,'

'I don't think he wants me there, Clarissa. I'll leave it for tonight. Maybe next time.'

'Don't be silly, of course he wants you there. We're a team. This isn't a personal thing, it's a work thing. We all work together and you should be there. People will notice anyway, if you're not, and ask questions.'

'What if I've got a prior engagement?'

'You haven't though.'

'Yeah, well, no one knows that.'

'I do.'

I sigh, watching Clarissa's open face. She's right, people will notice. Better by far to blend in, be one of the crowd. 'OK, just the one though.'

She shows me her dimples and glides back to her desk, pretending to do some work for a couple of minutes before easing her way over to Miles again, detouring via the photocopier to disguise her movements.

Let's look on the bright side.

As it is a work do: the Chlo won't be there.

Then again.

There she is, already wrapped around Miles by the time I get to the Bunch of Grapes. I was persuaded into this drink because we are a team, hooray, work colleagues, hooray, mining buddies, hooray, so what the fuck is she doing here?

'Stells? What're you having? Bob says there's enough in the swear box for one round.' Ringo stops me as I edge around the bar, trying to put as much distance between myself and Miles as possible.

'Gin and tonic. Double.'

I wasn't going to drink. If there is one day of the week when you shouldn't drink, it is Monday, yet here I am ordering a double. Pricey too, but as I am responsible for at least half of the cash in the swear box, I think it's fair. Ringo hands me a glass filled with ice, lemon and Gordons, along with a bottle of tonic. I splash a little in, not too much; if I am having this drink, I want to taste it. I need to taste it. Need that bitter bite of juniper to cut through the ignominy of the Melancholies.

Clarissa comes over and taps her glass with mine.

'Great way to start the week, don't you think? We should do this more often. Hey, Son, get over here and we'll have a girl's toast.'

Sonia, in dormouse gear not Goth gear, comes over and we clink and drink.

Clarissa then clears her throat, while giving a surreptitious nudge to Sonia. Oh, crap, what's coming now?

'We were thinking,' she says, 'that the Christmas party should be for plus-ones this year. Everyone should bring their other half.'

I look at her in furious horror. 'Some of us don't have *other halves,* thanks very much for asking. No plus-ones available. Like this drink,' I say slowly, trying to tamp down my anger, 'the Christmas party is meant to be for us, the workers, to get together and have a knees-up. If we invite other halves then it totally changes the dynamic.'

'Son was really hoping Barnaby could come. It'll be fun. We've never done it before. Robyn is working on some top-secret venue with dancing. At least it will be more fun than a restaurant and some rotten turkey and brussels.'

'Clay will never agree,' I say, scrabbling about for an excuse. 'Too expensive. All those extra people to pay for.'

'Well, actually,' says Clarissa, hesitating for one...two...three seconds before going on. 'Robyn's asked Mr Clay and he's agreed.'

'And your point in asking me, if it is a fait accompli, is?'

'I wanted you to feel involved. You've been very quiet lately. Feels like we're losing you again and we don't want to lose you.'

There is a pause while I absorb this and quickly grasp that there is only one acceptable reaction. 'You know what, you're right. Boring old turkey dinner, berk. And it's about time I met Barnaby properly.'

Sonia's face is transformed by her smile. She should try it more often, although her second life as a Goth probably requires her not to smile. Confusing. But I made the right decision, for once, surprising even myself. As Miles so pertinently put it before his departure, not everything revolves around me. And I refuse to go back to the aloof office grump that I embraced during the Jackson era.

'Oh, ma days,' drawls Clarissa, attempting an accent from the Deep South....not altogether successfully. 'Ah do de-clayer, Miss Steella is jee-oining the purrrrty.' She gives Sonia a high five. 'We were worried you'd be cross what with Miles bringing Chloe and everything,' she blurts, truth spilling out in her relief. 'Who will you bring? Angus?'

'Actually, I think I'll come on my own. I can keep an eye on Iris then.'

'She's bringing Olive,' she babbles, then seeing my face adds quickly, 'I only asked her today, so don't get your knickers in a twist.'

'All the more reason to come on my own. Those two are a right handful together, they'll be swinging from the light fittings and practicing their yoga on the bar.' Then I have an idea. 'I know, I could bring Colin!'

'You should find someone more your own age,' states Sonia, emerging from her Monday vow of silence. I swear I haven't heard her speak all day. 'I could ask Barnaby if he knows someone. Kind of blind date.'

'Yes!' screeches Clarissa. 'Son, you're a genius. A blind date, such fun.'

'Oh, yeah, right, with you lot all watching from the sidelines. An absolute riot,' I deadpan.

'Just think, it could be the start of something, you know, *special*. Call him now, Son.'

This is what happens when you drink large G&Ts on a Monday; you end up with a blind date for the office party called Aaron. Barnaby sent a photo; he looked OK and I capitulated. Actually, he looked more than OK: dark untroubled eyes, cute smile, longish hair. Bohemian. Nothing like Miles and the antithesis of all things Jackson, which was encouraging, so I recklessly agreed.

Then Barnaby asks for a photo of me. I am never at my best at the end of a day pandering to Feet-of so Clarissa sends me off to the loos for a refresh and then puts my photo through one of her selfie airbrushing apps.

'You can't send that,' I object. 'It looks nothing like me. Even I don't know it's me. Tone it down a bit, or he's going to be very disappointed. Just make me look a teeny bit nicer than normal so that he doesn't get cold feet before the big day.'

She does no such thing and Aaron now thinks he has a date with Elle MacPherson.

Another G&T later – I know, I know – I am feeling so empowered by my grown-up behaviour that I go and say hello to Chloe, and by default, Miles. Besides, ignoring her all night will only highlight how much I dislike, am intimidated by, am humiliated by, am driven to thus unscaled heights of envy by...

'Stella,' she growls. 'I was wondering when you were going to come and say hello.'

Now, I could reply that I was wondering the same thing, instead, as the adult, I smile sweetly. 'Sorry, got distracted planning the office party with Clarissa. Are you going to be joining us?'

'Of course, wouldn't miss it. Who can resist an office Christmas party? Especially when you get to go on the arm of the office hunk.' She gives Miles a wink, leaving me just enough time to cringe in private before she turns back to me. 'Are you coming with Angus?'

'No, I'm coming with Aaron.' And as the words leave my lips, I send up a quick prayer of thanks for Clarissa and Sonia and Barnaby. My eyes are fixed on Chloe so it is hard to see if Miles reacts to this news and, by the time I flick my eyes over for a quick assessment, he has turned his attention to George who is at the bar buying drinks.

Not bothered, would be my assessment.

Time to turn my attention to pastures new.

Starting with Aaron.

CHAPTER 32

Rehabilitate
/riː hə ˈbɪlɪ teɪt/
Verb: restore (someone) to former privileges or acceptance after a period of disfavour

Venue
Diamond Jubilee Tea Salon
Fortnum & Mason

Clinging on to my new grown-up persona like a life-raft in heavy seas, I have agreed to tea with Nina - and Kim (phew) - at the above, super-swanky venue. Nina invited us and the recently matured Stella accepted graciously. I can't fight Nina any longer; the prodigal is back. With baggage. Serious baggage in the form of the baby Ninja growing steadily in the still-flat Nina tum. We are not back to where we were pre-Hemplewood, but we are on the way. Kim created a new WhatsApp group for the three of us and a steady flow of mundane chit-chat has trickled in, including the invitation to tea. My immediate reaction, before the grown-up Stella reasserted herself, was, *you are fucking kidding me. Afternoon tea!* It was all too familiar with the Hemplewood fiasco for me until I remembered that Nina, pregnant, is hardly going to be game-on for a night out on the vino.

So, tea it is.

Nina is there when I arrive with no sign of Kim, which leaves the two of us, one-on-one, face-to-face, tête-à-tête, eeek. Unease crawls uninvited into my gut. Is this a set-up? Is Jackson going to slither out of the woodwork to brag about his progeny

331

and force-feed me house champagne? I look around urgently for Kim.

'Stella? Stella?'

Nina is on her feet, watching me warily. I don't move, can't move, so she slides out from behind the table and comes over to me.

'You look lost,' she says. 'I'm so glad you could make it.' And with that, she steps forward and pulls me into an embrace. I have half a second to react, a shred of time to hug the life-raft tighter and go with the current. As she holds me, everything about her is familiar, that perfume, the smell of her hair, the shape of her...except, wait, there it is, a pressure against my belly. I pull back, a smile tweaking my mouth. I haul it back in; can't be caving in too quickly.

'What?'

'Show me,' I demand.

'What?'

'Don't be coy. I can feel it. The baby Ninja. She's growing.'

'Ninja?' She is smiling now, hand to her belly.

Dammit, now I am smiling. It's a fucking love-in.

'That's what I call the bubba. Clever, no?'

'What's clever?' Kim is here, also smiling. If Devon were here, we would be in with a shout for a Colgate commercial.

'The baby Ninja. It's what I call her.' I poke Nina gently in the stomach. Then, daringly, I lay my hand against her and there is a perceptible bulge; not unlike my own tummy after a Domino's pizza, in fact.

'I won't be able to hide it for much longer And, anyway, how do you know it's a girl?'

'I don't,' I say. 'I've always thought of it as a girl. Not that I've thought about it, her, much, although I have of course, more than I wanted to, and there was never any question that it might be a boy, always a girl for some reason.' Nina and Kim arc watching me. Still smiling. 'Besides, Jackson would want a boy and we can't have him getting what he wants, can we?'

That breaks the spell. Smiles are pulled in, stowed. Frowns are installed in their place.

'What?' I cry. 'It's true. I bet he wants a boy. He does, doesn't he? Did he say?'

'Stella,' says Kim, crossly. 'Leave it.'

'No, I won't. If we are to be friends again then everything is on the table. No secrets. No taboo subjects. No hiding.'

A waiter comes and ushers us back to our table. We are spoiling the décor planted in the middle of the room like that, arguing. We all order tea and whatever delights the patisserie chef has cobbled together. Then Kim asks if we should have champagne.

'We're celebrating. We're back together. The three of us. Let's have champagne. Nina can have a sip and you and I will finish the rest.' She looks to me, expecting confirmation, but not this time.

'I'm going to CrossFit later. I promised Cliff.'

'Who is Cliff?' Nina looks interested.

'A man mountain who does CrossFit with us. We love him, don't we Kim? Everyone does, even if he is the teacher's pet.'

'Is he, you know, boyfriend material?'

'No, that was James,' says Kim. 'Although we haven't seen him for months now, have we Stells?'

'He's moved by to Singapore?'

'Singapore? Who is James bloke?' asks Nina.

'Just a man I met in CrossFit.' I dismiss James with a wave of my hand. He is, after all, history, and we never even got off the ground really.

'More than *just a man*. He was Stella's Knight in Shining, the very spit of Idris Elba, seriously sexy guy who stepped up and rescued her from a delicate situation.'

I need to clarify things here. 'Delicate situation? Delicate? You mean an intensely painful, humiliating and degrading situation than no one, not one person except James, lifted so much as a little finger to help me extricate myself. Kim stood around doing sweet FA, howling with laughter.'

'It *was* funny, but I'm not proud. I shouldn't have laughed and I should have helped you. Although, if I had, you'd never have met James. All those nights out on the rosé. He was a right dish,' she says to Nina. 'Quaffing with our Stells on a regular basis and giving her private tours around the gym equipment. They never exchanged bodily fluids, so she says - '

'Eoowww, Kim, that's gross. Not at the table, over tea and cakes. Fuck, Nina's gone white as a sheet. Are you alright?' I start fanning her with the menu. 'Is something wrong? Morning sickness? Afternoon puking? Kim, this is all your fault, *do something.*'

Nina takes a deep breath and puts up a hand to still my frantic waving. 'I am absolutely fine. Just got a little dizzy.'

'You don't look fine.'

'Just give me a minute. It happens sometimes.'

'Why does it happen?' I demand, fanning again.

'Because I'm pregnant, Stella. Now quit with that bloody thing. It's like being sat next to a wind farm.'

With a little colour returning to her cheeks, we chat about this and once Nina has got a cup of tea inside her, along with a doll-size strawberry tart, I decide it is her turn for some mild interrogation.

'OK. Let's get down to the nitty gritty. *You* are here. Jackson, I understand, is in New York. What's the deal? The real deal? You implied at book club that, well, that it's over. But knowing Jackson, and I know Jackson, there is no way he is going to let a child housing his DNA come into the world without getting involved. No way, José.'

She shakes her head.

'Is he interested at all?' I ask.

'Not,' says Nina, succinctly. 'Which suits me just fine. I don't want him involved. At all. Ever.'

Fuck. Right. Ok then. Honeymoon well and truly over.

Then again, how will he ever stay away if he knows part of him – *the great Lysander-Perry* - is out there?

'He might not be showing an interest now, but when she is here, the baby Ninja, he'll want to take over. I'd put my house on it. Olive's house.'

'Stella,' say Nina, softly. 'He tried very hard to make me get rid of it. We flew back here, to London. I didn't want to risk anyone at work in New York finding out and we went to a clinic, twice, but I couldn't go through with it. I just wasn't sure. I didn't know...I was so confused. It was awful, Stella. He pushed and pushed, and the more he pushed, the harder I wanted to push back. You can imagine how well that went. In the end, when I refused to go through with it, he flew back to New York in a rage, said he'd have nothing to do with it and if I wanted any child maintenance, he'd fight me all the way.'

'Bastard,' says Kim.

Nina shakes her head. 'I don't want him near my child. It has nothing to do with him now. I don't want him in my life and I'm sorry I was ever stupid enough to think I did.'

CHAPTER 33

Fool's paradise
/ˌfuːlz ˈpær.ə.daɪs/
Noun: to be happy because you do not know or will not accept how bad things really are

What was I thinking? Bringing an unknown plus-one to the office Christmas party. Sure, I have Barnaby's word that he is a good guy, except I don't actually know Barnaby either. Sonia likes him – a lot – but as someone in possession of a dual-personality and a set of fangs for nights out, I can't be sure that she is a reliable witness.

All good intentions to meet for a drink beforehand - to get to know each other - came to nothing as Aaron decided, without bothering to consult me, that it would be more fun not to. There is one small, teeny weeny, advantage to this plan in that he won't realise I look nothing like Elle MacPherson until the night in question, which gives him less room to engineer a cop-out.

On the other hand.

What. The. Fuck.

Clarissa and Sonia are sworn to secrecy. Even Olive and Iris don't know that I have never met the already infamous Aaron. He has made quite a name for himself around the office since our drinks in the Bunch a few short weeks ago and is now universally known as *Stella's new man* - no one seems interested in his real name, although they do want to know what he looks like. As I have only seen one picture of him myself, it's not hard to play it vague, keeping the focus on his character and innate kindness. This means that everyone is now convinced he is what might be termed *a character actor,* as opposed to leading man material.

Against all expectations to the contrary, the boss has allowed us to finish a whole hour early so that we can get ready for his big bash, due to be held at The Laboratory. This is a less-than-salubrious joint that triples as a bar/restaurant/nightclub – thus excelling in none of them - with a resident DJ named PyscO. A legitimate question would be whether this is a suitable venue for an office Christmas party? Not that it will be exclusively a Claybourne Estates gig; no, it has been agreed with The Laboratory that we worker bees will have the run of the place until 9.30pm, after which time it will be open to all-comers. Robyn tried to sell this to us as an amazing deal until John in accounts called her out and revealed that it never usually opens until 10pm and no one ever turns up before 11pm. At the absolute earliest.

So, here I am, in the office loos, with Clarissa and Sonia, donning our finery and sipping Prosecco from plastic cups. Robyn, *on it* as usual, came up with the highly original idea of a black and white dress-code, supposedly to distinguish us from all the other people wearing black and white. Although – and I say this in the strictest confidence as it goes against the grain to agree with anything that Robyn says – I am happy with black. Wearing black is like eating comfort food or lying on the sofa in pyjamas, drinking tea. It is easy, undemanding, manageable. Likewise, Clarissa and Sonia, putting on their out-of-office personas one false eyelash at a time, are entirely happy with black as they transform in to a dominatrix style sex-bomb and a Goth. Respectively. As for me, after a hopeless trawl through my wardrobe and on the off-chance that Aaron is worth dressing-up for, I have splashed out on a gorgeous long, black halter-neck dress, so outrageously flattering it would have been a crime to have left it in the shop. There is some particularly ingenious panelling from boob-to-butt that, in combination with my carefully engineered underwear, secures the entire wobbling mid-section in a firm but breathable embrace. The halter-neck gives me awesome boobs, my arms are miraculously - courtesy of CrossFit - free of bingo-wing and, despite a thigh high split in the skirt, the Halfpenny legs are under wraps.

As good as it is ever going to get.

Without fancy hair or complicated make-up to worry about, I am ready long before the others, so I sit on one of the loos with the door open, drinking Prosecco and offering free commentary and unsolicited advice.

'Your stockings aren't straight, Clarissa. Bit more, bit more, back a bit. There, you've got it.'

'No extra padding needed. You've got plenty going on there.'

'I think one dog collar is enough, Son. Less is more. Unless you're Clarissa, of course.'

'I can see your bra. Now, I can see your nipple. You can't go like that; the boss will have a coronary.'

Then, just when I think we are finally ready to leave, they set to work on me. My hair and make-up are deemed insufficient if I am to dazzle Aaron – ie. I am so unlike the photo Clarissa sent through, he will never recognise me. Their work is both exhilarating and unsettling. My hair is urged into a sleekly towering up-do and sprayed into place with such assiduity there is no chance of it moving for a week, while my face is transformed by Sonia's liberal hand with the slap. My eyes are kohled into smoky submission and my lips are red and surprisingly pouty, my skin smooth and pale as a carapace of some of the market's most sought after make-up is plastered on. I look fantastic.

Nothing like myself but fantastic all the same.

Ringo, hip in a black and grey checked suit, is waiting for us when we eventually emerge from the loos and we make our way to a pub where we are to meet Barnaby and Aaron. The Dog and Whistle – more dog than whistle - is heaving with

Friday night drinkers celebrating the arrival of the weekend and it takes a while to locate Barnaby, drinking with a tall man who I take to be Aaron. At least I hope he is Aaron, as I like what I see. He looks more exotic in the flesh, tanned skin, high cheek bones, wide spaced brown eyes, nice lips and long wavy hair down to his shoulders. He is wearing an open-necked white shirt over black jeans and biker boots, a multitude of bracelets jangling on both wrists.

He'll do, I think.

Then he spoils it. 'Well, well, well and which one of you beauties belongs to me tonight?' His eyes are playful, a suggestion of something seedier around the edges.

Please don't be an arsehole, I pray.

Barnaby wraps himself around Sonia before making the introductions. He looks much the same as he did all those months ago in the Uncorked, only this time he is wearing a black T-shirt with a picture of ET on the front with the slogan, *ET For President.* Having kissed Sonia – a proper French kiss, no peck on the lips for these two - he leans in to give me a warm hug, does the same to Clarissa, a fist-bump with Ringo, then calls over the barman and gets a round in.

Armed with a gin and tonic, I am ready to get this blind date rolling. He called me a *beauty,* that's good, surely? Mustn't let a ridiculous first impression get in the way of a good night. I turn to him, creaking my face into a coy smile and hoping a crack is not going to appear in the thick make-up.

He is looking at me intently as he breaks the ice by saying that I don't look much like my photo; which is true, but it is hard to know how to react because both the photo and the Stella standing here before him have been heavily edited. In fact, Aaron has no idea what I look like in real life. If things were to work out between us – just bear with me, for the sake of – and we were to go on a second date, who would I go as? My photo, today's apparition or the real me?

339

'Neither do you,' I say. Which is a complete lie as he looks exactly like his photo.

At least I can hope that he doesn't work in / on / or anywhere near a bank. They would never let him in the door with all those bracelets. He looks more like an artist or a photographer maybe. I am just indulging in a mini-daydream where he *is* a photographer and wants me to pose for him in a series of glamourous black and white photos, when he interrupts.

'What is it that you do, Bella?'

'It's *Stella*, actually.'

'I know, Bella, I know. But to me you look more like a Bella. Can I call you Bella?'

'Actually, I'd prefer Stella. I work with Sonia at Claybourne Estates.'

'You work with Barnie's Sonia, do you? She's a right cracker, isn't she? I'd have a go myself if he hadn't got in there first. That Goth stuff is pretty trippy. Knock-out.'

'Trippy,' I mumble, my brain too shocked by what he just said – out loud – to function properly.

He carries on, oblivious. 'We'd go well together. I've got a couple of looks that would complement her.' He sighs his regret and I wonder just who I have agreed to spend my evening with. 'So, you're an office worker, are you? Trapped in front of a computer all day. I've moved on from that. I'm a dog walker now.'

My eyebrows creak upwards. A dog walker? Is that a real job? 'That's interesting. Never imagined you could earn a living wage walking dogs.'

'It's not about the money, Bella, it's about the lifestyle. Anyway, I earn more now than when I worked in IT. Plus, I work for myself, I control the hours and I'm much fitter without paying any gym membership. I walk an average of 230 dogs a month, all at fourteen pounds a pop. Putting up my prices next year to fifteen an hour. Supply and demand, Bella, supply and demand.'

Frantically trying to work out his monthly takings, I try to ignore his satisfied (smug) expression.

'I'm also starting up a side line playing with cats, feeding fish and waiting for Amazon deliveries. Pays less but demands less. Some weeks I walk over fifty miles, ten miles a day if you can believe that. I take weekends off though. People don't need me then and I need some me time.'

'Wow.' I don't know what to say, astounded that people are willing to pay someone else to play with their cat. 'You should add Ocado and Tesco deliveries.'

'Got them. I'll wait for anything. New fridge, new sofa, I'm your man. You got a dog? I'll give you mates rates. Pretty prices for the pretty ladies, Bella.'

Ugh. Entrepreneurial dog walker maybe, but he also seems to work a side-line as a cheap lothario. I try and steer him back into the specifics of his job, mentally taking notes and wondering if Olive likes dogs. Only by the time we have to leave, I'm already having second thoughts; required attributes (according to Aaron, not shy in talking himself up in case you hadn't noticed) include; Olympic level fitness, photographic memory, adaptability, agility, problem solving ability on UN Security Council level, resilience, courage and, finally, you have to look good in sports gear (specifics on why this is important remain unclear).

Which all sounds a bit like working for Feet-of and exercising with the Sergeant Major.

When we get to The Laboratory, we find our Master and Commander has formed a one-man welcoming committee. I look around, wondering if he managed to persuade anyone to come as his plus-one, but there is no sign.

'Stella,' he takes my hand in his damp one. 'Welcome. Do come in. Make yourself at home. Here's a couple of drinks vouchers.' He squashes two scraps of paper into my hand and turns to Aaron. 'Hello, are you with Stella? I wasn't aware she had a new boyfriend. Go gently won't you. I need her back firing on all cylinders for Monday.'

'He is *not* my boyfriend,' I say, urgently.

'Not yet, but we've plenty of time,' murmurs Aaron, putting an arm around my waist and steering me into the room.

My first thought is that there has been an error. Are we in the right place? We have pushed through heavy double doors into a vast hall, empty space disappearing into the gloom, an infinity of air above our heads. The Laboratory, as far as I can make out, is actually a warehouse. An empty warehouse. So incongruously empty that I briefly wonder if there has been a robbery and someone has made off with all the furniture. The walls, as much as can be seen, the far walls being out of sight, are worn red brickwork, acres of it, full of fissures, entire chunks missing in places and crudely repaired with mismatched bits of concrete and wood. Emerging through the floor are giant rusting pipes that snake up the walls into the roof space where they criss-cross each other in an intricate dance to nowhere. A couple of them puff smoke as if still in use, lending a dirty haze to the obscurity and doing nothing to assist the inadequate spotlights roaming the floor area as if hoping to find someone dancing. Making up for the lack of visibility throughout the rest of the room is the bar, lit to dazzling and no doubt merrily burning through a small country's annual electricity supply every five minutes.

Clustered together at one end of this bar are the Claybourne gang, dressed to a man in black as far as I can see. No one appears to have taken up the white option in the dress code and the resulting gathering looks more ready for a funeral than a Christmas party. Aaron, still firmly attached to my side, is looking around the room with admiration. 'This place is going to be rocking later,' he says happily, giving me a squeeze.

'We should make it an all-nighter. Haven't done one of those in a while. I'll score us some E and we'll be good to go.'

'For fuck's sake, keep your voice down,' I hiss. 'And for your information, I don't do drugs and I don't like people who do.'

'No worries, Babe,' he sighs. 'Worth asking though. Brings me out of myself, you know?'

'I'm not a Babe,' I snap, horrified at the thought of him coming any further out of himself.

'Right on, Bella.'

'I'm Stella.'

'I know, Babe. Shall we get a drink?'

If Aaron is friends with Barnaby, I need to have a word with Sonia. And soon. Because you could only be friends with Aaron if you yourself are short of a raft of highly important grey cells.

We make our way to the bar, blinking in the glaring light like miners coming up from a shift, handing over our vouchers and ordering drinks. How typical of the boss to bring us for a Christmas party in an outsized mausoleum where, after two drinks, you are on your own with London nightclub prices. My bank account is going to take a serious hit as the only way to survive another couple of hours with Aaron is through a thick alcoholic haze.

'Look who I found,' a voice cries in my ear. Clarissa. I spin around to find Olive and Iris, both looking impossibly tiny in comparison, by her side. 'They were looking for you. I've already told Robyn she should cough up for a best-dressed prize. She says it's not fancy dress and there is no prize, even though she herself is dressed as a giant sausage.'

God love Olive and Iris. The whole black and white theme has completely passed them by. Iris, a ray of sunshine, is dressed in her yellow skirt with a dazzling red and orange flowered shirt that she recently unearthed in Oxfam, topped off with a red beret. On her feet, as ever, are in the faithful Doc

Martens, orange flowers tied to the laces. Olive too has upped her game with a pair of what look like green checked golfing trousers and a pink cardie, with one of Iris's berets sailing atop her grey curls.

I am about to give them a hug when Iris puts up a hand. 'Wait!' She looks at me with distrust. 'Is that you, Stella?'

'Iris! Of course, it's me.'

'Are you sure?' she squints up at me.

'Your skin looks like plastic,' complains Olive. 'And are you wearing a wig?'

No one can ever accuse me of getting above my station living with these two.

Aaron, now looking at me suspiciously, says accusingly, 'I said you didn't look anything like your photo.'

'I normally look much better than this.'

'No, you don't,' says Olive.

'She looks amazing,' cries Clarissa, stoutly. 'Just upped her game a little, didn't you Stells? Here, Miles, Chloe, doesn't Stella look like a dream?'

As if my evening couldn't get any worse.

And here they are, the royal couple. It is like George Clooney has just turned up with Amal on his arm; they throw shade on everyone around them. Miles carries off black without looking like someone died and Chloe is wearing some kind of skin tight white jeans or leggings, I don't really know what they are because they appear to be made of latex, moulded to every single inch of her perfect body. Nothing, and I mean *nothing*, is left to the imagination including more than a hint of camel toe. Up top, in keeping with the general leaving-nothing-to-the-imagination-remit, is a black see-through shirt and if she is wearing a bra, it is skin coloured, because I can't see one. She does a spin - unforgivable showing-off – reviving in me a desire to lash out and I regret not getting her with that cheese knife while I had the chance. I am about to look away, aware I am staring, when Robyn emerges from behind her like the ugly sister.

Mottled, bumpy flesh bulges in defiance of a stretchy, almost transparent, white catsuit. It is so unflattering that you have to wonder at what point Robyn thought this was a good look. Did she check herself out before she left the house? Did she get ready in the middle of a power cut? Did the words *butcher's block* or *Tesco's meat counter* not spring to mind when she saw her reflection?

'What happened to you?' says Robyn

Which, coming from her, is a bit rich.

'Son and I helped with the hair and make-up,' chips in Clarissa.

'I can see that,' drawls Miles, looking away.

'Didn't recognise you,' from Chloe, coming over to indulge in some air kissing. 'Did we, Babe?'

Babe? Oh, for fuck's sake, not another one.

'Yes, well, despite looking nothing like her photo, I am willing to make do.' Aaron, the dipstick, has just revealed to the whole world that we've never met before.

'Photo?' queries Chloe, with undisguised delight. 'Is this a blind date? Did you guys meet on Tinder?'

'Of course not,' I cry, relieved for the first time by the thick layers of make-up, now disguising my burning face. 'We've known each other a while, haven't we precious?' It's a gamble, I know. I cross my fingers, willing his conceit to the fore.

'Feels like I've known you forever, Bella,' he gushes, planting his lips on mine and – may his soul rot in hell forever - slipping his tongue in for a shimmy round my back molars.

I consider kneeing him where it would hurt. Want desperately to knee him where it would hurt, except it would only add a spotlight to an already mortifying situation. So, patting my helmet head as if absolutely thrilled with his oral examination, I make as dignified an exit as possible, citing an

345

urgent need to power my nose. As I teeter across the endless expanse of floor to reach the loos, I can feel fifty pairs of eyes boring into the back of my head, all thinking the same thing.

'*That hair isn't natural and who the hell is that muppet she's brought with her?*'

There is one of those machines selling tampons and condoms in the Ladies and, thank fuck, mini-toothbrushes. It costs me three quid, but it is money well spent. Just the thought of his repellent tongue exploring my mouth makes me want to heave, not to mention the shame, all those witnesses....Miles, Chloe, Robyn, Olive and Iris. In the mirror, I am surprised to see that I look much the same, except, wait, why is my head such a weird shape? I lean in closer and see that my hair has been pushed off its axis giving me a faintly extra-terrestrial look.

Back at the bar, the attention is thankfully on the Beatles, looking snappy in matching checked suits and performing an acapella version of Eight Days a Week. It is hard to tell how good or bad they are because DJ PyscO, no doubt pissed at the competition, has decided to ramp up the volume. Everyone has to resort to rudimentary sign language to communicate, which is fun for about ten seconds then just annoying and frustrating. After several failed attempts to broadcast our discontent to the bar staff, Devon – looking like he just strolled off the catwalk in fitted black jeans and a black T-shirt - takes control, frog marching a man who we think is the manager (he is the only one not doing any work) into the back office and within seconds the volume is reduced to more manageable levels. What is more, he emerges with two bar stools, provoking an unseemly stampede as half the office calls dibs. Robyn, claiming seniority, has just managed to heft her blanched backside onto one of the stools when Devon comes back with the two star guests – Olive and Iris – and we are all treated to the glorious spectacle of Robyn admitting defeat, revealing a small tear in her crotch as she clambers down.

'She the boss?' asks Aaron, now openly fondling my bum.

'No, she is not,' I reply, shifting to one side, only to have him move with me. I move again, and so does he. We shuffle like this for some time, skirting crablike around the Fab Four – now on to an iffy version of Penny Lane – until I stumble across Bob talking to Barnaby and Sonia. I offload Aaron, introducing him to Bob and telling a startled Barnaby that I am never speaking to him again.

And with that I am gone, hiding between Olive and Iris with Clarissa blocking his sightline.

'Bit of a tosser?' she asks.

'That man is a scourge on society. Shouldn't be allowed out in public.'

'Come on, let's get another drink. How many vouchers have you got left?'

'None. Typical bloody Clay. Two drinks each. As if that is enough.'

'Here.' She hands me a wad of vouchers. 'He's got thousands. Gave Miles a fist full.'

The evening takes on a brighter sheen then as a series of large G&Ts successfully takes the edge off just about everything. Including Aaron, who is thankfully starting to blur in the gin-soaked haze. Periodically, he tracks me down and finds some new part of my body to get a hold of. It is hard to properly get away as I also have to avoid the Clooneys and I would rather endure Aaron than spend time watching them admiring each other. DJ PyscO is steadily edging the volume up again so at least I am saved from having to listen to any more of his drivel. Not that he has stopped talking, it is just that I have stopped hearing.

As have Olive and Iris, now thankfully protected by two enormous pairs of headphones. If you want to speak to them, you uncover an ear and speak directly into the shell-like, otherwise they are blissfully sealed off from the worst of the mayhem. Occasionally, someone shimmies up, removes the headphones and carries them off for a short turn around the

347

dance floor. Bob impressed with a very nimble foxtrot, whisking Olive about with great authority, while Iris has shown a preference for a more casual approach, not unlike a traffic warden at a busy junction who has forgotten to use the facilities before their shift. This is proving a challenge for her partners; Marco was reduced to a confused sway and Paul kept dashing from one side to the other, as directed by her flailing arms. Dancing finished, they clamber back up to their lofty perches, don the headphones, sip a drink and then wave me over for an excited debrief.

It is past 9.30pm when a couple of waiters arrive bearing trays of sandwiches. Surprisingly good sandwiches, soft and plump, full of unexpected fillings. If only we were in a fit state to appreciate them. No one cares about the fresh bread and innovative flavours, they just want food, quickly please, so they can return to the more serious business of getting as plastered as possible before the vouchers run out. I wonder how Chloe will manage this gluten infested repast and discretely seek her out. Watching carefully, I see her select a small triangle of sandwich, inspecting it closely and, just as I am about to cheer to the rafters that she is an attention seeking fraud, she pops it into Miles's mouth with a sly, contented smile.

Fuck it.

Why am I bothered? Why do I still care?

I stuff in another sandwich as Aaron reappears and positions himself behind me, placing his groin right up against my bum.

'Awright, baby-doll?'

'Grrrrrr. Do not call me that,' I shout into his face, managing to spray a juicy piece of half chewed chicken curry sandwich onto his cheek.

'No worries, sweet cheeks. And ta for the snack.' He wipes his finger over his cheek and licks it, closing his eyes as if in ecstasy. It is only the sight of Miles coming over, Chloe firmly glued to his side as a fly to a particularly sticky piece of flypaper, that stops me from pulling away and attempting some kind of karate chop. Instead, I summon a smile and a wriggle, gritting my teeth as his arm pulls me closer. Miles, bastard, blanks me completely, but I am treated to a flash of Chloe's perfect teeth and, worse, a conspiratorial wink.

New low in a cycle of lows.

Her Babeness winked at me.

This was meant to be a fun night. I swore I would make up for all those Christmas parties past when I was more interested in getting home to Jackson in good condition, ie. not drunk, mascara still in place, and yet here I am having one of the worst nights in living memory, while Miles and his teeny bopping Chlo flaunt their perfect selves and their burgeoning romance.

Some days, life just sucks.

It is gone 11pm now and Clarissa, deciding we all need more drinks, goes to track down more vouchers from the boss. I am not so sure. Every now and then I keep getting a twinge in the region of my liver, probably packing its bags and planning a healthier life somewhere else. New arrivals are pouring in and inexorably lowering the average age. I can't see anyone outside of our motley group over the age of eighteen. It is time to go. Iris is a crumpled facsimile of her usual perky self and Olive looks like she has dozed off, eyes closed, head gently bobbing. As it is now impossible to speak, I write them a scrappy note to tell them I am calling a taxi.

Or I would if I had any battery.

Olive has not brought her phone, Iris doesn't own one, Clarissa is on the hunt for free drinks, Aaron is thankfully MIA, Bob is incoherent, Marco has left, Devon is causing a stir on the dance floor, Barnaby and Sonia are *as one* against the back wall and Robyn is making a move on Paul while his girlfriend is chatting up George, with Ringo watching on. In desperation, I ask Miles.

'You're going?' he shouts, his breath hot against my cheek.

Duh.

I shrug and nod and he shrugs and nods, tapping into his phone, a task made infinitely more complicated by Chloe draping herself around his neck and kissing his cheek every two seconds; peck..peck..peck.

Give it up, I want to shout. He's yours, you've got him, game over.

Eventually, Miles gives me a nudge. Sadiq, Renault Megane, twenty minutes.

I give a thumbs up, write another note to Iris, check that Olive is still breathing and disappear gratefully to the loo. When you've had too much to drink, the need to pee creeps up on you unannounced. One minute you're fine, the next you're crossing your legs and praying for deliverance. So, when I get to the Ladies and find a queue of about five hundred chattering girls, I know I am in trouble. I need a solution and soonest. There must be a staff loo somewhere, a bucket, a back alley where I can squat in peace.......I carry on past the near empty, as per, men's loos, past two doors marked PRIVATE – both are locked – past another door with a Zorro style lightning bolt and a DANGER sign, on to where the corridor ends in a black velvet curtain.

What lies beyond?

A brick wall? The cellar? Portal to a planet where Chloe doesn't exist?

The disabled toilet is what, empty, miraculously quiet, large and so clean I could curl up on the floor for a snooze. There is even soap in the dispenser and a full load of pristine hand towels.

I wee and wipe, wash my hands repeatedly in an effort to erase any traces of Aaron, and prepare for a final return to the fray to grab Olive and Iris and get the hell out of here. Then someone tries the door. I still, not daring to move. Aaron?

A knock.

'Occupied,' I shout. Bloody cheek. Why do people do that? A locked toilet door generally means that there is someone in there. Duh. Peeing.

'Stella? Is that you? Open up.' The door handle rattles again. 'Stella?'

Against the deep thump of the never-ending bass, it is hard to hear. Is it Aaron? Alone with him, unchaperoned, in a confined space, is a situation I am not willing to risk. The desire for violence has not yet left me and I could lash out. The way my luck is going, he'll topple over and crack his head on the sink and I'll get done for GBH; front page of the Daily Mail and five years. Olive will have to bring me cakes on her visits so I can use them to bribe the other inmates not to bully me and take all my things.

'Go away. I'll be out in a minute,' I shout at the door.

'Stella, it's Miles. Open up.'

Miles?

'I want to talk to you. Open the door. Please.' More rattling. 'Just give me a minute.'

What does he want now?

Having just seen the state of my face in the all-too-well-lit mirror, I flick off the light before opening the door. Miles is standing there, one arm braced against the door frame effectively blocking me in. No sign of his sidekick.

'No Chloe?' I ask, peering under his arm.

He tuts and I can sense his eyes flicking up to the ceiling even if I can't see them.

It winds me up. 'What do you want? If you need to go, I can recommend it. Spacious, spotless, reams of loo paper. Go right ahead, make yourself at home. Our cab will be here any minute and I need to get the gang home. Way past their bedtime.'

Miles doesn't move. I can see the whites of his eyes now, unblinking in the obscurity. He takes a deep breath, releases it slowly.

'Are you *with* that guy?' His tone is aggressive. 'What's his name?'

'Aaron. Aaron is his name as I am sure you know. Look, if you're going to have a pop, forget it. Job done. The man is a moron, even I know that. But hey, not my fault. Barnaby recommended him.'

'You don't even like him?'

'Give me some credit. I know you think I'm a complete loser, but even I won't sink that low.'

'Hard to tell given that he's all over you. All the time.' His antagonism bites deep.

'From the man who has spent the evening with his girlfriend wound around him like poisonous frigging ivy.'

'It's poison ivy,' he says, pedantically. 'And stop changing the subject. I asked you about Aaron.'

'What's it to you, Miles? You haven't said a word to me in months, you've shown zero interest since, since.....you know, *that night*, yet now you want to know all about my love life. Well, it's just peachy thanks. I'm peachy. Life is peachy, so button it and let me go home.' Quite the poet, aren't I? 'He's a nob, I'll admit, but fuck it, nothing ventured, nothing gained, right? I know your Chloe is perfect, but who wants perfect? I mean, where's the edge? What d'you get a hold of at night?'

There is a huff of indignation at this profound speech. Personally, I think it is pretty good for this time of night after a vat of G&Ts and some unidentified shots that Clarissa forced down my throat.

'Miles?' A voice emerges from the throb of music filling the corridor.

'Shit,' murmurs Miles, before I get a chance to say exactly that. Then his mouth is against my ear. 'Meet me tomorrow. Gabriel's Wharf. 11 o'clock.'

Before I can refuse, Chloe sashays into view behind him, winding her arms possessively around his neck and doling out a couple of her pecky peck pecks. She scrutinises him, his face in the shadows, before switching her gaze to me for a beat, then back to Miles.

'Babe? Everything alright?' she asks.

He ignores her, staring at me. 'Did you hear me?'

'Yes, I did and yes, Babe is just fine,' I snap.

And I run.

Out. Of. There.

CHAPTER 34

Scout's honour
Idiom: when you are trying to persuade someone that you are
telling the truth

I tried not to go.

Did not sleep a wink. Not one single bloody *tiddly wink* so busy was I listing reasons why I shouldn't go. I won't bore you with the details but rest assured that no excuse was left unturned. As the early hours crept towards dawn, I gave it one last try, mentally shutting down my mind and thinking about nothing. That lasted less than thirty seconds before full churning service was resumed, thoughts seething through my dehydrated, hungover brain, around and around, up and down, back to the beginning, back to the *why?* So, I gave up and got up, made tea, went back to bed and attempted to lose myself in Moby Dick, which Bart has chosen for book club – it is surprisingly gripping, just not gripping enough to wrestle my mind away from the *dilemma of the day*.

To Miles.

Or not to Miles.

Of course, it was a foregone conclusion, my curiosity piqued beyond any possibility of a no-show.

Not that I was in any condition to engage in such a demanding activity. I was fit for lying in bed all day and possibly, absolute tops, crawling downstairs to lie on the sofa and letting Olive administer to me with an endless parade of tea and snacks. Instead, I got up, drank five cups of tea before being able to even contemplate a shower – all that running water, all that noise, all those clashing colours – then dressed myself, applied make-up, etc, etc. Every movement was an excruciating reminder that drinking a sea of gin is a stupid idea. Iris then made me eat some toast and honey, which at least gave me the strength to put on my shoes. I didn't tell them where I was going; those raised eyebrows and accompanying questions would have sapped the little energy I had summoned.

I got the bus to Hyde Park Corner and then walked down to the river through Green Park, St James', past the Houses of Parliament, saluted Big Ben, over Westminster Bridge and onto the Queen's Walk. The meditative movement of my walk in the frigid December air cleared out the worst of the cobwebs and the toast was doing such sterling work calming my churning stomach that by the time I got to the London Eye, I was able to stop for a coffee. I was ahead of time anyway and there was no way I was arriving early. Ten to fifteen minutes late was my aim.

At 11.17am, as I approached Gabriel's Wharf with near perfect timing, panic set in, real panic, and it took another ten minutes perched on a damp wooden bench for me to calm down enough to contemplate moving on. I was now half an hour late and there was a real chance he might have already gone. How long would I wait, if it were me?

There is always a point when leaving, or staying, becomes a question of self-respect.

Miles has buckets of that, I thought, as I warily advanced towards the entrance to Gabriel's Wharf only to find there were about two hundred other people mooching about. I started scanning faces and looking for the familiar broad shoulders in amongst all the mums and dads, scrappy teenagers, foreign students, convinced that he must have already left.

'Stella!'

He was sat on one of the benches, about a foot from where I was standing, staring up at me.

He looked cold more than anything so, after a weak *hello* from me and a brusque nod from him, we left the crowds and walked briskly, silently, until we found a quiet coffee shop down a backstreet, as yet undiscovered by the throng of Saturday walkers. We installed ourselves in a table by the window with an uninteresting view of the street outside, the river now out-of-sight, both faffing about with coats and scarves for an age to avoid confronting the awkwardness of being there together. I got a coffee. Miles a pot of tea. We both ordered toasted teacakes and sat quietly while the young lad serving us, Richard, a badge pinned to his T-shirt announced, busied himself with plates, cutlery, sugar, milk jugs, butter, napkins. Finally, he put down my coffee and the tea, asked us if we needed anything else and scooted off, out of the frosty atmosphere pervading our table.

'I didn't think you were coming,' Miles said gruffly, warming his hands around his cup of tea.

'Neither did I,' I said. 'I tried very hard not to, tried and failed, my system weakened by lack of sleep and an excess of Christmas spirit last night. I think that's me officially done with office Christmas parties. I've done ten years of them and haven't enjoyed one.'

'You looked like you were having a good time,' he said, watching me closely.

I looked at him in disbelief. 'How could you possibly think that? Were you even at the same party as me? Oh, I know, you were so busy gazing into the dreamy violet pools of Chloe's eyes that you failed to notice the carnage going on around you.'

'Don't be absurd. And I saw more than enough.' He stopped to blow on his tea and then said churlishly, 'God, you weren't even being very discreet. In front of the office crowd too. And Mr Clay.'

'What? When he stuck his tongue down my throat?'

'That was just the start.'

'You can't think I enjoyed any of his over-enthusiastic attentions,' I spluttered, suddenly furious. I thought I had put last night behind me and now here we are hauling the less salubrious moments back into the light for another going over.

'You didn't put up much of a fight.'

'Strategic decision. Trying not to make a scene.'

He waggled his head at me to underline his disbelief.

I slumped back in my chair, defeated. 'Look, have you invited me all the way here to have a pop just because I brought a total nobhead to the office party? Is that what this is about?' I stirred my coffee and spooned in some sugar, wondering whether to simply flounce out. I don't need this, I thought. I could be home. On the sofa. With Olive. Iris. At peace.

'No. Yes. Kind of.' Then, with a surge of anger. 'Who is he, anyway? I thought you were with Angus?'

'For fuck's sake!' I cried. 'Angus is a friend, a good friend, he's been great these last few months. I just didn't want to invite him......for...various reasons. There. End of.'

'And?'

'And?'

'And, Aaron?'

'You're like a dog with a mangy bone. He's a friend of Barnaby's, someone whom I have no intention of ever speaking to again. I was going to invite Olive but Iris got there before me and then I was going to invite Colin, lovely Colin, right age bracket too, only Sonia and Clarissa persuaded me otherwise. Clarissa thought a blind date would be fun – which reminds me, never speaking to Clarissa again either.' I sighed deeply, exhaustion washing over me.

'Angus would have been a better bet,' he said then. Unnecessarily.

'Anyone would be a better bet than Aaron. But you know what, he looked alright in the photo and I thought I'd give it a go. Get out of my rut. Try new things, meet new people, not be a *stuck record.*' I looked at him crossly and got the same in return, his eyes less *blue-sky-day* and more *storm's-a-coming.*

'You can do better than him.'

'Oh, you're too kind,' I snapped.

'He was all over you like a bad rash.'

'I think that's my line, Mr Poison Ivy. I'm surprised you managed to disentangle yourself long enough to come here alone. Or did you sneak out while her Babeness was still topping up her beauty sleep?'

'Don't be bitchy. She's done nothing wrong.'

'Ha! That depends on your perspective. Anyway, what has Aaron ever done to you? You never even spoke to him last night.'

'He was with *you.*'

'Yeah, right,' I muttered, disbelievingly, as we glared at each other across the table, neither wanting to be the first to give in, look away.

It was the coffee that did it for me. I could smell it, a heavenly odour on a par with a Marco coffee, and I wanted coffee. Needed coffee. I dropped my eyes and drank deeply, revelling in the smooth taste with just enough bitterness, the hit of caffeine, the heat in my tummy. This was worth my time and attention; a lovely, unambiguous coffee, no mixed signals, no cryptic messages, just pure liquid heaven whose sole purpose in life is to comfort and restore. Miles, still silent, seemed for once to be out of his comfort zone, fidgeting and playing with the teapot.

For something to do, I started buttering a teacake. It was still warm enough to melt the butter so I was able to pack it on, watching it sink into the lovely squashy bun before adding more.

'Mmmm, fab-u-lous,' I hummed as I took a huge bite, melted butter dribbling down my chin.

'Stella, did you hear what I said?' (hint of exasperation in the voice).

As if I could have missed it. 'I'm not deaf yet, despite my advanced age. So, yes, I did. You said he was with me. Well, duh. I invited him. You yourself were joined at the hip with your date, *the Chlo.* Each to their own.'

He changed tack then. 'Stella, why are you here?'

'Tut, tut, tut, not so fast, sunshine,' I said, stuffing in another mouthful of doughy bliss. 'You asked me here, so you tell me, why am I here?'

Uncertainty made an unexpected appearance then, rippling across his face. What now? And did I want to know? As the wait for a reply expanded, Miles started looking distinctly troubled, uneasy even. Panicking, I decided to head him off at the pass. Distract him.

'Yum, yum. This teacake is perfection. You don't even need jam, the raisins do the job, adding that hint of sweetness to contrast with the butter. Now, unsalted wouldn't work at all. Bread, you see, needs some salt. Like a pizza - '

'Stella! Stop talking for five seconds. Jesus.'

'You asked me a question!'

'I asked you why you were here, not for an in-depth analysis of a toasted bloody teacake. Besides, you turned the question back on me.'

'Someone - '

'Shut up. Please.'

So, I did. Finishing the teacake and meticulously picking up all the crumbs onto a licked finger. When the plate was clean enough to go straight back into the cupboard, he still hadn't spoken and I was revving up for another monologue.

'Look. I've messed up and I can't seem to get back on track,' he finally croaked.

'Welcome to the club my friend. You are not alone,' I said, feeling both relieved and benevolent. Then I had a nasty thought. 'You're not pregnant, are you? You've not gone and knocked up the Chlo?'

He flicked his eyes up to the ceiling. 'Just keep quiet for a minute, *please*. Look, Stella, I am truly sorry that I belittled your pain, dismissed what had happened with your ex and how hard it was for you to let it all go.'

Was not expecting that. Dammit. Caught on the hop, I abandoned benevolence and went for sarcasm. 'Good of you to say so. And what brought on this episode of broad-minded enlightenment?'

'I've had a taste of it myself.'

'Oh, come on! I can't see how she can have peeled herself off you for long enough to have had a bloody fling with someone else.'

He banged his fist on the table, inviting the attention of every customer in the place.

'Easy, Tiger,' I whispered.

'It was seeing *you* with that man. That, *Aaron.*' Really, he wedged an impressive amount of contempt into that one small word. 'Seeing you with someone else. I was eaten up with envy.'

'Oh, per-leeze.' I scoffed, working hard to keep my voice steady, my heart accelerating into an unstable trot. 'That's just not going to wash. You were the school prom king and queen last night, lauding it over us commoners. She is clearly devoted to you and you were showing plenty of de-bloody-votion yourself.'

'It wasn't like that. Ever.' He tried to catch my eye then, but I refused to be caught. All too easy to be seduced if he decided to turn the blue lasers back on. 'When we met on the plane coming home, I thought she might be the one. Not *the one* but someone who could help me move on and forget you. She is smart, confident, beautiful, committed and I tried, I really tried to make it work, to like her enough. But in the end, she's still not *you.* No one is *you.* And you're right. She strives for perfection all the time and it drives me crazy. I miss you, Stella. Warts and all. I miss your edgy humour, I miss your sarcasm, I miss your terrible language, I miss everything. You suit me. I like you. I like the whole package.'

There was a long, stunned pause at this point as we considered the Halfpenny package, warts and all.

'I want the whole package, if you're still interested. If you'll have me.'

Undone and unnerved, I made a dash for safer ground. 'Do you want that teacake?'

'For fuck's sake, Stella. Are you listening at all? I just opened my heart and you're back on the teacakes.'

'Comfort food. I'll order another.' I raised my hand importantly, urgently, hoping and praying that young Richard would rush to my side so that I could talk about anything other than what Miles had just said.

'Stella.'

'Coo-eee, Richard!'

'Please, Stella.'

'I hear you Miles, I hear you. I'm just not sure what to say. It wasn't that long ago that you gave me very short shrift at the end of a particularly tortuous evening that resulted in me punching you. Told me you were done. We were done. Finished. Over. Nul points. Buggered off to Hong Kong just to make sure there was no possibility of bumping into the Halfpenny in the ensuing months. Only when some devious God put us side-by-side in the bloody cinema did I see you again, knotted together with the Chlo. Angus is a good friend and yet I am not sure I can ever forgive him for foisting that particular evening on me. Yet suddenly, I'm flavour of the month again? Forgive me for failing to keep up with the programme.'

I had been waving an arm enthusiastically throughout this lecture and Richard finally saw me and trotted reluctantly over; probably regretting he didn't have some oil skins and a sou'wester for protection against inhospitable elements swirling around our table. I ordered more coffee, a top-up for Miles and teacakes with a double ration of butter.

'I'll pay, just bring loads,' I said, begging him to be generous.

Fortifying rations ordered, I was obliged to turn my attention back to Miles.

'That evening with Nina, I really thought it was for the best, a move in the right direction for you and by default, for us. I didn't realise how raw it still was for you. Your reaction was so absolute, I - ' he paused, hunting for words. 'I saw the depth of your hurt and I was jealous that he could still draw such a reaction. From what you have told me, he wasn't a nice person and you weren't particularly happy, and yet you couldn't, wouldn't, move on. I thought we'd never get past him. So, I went to Hong Kong. Mr Clay offered me the chance to go and I grabbed it. I thought it would cure me of you if I took a break and buried myself in work out there. So, when I got on that plane to come home, I was upbeat. And in business class. A thank you from Clay. Sitting next to Chloe felt like a sign, like I'd done the right thing and what better way to wind-up my trip than to have met someone else. That way there would be no chance of falling for the Moneypenny again.'

Richard arrived at this point with refills, teacakes and butter a-go-go. Perfect timing because I hadn't taken a breath since Miles had started talking and I my body was screaming out for oxygen.

He went on. 'Then we went and bumped into you in the cinema. What are the chances? There you were with Angus who oozes class and ticks the right age box for you, him being older and therefore safer, and I could only think, stupidly, after I'd already told you we were over, after I had met Chloe, I could only think, I've lost her. How can I compete with someone like that? He clearly has money, he's intelligent, he's good company and he's a nice bloke. I hardly ate. Couldn't.'

I butted in here with a heartfelt tribute to the bread and cheese.

Got me a gruff smile. 'Yeah, it looked good. Maybe we can go back one day. Enjoy it this time.' He poured some more tea from the pot, thick and soupy with tannins. 'Then there was Aaron. When you announced that you were bringing some guy called Aaron to the office party, I knew I was in trouble.' He stopped again, putting his head into his hands. 'Stella, Stella, Stella. You turned up looking like a million dollars, even Chloe was put out, searching for faults and pointing them out to me.'

'That was all Sonia and Clarissa's hard work,' I huffed (pleased as punch).

Another half-smile. 'I prefer you without all that crap, you don't need it. Still, you looked fantastic and it was all for that *Aaron.*' He spat out the name again. 'All gypsy hair and laid-back attitude. That was when I knew for sure. That is why I'm here, Stella, stripped bare, laying out my heart. We were good together. Before. We didn't have long but what we had was good. And that's what I want. That is what I am asking for.'

So, here I am.

In my bed, curled on my right side with Miles tucked in tight behind me, his knees slotted in to mine, his left arm around me, his breath warm on the nape of my neck.

A change in my fortunes that was utterly unimaginable this time yesterday. We stayed in that coffee shop, Richard ferrying us an endless supply of tea, coffee and snacks, for most of the afternoon. As the groggy afternoon light faded to dark, we made a move. To Fulham. To the delighted surprise of Iris and the wary bewilderment of Olive.

'I don't understand, Stella,' she whispered, when Miles was safely out of the room. 'What about that Aaron? He wasn't my favourite but all the same. And that young Chloe?'

She gradually overcame her reticence as Miles worked his magic, gushing over her Shepherd's Pie, settling in to watch

The Poseidon Adventure – the original 1972 version with Gene Hackman and Shelley Winters, the four of us shedding a tear when she pegs it and asks Gene to give the pendant to her husband – and making tea for everyone in the ad break, as well as doing the washing-up. Come bed time, Iris whisked Olive off upstairs before she could get in a tizzy about whether Miles was staying the night or not.

Which didn't stop me getting in a tizzy about exactly that.

Should I ask him to stay? Was it too soon? Would that make me seem like a complete slapper? Should I escort him to the front door and send him out into the night? Besides, I desperately needed to sleep and how on earth would I sleep if he was there with me?

It was Miles himself who broached the subject as we sat alone on the sofa.

'Do you want me to go home?'

I pondered this as if I had not already been pondering it. 'Yes and no.'

'If it would help, I have no intention of touching you tonight.'

'You don't?' I squeaked, affronted.

'Nope. Not that I haven't thought about it. I have. Often. I've dreamt about getting down and dirty with you more often than I am comfortable admitting and, sometime soon, I would like to find out your deepest, darkest, sexual fantasies and bring them out into the light. But tonight is not the night? Am I right?'

My nether regions had swooped so low at this revelation they were able to start a tour of the Australian outback. Speech was not an option.

Miles, cool as, went on, 'Tonight, we both need to sleep. It's too soon and you're too tired and too tense. When I make love to you for the first time, I want it to be right. Relaxed. I want you to melt under my touch, not recoil in fright. But, if it's OK with you, I would like nothing more than to sleep beside you, to wake up with you tomorrow. A first night of many.'

A squeak of fear (excitement?) escaped me. 'Crikey, Miles. Let's not get ahead of ourselves. One step at a time.'

'One night at a time.' He gave me a soul searing look that threatened to melt my knickers, only recently returned from Down Under. 'Or I can sleep down here, on the sofa. Or I can call a cab. Go home.'

As if.

CHAPTER 35

Rammed
/ræmd/
Adjective: very full or crowded

Overexcited?
Olive ✓
Iris ✓✓

Having been denied a proper, full-on Christmas for as long as they can remember (and I have a suspicion that for Iris it is her first proper Christmas *ever),* Olive and Iris have decided to make up for the lost years, transforming No.6 Beatrice Avenue into a hot contender for the country's most over-decorated house. Highlights include a Nativity scene (front step), Santa's Grotto (living room), Elf Dormitory (Iris's bedroom) and a Fairy Circle (back garden by the giant rhubarb, also decorated to within an inch of its winter foliage life).

Iris has been particularly busy, visiting the Sue Ryder shop on the Kings Road twice last week where she secured a red and green sari (on visit No.1), which she somehow plans to turn into a skirt and matching scarf; a challenge given the short time frame and the available equipment, namely the Bernina sewing machine last used by Noah while doing some running repairs on the Ark. Visit No.2, after running out of cash on visit No.1, concerned a giant plastic Rudolph, complete with battery-operated light in his (red) nose, and now jostling for space with Mary and Joseph on the front step.

Olive has been digging out an endless supply of dodgy decorations from a series of well-hidden boxes – each dustier and more ancient than the last – and fretting about what to wear. After weeks of deliberations, she has selected a pair of (navy) trousers with a hideous Christmas jumper featuring a sequined kitten emerging from a Santa-style boot.

Mel 'n Kim are blasting out 'Rockin' Around the Christmas Tree' from the four-CD holiday special that Iris found under the stairs. Four CDs that we all know by heart having listened to them non-stop both at home and at work where she has persuaded Devon to set up a basic sound system.

'When can we officially stop playing Christmas songs?' asks Miles, buttering toast and grimacing as Mel 'n Kim give way to Shakin' Stevens. 'Is Boxing Day reasonable? We haven't got to go on to Epiphany of whatever it is, have we?' He flicks a drooping paper chain, living dangerously in close proximity to the toaster. 'That's if the house doesn't go up in smoke before then.'

'You'll have to consult Iris. She's in charge of Christmas Cheer. I'm going to try and distract her with the King's College Choir from Cambridge this afternoon. It's on the Beeb at four. At least it'll be a change.' Miles grunts. 'Hey, this is for Iris. And Olive. No holds barred. We agreed.' I shuffle over and put my arms around him. 'You missing your family?'

'Christ, no! I wouldn't be anywhere else.' He pulls me close. 'Mum and Roger will have all but moved into the Golf Club by now, terrified of missing a minute of gossip, and Dad will be hiding from Marina's family out in the garden shed and there's only room for one in there. I'm fine. Just tired.'

'Golden Boy,' I tease. 'You've been working your butt off for Feet-of since Hong Kong.'

'You work your butt off for him all day, every day. At least I like my job and the opportunity to go to Hong Kong was huge. I owe him for that.'

'Rubbish. He's lucky to have you. And he likes you.'

'You know he'd be lost without you? He just has a hard time showing it.'

'Ha!'

'Look, if you hate it that much, why not look for another job? I wouldn't mind so much now that I have my hands on you outside of the office.' He hugs me tight and I revel in the glorious feel of him. Grateful.

After a beat, I pull back, pinching a slice of his toast. 'I've thought about it. Often. But the grass is always greener, right? If I move, I might end up working for another Clay, only with bigger feet, and without you, or Clarissa or the Beatles. Bob. Or Marco and Iris. A working day without a Marco latté - '

'With an extra shot,' he adds.

'- with an extra shot, would be like living in a half-world, a kind of purgatory.'

'Is he still coming tonight?'

'With his wife, Ana. They did Christmas Eve with the family, so they're free today. One set of grandparents is here and they're happy to look after the kids. Devon has his family do though, so he's not coming.'

Miles starts adding up on his fingers. 'Just as well. Are we going to fit around the table?'

'If we all breathe in. And we need more chairs so Colin said he'd bring a couple.'

Kim and Bart are first to arrive with Reg, looking much perkier than when I last saw him. He says he owes it all to golf. Having given it up for the duration of his marriage, he is back on the fairways and chipping up a storm amongst the Senior Ladies. Weighed down by bonhomie and wine, Bart kisses everyone, including Miles, then dumps a huge sack of presents (in clear breach of the Secret Santa rules and regulations) under the tree.

Colin is next, sporting an impressive beard, a feature he has been working on since mid-October for his role as Father Christmas at a local school. He is bearing one gift – in accordance with the Secret Santa rules and regs – which he lays reverently beside Bart's sack.

Then the Von Trapps arrive. That is to say Marco, Ana, five – FIVE – mini-Marcos of varying sizes and sexes, plus one set of grandparents.

Eighteen for dinner then.

We are seven chairs, seven Secret Santa's and approximately seven feet of dining room short – in part because Olive has installed a Christmas tree so enormous, we had to chop off the top to fit it in. We stuff the Von Trapps into Santa's Grotto and get to work. Colin goes to get more chairs, Miles and Bart relocate the tree to the front garden via the French windows, giving a forest back-drop to Rudolph and the nativity characters, while Olive and I try, and fail, to locate the final section of the extendable table.

Time to think again.

We manage to squeeze a couple of chairs onto the end of the table for the grandparents and I ask Marco and Ana if they would mind the Minis eating off their laps in Santa's Grotto, with the Wizard of Oz on the TV.

Mind?

Marco thinks this is the best idea since someone decided to sell ready-sliced bread and Ana sheds real tears of gratitude, kissing me repeatedly and gabbling to her parents (or Marco's, not yet established who they belong to) in Portuguese.

When Nina arrives, dressed as the Ghost of Nina Past – she is white as a newly emulsioned wall – our party is complete. We put her in Olive's chair and instruct the mini-Marcos to keep their distance. Which is fine in theory but less so in reality - they hop, hither and thither, as unpredictable and unstoppable as fleas.

Olive is working a trench between the kitchen and a packed Santa's Grotto, Iris is upstairs fine-tuning her sari-conversion and I am wrapping everything from Olive's gift-drawer – who knew such things existed – to top up the Secret Santa stash. Stuck for choice, I can reveal that the Minis will each get a key ring or a bar of soap, the Marco/Ana father will be getting a Brazilian rainforest mug, while the Marco/Ana mother will be able to enjoy a pair of flipflops with the Rio Olympics blazoned all over them.

Coals to Newcastle, I know, but I'm out of options.

'Get the champagne flowing,' I whisper to Miles. 'I'm going to dig out Iris.'

Poor Iris is slumped beside the Bernina in the Elf Dormitory; the sari still remarkably sari-like, with just a whiff of toga. With the evening already in full-flow, I persuade her back into her (and our) favourite kilt, with my red ruffled shirt that she likes so much. It is way too big, but with the sleeves rolled up and a piece of sari around her waist as an impromptu cummerbund, it does the job and she at last feels Christmassy enough to join the fray. I grab her red beret on the way down, now sporting a snowman on skis for the holiday period, and pop it on her head just as she shyly slides into the living room. Marco sees her first and gives a whoop of appreciation, only to be bettered by a roar from Bart and a benevolent Father Christmas chuckle from Colin. Her happy beam has half of us weeping into our champagne; only the Minis look on dry eyed, stuffing in crisps without a flicker of emotion.

'A toasting,' cries Bart, his English deserting him in all the excitement. 'A toasting to our hosting Olive and Christmas cheering coordination, Iris. Everyone is with champagne? You need topping Olive. No toasting with half of glass.'

After toasting Olive and Iris five or six times, Colin whips out his Father Christmas hat, fluffs his beard and announces it is time for the Secret Santa gifts, tripping over a stray Mini on his way to the tree. It is safe to say that the last-gasp presents for the kids are not a success, but they perk up when Reg produces a tin of Quality Street and invites them to take two each.

The other Secret Santa's are more of a success:

Colin: red bobble hat with *Off-duty Santa* in white across the front

Iris: smart Brazilian Coffee Hut Barista apron with her name on the centre pocket

Olive: entry form for The Chase

Reg: golfing sun-visor

Bart: wine tasting voucher for two

Kim: silk scarf

Marco: Kopi luwak coffee beans – the ones that are swallowed and pooped out by a cute-looking animal and cost a mint, which makes me think they must be from Nina as no one else could afford them

Ana: spa treatment

Miles: vintage Levi's t-shirt

Nina: multi-coloured baby blanket, handknitted (by Olive, assisted by Iris who chose the colours so she could feel involved)

Grandad / grandma: as above

Me: bumper collection of Scandi crime novels

That should be that. But no, there is tons more as half of us have hidden stashes of extra presents. As a disbelieving but happy Iris disappears behind a mountain of discarded wrapping paper, I call for an interlude or we will never eat. And who knows what that turkey is up to; it has been in the oven since early this morning. Olive is trailing a slow-roast / low temperature technique, something I consider to be very brave (foolhardy) when you have invitees in the double figures and a giant bird full to the brim with *three* types of stuffing. One each for Olive, Iris and Colin.

Colin went for a mushroom flavor which he prepped himself, consulting most of Olive's collection of cookery books on the way and, controversially, putting it in some kind of bag he had procured from Mr Mukherjee to protect it from contamination by the other stuffings. This bag, made from potatoes, will magically dissolve during cooking. Apparently. Iris, opting for sage and onion, thought this was such a good idea that she used one too. This left Olive, put out by so much

371

freelance activity around her turkey, with a traditional chestnut offering that she proceeded to stuff into every available inch of not-yet-stuffed-turkey. We will be eating the stuff (no pun intended) for bloody weeks, not to mention the accompanying fart-quota. As it is, Iris only has to look at a can of baked beans to start tooting with abandon.

Feeling giddy from all the champagne, I prise Kim away from Bart, grab Nina and head for the kitchen. Apart from needing to check on the turkey and peel another batch of potatoes to feed the Minis, I want to find out what's wrong with Nina, now taking the porcelain look to a new benchmark of bleached nothingness. I issue aprons, potatoes and peelers and set them to work, while I gingerly open the oven.

The turkey looks good enough to eat, if frighteningly huge, glistening threateningly mere millimeters from the walls of the oven.

'Does a turkey expand when you roast it?' I ask.

'No idea,' says Kim. 'Never roasted a whole turkey before. I think everything expands with heat so it's probably fine. Nina's expanding nicely, although she could do with some of that golden colour.' She looks pointedly at Nina. 'Are you OK, really OK? You're the colour of glue and it's not a good look.'

'You were blooming and now you're not,' I add for emphasis. 'What's up? I know something's up and we agreed no more secrets, so give us your worst. Jackson hasn't made a comeback, has he? Demanding visiting rights and choice of prep school.'

She dredges up a smile and assures us that he is still safely in New York. Less good is that she has high blood pressure and the doctors want her to stop work and put her feet up.

'Then do it!' Kim and I cry in unison.

'Give me that peeler,' I snap, divesting her of such a heavy utensil. 'And, here, get your feet up.' I drag a chair over. 'Kim, pass me Olive's cushion. There. Now, *don't move.*'

'Stop being so bossy,' shouts Nina, standing up in protest. 'I'm fine.'

Three things then happen:

The paper chain around the kitchen light catches fire.

The turkey explodes.

Nina faints.

CHAPTER 36

Chaos
/ˈkeɪ.ɑːs/
Noun : a state of total confusion, without order

Festivities have been postponed until tomorrow when we will reconvene, without the Marcos or Nina but with the addition of Jeremy and Julia who were due for Boxing Day anyway. We have a new turkey (actually, two chickens from Colin's freezer, defrosting as we speak) and some new trimmings.

It all got hysterical for a while back there. Turns out I am rubbish in a crisis, which is something of a disappointment. I had always rather fancied myself as someone who could step nimbly up to the plate, as and when.

This was not the case yesterday.

As Nina lay unconscious on the floor, I sat in a panic, patting her face and shouting, eventually throwing a glass of water over her: none of which helped. Kim wasn't much better, dialing 999 and then bawling incoherently at the operator until Bart arrived and wrestled the phone from her – she didn't give it up easily – giving out clear instructions and full details of the situation in near perfect English. Meanwhile, Miles dealt with the small fire, slowly eating its way through Delia Smith's Christmas recipe book and Marco tried to extract the smoking turkey remains – they didn't give up easily either - firmly welded to the sides of the oven. Ana was nowhere to be seen, which left Colin and Reg to try and herd the Minis out of the kitchen and away from the action, something they were reluctant to do with so much drama in open play. Colin took to juggling tangerines as a distraction, while Reg tried the same with two pink grapefruits only to land one on the smallest Mini, who promptly keeled over and lay slumped on the floor beside Nina.

In the midst of this bedlam, Olive and Iris – stoic in the face of their hotly anticipated Christmas dissolving before their eyes - pinged around from one disaster to the next like a couple of over-juiced elves.

The emergency services came quickly and two competent paramedics took charge, loading Nina onto a stretcher in double quick time and bearing her off to the waiting ambulance. It was as they were negotiating the well-peopled front step that we found Ana, hands together, eyes closed, praying to Mary and Joseph.

No sign baby Jesus, although Rudolph was still standing loud and proud.

Now, gone midnight, it is just Miles and I, sitting it out in a cold, stark waiting room; hard plastic chairs in an uncomfortable shade of green, plants long beyond their best despite being fake and – of course, I am suddenly parched - an empty water cooler in the corner. Bart and Kim abandoned ship in the early hours; there is little point us all being here so they are going to come back and take over later this morning. I have promised, on pain of excommunication, to call the minute there is news. I have also tried to send Miles home a hundred times, but he refuses to budge.

'I want to spend Christmas with you,' he said, scoring a full 10-out-of-10 for romantic content, shortly followed by a 9-out-of-10 for romantic gestures when he brought me a Twix from the vending machine. I felt obliged to deduct a point as I really wanted a Mars. It packs a higher level of comforting sweetness; that biscuit layer brings little to the party.

Apart from us, there is a crumpled boy who cannot be more than sixteen - I am hoping he is a brother and not a father - waiting for news and a trio of anxious looking women who remain as a tight-knit group, refusing all overtures. They keep barking at each other in a language I cannot identify but which Miles believes is Croatian.

'How do you know? Do you speak Croatian?'

'No.'

'Have you ever been?'

'No.'

'Yet you have deduced they are speaking Croatian?'

'I heard her say Dubrovnik.'

You can see lucidity is hanging by a thread.

The witching hours between 2am and 4am are particularly tough. The Croatian team have left, destination unknown, the teenage lad is the terrified father of a healthy baby boy named Maddox (his girlfriend being a diehard Angelina Jolie fan, he explained to Miles, who was escorting him to see his son for the first time) and there are no new arrivals to help pad out the waiting room. An unnatural quiet settles over the whole place. No babies cry, no mothers howl, no soon-to-be-fathers pace. There are only the soft-shoed nurses humming silently through the darkened corridors, their voices hushed as if they are afraid of disturbing the calm and provoking a frenzy of births.

At 5.30am, a nurse comes to visit, apologising for the delay. 'We forgot you were here. Sorry. You can visit for five minutes now, that's all I can allow you.'

Miles and I follow her through a maze of right turns, left turns, right again – we will never find our way out – before finally stopping at room 602. She pushes the door open and gestures for us to go in. I don't move, suddenly afraid, and Miles has to give me a gentle shove in the back to get me moving, steering me through the door and over to where we see Nina, propped up in bed, looking serene.

'Hey, Nina,' I whisper, pulling up a chair as close to the bed as it will go.

She is sharing the room with another woman who is snoring loudly under a white cotton sheet, her immense belly expanding across the bed with her every rumble. Miles pulls a horrible blue nylon curtain around Nina's bed, as if that is going to make a difference – it doesn't - and then says he'll wait in the corridor.

'No, wait, Miles. Please.' Nina holds out a hand to him. 'Don't go. Thanks for waiting with Stella all this time. I didn't know you were even there. They never said.'

'Of course, we are here. Bart and Kim were too, but we decided it was stupid us all waiting so they're coming back for the morning shift. The second morning shift, if you like.'

'Will you apologise to Olive and Iris for me? I ruined their Christmas.'

'You can't hog all the credit. There was also a small fire and an exploding turkey. And we nearly lost one of Marco's little ones to a pink grapefruit. However, we are reconvening tonight for another go with a couple of chickens from Colin's freezer selection.'

She squeezes my hand and attempts a smile.

'What the fuck's going on, Nina? And why the hell aren't you being pampered to in some fancy private hospital? This is all most unlike the Nina I know,' I pause, gather my strength. 'And love.'

She presses my hand harder.

'I'm good here. And Jackson's far too much of a snob to set foot in an NHS hospital.'

She is right. 'Good thinking. I'd never have thought of that. He doesn't know you're here though, does he?' She shakes her head emphatically. 'Thank fuck, now, what's going on? What's with the fainting? Don't tell me it's normal, I know it's not. Nearly gave me a heart attack.' I press my hand to my chest to emphasise the point.

'A little high blood pressure again, nothing to get het up about. We're fine. Both of us. Dandy.'

I am immediately suspicious. Nina doesn't use words like *dandy*.

'Don't give me dandy. What are you hiding? I'll go and see the doctor and stage a sit-in until I have the low-down. As a recently reinstalled best friend, future godmother to the Ninja,' something we have not discussed, but I thought I would slide it in while she is feeling vulnerable and grateful, 'I have a right to know the truth.'

She looks at me, her eyes unnaturally big, her face strained with anxiety and I know something bad is coming. Why didn't I just accept the fine and dandy story? I don't need to know any more.

Details can muddy the picture.

'I've got a weak kidney and it's buckling under the pressure. Got sick when I was young, a urinary infection that wouldn't go away.'

'What are you talking about? You have never mentioned a dodgy kidney. All these years, Nina, not a word,' I accuse. Then I have a thought. 'Is that why you have to pee so often?' We always used to joke that Nina had a weak bladder and now it turns out she sodding well *has* got a weak bladder. 'Why didn't you tell us? *And* you've been working all hours. Living out there in the remotest corner of the docklands on your own. It's madness. Why would you do that?'

She gives a tired shrug. 'Didn't want any pity, didn't deserve any. I just wanted it to be like before, with us. Friends.'

'That's just stupid,' I say, although it isn't. Not long ago – to my shame - I would have crowed with delight at all this bad news.

'But, listen, Stella, if something happens, will you and Kim take care of her? I want to make you her legal guardians, just in case.'

'Jesus, you're scaring me. Nothing's going to happen. Right, Miles?'

'She's called Mia,' goes on Nina, ignoring me. 'Mia.'

CHAPTER 37

Same old, same old
Informal: a situation or someone's behaviour remains the same, especially when it is boring or annoying

'How was your Christmas, Stells?' Clarissa parks herself on my desk, nudging a pile of papers to the floor, which she chooses to ignore.

'Busy.'

'A good busy, right? Not a bad busy?'

'Busy busy. There was good, there was bad and there was downright ugly. Christmas disintegrated with a fire, an exploding turkey, a fainting mama-to-be, a low-flying grapefruit, a 999 call, ambulance, flashing lights, the works. My Christmas dinner was a Twix from a vending machine. Not a resounding success. We had a second stab on Boxing Day, which went a little better even if Rudolph did overheat and melt all over Mary and Joseph on the front doorstep, and we never did find Baby Jesus after he disappeared. Olive thinks it was next door's cat.'

Clarissa is flapping her hands about, trying to shut me up. 'What are you talking about?'

'Nina keeled over and we were obliged to call in the paramedics. It was high drama, I can tell you. She's got to put her feet up until the Ninja arrives, so we spent a hectic few days doing up Colin's spare room and moving some of her stuff from the Docklands to Fulham.' I pause to check she is following. 'It's been what you might call, all go. Olive and Colin have abandoned life as we know it to squabble over who should mop the Nina brow or make the tea she likes, as she likes, when she likes. Iris has called a strategic retreat on the nursing front and taken charge of entertainment instead. This involves leaving lots of books in handy locations around the house guaranteed to trip up Nina on one of her frequent visits to the loo. Then there is a well-thumbed copy of the Radio Times with recommendations highlighted in yellow and must-watches in pink. She even goes back to change the channels sometimes to make sure they're keeping up with the schedule. Colin no longer gets a look-in. Not that he minds; he is too busy plumping cushions and checking that the Nina brow doesn't need another wipe.'

Clarissa is, understandably, looking more and more confused at every revelation.

'Hang on, hang on. Nina, Swedish Strumpet and persona non-grata, who was confined to Coventry until the end of time, is now shacked up with the heavenly Colin? With Olive and Iris tending to her every whim?'

'And Colin. He's top whim tenderer given that she's in his house.'

'What the fuck? I know you were making an effort, but don't you think you've gone overboard? Just because she's up the duff it shouldn't eradicate all past sins. And I'm surprised at Olive; I didn't think she'd cave so easily.'

'I didn't think I would either, but there you are. Felt like I was taking something back from Jackson and we have been friends for a long, long time. Turns out that counts for something after all.' She nods at this and I go on. 'Any lingering resistance to her disappeared when she toppled over at Christmas and was carted off in an ambulance.' Feeling emotion building, I try for nonchalance. 'Hogging the limelight as usual. Turns out she has a kidney problem though and is under orders not to move a muscle for the next two and a half months. First, she was going to go to Kim and Bart's, but they're out all day and she'd be on her own. Then she was coming to Olive's, but it's a mad house and we're three already, four sometimes with Miles, and finally Colin stepped up and offered his room. It's the perfect solution, almost next door and much quieter. In principle anyway. In reality, everyone has decamped to help out and it is pandemonium most of the time. And Colin's house is not what you'd call modern, so we did some emergency repairs, sprucing up the spare room. Miles repainted half the house in the end. He's very handy with a paint brush, don't you know.'

'Crikey. I thought he was looking tired. Put it down to too much holiday sex,' she sniggers.

Without blushing.

Unlike me. My face is instantly aflame as, aside from the numerous hospital visits, house redecorating and ridiculous amounts of Nina mollycoddling that had to be factored in to every day, Miles and I did manage to indulge in plenty of holiday sex, covering my every sexual fantasy and several of his. It has been enlightening, unreasonably pleasurable and, yes, dispiriting. Miles has put the bar so high, it is now out-of-reach, and I am going to have to polish my Moneypennyness daily to hang on to him and avoid a future of disappointing sex. Or more likely none at all. I think it's sex with Miles or celibacy from here on. He made me feel so comfortable, at ease, crooning over my every curve and insisting on kissing the parts I hate –

'Stella? I lost you there. So, Nina is fully back in the fold? What about *him,* you know, *the father?*' She leans in to me and whispers, 'Jackson.'

'New York. Wants nothing to do with anything. So, Nina thinks. I don't trust him. He won't be able to stay away once the Ninja decides it's time to join the real world. He'll want control.'

'Gawd, it's like a soap. EastEnders has nothing on you lot. What about presents? What did you get? More importantly, what did Miles get you?' Before I have time to answer, she sticks her generous bosom into my face. 'Look what Ringo got me.' She flashes a bright red lacy bra two inches from my nose.

'Matching knickers too. Well, a thong to be precise. And a suspender belt, with fishnets. Not quite got to grips with them, the little poppers keep pinging open and down they go, faster than a whore's drawers.' She lets rip with a filthy cackle. 'But Ringo loves them, so I wear them at home, at night.'

'You sleep in them?'

'Yes!' she squeals. 'And usually he doesn't like me to wear anything in bed.'

'Too much information, Clarissa.'

'He's made an exception though for the red thong and the fishnets.'

'Still too much information.'

'I have a black set too, which I cook in with my Game of Thrones apron over the top. We've been fine tuning our role-play too. My new favourite is when - '

'Waaaaay too much information. It's not even 9am.'

'Don't you guys do role play? You could be kidnapped and Miles could be a sexy assassin who storms in, kills the baddy, then has his wicked way and kidnaps you himself.' Her voice is full of relish as she lays out this scenario. Clearly an old hand.

'And that's fun, is it?'

'Fuck, yes!'

'Clarissa,' intones Bob. 'You have the honour of making the first donation to this year's swear box. Fifty pence please. And you, Stella. I've had my ears syringed so nothing will escape my attention now.'

Why does everyone in this office feel the need to share so much personal information?

'We've also been working on some of the scenes from Fifty Shades,' Clarissa goes right on sharing. 'We need more equipment though. I've just ordered a clitoral clamp and some jiggle balls.'

See what I mean?

'So, come on, what did you get?' she demands.

I am reluctant to show her what Miles gave me. He handed it to me in the wee small hours as we sat waiting for news of Nina. It is the most beautiful thing I have ever owned and I want to keep it to myself. Here at least. At home, Olive and Iris demand to see it every two minutes.

'Give it up, Stells. What d'you get?'

I pull back the collar of my shirt.

'Fuck me,' she murmurs, breathily.

'Clarissa,' thunders Bob. 'That's a pound now. In the box.' He gives it a rattle. 'I'm also thinking of putting up the prices. Got to try and keep you two in check.'

She flashes a V sign at Bob and leans in for another look. 'That is the most romantic thing ever. It's like James Bond. Which one was it? Casino Royale? That's the one. Daniel Craig.' She plants herself back on the desk. 'Now he's one I wouldn't turn away. He can do me any time he likes. Ringo would make an exception for a Bond.'

'Good morning, Clarissa.' Crap, the boss is here. 'What's that about a bond? Have you been investing?'

'Barry's been advising me on the best placement of my assets,' she says, straight-faced.

'Didn't know Barry knew so much about it,' he huffs.

'He's been doing an in-depth study of my utilities, Mr Clay. Top to bottom. Inside out. Figuring out the best way to exploit them.'

'I could advise from the sidelines, if you like.'

'We've discussed inviting a third person in to the room, it's an interesting option. For the time being, though, we've decided to keep it to the two of us.'

The woman has enough sass for ten. The boss, oblivious, looks pleased with his early morning altruism. Then he turns his attention to me.

'What are you smiling about, Stella? Happy to be back, I trust. We've lots to be getting on with, so I hope you are well rested. First and most importantly, my car, the Morris Minor, it's due a service and I need it back before the weekend. Got a wedding in the Cotswolds and I promised I'd bring Morris.'

'That's going to be tight. You know they need more notice than that.'

'Wrong! You see Mr Martello lives and breathes cars like mine. He'll find room for me. Give him a call. Need it arranged as soon as.' And he wobbles off into his office.

I reluctantly phone Mr Martello who laughs in my face and tells me he could fit us in at the beginning of Feb. At the earliest. Taking a deep breath, I tell him it is *the* Morris Minor. Malcolm Clay's. 'I don't care if it's for Prince William, love. February. Can't do better than that.'

Feet-of is not happy. Go figure. 'Did you tell him who it was for?' I nod. 'Did you tell him my name?' I nod. 'Does he know it's Morris?' I nod, edging towards the door. 'Ring him back. You've not made it clear who I am.'

Instead, I go and see Miles for a morale boost, then pop down and see Iris and Marco, both run off their feet as everyone tries to fuel their post-holiday slump with large coffees and muffins. Overcome by a wave of goodwill to all men, I buy coffees for Miles, Devon, Clarissa and Bob. Sonia is away in Amsterdam with Barnaby; they went for a New Year's Goth festival and haven't been heard of since. Ringo can get his own. If I get him one, I'll have to get all the other Beatles one and there is a limit to my munificence.

Back in the office, Bob is busy reading the Guardian and Clarissa is drawing up the first sweep stake of the year.

'Getting organised early,' I say, scanning the list and handing out coffees.

'Ooooh, Stells, you legend. You can have first pick. The Australian Open will be upon us before we know it.'

'Thank you, Stella,' says Bob. 'Although I disapprove of bribery, so don't expect any favours.'

We discuss our favourite tennis players for a while until I figure the boss has been left to stew for long enough.

'They can't fit you in until February,' I announce.

'Next time Stella,' he tuts, 'it would be useful if you could think ahead and phone the garage with plenty of notice. They're going to be very disappointed. Who will drive Caroline to the church now?'

And it is not even 10am. On 2nd January.

Going to be a long year.

CHAPTER 38

De trop
/də ˈtrəʊ/
Adjective: in the way, not wanted

Iris, after months of procrastination and ever more inventive delay tactics, finally admitted that she didn't want to collect any belongings from the shelter. Couldn't think of anything she wanted to do less, not to mention the fact that they do not hold on to the endless bits and bobs that are left on a daily basis and would I mind moving out of the way because she had better things to be getting on with than discussing this with me.

Again.

Which is a fair call. I have been unreasonably dogged about this, proverbial hound with a tasty bone, certain that she must have something from her old life that was worth tracking down. However small, however insignificant. Although, of course, the smallest things are often the most significant, like Iris herself. She has been robust in a proclaimed lack of sentimentality, saying that the people and possessions she has acquired since she moved in with Olive and I hold more value for her than anything from her old life.

'Although, I would like to see Ron,' she conceded.

'Ron?'

'From Ron's Café. I had a cup of tea there most days and he could always bring a smile to my face could Ron. Lovely man. Makes the best bacon sarnie in London too. Thick white bread, plenty of butter, crispy bacon, Brown sauce.'

So, Olive, Iris and I are all going for bacon sarnies at Ron's one weekend. All fine by me, as long as I don't mention it to the Sergeant Major, who recently warned us all off white bread. Not to mention the Brown sauce, which I can't imagine features high on his list of approved fare either.

I am explaining all this to Clarissa, partly to avoid doing any work. I've had enough for today. Nothing I do is right or good enough or how he would have done it – which is rich as he does precisely fuck-all most of the time.

This morning he rolled leisurely in at 10am to demand that I find out if the sales were still on in Hugo Boss. I resisted asking if this was, a) part of my job description and, b) whether Hugo Boss was the right fit for him, and went to phone around and find out. It was, after all, a better task than drawing up a spreadsheet of his average travel expenditure for last year – something that would have been infinitely easier had he asked me this time last year and I could have updated it trip by trip, flight by flight, taxi by taxi, coffee by coffee.....

Yes, I happily reported, sales are still on and the nearest one in Eldon Street had informed me that there was plenty of bargains still to be had.

'Right,' he sniffed. 'Are you sure? Because if I go all the way over there and the sale isn't on, I'm not going to be happy.'

'Well, I just spoke to them on the phone and they confirmed that they have plenty of stuff on offer. Keep calm and wear Hugo Boss!'

'Don't be facetious, Stella.'

'It was one of their Ads!'

'I just want to know if the sale is on.'

'It is.'

'Are you certain?'

'That's what they said.'

'Hugo Boss?'

'The very same.'

You see my point. There is only so much of that you can take in the average day.

Clarissa is just inviting herself to join us in Ron's, with Ringo too, when my phone rings. For a second, I think it must be the boss calling to have another pop about Hugo fricking Boss so I answer with a curt, 'Stella speaking.'

'Stella?' a small voice wobbles.

'Olive?'

'Stella?'

'It's me, Olive. Is something wrong?'

'Nina's fainted again,' her voice shakes with fear. 'Colin has called an ambulance.'

It took an age to get to the hospital. Iris wanted to come, but I managed to persuade her to go home to keep Olive company, putting her on a bus with a promise to keep her posted via texts to Olive's mobile. I then fought my way down to the tube, squeezing myself onto an already full train. Once we were packed in, sardines to a man, the train driver kindly took it upon himself to make an unscheduled stop just outside South Kensington station for us to admire the view – a brick wall - for over twenty minutes. Then, when we finally made it to my stop, I emerged into a deluge of such biblical proportions that I nearly got swept away by a rogue wave flowing down the ramp from the hospital entrance.

When I eventually squelched into the maternity wing, hysterically demanding to know where Nina was, I was firmly told by an intimidating matron, one bearing an uncanny resemblance to Nurse Ratched in One Flew Over, to calm down (her exact words were, *stop shouting or I will ask you to leave)*, to speak quietly (*you are still making too much noise),* to clean up after myself (*I'll thank you for mopping up that puddle)* and to take a seat in the waiting room (*now sit down like everyone has managed to do).*

That waiting room. The one with the unforgiving chairs and atmosphere of an A-level examination room, today peopled with fraught families, faces waxy in the artificial light.

Waiting is awful.

Waiting on your own is doubly awful.

Where is Kim? Every minute seems to last ten. I keep looking at my watch, shaking it and peering to see if the second hand is still moving, disbelieving that time has been reduced to this sluggish crawl. Unable to stop fidgeting, I try pacing to see if it moves things up a gear, counting my steps back and forth across the worn linoleum, up to a hundred and then back to zero but it gets me nothing except a terse telling-off from one of the other inmates.

Gradually the faces around me start to change: one couple leaves, faces bright with joy, while another older couple – grandparents maybe – arrive, stiff with anxiety.

Where is Kim? I ping off a text and start mentally preparing to try my luck with the scary matron again when, as if by telepathy, her sour face pokes around the door.

'Ms Halfpenny? Is that you? I'd like a moment.'

Her tone is soft, polite and I know instantly something is not right. Following her straight back up the corridor my mind ticks through a hundred questions; Where are we going? Is this normal procedure? Am I being taken to be introduced to baby Mia? How is Nina? Why didn't she talk to me outside in the corridor like everyone else?

With my attention focused on Matron's poker-straight spine, I almost bump into Kim and Bart, hurrying towards me from the opposite direction.

'Where are you going?' I cry.

'We're looking for you. Where are you going?'

'No idea, but you're coming with me.' The relief that I am no longer handling this alone is immense. As it is, my heart feels like it is trying to climb up my throat, bulging into my windpipe and blocking the air flow. I thump my chest as we walk, trying to loosen things up, get some much-needed oxygen into my lungs.

'Is something wrong?' Matron asks me, before noticing that one has become three and not looking happy about it.

'You tell me,' I say to her, as we get to her office. 'And they're with me. With Nina.'

Kim and I slump into chairs and Bart drags in another from out in the corridor while Matron installs herself behind an impressive desk and starts rearranging perfectly arranged bits of paper. I sense a delay tactic. Being something of a specialist myself in this domain, it is of no comfort. You only delay bad news. If the news had been good, we would be clucking over the baby Ninja by now and trying to snap discreet photos of Nina looking less than perfect.

Finally, she puts her fingertips together and assumes a dour expression. 'Please try and hold it together, Ms Halfpenny. Miss Bergdahl is making less fuss than you and she's just endured an emergency C-section.'

'Oh,' I cry, 'so she's alright? If she's not making a fuss then she must be OK. Right, Kim? And the baby Ninja? How's the baby? Why haven't you mentioned the baby.......' I run out of puff, giving my chest another good whack to get things moving again.

Looking pained, Matron turns to Kim, appealing for help. 'Is she always like this?'

Kim nods and shakes her head, nods again, then tells her to get on with it.

Piqued by Kim's lack of support she remarks pointedly, 'This is all most irregular.' There's a pause, then she goes on in a softer tone. 'Your friend Nina Bergdahl is quite alright. Weak and exhausted but absolutely fine.'

'And the baby?' asks Bart.

'Her baby is also fine. Remarkably healthy for thirty-four weeks.'

I swivel around on my chair and gaze at Kim. 'We're aunties!' I squeak excitedly. 'And you're an uncle, Bart. Uncle Bart. Has a natural ring to it. I bet you'll be her favourite too, it'll be Uncle Bart this and Uncle Bart that, where is Uncle Bart?' I raise a hand to high-five Kim, stopping half-way there.

'Wait.' I spin back around to Matron. 'Why are we here? If it's all it's all hunky dory, why are we here?'

'Hunky what?' she asks, confused.

'You know, in order. If everything's alright, why are we here in your office?'

She looks shifty all of a sudden and I wonder what on earth she can be going to say. We watch her impatiently as she rifles through the immaculate stack of documents on her desk and extracts a small piece of flimsy paper.

'The reception received a call this morning from one...' she trails off, adjusting her glasses and moving the scrap of paper nearer the light. 'Um, Mr Jackson Ly.......slander-er-Pelly, who was calling to enquire after the situation with Miss Bergdahl. Now, we do not give out information over the phone as I am sure you will appreciate, which did not please Mr Sly-er-land-er-Pelly one bit. He was very rude.'

'Running true to form then,' I quip.

'You know him?' she asks. 'Miss Bergdahl advised me that there was no father involved and she would not be naming one on the birth certificate. In fact, she mentioned that she was unsure who the father was.' Disapproving sniff. 'Something I took to mean that she had made recourse to an anonymous sperm donor.' A look of distaste flits across her face. 'However, this, er, what's his name?'

'Sly-er-man-duh-Pelly. Something like that.'

'Yes, indeed, and he stated that *he* was the father of the child and would be flying in from New York tonight.'

'Oh, crap,' breathes Kim.

'Oh, shit,' puffs Bart.

'Oh, fuck,' says I.

'I will thank you to watch your language whilst you are in my office,' snaps Matron.

We all mumble apologies and sit up a little straighter, minds whirling with disbelief. Jackson? Really? He is actually going to do this? He is going to stick in his great unwanted, controlling oar, making giant waves and generally rocking the boat.

I feel seasick just thinking about it.

'So, who is this man and does he have a rightful claim as father of Miss Bergdahl's newborn? It's not good enough for her to want to cut him out because they are no longer together. If she denies he is the father, he will of course have to establish paternity via the appropriate channels and a judge will then decide on his rights as father, etcetera, etcetera.' She gives me a knowing glare as if I am personally responsible. 'What I do not want is an unseemly episode in my maternity wing.' She switches a flinty eye to Kim and I let out a breath I hadn't realised I'd been holding. 'Would someone care to elucidate?'

'Er, no,' says Kim, nonchalant as you like under that harsh gaze. 'Elucidation not possible. We are as much in the dark as to the papa of the baby Ninja as you are.'

'Ninja?'

'Mia. Nina's baby. But I don't like the sound of this Sallymander-Pelly bloke ringing up like that out-of-the-blue and making outrageous claims. When you think about it, anyone could call up and say, *I'm the father.* It's too easy. He shouldn't be allowed in the building unless he can prove paternity. He might be a stalker. He could steal the baby. Imagine that! She is a very beautiful woman as I am sure someone of your perspicacity and experience has not failed to notice and that can lead to passions running amok.'

Matron, visibly preening now under Kim's praise, says keenly, 'I couldn't agree more. High passion can get the better of the strongest and sanest among us. I will advise Miss Bergdahl of Mr Salamander-Pelly's assertions and we will of course remain vigilant.'

CHAPTER 39

Bombshell
/'bɒm‚ʃel/
Noun: unexpected and shocking news or event

In the end, we were sent away last night without even having set eyes on the little Ninja; she had been whisked off to the Neonatal intensive care unit (NICU), the entry to which was blocked by a woman who made Matron look like Tinkerbell. We were however allowed a short five minutes – Matron stood at the door with a stopwatch – with Nina, looking fragile yet exquisitely beautiful, her skin aglow, as if a fire had been lit within. She was too weak to do more than whisper to us how beautiful Mia is, before closing her eyes and all but dismissing us. We debated whether to sit it out and wait for her to rally her forces, before finally retreating home to recharge our batteries ready for an assault on the NICU this morning.

Now though, I wish we had stayed, pacing the corridors and keeping a watchful eye out for the dodgy Salamander bloke who I have the displeasure of finding planted in the middle of the Maternity Wing's reception, out of place in an expensive suit and speed typing into an iPhone with his thumbs. Kim and Bart appear at my shoulder and we all stand and stare.

Feeling the weight of our glare upon him, Jackson eventually looks up. His eyes stroll from Bart to Kim and on to me as he casually types a few more words before blanking the screen and putting the phone into his pocket.

'Well, well, well,' he drawls. 'The Three Amigos. I wasn't sure if you'd be here, Stella. Thought you might have sworn off

Nina for life given her recent behaviour. But then you never could see anything through to its conclusion.'

'Oh, shut it, Jackson. For once in your life, stop being such an arse.'

'Once an arse, always an arse,' jeers Kim. 'Although I think you should bugger off and be an arse somewhere else because last I heard, neither Nina, nor baby Mia, want - '

'Mia? We never agreed on Mia.'

'Agreed? You haven't even spoken to Nina for months,' I say, incredulity making my voice go up a full octave. 'I think you'll find you relinquished your rights to choosing a baby name when you stormed out of the abortion clinic because she wouldn't get rid of it.'

Bristling, he steps over to me, sticking his face into mine and snapping aggressively, 'Don't you dare speak to me like that. You know absolutely nothing about anything, Stella Halfpenny. Butt out.'

'Oooh, get you, bringing out the big guns......butt out. He told me to butt out, Kim, can you believe that? The language. Call the navy, alert the army!'

'What have I missed?' Miles glides to my side and puts an arm loosely around my shoulders, his eyes on Jackson. 'I don't think we've met. Miles.' He holds out a hand.

Jackson ignores him, so Kim steps forwards and makes the introductions. 'Miles, as you've probably guessed, this is the infamous Jackson. Currently Jackson Salamander-Pelly, although he used to be known as Jackson T. Lysander-Perry and before that he was plain old Jason Lander.'

'Jason Percy Lander,' I correct.

Jackson flushes, a deeply unflattering scarlet from Adam's apple to hairline. 'I haven't the time to waste listening to your drivel. Just tell me which room Nina is in. You can wait for me here. I'd like to see my child alone, with Nina. No gawkers. No hangers on.'

Relieved, I feel like whooping and cheering to the rafters; he doesn't even know which room she is in. Doesn't know that Nina has already chosen a name. Doesn't know anything. He was standing here waiting for us, waiting for clues, waiting for someone to let him back in to Nina's life.

Jackson is on the outside, knocking and trying to get back on the inside.

'Ms Halfpenny?'

Ah, my old friend Matron. I never thought I'd be happy to see her, but there is no one I want to see more right now.

'Matron,' I say, packing in as much deference as will fit. 'Just the person. Do you remember our conversation yesterday? About Miss Bergdahl and the stalker? Well - '

She cuts me off. 'That is exactly what I'm coming to see you about. My reception tells me a man of that name, what is it again?'

'I'm not sure. It keeps changing. Something I find highly suspicious.'

'I quite agree. And, he is here. In person. I have advised Miss Bergdahl and, *against* my recommendations, she has agreed to see him.'

Kim and I look at each other, eyes full of horror, wanting to protest but unable to articulate the words.

Bart takes up the slack and manages a weak, 'Nina want to see him? Are you sure?'

'Of course, she's sure. You heard the woman. Nina wants to see me. I am the father of the child after all.' He addresses Matron directly now. 'My name is Jackson Lysander-Perry.' He offers her his hand, which she takes with the very tips of her fingers. 'I am the father of the child and I would thank you for taking me to her directly. This rabble can wait. I have priority.'

Matron is not just unimpressed by this statement, she looks completely nonplussed. 'I'm sorry, I don't understand.

You are Mr er Ly-mander-Pelly? And you say you are the father of Miss Bergdahl's child?'

'Ly*sander-Perry* is the name,' huffs Jackson, digging into his pocket and pulling out a business card. 'I'll thank you for remembering. Now, can you now please take me to see my offspring. I've been waiting here long enough.'

Matron continues to look at Jackson as if he has grown a second head.

'*Now* would be a good time, Matron, if you would be so kind.'

'This is most irregular. I don't know what to say. I think you had better come with me.' She waves a hand around the group. 'All of you.'

'That won't be necessary. They can wait. I would like to see my child and my fiancée alone.'

'Fiancée?' I choke. 'Did you say fiancée?'

'She will be,' he says confidently, patting a bulging pocket. '*Now*, Matron, if you don't mind. I'm ready.'

'Indeed, I can see you are. However, I'm in charge here and I say everyone comes. *Quietly.*'

We file off, Matron, Jackson (protesting loudly), Kim, Bart, me, and Miles bringing up the rear. Two corridors and one tense ride in a lift later, we stop outside a door with Nina's name on a printed sheet above the handle. Matron maintains control by holding up a beefy hand and telling us to wait. Jackson tries to get in first and push past her, but she is having none of it.

'That includes you,' she says firmly, hand upon his chest – a move I can but admire. She eases through the door and it clicks shut behind her. I am desperate to talk to Kim but I can't, here, in front of butt-out-Jackson.

The only thing keeping me calm is Miles; solid and reassuring. Here.

For me.

Who needs Nina?

If she goes back to Jackson, this will be the first and last time Mia ever meets her Auntie Stella.

What feels like an hour later, the door edges open and Matron is back, nodding us forward and holding the door wide as we bulldoze past her. Nina is propped up in the bed, her pale face flushed, anxious. She watches us wide-eyed for a second, taking in the crowd, before turning her attention back to the tiny bundle in her arms, murmuring gently, a finger adjusting the little white beanie. Kim and I jostle carefully with Jackson, all trying to get the best position by the bed, while Bart and Miles hang back and Matron takes up a position at the end of the bed, like a Sentinel.

'Oh, Nina,' breathes Kim. 'You're a mummy. Hello, little Mia.' She stretches out a hand, stroking the blanket, pausing where her tiny feet must be. It's impossible to see anything, so completely is she bundled up in a pale-yellow blanket.

'We're not calling her Mia,' says Jackson crossly. 'We'll discuss it later, darling, find something we both like.'

Darling? She is really going to let him do this?

'Nina?' I plead. 'What are you doing? Please don't be that person, please don't do this. I can't stand by you if you do. I'm sorry, I really am, it's your life, but I can't be part of it.'

Nina just smiles, her eyes wet with tears. 'It's OK, Stella, it's going to be OK. Here, take her Kim, I want you to meet my beautiful Mia. It's my mother's middle name.'

Jackson starts to protest but is silenced as Nina carefully unwraps the blanket, easing off the white cap to reveal a surprising thatch of black curls, pausing to delicately kiss the teeny head and then holding her out to Kim.

We all stand, transfixed, unable to speak with wonder.

The silence stretches, home to a thousand questions.

It is Kim who eventually breaks it. 'Trust you to have an ace up your sleeve,' she whispers proudly, turning to Bart and Miles so they can see her properly. They both press forward, edging a mute Jackson to one side, Bart muttering in Polish and crossing himself repeatedly.

There is a final expanse of hush as Kim cradles the wee Ninja, a lull before the lid comes off.

With no warning, Jackson launches himself at Nina and it is only because Bart and Miles had managed to get in front of him that he is unable to get a clear run at the target. His impetuous lunge costs him dear as Miles, instincts honed by all those hours of Krav Maga, has him in a neat headlock before he can say, butt out.

And that was just the beginning.

Jackson, in a fantastic loss of T Lysander-Perry, reverts to pure Jason Lander and utters so many fruity and unusual swearwords that I regret not having a pen and paper to hand to take notes. He puts up a ferocious fight and Miles has to dig deep into his bag of tricks to contain him – with Bart helpfully cheering from the sidelines – before eventually manoeuvering him to the door.

'You mothercunting fuck,' he bellows, as Miles struggles to hold him while opening the door at the same time.

'All those years of only swearing at work, Stells, and you had this hiding at home,' says Kim, calmly. 'Woo hoo, good job, Miles. Bart, you need to start going to that Magna Krav-bot thing with Miles. He's totally got this.'

'I'll kill you, you filthy dickhole, you - '

'Enough,' roars Matron, yanking open the door. 'Security is on the way.' And with Miles and Bart, she manhandles Jackson out into the corridor.

Which leaves the three of us.

And Mia.

Cutest button on the planet, Mia is undoubtedly Nina's; her sweet face, the curve of her lip, the shape of her nose, it's all Nina.

Only Jackson is categorically not the father.

Despite the perma-tan, there is absolutely no way that Jackson could have given Mia such beautiful, dark dusky skin and so many luscious black curls.

CHAPTER 40

Composition

/käm-pə-ˈzi-shən/

Noun: something that is made from separate parts or
elements to form a whole

'I'm going to put Mia here, by the snacks, so that she feels
involved,' says Olive, carefully putting her down by the coffee
table and fussing about with the blanket – the latest, a brightly
coloured affair, crocheted by Iris. 'She'll want to listen in to the
book discussion too. It's never too early to start. They hear
everything you know.' She stands up, her face creasing with
concern. 'I worry we should have chosen a more child
appropriate book. Colin wasn't thinking straight. Fishing and
death are not suitable subjects for a young girl.'

'I don't think she'll be following the debate that closely,
Olive.'

'Still. The Old Man and the Sea is hardly fun reading.'

'Mia, if she's awake, which is unlikely, will be soothed by
the murmur of our voices. We'll put Bart beside her; he can
send her to sleep in minutes with his low rumble. Anyway,
short was the only directive we gave Colin and he complied. It
was all rather man v nature after Moby Dick but predictably I
couldn't put it down and I can tick it off the next time I do one
of those *one hundred books you must read before you die*
lists.'

Iris shuffles into the room straining under the weight of
one of Olive's showstopper cakes. 'How many pounds of
carrots did you put in this?' she puffs.

'One or two. Then I added a sweet potato and a red
pepper as well. They looked lonely in the fridge after all the

carrots had gone,' says Olive, helping Iris lower the enormous offering to the table. 'Miles is partial to a bit of carrot cake. He can take the leftovers to the office on Monday.'

Iris looks at her watch. 'Colin's running it fine. He's got some fishing themed decorations to set up before we get started. He thinks it might help us get into the spirit of the book so I said I'd lend him my shell collection.'

On cue, the doorbell rings and the front door opens, Colin yodeling a jolly halloo and stopping for a brief pose in the doorway so we can all admire his outfit. He is wearing jeans (a first) tucked into welly boots (*Brand new, so they won't dirty the carpet, Olive*), an Aran jumper, a yellow rain jacket and a jaunty corduroy skipper's cap on his head.

'You're taking this book club lark to a whole new level, Colin,' I tease, as he does a twirl. 'Perhaps we should open a few windows though? Don't want you overheating in all that wet-weather gear.'

'This can be the center-piece,' he announces gravely, ignoring me and placing a ship-in-a-bottle on the coffee table. 'It will add a certain gravitas to proceedings.'

'Colin, you do remember who is coming tonight, don't you? Gravitas is going to be a stretch for the likes of Bart and Kim, not to mention Clarissa. And Ringo. He's more of a Games of Thrones or Breaking Bad man.'

'I thought he was called Barry? Anyway, Hemingway invites a level of solemnity whoever you are, Stella. Now where shall I put my fishing nets?' His fishing nets are, to give you the full picture, three shrimping nets, the kind used by kids on the sands at low tide, and a bundle of black tulle netting more usually seen in the fashion industry to puff out a skirt. Inspired, Olive goes to dig out an old fishing rod of Derek's, provoking a sigh of delight from Colin as he arranges it next to his chair – that is to say, Olive's chair, which he has commandeered for the evening.

401

'Should we call you Santiago, so as to really get in the mood?' I ask.

I can see Colin summoning a withering reply when he is put off by the arrival of Bart and Kim. In force. They not only have Reg with them but a surprise guest.

'Eric!'

I have been speaking to him often and knew he and Reg still meet up regularly for wine and Scrabble, but I had no idea he was coming tonight. What surprises me most is how moved I am to see him in person. I go and give him a big hug, choking back a tear when he rasps, 'And how's my 'alf Pint?'

'Colin,' says Kim, 'this is our dear friend, Eric. Cracking outfit by the way, Col. Book club keeps getting better and better.' She makes her way around the room issuing kisses like a fairy godmother, finally getting to Mia. 'Hello my precious,' she whispers. 'Have you got a smile for Auntie Kimi? Oh, you get more gorgeous every time I see you. Shall we have a quick round of Mamma Mia?'

Kim has taken to singing Abba's Mamma Mia every time she sees the little Ninja. It was fun at first, but the originality is wearing thin.

'Not tonight, Kochanie,' breaks in Bart gently. 'Let's have a night with no Abba. Eh?'

Kim, in the grip of a late-blooming Abba obsession, is about to give it hearty go when the doorbell signals the arrival of Clarissa and Ringo. Iris shoots off to let them in and returns with the two of them, both dressed to the nines.

This is book club, for fuck's sake, I want to cry. Book club!

Clarissa is encased in a shimmering grey sheath that swaddles her right down to her knees where it bursts out into an enthusiastic frill, boosted by a froth of tulle.

'What do you think?' She preens, hand on hip.

'Are you a mermaid?' asks Colin, admiringly, eying up her costume and no doubt wondering if more decoration has just walked in the door.

'I am,' she puffs, collapsing onto the sofa and trying to find a workable position. 'Loving the look, Colin. I tried to get Ringo into something fishy, but he's been working on a new look for Lord of the Rings lately. We've done as much as we can with Fifty Shades. He's a very convincing Christian you know.' She absently rubs her hand over her bottom. 'Have you read the books?'

Colin shakes his head, oblivious. 'Is it about an artist? Some of Monet's most famous paintings are all about the art of shading.'

We are saved from having to explain further by Miles coming in with a tray of glasses and a bottle of something chilled. Not that one bottle is going to be nearly enough. Won't even wet the sides with this lot. I look around the room, marveling at this wonderful, diverse, hodge-podge of people who I now consider my family. Who is missing?

Mummy Nina is yet to arrive and you would be forgiven for wondering where Angus is.

Oh, Angus. Blotted his copy book he has. Scratched off the coveted book club roster and all other social gatherings until the end of time. Or at least until he comes to his senses. He came around for a drink not long ago with his new girlfriend. Now, Olive and Iris love pretty much everyone but even they crumbled under the shameless self-satisfaction and complacency of the *Chlo.*

Not a typo. Unfortunately.

The Chlo has hooked herself (in keeping with today's fishing theme) another good one. She was undeterred by the twenty-year age gap and tracked an unsuspecting, but uncomplaining, Angus with as much obsessive dedication as Ahab gave to hunting down Moby Dick. Only with better results.

So far.

We still live in hope that he will see the light and return to the fold.

'Colin, where's Nina?'

'Checking the street for any For Sale boards,' he tuts. 'Doesn't trust me anymore.'

Nina is selling the Docklands property and wants to find her own house in Beatrice Avenue, much to Colin's distress. He had dreamed up a scenario where she moved in permanently with Mia. Even after she announced she was making a go of it with the daddy, he refused to give up, getting up early most mornings to patrol the street for any sign of a For Sale board. He even offered to move out of the master bedroom and everything but Nina, understandably, wants her own home.

A family home, with a mummy bear, a baby bear, and of course a daddy bear.

Never had we been given the slightest suspicion that there was the vaguest possibility that Jackson might perhaps not after all be the father of the forthcoming Ninja. While being thoroughly pissed off that we, Kim and I, had been kept out of yet another important Nina-loop, I have forgiven her, mainly because pulling that particular stunt on Jackson – with us there in the front row seats – was a masterstroke.

Also, I can still call the little poppet my Nin-ja.

Nina and – James arrives with a bottle of rosé, a book tucked under one arm.

Yes, James, my James, from CrossFit, although of course he was never really *my* James, but I like to tease Nina. They met in Cancun where she was delivering the keynote speech about money laundering across the foreign currencies. Clever girl, our Nina; the nearest I get to money laundering is writing a step-by-step guide for the boss for his Hotpoint.

'I didn't know you even knew him, Stells, I promise on Mia's life. I would never have got involved if I'd known. He was *so* lovely – you know that. So different from Jackson. I couldn't help myself. I was so unhappy and every minute I spent with him felt like I was being cleansed of Jackson. Then he told me about you, how you'd met at CrossFit, gone for drinks, and the bubble burst. I'd been shown this heaven-on-earth but the entry price was one I wasn't willing to pay. And that felt....' she paused, making sure to catch my eye. 'Right. My due. My penance. I begged him not to tell you, pleaded, then I cancelled my final talk, flew home, changed my phone number and slept with Jackson.'

'You thought that might help? Sleeping with Jackson?'

'Felt like my penance for sleeping with James. Then I found out I was pregnant and I thought, more penance. You reap what you sow.'

'And you were sowing without the necessary precautions?'

'I'd been sick in Cancun, an upset stomach, but it never occurred to me that I was at risk. Not that I would have cared. We were delirious, careless. Carefree.'

'Crikey, Nina, I thought rosé after CrossFit was carefree, or careless if you listen to the Sergeant Major, but careless shagging is a whole different ballpark of carefree.'

She didn't even look embarrassed. 'Then I didn't know who the father was. Terrified it was James, even more terrified it was Jackson.'

Not so clever then, after all.

'Order, order,' shouts Colin, tapping his glass with a teaspoon. 'I would like to call the room to order. Now, are we all here?'

'Nina will be here in a minute,' says James. 'Rumour has it Mr and Mrs Smallwood opposite are thinking of moving to Scotland to open a bed and breakfast.'

Disquiet flits across Colin's face. 'I don't think Abigail is suited to the Scottish climate at all. I'll have a word.'

405

The room bursts into such a heated discussion about the merits of moving to Scotland (Oban, according to James) that Nina's arrival goes almost unnoticed. She makes a quick stop to tickle Mia's cheek, then moves over to Colin, tugging his cap and kissing him on the cheek. She takes his hand and they exchange a long look, the room stilling to quiet around them.

'We'll only be a few doors down,' she says softly. 'And you'll be top of the list for baby-sitting duties.'

'Ahem,' Olive clears her throat. 'Iris and I would also like to be considered for baby-sitting duties. I'm free all day, don't forget, apart from Thursday afternoons when I have my Pilates class, and Iris is ready for any evening shifts. You'll want to go out to dinner sometimes, won't you?'

Things erupt again then as Kim and Bart stake a claim for Friday and Saturday evenings, provoking a lively protest from Iris. As they banter back and forth, Eric comes over to me.

'What about you, 'alf Pint? Or you planning your own now, with Miles?'

'Don't be silly, Eric,' I scoff, giving him a playful punch.

'Well, don't wait too long. I'd like to meet my 'alf Pint's 'alf pint, and I won't be 'ere forever.'

'Alright, Eric?' Miles comes over with a bottle of wine. 'Did you see what James found?' He holds out the bottle to show us the label. *Mia,* it reads.

'Looks like you're not the only one with your own wine, 'alf Pint,' sighs Eric. 'I'll have to get some in for the pub.'

We stop for a minute to survey the room, still busy discussing the details of Mia's already busy weekly schedule.

'We're not going to get a look-in, are we?' says Miles, drawing me in close.

'Absolutely none at all,' I say. 'Until she starts teething and spends all day and half the night howling. Then we'll be called into action and berated for not doing our bit.'

'Can't wait,' he says. 'Good practice, eh?'

I give him a dig in the ribs, both alarmed and elated, as Colin, brandishing the ship-in-a-bottle, once again tries to get everyone's attention back to the book, back to Hemingway.

'Funny how it's all worked out,' says Miles, quietly. 'Look at us all. We're a right motley crew.'

'You don't mind?' I ask. 'Do you?'

'Wouldn't change a thing. It is unexpected but surprisingly,' he pauses, searching for the right word, 'stellar.'

'Stella? That doesn't make sense.'

'Stella-rrr. With an r.'

'Very clever,' I say, looking around the room. 'I can but agree; it is both unexpected and, yes, absolutely stellar.'

Emma Henry

ABOUT THE AUTHOR

Emma Henry is a first-time author. She was born in the UK and now lives in Switzerland with her partner Thierry.
Ps. A lot of wine (red) was consumed during the writing of this novel.....

THANK YOU FOR READING

I sincerely hope you enjoyed the ride. Please do take a few minutes to write a review and let other potential readers know your thoughts....

Printed in Great Britain
by Amazon

52048801R00251